THE DIAMOND FRONTIER

British redcoats brave a ruthless enemy on the battlefields of South Africa...

It's 1880 and the atmosphere is volatile in the Transvaal. The discovery of diamonds has bred greed and violence, while a strong anti-British feeling is taking hold amongst the Boer farmers. War-weary from service in Afghanistan, Simon Fonthill and his servant '352' Jenkins are homeward-bound when the cry for help comes. An old friend has been kidnapped in Kimberley, and the pair must go to her aid before redeeming a promise to act as army scouts. When General Wolseley decides to attack the stronghold of the bePedi tribe, Fonthill and Jenkins once again find themselves marching to war.

THE DIAMOND FRONTIER

THE DIAMOND FRONTIER

by

John Wilcox

Magna Large Print Books
Long Preston, North Yorkshire,
BD23 4ND, England.

British Library Cataloguing in Publication Data.

Wilcox, John
  The diamond frontier.

  A catalogue record of this book is
  available from the British Library

  ISBN   0-7505-2589-4
  ISBN   978-0-7505-2589-3

First published in Great Britain in 2006
by Headline Book Publishing

Copyright © 2006 John Wilcox

Cover illustration © Mary Evans Picture Library

Published in Large Print 2006 by arrangement with
Headline Book Publishing Ltd.

Magna Large Print is an imprint of Library Magna Books Ltd.

Printed and bound in Great Britain by
T.J. (International) Ltd., Cornwall, PL28 8RW

For my sister Margaret

Acknowledgements

As always, I owe gratitude to the staff of London Library for allowing me to delve, via their shelves, into the minutiae of life in Britain, India and South Africa in 1880; to my agent, Jane Conway-Gordon; and to my meticulous and constructive editor at Headline, Sherise Hobbs, for helping me to put the results on paper.

Research overseas is an expensive but necessary (and fun!) part of the business, and I received an enormous amount of help in South Africa. I wish to think Mrs K. Dumminy of the Kimberley Africana Library, and Ms Celeste Feder, the de Beers Archivist, for providing me with so much evocative documentation about old Kimberley; Avril Morris, PA to my old friend, publisher Alan Ramsay in Cape Town, for easing the logistical nightmare of covering so many miles in such a short time; and Toyota South Africa, for providing reliable transport which took me in comfort to the remote Mpumalanga/Mozambique border. Once there, I received expert help and splendid company in Sekhukune land from guide Ben Fouche, and Orphrus Ntjana, a member of the bePedi race. Lastly, as ever, my love and thanks go to my wife Betty, who accompanied me on these travels and proof-read with diligence every word I wrote.

For those who would like further reading on the subjects and territories covered in this novel, the following very short bibliography may help: on Bombay, *City of Gold* by Gillian Tindall (Temple Smith, 1982); on diamonds, *The Book of Diamonds* by Joan Younger Dickinson (Frederick Muller, 1965); on Old Transvaal, *The Veldt in the Seventies* by Sir Charles Warren (Isbister & Co, 1902), and *Life of Sir G. Pomery Colley* by Sir William F. Butler (John Murray, 1899); on Cecil Rhodes and the early days of Kimberley, *Rhodes of Africa* by Felix Cross (Cassell, 1956), *Cecil Rhodes* by John Flint (Hutchinson, 1976), and 'Rhodes C.J. Last Will and Testament' (ed. W. T. Stead, 1902, *London Review of Reviews*); on Wolseley and the Sekukuni campaign, *Wolseley* by Sir F. Maurice and Sir George Arthur (Heinemann, 1924), and *The Colonial Wars Source Book* by Philip J. Haythornthwaite (Arms and Armour, 1965).

Many of these books, alas, are now out of print, but the London Library – and almost certainly the British Library – should be able to provide most if not all of them.

J.W.
Chilmark,
August 2004

South East Africa 1880

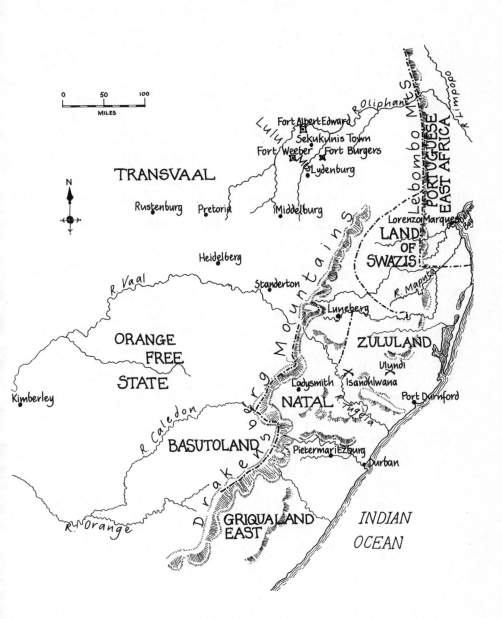

Chapter 1

Bombay, 1880

The waiter, conspicuous in his white kurta among the soberly suited Parsee merchants conversing at their tables, positioned the glass of whisky and soda precisely in the centre of his silver tray and looked around for his customer. There he was, at the far end of the lounge, sitting alone and slightly cramped on the narrow balcony, partly outside, one boot on the carved wooden rail tilting back his chair, his head turned as he looked fixedly down at Parsi Bazaar Street. He presented a picture of a man completely absorbed by something at the distant end of that teeming thoroughfare and unaware of his immediate surroundings, or, indeed, of the speculation his presence at the hotel was causing.

Picking his way between the tables, the waiter regarded the static figure with curiosity. Europeans were rare residents of this little hotel – if this man *was* European, that is. His skin was dark, whether from sunburn or ethnic origin was unclear. And that was the point. He didn't quite seem to fit in, even here in eclectic, expanding Bombay – now vying with Calcutta to be the largest city east of Suez until Tokyo and the largest in the British Empire after London. It was a city full of the wealth of East and West and of the poverty and vice of both, where the hands of the gods Vishnu the Preserver and Shiva the Destroyer were evidenced daily. A breeding ground of millionaires but also of plague. Here in the heart of that city, this cramped, ancient hotel, with its extravagant wooden Gujarat carvings, set in the middle of the Fort away from the white men's clubs, was accustomed to welcoming ethnic misfits and exotic travellers from the far fringes of the Indian Ocean. In this room, the waiter had seen Mosselmen from Arabia furtively drinking brandy and giant negroes from the African coast talking of gold. He had served suave Persians and, occasionally, an Anglo-Indian bureaucrat entertaining a coy Hindu lady. But this man fitted no pattern.

He wore the crumpled white cotton suit of a Eurasian civil servant, yet his bearing was that of a pukka sahib: erect and with a slim build that made him seem taller than his five foot nine inches. He had been commanding and confident in his requests. Yet he did not bark orders like the English. He spoke softly and politely, though he rarely smiled and his sad eyes were brown, not black like those born of the union of British Tommy and Hindu bazaar girl. The hair was brown, too, although obviously bleached by the sun, and it was worn long, not in the harsh, short cut of the Englishman. It was the face, though, which had caused the most speculation among the staff of the hotel. The waiter studied it again as it came into profile as he approached the guest. The broad cheekbones narrowing down to a small but firm jaw were commonplace enough, as was the thin-lipped mouth, although it did perhaps betray a sensitivity

16

unusual in those ruling the Queen Empress's Raj – if, that is, he was of that class. But the nose had been broken, seemingly quite recently, for it still bore a white scar across the bridge that stood out savagely from the tanned features. The result, however, had not been to spread the nose across the face, but rather to hook it downwards, so that it gave a predatory expression to the visage. He looked, in fact, like a Pathan warrior in a suit, a man of the hills who had descended to the plains. A hunter resting between kills.

'Whisky soda ... ah ... sahib,' said the waiter, deciding to give his customer the benefit of the doubt and carefully placing the glass on the rattan table.

Simon Fonthill whirled round. 'Thank you. Oh, no ice?' To Fonthill, who had been in Bombay only two days, the rare luxury of ice after so many months on the dry plateaus and dusty scree of the Afghan hills had been a revelation and a delight.

'Sorry, sahib. Bombay ice house is empty. But I have wrapped glass in damp towel.'

'Very well.' Fonthill looked away again, along the crowded street below him, and then back to the waiter. 'Would you do me a service, if you have a moment, that is?'

The waiter inclined his head, flattered at the politeness of the request. 'Of course, sahib.'

'Thank you. I am watching for the arrival of someone and I do not wish to leave the balcony. Here is the key to my room. On the table inside – on the right-hand side of the door – there is a small field telescope. Please bring it to me.'

For a moment, the Hindu looked astonished.

17

Would he not rob the room, taking all of the belongings of this strange white man – if, again, he *was* a white man, that is? Would he not delve beneath his shirts and look for that wallet which, he had been told, was always there? Would he not take his socks and his spare shoes and sell them in the bazaar? He stared into the brown eyes that regarded him with just a trace of amusement.

Fonthill smiled fully now. 'You are a man to be trusted, of course,' he said and turned to redirect his gaze up the street.

The waiter bowed and was gone. Simon frowned and concentrated hard as he looked for that familiar face among the crowd stretching away from only twelve feet below him. That thronged street seemed, indeed, like the Biblical river of humanity, as though some giant hand had swept up examples of all the races of the Levant, the Orient and India and sprinkled them down, struggling north and south along Parsi Bazaar Street, two currents surging in random urgency. Arabs and Afridis from the north, all with precariously wound turbans, jostling with red-turbaned Banians and Persians in silken vests; prosperous Jains, in their snowy robes, using their tall staffs to make their way; fakirs, their eyes hollow and hypnotic under their mud-tangled hair, being allowed respectful passage; black-capped Jews hurrying towards another negotiation; and Parsees in gaily painted buggies carving swathes through the slow-moving pedestrians. The horse-driven trams, made in England and introduced to Bombay only ten years before, had not yet reached the crowded canyons of the Fort, but humped oxen, like ponderous islands in the stream, were doggedly pulling their loads, their drivers occasionally slipping down to wipe the muzzles of their beasts to avoid them suffocating from the froth that formed there in the heat.

Simon Fonthill unthinkingly took in the pageant. After the dun greyness of the Hindu Kush mountains, the colour almost hurt his eyes. But his mind did not record it. His brain was dominated by one question: where the hell, where the bloody hell, was Jenkins?

Ex-Sergeant Jenkins, once of the 24th Regiment of Foot and latterly of the Queen's Own Corps of Guides, Indian Army – '352' Jenkins, always so-called (his Christian name hardly known and never used) because the last three units of his army number were the only means of identifying him from the other nine Jenkinses in the 24th, this most Welsh of regiments – had been away for nearly five hours now. The mission had been simple: gathering poste restante mail from the army collection point and picking up the tickets from the steamship line for their onward passage back home to Britain. Both destinations were only twenty minutes' walk away from their hotel.

Simon's brow wrinkled at the thought. Jenkins, the bravest of warriors, the most caring of servants and the warmest of comrades, had two great failings: a penchant for beer and an inability to find his way from A to B, even if the path was marked by flaming beacons. Somewhere out there, amongst the multitudes in this most populous of cities, was Jenkins – lost and probably drunk. It was not that the man could not take care

19

of himself. Although only five foot four inches tall, the Welshman was as broad as a chapel door and hardened by years of adversity and of fighting in barracks and bar rooms and on battlefields around the world. Simon had seen him, unarmed, completely demolish a huge spear-carrying Zulu in single combat. Oh, Jenkins could fight all right! But drink never improved any warrior, and Simon knew that in a city like Bombay this could be dangerous. He was well aware that the cult of Thuggee, practised by the followers of the Hindu goddess Kali, had never been completely eradicated by the British. The Government formally boasted that the campaign of Lord Bentinck back in the thirties had finally crushed the cult. But anyone who spent any time in India knew that it had lingered on in the rural hinterland of the subcontinent, with news of the garrotting of rich farmers and even, occasionally, of white men being reported and, usually, suppressed. Now, it was rumoured, the Thugs were creeping into the new cities, of which Bombay, with its thirty new textile mills and cotton fortunes being created by the month, must be a target. If Thugs were out there somewhere they would see a lone, drunken European as easy prey. They never hunted alone, and even Jenkins, an unsteady, unarmed Jenkins, would be no match for a group of them. Simon squinted against the sun and tried to focus into the distance, his worries now building.

'Your eyeglass, sahib.' The waiter was smiling now, with the shared intimacy of a man who had been trusted and had passed the test with glowing colours.

'Ah, thank you.' Simon put a handful of coins on the tray and picked up the telescope. He extended it and put it to his eye, looking to the south, the direction from which Jenkins should emerge. But all he could see was a mass of multicoloured turbans, bobbing away into the distance. Disheartened, he swung the glass in the other direction, away from the docks and the Post Office. At first, nothing. Then he stiffened. He focused the lens to gain a clearer definition – and there, heading in his direction, was the man himself: 352 Jenkins, his black hair sticking up like corn stubble in a newly fired field, his huge moustache curving away under his nose, his head atop that short, wide body appearing and disappearing in the middle of the crowd. A Jenkins who was, it could now be seen as he came closer into focus, staggering slightly and, by the look of it, singing. A very happy, drunken Jenkins.

'Oh lord!' Simon snapped the telescope shut and took a deep pull at his whisky and soda as he faced the prospect of sobering up the best yet most awkward friend in his life. It was drink which had led the young Jenkins, then a corporal, to hit a colour sergeant of the 24th Foot and spend a year in 'the Glasshouse', the new and violent detention centre in Aldershot. Reduced to the ranks on his return to the regiment, he had met Simon in the depot hospital at Brecon, Wales, when Simon was on his sickbed. As batman, it had been the older and barrack-wise Jenkins who had been Simon's mentor through the long period of the young subaltern's persecution by his commanding officer, Colonel Ralph Covington, the man who had remained Simon's enemy ever since. Together Simon and Jenkins had fought through the Zulu War and the Second Afghan War, each saving the other's life and forging a bond of friendship virtually unique in the class-structured army of Queen Victoria. Now, having left the army, they were homeward bound to Simon's parents' house in the Welsh borders, where Simon hoped that he could recover from the scars – both physical and spiritual – which he had sustained during those campaigns and where they could decide where next to seek their fortunes. They could, that is, if Jenkins could sober up.

Relaxed now to know that, at least, 352 was almost home, Simon put the glass to his eye again. No doubt about it. Jenkins was drunk right enough. He was happily rolling through the crowd, his mouth opening and closing in what Simon knew would be a completely tuneless rendition of 'Men of Harlech' (Jenkins was one of the few Welshmen known to Simon who could not carry a melody). Simon refocused the lens slightly and idly regarded the faces around the little Welshman. No one seemed concerned, unless... He sat up and looked again. There were three men in black turbans immediately behind Jenkins, two of whom, as he watched, moved to either side of 352. Each put an arm around him, as though in a friendly, jocular manner, and then, to Simon's horror, moved him out of sight into a side alley in one smoothly executed movement. The third stayed behind for a moment, smiling and speaking to someone in the crowd, before he too slipped away.

With a crash, Simon sent his side table flying and, with one hand on the wooden rail before him, vaulted unthinkingly into the crowded street below. The fall could have fractured an ankle at least but it was broken by a stout Parsee, whom Simon sent crashing into his companions and then to the ground. 'Sorry,' gasped the Englishman and then, shouting, 'Make way!' he began to run as best he could through the jostling multitude, thrusting men aside without care.

Simon had covered some 250 yards before he realised that he had taken no bearing on the side street into which Jenkins had been thrust. He had no way of knowing which of the many turnings he should take. He stopped at one corner, his chest heaving, unsure whether to waste precious time by delving into its shadows, when he caught the eye of a small ragged urchin who beckoned to him. Should he follow? Could it be a trap? Simon shook his head in frustration. This was no time to ponder. He had to take the risk. The boy was difficult to keep in sight because he was able to weave more skilfully through the crowd, but Simon hung on until, eventually, the lad stopped and, with wide eyes, pointed down an alleyway. Simon looked behind him towards the hotel, attempting to gauge the distance covered, but one multi-storeyed, overhanging building looked much like another to him. With a nod to the boy, he ran down the turning.

There was an immediate opening to the right. It seemed to be a carpet shop, for brightly woven floor coverings were stacked all around and were hanging from the ceiling, yet the place seemed completely empty – and strangely quiet. Until, that is, there came a high-pitched scream of pain and then a crash from behind a low doorway, half concealed by vertical strings of beads.

Tearing the beads apart, Simon sprang through the opening. The scene within was inanimate just for the moment, as though the players were performing a tableau and had stopped to milk applause. Jenkins was standing with his back to a wall, his once-white cotton jacket wrapped round his left forearm, which was thrust forward, as though in a mediating gesture. Yet his frown and the gleam in his black eyes betrayed that he had no intention of mediating. Further proof lay at his feet, where one of the Hindus was lying completely still, his eyes and tongue protruding from a head that was twisted unnaturally. In one hand he still gripped a length of narrow black cord, clearly a garrotte. Blood poured from Jenkins's left shoulder. The other two men were standing before him, garrottes dangling from loops around their wrists and knives in their hands. One of the blades was bloodstained.

The two men whirled round on Simon's entry. Jenkins looked across and beamed. 'Sorry I was a bit late, bach sir,' he said. 'Glad you've dropped in, though. Mind what you're doin' now. These lads are a bit rough, look you.' It was clear that, if Jenkins had been drunk before, he was not now. For him, action and danger had always induced sobriety far quicker than cold water and the lashing of a sergeant major's tongue.

The taller of the two Thugs gestured to the

24

other and then to Jenkins. The smaller nodded. Then the first turned and began to walk softly towards Simon, limping a little, his knife held low. He was dressed all in black, the colour of his loose garments matching his eyes.

Simon looked at the blade of the knife and felt his mouth grow dry. He took an involuntary step backwards.

Then the voice of Jenkins, anxious now and almost mellifluous in its urgent Welshness, broke in. 'Don't 'ang about in 'ere, bach. I can 'andle these two. See if you can find a Peeler, eh?'

Simon came back to his senses before that old demon of fear had time to take hold. The Thug was now quite close, the knife still held low and his other hand stretched out in balance, as he trod forward slowly like a cat, his slippered feet making no noise. In desperation, Simon looked round for some kind of weapon. The room, it seemed, was a store place for the carpet stocks. From the corner of his eye Simon saw Jenkins edge between two piles of carpet and, as he did so, begin removing a green glass bottle from his back trouser pocket. He had no time to record more, for the Hindu stalking him now made his move, springing forward, the knife drawn back for a series of thrusts.

In turn, Simon danced back – straight into a stack of Afghan rugs. They caught him behind the knees and sent him sprawling, so saving his life, for as he fell, he threw out a despairing hand. This caught the edge of a deep-pile carpet which was hanging on display along a line strung from the ceiling, and Simon's fingers clutched it, bringing down line and carpet. The heavy fabric

25

crashed on to the Thug, knocking him off balance and sending his knife spinning across the earthen floor. Immediately, Simon threw himself at the figure struggling beneath the carpet, sending both of them crashing down. The Hindu was momentarily winded as Simon landed on top of him but he fought like a trapped tiger, wrapping both hands round the Englishman's neck and then slipping one end of the garrotte cord under Simon's throat. As he did so, Simon pulled back his head and then sent his forehead crashing into the Indian's nose. The crack as the bridge shattered was closely followed by another, as a beer bottle was brought down sharply on to the man's head, knocking away his turban and sending a stream of blood from his broken nose into Simon's eyes, momentarily blinding him.

It took perhaps twenty seconds before Simon could wipe the blood away and regain his vision. Blinking, half fearing what he would see, he looked around. Close to him, Jenkins was perched on the edge of a pile of rugs. His head was back and perspiration was pouring down his face. But his eyes were closed in an expression of divine ecstasy as he drank from the now-opened beer bottle, which protruded from under his great moustache as though it had been wedged there as a permanent fixture. Of the two Thugs there was no sign, although their comrade still lay where he had fallen.

'Good God,' exclaimed Simon. 'Where have they gone?'

Continuing to drink, Jenkins opened his eyes and waved his hand to Simon. Then, with a great sigh, he put down the empty bottle and wiped the back of his hand across his moustache. 'Sorry, bach sir. I needed that, see. Though just as well I 'ad it in my back pocket, isn't it? I always say that a feller should carry a bottle o' booze in 'is back pocket. You never know when you are goin' to need it ... one way or the other, that is.'

'Oh do shut up, 352. If you hadn't been drinking we wouldn't have got into this mess in the first place. Now tell me. What happened?'

'Ah well, look you, when I pulled out me secret weapon – this fine but alas now very dead bottle of Indian pale ale – and when you cleverly pulled that carpet thing down on to 'is mate, my chap turned round and hoofed it.' Jenkins spread a large palm across his face and flicked away the perspiration with his fingers. 'I thought you 'ad probably knocked off your bloke with your 'ead, like...' A huge beam spread across the Welsh-man's face. 'An' I must say, bach sir, what a great dirty fighter you're turnin' out to be. Nobody would think you was an officer, see.'

'Oh for goodness' sake, just tell me what happened.'

'Well, like I said, I thought you 'ad finished off your man, but, just to be sure, I clouted 'im one across the turban with me bottle – though not too 'ard, see, because I didn't want to break it, did I? But it looks like I should 'ave 'it 'im 'arder, because no sooner 'ad I opened the top an' taken the first gulp than 'e was off like an eel, the perisher, trailin' blood all over the place.'

Simon gestured to the dead Thug by the wall. 'What about him?'

27

'Ah yes, 'im. Well, when they sort of pushed me into 'ere, I let on that I was more drunk than I was, see.' Jenkins frowned earnestly. 'Though I never really was very drunk, see, sir. I just 'ad a couple o' jars with some lads from the Buffs I met when I was tryin' to find me way back to the 'otel. I was never really–'

'Oh yes you were. But just get on with it.'

'Very well. So I pretended to stagger a bit an' 'alf fell over. Then they tried to get me up an' was feelin' inside me jacket for me wallet, while one feller started to put this black string stuff round me gullet.' He blinked for a moment. 'Cor, that didn't 'alf 'urt, I'll tell you. So I kicked one chap in the ballookers, threw the feller with the string over me shoulder – I was worried about me beer bottle then, I can tell yer – and the third one came at me with a knife. Got me in the shoulder, see, just 'ere.' He pointed to where the blood had congealed on to his shirt. 'Luckily it wasn't much, so I was able to get 'old of 'im...' he paused, as though in some embarrassment, 'an' ... er ... just break 'is neck, see. I think 'e's a bit dead now. But he shouldn't 'ave knifed me, look you. I don't like fellers who fight with knives.'

Jenkins sat back with an air of indignation and drained the last dregs from the bottle before throwing it away. Then he looked at the floor and spoke shyly. 'Sorry, bach sir, for all the inconvenience, like. But I'm very grateful, see, for you comin' after me an' all. I might 'ave 'ad a bit of trouble seein' off three of 'em.' He looked up, with the air of a terrier who had run after a rabbit and returned very, very wet.

28

'Don't mention it, I'm sure.' Simon's eyebrows shot up. 'Here we are, stuck in this strange city. You have gone off and got blindingly drunk, killed a local inhabitant and wrecked a carpet shop. No one will believe they were Thugs because the state always claims that they've been stamped out. I'm glad you're sorry, because we will probably be thrown into jail any minute now.'

Jenkins screwed up his face. 'Yes, well, I don't think it was completely my fault, see. I wasn't interfering with those fellers in their black nighties, now was I...'

Lecture delivered, Simon relented. 'Of course you weren't. Let me think.' He rose to his feet. 'To be honest, I don't quite know what to do about it. We *could* go to the police, of course, but whichever way you look at it, we've killed a man and there he is. Mind you, there don't seem to be any witnesses. Which is strange in itself.' He looked around. 'Where the hell are the people who own this shop – if that's what it is? Why is it all so quiet and empty?'

'P'raps they're part of the plot. These bastards knew where to take me, look you.'

'True. Either way, we'd better get out of here, because I don't want trouble with the army. That shoulder needs attention anyway–' Simon held up his hand. Just beyond the beaded curtain they heard the sound of a soft footfall. In an instant, Jenkins had leapt to his feet and was silently moving to the edge of the doorway. Then he plunged through, and when he returned, he was holding by the ear the urchin who had pointed the way for Simon. The boy made no attempt to escape but regarded Simon with large luminous eyes.

'Let him go,' said Simon. 'He saw you taken and showed me the way.'

'Did you now, young feller.' Jenkins's face broke into one of his expansive grins, so that his black moustache seemed to stretch from ear to ear. 'Well, I regard that as neighbourly. Thank you very much, bach. 'Ere, let's shake.'

The boy looked at the huge outstretched hand without expression. Jenkins seized his matchstick-thin arm and shook the tiny hand. 'Well done, bach.' Slowly a smile spread across the boy's face as his arm was pumped.

'All right,' said Simon. 'Let's go.' He put his hand on the urchin's shoulder and pointed to the body on the floor. 'Do you speak English?'

The boy remained expressionless. Then he opened his mouth and pointed inside.

'Oh, the poor little devil's dumb. Here.' Simon reached into his pocket and pressed several rupees into the tiny palm. Then he indicated the body again, put his fingers to his lips and slowly shook his head from side to side. 'Understand?' he asked.

This time the urchin, his fingers clenched tightly around the coins, nodded vigorously.

'Good. Let's be off. Put your jacket on, 352. We don't want you dripping blood on the carpets and attracting attention.'

The three of them walked through the outer room and then into the alleyway. Once in the main street, the urchin slipped away and was gone in a flash, like a trout returned to a stream. The two men walked as nonchalantly as they could back to the hotel, where, once in Simon's room – Jenkins had the one next door – Simon helped the Welshman off with his shirt and examined the wound.

'Hmm. You're right. It is only a flesh wound.' He began gently washing the incision with soda water, poured on a little iodine and applied a gauze pad to the wound with a clumsily bound bandage. 'There, keep your hand in your pocket so as not to open the wound again. That should fix you up until we can see a doctor. Which reminds me: did you get the tickets? When do we sail?'

'Ah, sorry, bach sir. I quite forgot about all that, with all the fuss an' all. Yes, two tickets for London and we sail in six days' time. Through this Suez Canal place, which should be somethin' to tell your folks back home. Ah, I forgot again. Two letters for you as well.'

He fumbled inside his jacket and produced the tickets and two envelopes. Simon checked the tickets. 'Damn. I had hoped that we could be on our way within a couple of days. You're sure there was nothing sooner through the Canal?'

Jenkins shook his head. 'Goodness, lucky to get on board at all, look you.'

'All right. Well, I think we both deserve a whisky. See if you can get the boy to bring us two here.' Jenkins beamed and was gone and Simon looked at the two envelopes. The first, addressed to 'Captain S. Fonthill, Queen's Own Corps of Guides, Afghanistan', bore the distinctive, boldly sloped handwriting of his mother. The second, made of coarse paper, carried an indecipherable postmark and was merely addressed to him 'Care of the British Army, India'. He did not recognise

31

the simple hand. He laid it to one side and, dutifully, read his mother's letter first.

He had written to her from Kabul, explaining that he and Jenkins had resigned from the army and that they were on their way home, although he had given no estimated date for their arrival. This was just as well, because the pair had then become involved with General Roberts's epic march on Kandahar, smuggling the plucky war correspondent Alice Griffith with them across the mountains. Alice ... ah, Alice! He shook his head and continued reading. Predictably – and here he smiled – Charlotte Fonthill was 'shocked, no, astonished' at his decision to resign and urged him to reconsider. She demanded to know the reason behind the decision (Simon had only hinted at his dissatisfaction with the army staff) and why he was buying out 'this servant person' whom he was bringing home with him. She was not at all sure that there would be room for Jenkins in their house, although 'your father believes it will be quite possible to fit him in – despite the fact that Papa, of course, knows nothing about the running of this establishment...' They were both well, and she closed not with affection, of course, but 'sincerely'.

Simon smiled again and turned to the other envelope. Looking again at the postmark, he made out the words 'Cape Colony'. He tore open the envelope and scanned the single sheet of paper, ruled as though torn from a child's exercise book. The letter was undated. Anxiously, he read:

Dear Simon,
I do not know if this letter will ever reach you

32

but I am in desparate trouble and can only turn to you. I cannot write you a long story but Papa came to this place after the break-up of our farm in Zululand. He hoped to dig diamonds. He sent for me to come here and help him but when I came here Papa was gone and a Big Man has the house and says that he is Papa's partner and Papa is away on business but he keeps me here and is not nice. Papa has been away a long time and this Big Man is bad to me and hurts me and there is no law here. I have smuggled this out to post and pray it will reach you somehow. Oh Simon you remember that I helped you once. Can you help me now?

Your freind Nandi

Simon looked up and stared hard at the wall of the room. But he saw nothing of the whitewashed plasterwork, only the vision of an exquisitely small coffee-coloured face, flashing a smile with tiny white teeth in sun-dappled shade. Nandi, with her warm trust of everyone, Nandi, who loved her country with as much passion as any jingo did England but who would not harm a soul. Nandi, whose courage was hidden behind a sweet gentleness. Nandi, who was now being–

He clenched his fists in an agony of frustrated anger and then looked again at the head of the paper, where she had scrawled, in her schoolgirl hand, '5 Currey Street, Kimberley'. Kimberley? He frowned. He had never heard of it – or had he? Something about diamonds came into his mind. But where the hell in the vast Cape Territory could it be? And how long ago had she penned this *cri de coeur?* He bit his thumb as he tried to grapple with the logistics of reaching her, but his efforts to concentrate were ruined by the memories which, unbidden, came rushing back.

This half-cast Zulu girl, daughter of John Dunn, a white hunter who had made his home in Zululand and become a trusted *induna* or chief to King Cetswayo, had helped them both escape from Ulundi, the Zulu capital, where they had been imprisoned by the King at the beginning of the Anglo-Zulu War. Then, with Alice Griffith's connivance, Nandi had intervened at the last minute at a court martial brought against Simon by Colonel Ralph Covington. Her evidence had saved him from being shot for the false charges of cowardice and desertion. Simon had half fallen in love with her – despite his growing feelings for Alice – and Jenkins, he knew, had always been completely enamoured of this fey, brave girl. There was no question but that they should go now to her aid. But where the hell was she, and would they be too late?

His brain was still seething when Jenkins returned, beaming and carrying two large tumblers. Resourceful as always, he had found precious ice from somewhere.

'Oh, not bad news, I hope?'

'The worst. Here. Read for yourself.' He threw the letter down on to the table.

Jenkins put down the tumblers and picked up the notepaper. His brow immediately furrowed and his lips moved silently as he tried to follow the words.

Simon stood and retrieved the letter. 'Sorry,

352. I'd forgotten.'

'No. No. It's all right. It's just the big words, look you.' But he made no attempt to take back the letter and Simon began to read it aloud. At the reference to Nandi being hurt, Jenkins let out a cry of anguish and snatched the letter back, finishing it himself. When he looked up at Simon, there were tears in his eyes.

'Whoever 'e is, I swear I'll kill the bastard,' he said. 'We've gotta go now, bach sir. Right away, isn't it?'

'Right away. We must change those damned tickets.'

'Very good, sir. Kimberley, is it? Is that a port then?'

'I haven't the faintest idea, but I don't think so. It must be in the north somewhere; in the Transvaal or the Orange Free State. I think they've found diamonds there.'

'Is that where we were – with the Zulus?'

'No. Much further north and west. But I don't really know and we must find out – and quickly. Are you sure you want to come with me?'

Jenkins lowered his gaze and spoke quietly. 'I'd do anything for that little girl. You know that.'

'Yes, I'm sorry,' said Simon. 'I knew you would. Right. Go to that shop in the Fort where they sell everything. You know, the one with … no. You'll get lost again. I will go. We need a map of South Africa. But can you find your way back to the shipping office? Honestly?'

''Course I can.'

'Good. Change these tickets. Better book us to Durban. If we find we have to go on to Cape

Town we can change later. But find the very first ship that is leaving and get us on it, because we have no time to lose. Leave the whisky. Go now.'

Without a word, the Welshman turned on his heel and was gone.

The all-purpose shop, kept by the good and famous Parsee Jangerjee Nusserawanjee, sold everything from candied fruits to French clocks. It even possessed a much-folded map of South Africa. But the northern territories were blankly white and Simon could find no trace of a town named Kimberley. He bought the map anyway and returned home to pen a quick letter to his parents, explaining that alas, once again they would have to postpone their journey home to the Welsh borders – he hinted at urgent business but gave no other reason.

This time, Jenkins returned within the hour and triumphantly announced that he had secured passages for them both on a steamer that was leaving the very next day, bound for Durban, Port Elizabeth, Cape Town and London. They rose early the next morning, just as the half-naked *halalcore* Kolis, the lowest of the Untouchables, were sweeping the streets, and Simon bought a copy of the local daily newspaper. He read it with some anxiety but there was no mention of a body being found in a carpet warehouse, nor any raised eyebrows when he announced at hotel reception that they were leaving early. Eccentrics who left their whisky and leapt from twelve-foot-high balconies were, it seemed, accepted as part of the rich pattern of life in bouncing, burgeoning Bombay.

They took a gharry, complete with leather hood and buttoned upholstery, down past the grand new Yacht Club to Apollo Bunder, where a bunder boat was waiting to take them out to the steamer riding at anchor in the bay. In what the experienced India hands called 'the good old days', the journey home under sail round the Cape of Good Hope could take nine months or so. Now, since the opening of the Suez Canal eleven years before, the passage by steamship and via the Mediterranean could last as little as seventeen days.

The best ships, of course, were now plying that route, and it was an older vessel, with sails and spars still rigged to act as an auxiliary source of power – as well as a stabilising influence, where necessary – which awaited them out in the placid turquoise waters of the bay. Jenkins, no sailor, noticed rust patches on the waterline of the vessel as they climbed the ladder up its side.

'Indeed to goodness,' he muttered, 'I don't fancy this one little bit, bach sir.'

Not for the first time, Simon noticed how Jenkins's Welshness increased the more agitated he became. He smiled. 'Nothing to it, 352,' he said. 'Just a pleasure cruise across the Indian Ocean, that's all.'

'Humph. That's what you said last time. And then we sank, look you.'

'That was the Atlantic. This will be different. Sunshine all the way, you'll see.'

Their cabins were spartan but comfortable enough and seemed luxurious to Jenkins, who, on the outward passage, had shared the *Devonia*'s fo'castle – a Stygian, plunging steel shell – with some 250 other troops. Nevertheless, Simon was less than happy at the age of the ship. The voyage to Durban would be slow and he was anxious to make all speed to go to the aid of Nandi. Goodness knows what might have happened to her, he mused, since she had penned her cry for help. And would they be able to find her on those vast plains of the northern Cape?

His state of mind was not improved when the appointed time for their departure in the late afternoon came and went. Steam had been raised but they remained moored to the giant buoy riding in the centre of the bay. Why the delay? He sought out one of the ship's officers.

The man shrugged his shoulders. 'Unusual, I agree,' he said, 'but not so vital these days when we don't have to catch the evening breeze to sail or worry so much about the tide at this anchorage. We are waiting for a last-minute passenger. We understand that she is on her way and should be out with us within the half-hour. Then – a toot on the steam whistle and we're off!'

Simon frowned. Time and tide, it seemed, waited for no man – but it could for a woman! While Jenkins unpacked their belongings down below, he walked to the stern and looked out at Bombay, the gateway to India for most Englishmen, where he and his servant had landed, it seemed years ago, but in fact only some ten months before. They had been shuttled off immediately to Gharagha, in the hills, for a lamentably short spell of training in the art of

38

spying on the North West Frontier of India. Both he and Jenkins still bore, under their eyes, faint traces of the dye that had been applied to their skin to make them look like natives of that wild country. He gazed now over the pretty yellow and cream houses of the city to the white-spired Scottish church. The view was charming but he took little of it in. In his mind's eye he saw the low mountains of Swat and the more terrifying jagged peaks of the Hindu Kush. The famous late-afternoon breeze that brought succour after the heat of Bombay's day touched his cheek but it went unnoticed. Instead, he winced as he felt again the musket barrel crashing into his nose and remembered the torture he had endured in that Afghan village. He had been lucky to survive and would always bear the scars. He heard nothing of the steam whistle sounded by a passing vessel, only the pitch of Alice's voice in the fort at Kandahar as, hurriedly – to prevent him interrupting with his own proposal of marriage – she explained that she had accepted Covington's proposal and had resigned from the *Morning Post* and her hard-won position as foreign correspondent to journey home to prepare for her wedding. His knuckles tightened on the stern rail. Well, that was that and it was all over now. He was glad to be leaving India. Good riddance to it, and to the British Army!

From the quay he saw now a bunder boat pulling towards them. He could just make out the figure of a woman sitting in the stern. Thank God for that! Now they could get under way. He turned and walked to the other side of the ship and

39

looked out across the bay, where shallow-draught tramp steamers and coasters were anchored, waiting for their turn to pull in and unload. Beyond them stretched the line of the horizon where the light blue of the sky met the darker colour of the ocean. He couldn't remember how long the voyage was expected to take – a week, perhaps, and then the trek to the north to find Kimberley. He still had no idea where this little township lay, but he suspected that the nearest point for disembarkation would be Durban, from which they could strike north-west towards the Transvaal border. They should be able to buy a map and horses at Durban, where the army would still have a strong base following the resettlement of Zululand. They would need rifles, too – and not just for hunting. This Kimberley sounded like a rough-and-ready border settlement and they would probably need guns to rescue Nandi.

His speculation was interrupted by a cry from Jenkins, who had materialised and was now standing in the space between two deckhouses, beckoning him to come to the starboard side. 'You'll never believe this, bach sir,' he called. 'Quick, come over.'

Simon hurried to join the Welshman and together they looked down at the little boat gently rising and falling by the side of the boarding platform.

'Good lord,' exclaimed Simon. 'Alice!'

Hearing her name, the young woman balancing in the boat looked up and then put her hand to her mouth in consternation. The movement did not prevent a blush from spreading across her cheeks. Then she gave a half-wave at the faces looking down at her and spoke quickly to the bunder boat boy, who nodded affirmatively.

'Yes,' called down Simon. 'Bound for Durban. But you as well?'

Momentarily she frowned, and then nodded. She grasped the hand extended to her by a sailor and stepped on to the platform at the bottom of the companionway, pulling her light shawl tightly across her shoulders. She made a graceful figure as she mounted the steps, climbing without hesitation, the sunlight shining in her blonde hair and the simple shift dress she was wearing accentuating her slimness. The flush was still on her cheeks as she greeted the two men waiting for her as she stepped on to the deck.

'My dear 352,' she said, and kissed the beaming Welshman on both cheeks. It was with a little more restraint that she saluted Simon similarly, and her grey eyes were slightly troubled as they looked into his. 'You were the last two people I expected to see here,' she said. 'I thought you would be well on your way along the Suez Canal by now.'

'No,' said Simon, not knowing whether to feel delighted or despairing to see so unexpectedly the loved face he was now so used to banishing from his mind. 'Our plans have changed – or, at least, have been changed for us.'

'But South Africa! I thought you were going home.'

'I could say the same of you. You told me that you were returning to England to marry Covington.' A sudden, heart-lifting thought occurred to him. 'The, er, wedding ... it's not been cancelled,

41

has it?'

She looked away quickly. 'No. Merely post-poned.'

'Excuse me, madam,' a ship's officer inter-vened. 'We have been waiting for you to board. If your baggage can be unloaded from the boat quickly, if you please, then we can get under way. I will show you to your cabin and you can meet your friends at dinner.'

'Oh, I am sorry. Yes, of course.' She turned back to Simon and Jenkins. 'We will, then, exchange our stories over a glass of wine. Please excuse me.' She gave a rather stiff smile and turned away.

'Wonderful to 'ave you on board anyway, miss,' Jenkins called after her, his face beaming.

Alice looked back over her shoulder. 'Ah, it's so good to see you again, Mr Jenkins – oh, sorry, I mean Sergeant.' And this time her smile was wide and genuine and she waved as she disappeared down the companionway.

Jenkins was still beaming as he turned to Simon. 'Well, bach sir, that's a turn-up for the book, eh? You must be as pleased as punch.'

'I don't know why you should say that.' Simon's voice was cold as his mind grappled with the renewal of his disappointment. 'Miss Griffith is engaged to be married and means nothing to me now. Have you unpacked?'

'Yes, everything stowed and shipshape. All ready for the bleedin' shipwreck.'

'Very well.' The second and last of Alice's bags – she travelled amazingly light, noted Simon – was put on to the deck and taken down below. Then the anchor chain rattled and a steam whistle on the funnel sounded its farewell to Bombay and India, and slowly the big ship began to gather way. 'I'll see you down below in a minute or two,' said Simon curtly and he strode away towards the bow.

'Suit yerself, bach,' muttered Jenkins to himself. 'But it's no use mopin'. She's a strong-willed lass. She's goin' to marry 'im, that's for sure.'

The three met up again some two hours later as sherry, wine and whisky were dispensed to the first-class passengers in the lounge before dinner. In deference to Jenkins, who, of course, possessed no evening wear, Simon did not dress for dinner. But Alice was looking radiant in grey taffeta which matched her eyes and revealed well-rounded shoulders of astonishing whiteness compared to her face, which, despite a light coating of powder, still showed a tan from the Afghan sun. Alice was Simon's age, but she carried herself with a maturity that belied her twenty-five years and reflected, perhaps, something of the hardship of the campaigns on which she had reported in Zululand and Afghanistan over the last two years. Her face beneath its halo of shining hair smiled easily, but to Simon, her eyes seemed a little sad as they stood together, slightly self-consciously and apart from other passengers, Jenkins in his best white drill suit, formally at ease, army style, hands clasped behind his buttocks.

'Now, Alice,' said Simon, 'do tell us why you are sailing for South Africa when you should have been sailing home to England.'

'Please,' said Alice, looking out of the porthole

43

as though to seek inspiration on how to start her story. 'You first.'

Simon related the story of Nandi's letter and of their decision to go to her aid. Alice's face clouded as she heard of the girl's desperation. 'But are there no police or government people she can turn to?' she asked.

'Apparently not. This Kimberley place sounds like some sort of frontier town from the American west. She does not seem to have help at hand. I only hope that we can find her and that, if we do, we are in time to be of some use.'

Alice grasped Simon's arm impulsively. 'Oh, my dear. I want to help you find her.' Then she paused. 'But I am afraid that I cannot come with you. You see...'

'Yes. Tell us what has happened.'

'Very well.' The words were spoken with a sigh, as though she was not particularly proud of what she was about to relate. 'Shall we sit at the table?'

They sat and Alice began. She spoke without looking at either of them, her eyes downcast. 'You will remember that after ... after you had so bravely taken me over the mountains to report the battle of Kandahar, when General Roberts forbade me from accompanying his column and...' She paused.

The two nodded, although Alice was still staring at the tablecloth. 'Well, I felt that I had had enough of killing – what with endangering your lives and all.'

'No, no,' Jenkins interrupted, his black eyebrows nearly meeting his moustache, so fierce was his frown. 'You mustn't blame yerself for all that, miss. These things 'appen in war, look you.'

She turned on him quickly. 'That's just the point. I didn't want any more of it. Writing about killing and even being involved in it. I felt sick of it all. And then...'

'And then?' prompted Simon.

'Yes, well,' her eyes returned to the tablecloth, 'then Ralph proposed to me and it seemed the way out. So I cabled to my editor at the *Morning Post* and resigned my job. He responded by trying to change my mind, but I refused. Then, I was packing to leave when I received another cable from him. This contained an urgent plea to "deviate", as he put it, to Durban on the way home and file a couple of reports from there on the situation. It seems,' and here her eyes began to light up as she turned to each of her listeners in turn, as though to share her excitement at the task offered her, 'that there is a chance of war with the Boers of the Transvaal, who want their independence back. But before that, General Wolseley, who, as you know, is in command in South Africa and is at Durban, is determined to put down the bePedi tribe.'

'Who are they, then, miss?' enquired Jenkins.

'They are people very like the Zulus who live in the north-eastern part of the Transvaal, near Portuguese-Mozambique territory. They raid and maraud from the mountains there and have been attacking farms. Both the Boers and the English have sent expeditions against them and been well and truly defeated by this tribe. Wolseley believes that he must put them down before he can even begin thinking about the problems with the

Boers.' She smiled. 'There must be a touch of the good housekeeper about this general.' Then she shrugged her shoulders. 'It doesn't really seem like a great international incident to report – perhaps just another little colonial bush fire – but the point is, William Russell is there, with Wolseley.'

'William who?' asked Jenkins.

'Russell, the great special correspondent of the *Telegraph*. You will know of him, Simon.' Simon nodded, as Alice went on. 'He made his reputation on the *Times* in the Crimea by revealing just how poorly led and badly organised was the British Army in that war.' Alice's face became even more animated. 'If it hadn't been for his reports from the front line, none of the reforms of the army, such as Cardwell – you know, the introduction of formal officer training at Sandhurst, and so on – would have happened. Russell is a great journalist and someone I have always admired. But the point is that if he is there, there must be something up. He smells stories from continents away. It may be that he believes this little bePedi campaign could turn out to be another Isandlwana, and if that is so, the *Morning Post* mustn't miss the story. That is why...' she paused rather self-consciously, 'my editor has asked me to go.'

The three sat silently for a moment. Then Simon cleared his throat. 'But Alice,' he said, 'I thought you had had enough of fighting and wars. What has made you change your mind?'

Alice studied the tablecloth again. 'Yes, I know. It seems perverse. Perhaps ... oh, I don't know.' She looked up defiantly. 'One can't turn off being

46

a journalist just like that, you know, as though twisting a tap handle. Anyway, I was the nearest member of staff to South Africa, the others having gone back long ago after the end of the Zulu War. I could not let my editor down.'

'What did Covington say?'

Alice flushed and was silent for a moment. 'He did not like it, of course. But he understands. Anyway,' the defiance came back into her voice, 'the wedding is only postponed. Not cancelled.' She stared fixedly out of the porthole.

They spent the rest of the meal attempting to make light conversation, but the atmosphere between them was uncomfortable. And it continued to be so throughout the voyage, which, as Simon had prophesied, turned out to be calm and uneventful. Alice increasingly took her meals alone in her cabin and seemed to avoid Simon, although she sometimes spent minutes leaning over the ship's rail with Jenkins, listening as he regaled her with stories of his early life as a farm worker in Wales and as an itinerant bricklayer. Jenkins himself received attention from the ship's doctor for the flesh wound in his shoulder, which, given rest for his arm, began to heal rapidly. Covington's name was never mentioned again by any of them, and it was almost a relief when they rose one morning to find the surf booming on Durban's beach on the far side of the bar.

Chapter 2

The bar and the surf caused difficulties in landing
and they all had to go ashore in a longboat, riding
the surf and getting wet in the process. Alice sat in
the stern of the boat, in riding breeches and
boots, her hair tied back in a scarf and her eyes
shining with the excitement of shooting the surf.
Simon thought that he had never seen anyone
look so beautiful, and he bit his lip and cursed the
salt spray that drenched him. He vowed to get out
of Durban as soon as he could buy provisions and
transport. He wished to leave Alice, with her
troubled grey eyes, as far behind him and as
quickly as possible.

The trio split up as soon as they had booked
into a modest timber hotel, sited near the shore
so as to allow the sea breeze to reduce the
humidity somewhat. Durban, indeed, bore some
resemblance to Bombay in that the atmosphere
was moist and, surrounded as it was by sugar and
coffee plantations, the streets were full of Indian
coolies who worked in the fields. But it possessed
none of the vitality and obvious prosperity of the
Indian city. It oozed sleepiness, and even the
presence of Wolseley's troops gave it no sense of
purpose or vitality. If there was going to be a war,
it would be far away and of no great import to
Natal, relieved and relaxed as it was after the
threat of Cetswayo's Zulus had been removed.

Alice immediately went to Wolseley's headquarters to present her credentials, resigned to meeting once again the initial incredulity caused by a woman – and a young and attractive one at that – representing, as a war correspondent, a newspaper as traditional and important as the *Morning Post*. On this occasion, however, she knew that her reputation would have preceded her and that her editor would have cabled the General's staff and, to some extent, prepared the way for her.

Simon and Jenkins meanwhile set about equipping themselves for their long overland journey. A quick study of a locally bought map showed Kimberley as a small dot in the centre of southern Africa, at the far north of the Cape Colony, sitting by the Vaal River in a territory previously unknown to Simon called Griqualand West. To its north stretched the Transvaal, and to reach Kimberley they would have to traverse the Drakensberg Mountains and cross Basutoland and the independent Boer Republic of Orange Free State which fringed it to the east.

'Funny name, that,' said Jenkins. 'Lots of oranges there, is there? And do they give them away?'

'Not quite. It's pretty barren, flat country, I think. Many of the Boers trekked there from the south, to get away from English rule. They established a new homeland there, and because they were originally of Dutch origin, they named it after the royal family of Holland. Something like that, anyway. It's going to be a journey of five hundred miles or more, and there's no railway

49

and precious few roads by the look of it.'

It would mean travelling on horseback or by cart and oxen. The latter would be less uncomfortable, but Simon disliked the thought of outspanning. Their pace would be slow enough as it was, without the need for uncoupling and coupling harnesses night and morning and putting the team of oxen out for grazing. They therefore purchased three riding horses, one to act as relief, and a pack mule. Simon knew that the high veldt country (it was marked on their map as 4,000 feet above sea level) could be cold, so they exchanged their light cotton clothing for flannel shirts and hard-wearing corduroys, and bought wide-brimmed Boer hats. At a gunsmith they were advised that they might cross lion country and should take heavy-calibre elephant guns, but Simon found, at the back of the store, two old ex-army Martini-Henry rifles. The gunsmith was reluctant to sell – they were probably illegal weapons – but Jenkins was adamant and Simon needed little persuading to pay the heavy premium demanded. Both men had fought with these single-shot breech-loading guns against the Zulus and the Pathans, and valued them highly. It was true that at ten pounds they were heavy, and with eighty-three grains of black powder behind each slug they kicked like a mule when fired, bruising the shoulder when in constant use, but they were proven man-stoppers. They could be accurate at a thousand yards and deadly at six hundred, firing .45 Boxer cartridges with a heavy lead slug so soft that on impact it spread to cause the most fearful wound. They would see off both lions and hostile natives, but as an afterthought Simon also bought a brace of Navy Colt pistols.

'We goin' to war again then, bach sir?' enquired Jenkins with a sniff.

'We may just have to. I don't like the sound of the "Big Man" Nandi wrote about. And we're going to be crossing pretty wild territory. Come on. We're wasting time.'

A couple of low tents, groundsheets, blankets and basic provisions – including biltong, the dried beef which was the Afrikaner's staple when on trek – completed their preparations, and they decided to set off shortly after sun-up the next day. In both men's minds was the thought of the time that had elapsed since Nandi had posted her plea for help. Anything could have happened to her. Time was at a premium.

They were delayed, however. Alice was waiting for them when they arrived back at the hotel. She too was concerned about the Zulu girl and had tried to make enquiries about her at army head-quarters. Although John Dunn, Nandi's father, had lived in Zululand as one of Cetswayo's chiefs, he had been pressed into service by General Chelmsford to be head of intelligence for the British force that had reinvaded Zululand from the south after the disaster of Isandlwana. He was, therefore, known to the British staff. But he had disappeared after the dissolution of the Zulu kingdom and no one knew where he had gone.

'I understand,' Alice told Simon, 'that Catherine, his number one wife, still lives on what remains of their farm in the south of Zululand. But no one has seen Dunn for some months now,

51

and wherever Nandi is, she is not back on the farm.'

'Thank you,' said Simon, 'but I'm afraid that doesn't take us any further. We shall just have to set off and hope that she is still in Kimberley. We leave tomorrow.'

'Oh no. You can't do that.' For a moment Simon's heart leapt. Did she, *could* she care? Certainly Alice's eyes were wide. Then her lids dropped. 'What I mean is,' she continued, 'the General wishes to see you in the morning.'

'What? Whatever for? Well, I don't wish to see him. I've had enough of British generals. We leave at dawn.'

Alice leaned forward. 'No, Simon. You forget that this man now virtually controls South Africa. He is High Commissioner for South-East Africa, as well as army commander. If you went off without seeing him, he would send an army patrol after you and have you back within the hour. He is no Chelmsford, you know. He is a great reformer with a high reputation. He is very determined and absolutely ruthless. You must know about him.'

Simon nodded his head slowly. He did know about Sir Garnet Wolseley. So did every officer in the army. He was the nation's most high-profile general, with a reputation for valour, efficiency and reforming zeal which infuriated the Duke of Cambridge, the Queen's cousin, who commanded the British Army from a hidebound Horse Guards in London. Without patronage or a friend in high places, Wolseley had made his own way. He had lost an eye in the trenches before

Sebastopol in the Crimean War, and in 1859, at the age of twenty-six had become the youngest lieutenant colonel in the British Army. He had made his name by leading the Red River Expedition in Canada in 1869, taking a small force 1,200 miles through forest and across lakes and prairie to crush a rebellion of French-Canadian Indians. What was more, he had done so without firing a single bullet in anger or exceeding his budget. The British Government loved him for that, whatever the feelings of the Duke. Following that he had won a difficult jungle war in Africa against the Ashanti, despite facing overwhelming odds. He was England's hero, and at this very moment, Simon had heard, he was being affectionately satirised on the London stage by Gilbert and Sullivan as 'the Very Model of a Modern Major General'. Now here he was, cleaning up after the Zulu War and, unofficially, softening up the Boers for confederation of the whole of South Africa under the British flag.

Oh, Simon knew about Wolseley all right. But he regarded him with ambivalence. Simon hated the conservatism still at the heart of the British Army – the power of the aristocracy and the unprofessionalism of many of the senior officers, displayed alarmingly when spear-carrying Zulus had wiped out a well-armed but badly led column of British soldiers at Isandlwana. To the extent that Wolseley was a moderniser and a radical, a man who argued that the army had fought too long 'in the cold shade of aristocracy' and that an officer should understand ways of providing shelter, good health and even clothing for his men

53

– these views Simon, as a young subaltern, had applauded. They were rare among senior officers, most of whom valued the pleasures of the hunt and the levee before the study of military tactics. But he also knew that the General had his favourites, and that if you were outside his circle of approval it was difficult to rise to the top in his command. In the Ashanti War he had surrounded himself with officers who ever afterwards received his patronage. They were called 'the Ashanti Ring'. Colonel Covington had fought against the Ashanti. He was one of the Ring.

'Yes, I know about Wolseley,' Simon said. 'But why on earth should he want to see me here? Did you tell him anything about me?'

Alice shook her head. 'No – well...' She lowered her gaze again, then lifted her head and looked at him with that air of candour that had so intrigued him from the moment they'd been introduced by their parents, all those years ago in Wales. 'I did say that I knew you to be a most brave man and that the charges brought against you in Zululand were unfounded. Mind you,' she smiled, 'Wolseley hates journalists, and he told me that if it suited his purposes he would feed them false information on a campaign, so I doubt if my opinion would influence him either way.'

Simon felt his aloofness melt as he looked into those familiar grey eyes. 'Well, thank you, Alice. But I can't understand why he should ask about me or want to see me. Do you know why?'

'No. But he knew that you and dear 352 – yes, he'd heard about him, too – were on the ship. He's very shrewd, Simon. He seems to know

54

everything that happens down here. Don't underestimate him. Oh! One other thing. I think he dislikes General Roberts. I think he is jealous of him after Kandahar.'

They both laughed. 'Good,' said Simon. 'That's one thing in his favour, anyway. What about you? Has he accepted you?'

'Yes, but he doesn't like it. He clearly doesn't favour women anywhere near the front line, and in fact he has told me that I will never see the actual fighting – well, we'll see about that.' Alice stuck out her jaw. 'But, as I have said, he doesn't like journalists reporting on him anyway, although it is as a result of people like me writing about him that his reputation is so high. And the Horse Guards have accredited me, so he has to take me on his advance. The other thing is that I am sure he has heard that I upset Roberts in Afghanistan. There was a definite twinkle in his eye when he asked after the General.'

'When is he going to the north?'

'Soon, I think, for his camp is in a turmoil. But Simon, he definitely wants to see you first thing in the morning. He suggested eight a.m.'

'Damn. Very well. I shall see him, of course.'

The next morning Simon made no concessions to formality, and arrived at Wolseley's HQ – a charming old house set in flowered gardens on the outskirts of Durban – dressed in his travelling gear. He was made to wait, for the General, it seemed, was still playing tennis. Simon perched on the edge of his chair in an anteroom, contemplating the fact that his vital journey was being delayed while some pompous English staff officer was hitting a ball across a net.

But Wolseley was not pompous, nor did he look like a general. He came bustling through a door, dressed in white flannels and cool shirt, rubbing a towel through his hair.

'Sorry to be late, Fonthill,' he said – and then, suddenly, 'No I'm not.' He looked at the wall clock. 'Three minutes to. You're early.'

Simon stood. 'Yes, sir. I have to travel to the north-west and don't have much time.'

'Right you are, then, we won't waste time.' Wolseley advanced, one hand outstretched, the towel in the other. They shook hands. 'Come on through. Forgive me if I don't change.'

Simon observed the man with interest. England's hero was just below middle height – perhaps five feet seven inches – and was sturdy and well proportioned and bounced rather than walked. His features were clean cut with a fresh complexion, ruddy now from the tennis. He had a broad and lofty forehead topped by wavy chestnut-coloured hair. His one good eye was bright, penetrating and rather bulbous – the other was obviously made of glass – and he would have been very handsome except that his chin and jaw looked weak, surprisingly so considering his reputation for fortitude and resoluteness.

Wolseley sat in a large chair behind a desk and gestured to Simon to take the one opposite. 'North-west. North-west? Where exactly are you going and what are you going to be doing there, eh?'

Simon shifted uncomfortably. 'None of your

business' was the first retort that ran through his mind. Then he remembered Alice's warning. 'I have to journey to a place called Kimberley to do some personal business there,' he explained.

'You goin' to be a digger?'

'A what? Oh, I see. No. I am not going to try and find diamonds. I, ah, want to try and find someone to whom I owe a debt. Then I shall return immediately to England.'

The one good eye regarded him intently. 'Why did you hit Covington?' The question came out of the blue, without warning. This man obviously did not beat about the bush.

Simon shifted awkwardly in his chair. 'He had placed me under arrest, out in the field, just after Isandlwana. He would not believe me when I told him that our column had been completely wiped out and that he should alert General Chelmsford up in the hills. I was on my way to warn the mission station at Rorke's Drift that a Zulu impi was on its way to attack it and, probably, invade Natal. He was stopping me from doing so by ordering my arrest and I felt that, because of his obduracy, many lives would be lost. I'm afraid I saw red and hit him and then rode away to get to the Drift.'

A half-smile came over Wolseley's face. 'I know Covington well. He served under me in the Ashanti. He's a brave chap – big one, too. Must have been quite a blow, eh?'

Simon did not return the smile. 'I know him well too, sir. I'm afraid that I would do it again, given the same circumstances.'

'Hmm.' Wolseley kept his eye fixed on the young

57

man opposite him and neither spoke for some seconds. 'It doesn't do, Fonthill,' the General said at last, 'to hit senior officers, but then you were court-martialled for it and will know that. Nevertheless,' and his voice took on a musing tone now, 'I don't know of anyone else who served at both Isandlwana *and* Rorke's Drift. Then I gather that you and your man Jenkins did well acting as scouts for the Eshowe column in the south before the Battle of Ulundi.'

Simon remained silent. This man was after something and he felt it best to keep quiet until it emerged.

'Yes,' continued the General. 'Did well. And then you both, ah, metamorphosed, so to speak, as spies behind the Pathan lines in Afghanistan, serving Roberts with distinction from what I hear.'

Simon shrugged. 'We did our duty, sir. That was all. But now we are out of the army and wish to do other things. And forgive me, General, but we are rather in a hurry just now.'

Wolseley had been languidly leaning back in his chair but now he sent it crashing forward. 'Yes, well, dammit, so am I. You spoke of duty. Well I have a duty to do as well, young man.' He stood up and paced around the room, circling Simon like a stalking tiger, his dishevelled hair and white tennis garb sitting incongruously with the passionate way he now spoke.

'Look here, Fonthill. Everyone assumes that I am the radical that I am painted. Well, I detest radicals. Men of Gladstone's stamp are abhorrent to my instincts. They are vestrymen rather than Englishmen. I am a Jingo in the best acceptance of that soubriquet and yet I am represented as precisely the reverse.' He swung the towel around his wrist as though about to hurl a stone from a sling. 'I am so tired and wearied of Mr Gladstone and his cabinet of vestrymen, with their plans, their littleness and their indifference to the honour and greatness of England. I am no great lover of life but I would like to do something for England before I die.'

He paused by the window and continued, looking out, speaking softly as though to himself. 'How much pleasanter is death from clean bullet wounds than from loathsome disease. To be killed in the open air with the conviction that you are dying for your country – how different from rotting to death in some hospital or dying like a consumptive girl in an artificially heated room.' He stopped and remained staring out at the garden, full of its English roses.

The silence hung in the air, almost like an accusation, and Simon shifted in his chair. *Was* it an accusation? Had he been interrogated, put in the witness box, so to speak, now to receive some great crushing condemnation because he had not served his country well enough? Simon was familiar with jingoism – patriotism being worn as a badge of courage by men who despised other races and, as likely as not, would run at the first whiff of gunsmoke. But Wolseley had more than won his spurs on the field. His bravery and dedication were renowned throughout the Empire, and it was as unnecessary for him to protest his patriotism as for the Queen to suggest that, perhaps, she was royal. And yet that strange, almost disloyal, attack on the Prime Minister...

Suddenly Wolseley turned, as though remembering Simon's presence. 'Eh?' he said. 'What?'

'Er, yes, sir. Of course.'

'Very well.' Now full of decision, the General threw the towel into a corner and returned to his chair. 'Now look here. There is a further service that your country demands of you, Fonthill. You know that we annexed – there is no other word for it – the Boer independent state of Transvaal about three years ago?'

Simon felt his heart sink. Not another call to arms! 'I understand so, yes,' he said.

'We did it because the Boers are poor managers. They couldn't organise a prayer meeting in a monastery. They won't accept being taxed and hate interference of any kind in their personal liberties, which is all very well and good when you're running a farm miles from anywhere but not when you're trying to build a country. They act like children and the damned place was virtually bankrupt, so we took it over – with their agreement, of course.'

'Oh, of course, sir.' The irony was lost on Wolseley.

'Well, now that we've got the place more or less up and running, they want their independence again, of course. We can't let 'em have it – we have gone too far down the line to put the engine into reverse, so to speak. Things are building up a bit round Pretoria, the Transvaal's capital. I don't think it will go as far as a fight, but it may do. They were of precious little help to us during

60

the Zulu War, and the sensible thing for them to have done, if they wanted us out, would have been to rebel against us when we'd got our hands full with Cetswayo and his impis. But that's a soldier speaking, and the Boers are not soldiers.'

'No,' Simon intervened, 'but I hear they are damned fine shots.'

'That's as maybe, but they would be no match for British soldiers of the line.'

Simon sighed, and in his mind's eye he saw a red-coated colonel sitting in a tent under the giant rock of Isandlwana, and heard him say again, 'I hope Johnny Zulu does attack – I'll give him a bloody nose.' Would the British Army never learn? But the General was continuing.

'The point is, I don't want to fight 'em. I doubt if there'd be support from the Government back home for doing so. What I want to do is to impress them; show 'em what British troops are capable of.'

'Ah,' said Simon. 'The bePedi.'

Wolseley looked at him sharply. 'What do you know about them?'

Simon coughed. 'Very little, sir, but I think I get your drift.'

'Right. They're a tribe right up there in the north-east, near the northern Drakensbergs, led by a chief called Sekukuni who supported Cetswayo in the recent fight – although he never went as far as sending troops. They're a canny lot. They threw out bunches of German missionaries in the sixties and have never come to terms with the Afrikaners – the Boers – who settled in their territory.'

61

'Seems reasonable.'

'What?'

'Nothing, sir.'

'Well, they have made a nuisance of themselves for years, raiding farms and so on. The Boers managed to get themselves organised back in '76 and a pukka Boer army attacked them in their stronghold, a sort of fortified hill called Ntswaneng, known to the Afrikaners as the Fighting Kopje.' Wolseley looked up. 'You know what a kopje is – a sort of conical hill, eh?'

'Yes. I was in Zululand.'

'Course you were. Sorry. Anyway, the Boers were beaten back. We had a go a few months ago when we sent a column under Hugh Rowlands – he got a VC at Inkerman. Too old now, that was the trouble. Anyway, he had to crawl away too.'

Despite his dislike of the army, Simon found his instincts being aroused. The infantryman in him was not quite dead. 'They sound a hard bunch to beat, I must say.'

Wolseley reacted quickly to the interest he had kindled. 'Quite right.' He leaned forward in his chair. 'Trouble is, Fonthill, these tribesmen are not your spear-carrying Zulus. They may, in fact, lack the organisation and the sheer blind guts of Cetswayo's chaps, but what they have, and what the Zulus lacked, are guns. For years the bePedi have lived in the shadow not only of the Boers but also of the Swazis, their neighbours, who are also a war-like lot. So, shrewdly, the young bePedi menfolk have fanned out across the whole of what you might call civilised South Africa. They've worked on the plantations in the south and they've dug for diamonds at Kimberley. And they've sent rifles and ammunition back home. Anyone who attacks them is up against a bit of modern firepower.' He sat back.

'So you are going to knock them over?'

'Absolutely. Shouldn't take me long.'

Simon hid a smile. The tennis player opposite him saw no contradiction in his admiring description of the military prowess of this tribe who defended its fortress capital so fiercely, and his own belief in his ability to defeat them. He wondered anew at the ingrained confidence – the arrogance – of the British military ruling class. Yet part of him admired it and respected the tradition and long years of attrition that had given birth to it. Wolseley had never failed yet. Why should he consider failure now?

'I am sure it won't, sir. But I have left the army now. Why do you want to involve me? I am afraid I cannot help you.'

The General leaned forward again, his good eye gleaming. 'Oh, but you can, Fonthill. You see, although I have no doubt at all that we can successfully attack the bePedi, it is absolutely vital that no stupid mistakes are made this time, such as poor Chelmsford made in Zululand, or, for that matter, Rowlands not so long ago. If we trip up in any way, those Transvaalers, sitting in the grandstand, so to speak, will laugh us all the way back to Cape Town. If you will pardon the pun, it will give them Dutch courage and even perhaps prompt 'em to have a go at us themselves.'

'So...?'

'So, I need good scouts. The best I can get.

63

From what I hear, you and your Welshman are probably about the best I can lay my hands on in this part of the world.'

'But that can't be true, sir. We don't know the territory, and–'

'Stuff. One kopje is very like another – and you found your way round Zululand right enough. And when it comes to mountains, there can't be any more formidable than the Hindu Kush, where, from what I hear, you strolled around for months lookin' like damned Arabs. If you did that for Roberts, you can do this for me.'

'But what about the Swazi? They will know the area like the back of their hands. Or the Boers...?'

'Can't trust the black fellers completely, although we can use one or two of them as guides, don't you know. And as for the Boers, I want to do this show without using them in any real way, so that they can't take any of the credit. Don't forget, I want to impress 'em. No, I want you and your Welshman. You can stay as civilians and the pay will be as good as I can manage, given the miserable budget the Horse Guards is allowing me. Now come along, Fonthill. Your country needs you one more time.'

Simon closed his eyes in frustration. This was the very thing he feared: another appeal to his patriotism, another bugle calling him back to duty. The army was like a vast spider's web. As soon as you felt you were out of its sticky, clinging reaches, another strand was spun to reel you back in again. Well, this time it wouldn't work. He had Nandi to think about.

'I am sorry, Sir Garnet. I would like to help

you, but I fear I cannot.'

The silence was cold. 'Why not? It is your duty.'

Simon sighed. Should he tell him about Nandi? No. The girl could be in great danger and he did not want the authorities crashing around heavy-handedly until he knew exactly where she was and how acute was her position. In any case, it was none of Wolseley's business. 'I am sorry, sir,' he said, 'but I have a mission to complete which concerns someone else and I am not at liberty to discuss it.'

Wolseley regarded him silently for a moment longer, then he leaned forward to his desk, opened his blotter and selected a piece of paper from inside. He put on spectacles and read it silently before lowering his chin and regarding Simon over the top of the glasses.

'This is a cable from the military authorities in Bombay,' he said. 'It seems that a man was found dead in a carpet warehouse in the heart of the city. His neck had been broken and there was blood everywhere. It was obviously a case of murder. Two men fitting almost exactly the description of yourself and ... what's-his-name – Jenkins – were seen leaving the warehouse shortly before the body was discovered. The next day you abruptly left your hotel. I am asked to detain you for questioning about the matter. It looks as though I must do so – although, of course, if I have already despatched you to the north as my scouts this will not be possible.' The General regarded Simon stonily. 'Do you know anything of this business?'

Simon returned the stare without flinching. 'Of

course not,' he said.

'I think, Fonthill, that before I make up my mind about the action I must take in this matter, you should tell me exactly what it is that compels you to go to Kimberley.'

For the second time in his short life, Simon realised that he was being blackmailed by a high-ranking officer in the British Army. Did they all take a course in dirty tricks before reaching staff rank, for God's sake? He sighed again. 'Very well, sir.'

Slowly he began to relate how Nandi had contrived the escape from Ulundi and had intervened decisively at his court martial. Although Simon had been admonished for his attack on his superior officer, his plea of mitigating circumstances had been accepted and the main charges had been accordingly withdrawn. Then he spoke of Nandi's letter and her cry for assistance – an appeal that must now be weeks old – and of how the need to go to her assistance was not only urgent but needed to be handled with care.

Wolseley heard him out without interruption. Then he stood and once again looked out at his roses. 'Well,' he said eventually, 'I knew much of the detail of the court martial – it was a strange case, and when I arrived here regimental messes all over Natal were still buzzing with it. But I was not exactly aware of this young lady's part in it, and, indeed, nor did I care. I had other things to do.'

He turned and sat again, leaning across the desk and fixing the young man opposite with a glare which, now, was not unkind. 'I am desperate for your help with this campaign, Fonthill,' he said. 'But I like to believe that I am a gentleman. And a gentleman must always help a lady. Of course you must go to Kimberley.' As he spoke, he slowly tore the cable up into small pieces and deposited them into an ashtray. 'This man was a Thug anyway. Good riddance to him. Now, show me your route, because this could be a difficult journey.'

Beckoning Simon to follow him, he strode to the end of the room where a large map of South Africa dominated the wall. 'Let's see,' he mused. 'Kimberley. Hmm, it's not really north-west, is it? More west-north-west, which means that you don't have to tackle the Drakensbergs at their worst. There's a pass here,' he jabbed at the map with his finger, 'which is comparatively easy to cross. However, I doubt if you'll find any real trails, not to mention roads, until you reach the Orange Free State, here. Then it's open veldt country where you should be able to get accommodation from isolated Boer farms.' He snorted. 'They'll charge you through the nose for putting you up and feeding you, but they'll be hospitable enough once you get talking. No, the problem will be here, in Basutoland, which you'll have to ride through.'

'I was not anticipating trouble with natives anywhere,' said Simon.

'Well, you should. The Sothos are as well armed as the bePedis. Their tribesmen have been working in the mines too, and have also fed rifles back to their homeland. The people in the Cape have been trying to disarm them and there has been a lot of trouble there recently, after an

67

attack led by Cape Mounted Riflemen killed their chief Moorosi last year. The Cape Government – nothing to do with me, this, I am glad to say – has been trying to negotiate a formal peace treaty, but nothing has been signed and it is dangerous country. You may also find lion there. You really ought to have an escort to get across the country because the Sothos are pretty cocky just now. What's worse is that they also have no central leadership, which means that you could meet groups of tribesmen who will lack discipline.'

The General frowned, hitched up his flannels and shot Simon a rather embarrassed look. 'Trouble is, I can't really spare you any men – at least not right away. Now if you can wait a bit–'

Simon interrupted quickly. 'I'd rather not have them anyway, thank you, sir. We really can't wait any longer, and in any case, two of us can ride more quickly and more discreetly than a group. Jenkins and I can keep out of trouble.'

'What sort of weapons have you got?'

'We have a couple of rather ancient Martini-Henrys.'

'Not good enough. Here.' Wolseley bounced back to his desk and began scribbling on a pad. 'Take this to the Quartermaster – the sentry outside will tell you where he is – and get yourselves a couple of modern rifles. They could make all the difference. Now, off you go.' He strode to the door and held it open. 'I hope you find this young lady. And when you are free, I shall count it a favour if you will come across country and join me. It will probably be a month at least before I can mount an attack. I am going to Pretoria first, of course, and then you will find me to the east, in or about Lydenburg.'

He held out his hand. 'Good luck, my boy.'

'I am really most grateful, sir.'

'God be with you.'

Once in the anteroom, Simon blew out his cheeks. From virtually being accused of murder he had progressed within minutes to becoming what seemed like the bosom friend of the most influential man in South Africa. Had he committed himself to Wolseley? He thought not. But he had learned something about the men of power in the army of the Empire. They were not all without heart or the ability to see beyond what could benefit their careers. A Very Model of a Modern Major General indeed! He spoke to the sentry and hurried to find the Quartermaster.

Later that day, Simon and Jenkins rode out, leading their spare horse and pack mule, along the road which led them north-west and out of Durban. Simon had contemplated waiting to say goodbye to Alice, but thought better of it and instead left her a note explaining how helpful Wolseley had been. He urged her to handle the General with care and implored her to keep out of the line once the fighting began. Then the two men set off to begin their search for Nandi.

Chapter 3

For the remainder of that day and throughout the next, they rode through the verdant countryside of Natal, passing the small town of Pietermaritzburg and then, turning west, heading towards the Basutoland border, unmarked but somewhere up there in the blue smudge on the horizon which was the Drakensberg range. At first they rode between sugar and cotton plantations. Then the roads gave way to dusty tracks that wound their way through farmland on which sheep and cattle grazed. It was warm but became less humid the higher they climbed into the foothills. They could have been in the border country of Wales, and even Simon, a poor and uncomfortable horseman, found himself enjoying the journey.

On the second day, however, they faced the barrier of the mountains. As the General had predicted, the Drakensbergs here were not as fearsome as further north, where the early Boer voortrekkers had taken their oxen and waggons down a steep pass in 1837, to meet a cruel death at the hands of the Zulu king Dingane. Nevertheless, the pass that Wolseley had called 'easy' looked like a broken staircase to Simon, as they picked their way upwards between fallen rocks and tumbling streams. This was hardly a track, more a declivity between slabs of stone that seemed to climb perpendicularly to the heavens.

It was hard toil, and Simon, following Jenkins, looked with admiration at the broad back of the Welshman as he sat, perfectly at ease on his horse, gentle hands letting the animal find its own way across the shale and between the boulders.

Jenkins was a fine horseman, unlike Simon, who, despite his training as a subaltern, had never come to terms with the business of sitting astride a living, moving animal. Early work on farms had bequeathed this skill to the Welshman but, reflected Simon, Jenkins possessed a happy ability to come to terms with many challenges in a life which, in theory, should not have equipped him to handle them. He could talk confidently about wine (a by-product of his days as officers' mess corporal) and military law (a result of studying for his Army Certificate while in the Glasshouse) and his natural egalitarianism enabled him to chat equably with British generals and Indian Untouchables alike without causing offence to either. Jenkins had an innocence that left him content to be Simon's servant in tranquil times, polishing boots and laying out shirts, but to become his brother-in-arms when danger threatened. Musing on the future as the only just recognisable tune of 'Men of Harlech' drifted back from ahead, Simon wondered what his mother and father would make of this unconventional friendship when they reached home. He smiled at the thought.

'I don't know where the 'ell I'm goin', look you.' The Welshman interrupted his reverie. 'I think you'd better lead in case we end up back in Isandhwannee or whatever.'

'Don't worry. Just keep climbing.'

They did so, and eventually they came to the summit of the pass. The air was noticeably cooler, and although there was no definable frontier, Simon had the feeling that they had crossed from Natal into the independent native kingdom of Basutoland. They had reached a rocky plateau that bore no sign of human or animal life, apart from several tawny eagles that rode the thermals high above them. Occasionally, far on a peak, they glimpsed a mountain goat, but it was a forbidding, lonely spot which, except for the absence of snow, reminded Simon of parts of the Hindu Kush. The mountains seemed to encircle them and it was not until they had ridden for another two hours that the plateau began to give way to a gentle, sloping terrain and the hoofs of their horses trod on welcoming, khaki-coloured moss. Below them a valley stretched away before rising again to a lower range of hills in the distance. Simon realised that Basutoland was a rocky fortress that bore no resemblance to the rolling grasslands of Zululand. No wonder it remained more or less unconquered.

'We will follow this stream down and camp within the hour,' he called to Jenkins. 'But I think we had better not light a fire, because we must be in Kaffir country now.'

In the event, however, they were able to find a mossy bank, surrounded by rocks and close up against a stone face in which a chimney-like fissure enabled them to light a fire without the smoke curling for all to see. They hobbled the horses, brewed tea and ate the last of the cold meat, fruit and cheese they had brought with them from Durban. It would be biltong from now on. Then they stood watch in turn throughout an uneventful but bitterly cold night.

They had been in the saddle for at least an hour when the sun rose behind them, kissing the top of the mountain and immediately suffusing their bodies with warmth. In the valley, the way was easier and, using the spare horse to spell their mounts, they were able to make quick progress along the springy grass. There was no sign of fixed habitation, but here and there, they passed the cold ashes of camp fires.

'I know nothing about these Sothos,' confided Simon, 'but it could be that they are nomads.'

'I don't care if they're Church of England,' replied Jenkins, sucking in his moustache, 'as long as they keep their spears to themselves.'

'It's not spears I'm worried about. According to the General, these fellows have got rifles, so keep your eyes open.'

The inevitable encounter came at about noon, when the two were looking for a place to stop for a midday meal. From around a copse of stunted trees loped a party of six Sothos. To Simon, they looked exactly like Zulus in that they all wore the *umuTsha*, a thin belt around the waist from which strips of dressed hide hung down front and back, and white cow-tail fringes decorating their calves. They carried shields, although none had the Zulu *isiCoco*, the fibre ring sewn into the hair to signify maturity. Four of them were armed with the Zulu-type *iklwa* or short stabbing spears and the other two had rifles, though not, Simon noted with relief, Martini-Henrys but the older, less accurate Sniders. Their comparative lack of decoration meant in Zulu terms that they were stripped for battle, but Simon was not sure if this carried the same significance in Basutoland. The six spread out to bar their passage.

'Keep me covered,' said Simon quietly, 'and pull the pack animals in on a short rein. Don't shoot unless you absolutely have to.'

'Be careful, bach sir,' said Jenkins, gently easing his Colt from its holster and partly covering it with his hand holding the reins. 'I don't like the look of 'em.'

Simon held up his hand and trotted towards the six men, all of whom regarded him with expressionless faces.

'Do you speak English?' he asked, in conversational tones.

No one spoke and no flicker of expression crossed their faces. Slowly Simon reached behind him into one of his saddle bags and produced a small buckskin pouch, loosely tied with cord at the neck. He had bought it in Durban on a last-minute impulse and was glad now that he had done so. He unknotted the drawstring, reached inside, took a pinch of snuff and then leaned down and offered it to the nearest warrior. The man waited for a moment, regarding Simon from black pupils set within amazingly yellow eyeballs. Then he took a pinch and sniffed, and then took another. He made as if to hold on to the bag, but Simon gestured for him to pass it to his fellows. He did so, grudgingly, and they all indulged.

'Where you come from?' The question came in stilted English from a man in the middle of the

74

semicircle. He held his rifle with one hand, as if it was a revolver, pointing at Simon's midriff. Simon noted, however, that the cocking hammer was not pulled back. The second needed to do that would give Jenkins time to fire.

'From Natal,' he replied, twisting in the saddle to point behind him. 'We are not soldiers and we come in peace. We cross your land because we journey to the Boer country of the Orange Free State. We do not stay here.'

The Sotho continued to regard him unblinkingly. Then he pointed. 'If you not soldiers, why you have soldiers' guns?'

'It is possible to buy these in Natal. We need them for protection against lions.'

For the first time an expression crossed the man's face. It seemed to signify contempt. Of what? The white man's fear of the big cats, or just his ignorance?

'No lion here,' he sneered. He pointed to the north with his rifle. 'Many miles that way.'

'We did not know that. We have never been to your country before. We only cross it. We do not stay.'

The impasse continued. Simon held the man's stare and allowed a faint expression of truculence to creep across his face. He would not be bullied.

The Sotho gestured to the Martini-Henry in the saddle holster. 'No lions so you no need that gun,' he said. 'You give that gun to me.'

Simon slowly withdrew the rifle from its holster. Still holding the Sotho's gaze, he pulled down the lever behind the trigger and gently brought the barrel up so that it was pointing

75

directly at the native's chest. 'No,' he said.

The Sotho broke the stare and looked at the muzzle of the gun. His companions had not moved during the confrontation and they all now regarded their leader. At last he looked up, back at Simon, and then stepped to one side.

'Thank you,' said Simon. And he gently urged his horse forward, looking directly ahead.

'Good afternoon, gentlemen,' said Jenkins, giving the Sothos the benefit of one of his beaming smiles. But as he rode through them, following Simon, he turned in the saddle and, still beaming, covered them with his Colt. The natives stayed in their semicircle, watching them go.

When the Sothos were out of sight, Jenkins eased alongside Simon. 'Just as well we didn't 'ave to gallop, look you,' he said. 'You would 'ave to 'ave 'ung on to 'is neck.'

'Oh, do shut up. Can you still see them?'

'No.'

'Right. That seemed too easy. They shouldn't be able to catch us without horses, but if they're anything like the Zulus, they'll be able to move over this ground very quickly. We need to move fast. Come on.'

The two men eased the animals into a trot, with the pack mule protesting at the rear so that Jenkins had to drop back and give it a kick in the rump. The mule now became a hindrance in that every time the horses trotted, he pulled back on the lead rope and dug in his front hoofs. Only curses and blows from Jenkins would persuade him to go forward at anything above a leisurely walk. Both men now became concerned at their

76

lack of progress and they forsook their midday meal to put distance between themselves and the Sothos. Constant scrutiny with the telescope of the landscape behind them, however, revealed no sign of pursuers, and Simon eventually decided that it would be safe to stop just before nightfall at what appeared to be a reasonable campsite, within a small cluster of trees which afforded them good cover and where they could tether the horses. But they lit no fire and the man off watch lay with his hand on his rifle.

Simon took the first guard, and as he watched the daylight disappear, he debated with himself whether he had mishandled the confrontation with the Sothos. After all, by the sound of it, these people were still in a state of some kind of hostilities with the Cape authorities and they would argue, no doubt, that they had every right to disarm strangers who rode through their land. Yet, clearly, he could not have surrendered their rifles, for, from what Sir Garnet had told him, it was the very question of the possession of firearms that had provoked the hostilities in the first place. On the other hand, he had threatened the leader of the party with his Martini-Henry. Would he have caused this man to lose face in front of his tribesmen? Had he thrown out some kind of challenge? Simon's chin sank on to his chest as he considered the question. The answer was probably yes. The English-speaking Sotho had been faced down. In Zululand this would have evoked revenge. Given that the Sothos were virtually neighbours of the Zulus – they certainly looked and dressed alike – the same standards probably applied here. There would have to be an accounting. Almost certainly, then, they would have been pursued – and skilfully, for there were no signs of them being followed. The watch would have to be keen.

It turned into an extremely uncomfortable night for Simon, who now found his attempts to sleep when off watch disturbed by his preoccupation with those implacable black faces. The sight of the spear tips up close to him had stimulated his imagination and, perforce, he lived again the sharp, searing pain of the assegai wounds he had suffered in the Zulu War. The night was cold but he found perspiration trickling down his forehead on to his blanket. He had told Jenkins that he felt they had left the six warriors far behind them, but his every instinct now told him otherwise.

After lying wide-eyed in the darkness, it was a relief to come back on watch, and Simon looked with envy at Jenkins, who slipped into sleep as soon as his head touched the rolled jacket that served as a pillow. Peering out into the valley from the safety of the trees, Simon could see very little. He was gambling that the Sothos, if they had followed them and were planning to attack, would wait until dawn. Certainly, Zulus and Afghans both followed this precept. If the natives of Basutoland were different, then he and Jenkins stood little chance, because attackers would be upon them in the darkness before they could raise their rifles.

Simon had stood night guard many times in his army career, but this vigil was the worst he had experienced. It was like keeping watch in a graveyard, for this valley seemed to be bereft of nocturnal animals, and light cloud hid the moon and stars. Little broke the silence, except the gentle rhythm of Jenkins's breathing, yet Simon sensed that somewhere out there in the velvet blackness, those spearmen were waiting, biding their time. His tongue felt like a lump of dough inside his dry mouth as he leaned against a tree, his rifle across his knee, straining his eyes into the blackness.

It was almost a relief when he saw the Sothos. It was just after dawn, as the sun, still hidden behind one jagged peak, was shooting spokes of bright light into the dark sky, that Simon's tired eyes caught a movement, somewhere out on the plain. His hand reached out to touch Jenkins, who wriggled out from beneath his blankets in a second, rifle in hand.

The Sothos were crawling on their bellies, making clever use of dead ground. They were spread out and approaching with extreme caution.

'How many can you see?' whispered Simon.

'Just three.'

'Agreed. If there's still only six of them, then the other three are probably on the other side of the trees, coming to take us from there.'

'Is there time to mount up and make a run for it?'

'No. Not a hope.'

'Shall I try and pull the horses down, in case they start firin'?'

'No. They will want the horses as much as the rifles, so keep them standing. They won't want

79

them killed so it may deter them from using those Sniders. They will probably try and rush us in the hope that we're still asleep. We'd better stay back to back. We mustn't lose each other in this brush.'

Jenkins sniffed. 'Wish I'd got a lunger.'

Simon swallowed at the mention of cold steel. 'I'm not sure bayonets would be much good, two against six. We must try and bring them down before they reach us. How's your shoulder?'

'Bit stiff, that's all. It could do with a drink.'

The Sothos had disappeared from sight for the moment, and Simon felt certain that now that the sun was up, they were spreading out to attack the copse from several sides. It was time to flush them out. Yet still he hesitated. He was in their country. Until they showed actual signs of aggression he did not wish to kill, but if he allowed them to come nearer they could charge and be in the trees before he and Jenkins had time to reload.

Suddenly he stood up. 'Do not come any further, or we will open fire,' he shouted. 'What do you want?'

'For Gawd's sake,' gasped Jenkins. 'Don't give them a target.'

A hand carrying a spear rose from the ground, frighteningly near, and suddenly three natives sprang from concealment and rushed towards Simon. He hardly had time to gasp, 'Watch the rear,' before the Welshman's gun roared and the nearest attacker fell. Simon brought down the second, but as he had feared, the third warrior was upon him before he could reload. He heard Jenkins's rifle fire again behind him and he just had time to pick up his Colt before the Sotho pushed the stave-tip of his shield under his arm and spun him round. It was the typical Zulu tactic devised years ago by the great Chief Shaka: the shield used as an offensive weapon in close-quarter fighting, the tip tucked under the other man's shield to twist him off balance and open him for the spear thrust under the ribs. But Simon had no shield to encumber him, and as he was spun, he cocked the revolver with his thumb, pointed it blindly behind him under his elbow and pressed the trigger. At that range he could not miss and the native folded across Simon's back, drenching him with blood.

He pushed him away and whirled round. At the foot of a tree, some fifteen feet away, lay another warrior, his blue-blackness somehow accentuated by the red blood that flowed from the bullet hole in his chest. He lay very still. But there was no sign of Jenkins nor of the other two – and perhaps there were more – Sothos.

Simon stood stock-still and listened. The horses were whimpering, and then they fell silent. He found himself shaking and he thumbed back the hammer of his Colt once more but that click was all that he heard. Where, for as long, perhaps, as half a minute, there had been shrieking and firing, now there was only silence. He gulped and dropped on to one knee, the better to peer through the low bushes and brushwood in the clearing. The action saved his life, for as he did so, a spear thudded into the tree behind him, vibrating with the force of the throw.

Immediately, another shot rang out; the un-mistakable crack of a Martini-Henry, and Simon saw a thin curl of blue smoke rise languidly into the air between the low branches of a bush to his right. Thank God, Jenkins was still alive! Neglecting caution, Simon ran bent double towards the bush and, for his pains, a Snider bullet – creating a higher, lighter report than that of their rifles – whistled over his head. He threw himself down in the bracken, his revolver poised.

'352,' he called. 'Are you all right?'

'Yes, bach sir. Still thirsty, though.'

'I can't see you.'

'Aye, well that's the idea, see. One of the buggers is still 'ere in this wood somewhere an' I can't flush 'im out. You 'elped me with that one, just a second ago, an' I got 'im. But if you'd like to dance around a bit more, like a fairy, look you, I could get the last one.'

'Are you sure there are no more?'

'No. I'm just 'opin' like.'

As he spoke, the Snider fired again, to their left. Knowing that it took perhaps all of twenty seconds to reload that model, Simon immediately sprang to his feet and ran towards where he saw the smoke rising from the hidden rifle barrel. But he was too late. Jenkins's own rifle had barked and a man crashed from behind the bush and fell, face down, on to the ground, his head shattered.

Simon knelt beside him and turned him over. It was the leader of the Sothos, the man who had demanded his rifle. Slowly Simon rose, revolver at the ready, and looked around. The horses were whinnying again after the renewed firing but there was no other noise or movement until

Jenkins, treading carefully, eventually joined him.

'You all right, bach sir?'

'Shaking a bit, that's all. Oh damn. You've been hit.'

Jenkins looked down at his shoulder. 'No. All the fuss an' rushin' around in this wood like Red Indians 'as bust me stitches. Nothing new, look you. Phew! That was a bit warm while it lasted.' He lifted his great black eyebrows in indignation. 'Fancy them comin' in on us like that – an' after you'd given 'em snuff an' all. Ungrateful bastards! Just as well you thought of the devils coming from the back of us, otherwise we would be lookin' like pin cushions now.'

Simon found himself trembling but returned the smile. 'My dear old 352, it was your shooting once again that got us out of this mess. But come on, better get moving. I think those six were on their own, but you never can tell. Let's make for the border as fast as we can.'

Cautiously, the pair scouted the interior of the copse and, finding nothing, Simon applied a rough dressing to Jenkins's shoulder. Then they examined the bodies of the Sothos to ensure that there was no binding of wounds to be done there. All six, however, were dead. Simon thought for a moment of burying them, for a vulture had already begun to circle overhead, but they had no digging tools – nor could they afford the time. So they dragged the corpses into the wood, piled as many stones as they could find over them and set out westwards, towards a lower range of hills that Simon hoped would mark the border with the Orange Free State.

In fact, as far as the travellers could tell, it did not do so, for the range only masked yet another ridge of peaked mountains which rose from a rock-strewn plain ahead of them. The country was inhospitable in the extreme and Simon wondered how its natives scratched sustenance from the hard, infertile soil. His answer came the following day when they descended into a much wider valley, covered with long, straw-coloured grass on which bony, high-shouldered cattle grazed. These were tended by semi-naked boys who watched sullenly as the two white men passed. But they returned no greetings nor was there any sign of habitation or adult warriors. If the Sothos had aggressive intentions towards the strangers, they had either been frightened away by the carnage in the copse or they were waiting for a more suitable place for ambush.

There were plenty of these, for the pair toiled for another day through defiles and between rocky crags that could have provided sites for half a dozen attacks. But their only visible companions were large, pale Cape vultures, circling high overhead, and, less frequently, the ubiquitous mountain goats, the latter too shy and distant to provide any chance for a shot and an evening meal. It was with all kinds of relief, then, that the two men eventually descended on to a grassy plain that undulated to the horizon, broken only by an occasional kopje. Rising unsteadily in his stirrups to look ahead into the setting sun, Simon felt that, at last, they had reached the veldt country. This must be the independent Boer Republic of the Orange Free State.

And so it proved. The air was crisp, dry and refreshing and it took them little more than an hour of easier riding to come upon the first Boer homestead. It was a simple wooden shack, with outlying rocky kraals to house sheep and cattle, although no animals were to be seen. As Wolseley had predicted, their welcome was not particularly warm, but for four shillings and sixpence ('Bit steep that, bach,' murmured Jenkins) they were given soup and mutton and allowed to lay their blankets on straw in a dry-stone barn.

The experience was repeated six times as they followed Simon's compass bearing towards the west, and these encounters provided Simon with his first real opportunity of studying the Boers. He had met them in Natal, of course, but those who were attached to the army there were horse wranglers, adventurers acting as scouts, and other drop-outs from the mainstream of the Dutch pastoral economy. But it was here, in the Free State, that the voortrekkers had first outspanned their waggons in the course of their 1830s exodus from the English in the south. Others had gone north to create the Transvaal and some had peeled off north-east and then south again, down the Drakensberg passes, to keep their awful appointment with Dingane's impalement stakes. But the Free Staters were the first settlers of the plateau country. Here for Simon were the *real* Boers, the surly, fundamentalist farmers who considered that God had given them the land and who wanted no interference in their freedom to farm it how they liked and to treat the indigenous black people as their inferiors, created to provide them with cheap labour.

As they neared the interior of the state, the farms became more numerous, perhaps twenty to thirty miles apart, and most of them almost primitive. The homestead was usually a square building with a *stoep* or veranda on one side, on to which the great room – usually twenty-five feet square and some twelve feet high – opened, with small rooms about ten foot square on each side. Rough boards provided the ceiling to the main room and in these was set a hole, reached by an unfixed ladder. On these boards were kept the farm produce and stores: forage, mealies and the like. From farm to farm the inhabitants were remarkably similar. The men wore old corduroy suits with wide battered hats, and they punctuated their few words with a gob of saliva, spat outdoors and in. The women were dressed in shapeless black dresses and, as the sun went down and the temperature fell, shawls across their shoulders. Hands were soiled and the farmhouse usually bore a disagreeable odour of sour milk.

The ritual of arrival rarely changed. The visitors were welcomed to the family table, where, with plates turned bottom upwards, the patriarch would put his hand to his forehead and say grace. The women of the family served the food and grace would be repeated after the meal, which bore a remarkable sameness from house to house: fat mutton washed down with milk, sometimes with bread but rarely with vegetables. Occasionally, pumpkin was served, and there was always a tureen of fresh milk on the table. Wines or spirits were never offered, although this did not stop

Jenkins from scanning each new room, as they entered it, in case a blessed miracle had occurred.

Their arrival was never met with enthusiasm, but the travellers began to realise that this represented no lack of hospitality, basic though it always was, but more an initial distrust of intruders – an attitude that usually relaxed once the price for the accommodation had been established. Conversation, at first stilted, monosyllabic and offered by the hosts in strongly accented English, always became easier when coffee was offered from a metal pot after the meal. The Boers seemed remarkably uninquisitive about their visitors (no comment was made on that first morning when Jenkins washed his bloodstained shirt and dried it before saddling up) but were quick to express their distrust of the British Government in London and its colonial representatives in Cape Town. Simon realised that, to these simple people, living in isolated family groups, the Great Trek to escape the British was as yesterday, although it had happened nearly fifty years before. Nevertheless, this prejudice never prevented care being taken to see that the guests were as well fed and made as comfortable as possible, given the spartan conditions under which they all lived. Simon was uneasy at their stubborn insularity, but he liked the Boers' bluff courtesy and, once established within the house, Jenkins's huge smile never failed to break down whatever barriers remained.

The pair made their way by compass bearing to the west, over the open veldt. It was not difficult riding through the karoo bush, picking their way between the white ant heaps and glorying in the keen, fresh air that made their cheeks tingle. Jenkins's robust constitution soon made his shoulder dressing redundant and he returned to his self-appointed, if unwelcome, role as Simon's riding master: 'No, no, bach sir, grip with your knees a bit more, see, an' don't slouch, 'cos that will make your back ache...'

The air was good but the countryside now was dreary: endless plains broken here and there by small, flat-topped hills. There were no cornfields, no terraces or vineyards. Some thorny mimosa and wild jessamine poked through the thin, sandy soil but the travellers passed no ruins or other vestiges of the past. It was as though no one had ever lived there. It was country under-developed in every way.

Simon had set their course too far north, and they realised that they had crossed the unmarked border between the Free State and Griqualand West when they saw the first evidence of diamond diggings near the Vaal River: scratchings on the river bank, some hollowed down to five feet and long since deserted in favour of the greater riches to be found from the vertical-shaft mining in Kimberley itself.

Despite his original ignorance of the where-abouts or even the existence of Kimberley, Simon, like the rest of the readers of the British press, possessed vague background knowledge of the discovery of diamonds in this area years ago: the finding by the boy Erasmus Jacob of 'a large shiny pebble' – a stone which became the Eureka Diamond. And then, forty years later and only ten years ago now, the discovery of the great 83.50

carat Star of South Africa, 'big enough to have choked an ostrich', which sold for 55,000 dollars and prompted the beginning of the great South African diamond rush. He had expanded this knowledge on the ride through the Free State by gentle questioning of the farmers with whom they had lodged. One of these Boers, in fact, had previously farmed land by the Orange and Vaal Rivers and even, further south, in Kimberley itself, but, disgusted by the diggers' greedy ways – their clumsy, noisy waggons, their shanty towns of portable iron houses brought from the coast, their mixtures of languages and currencies, their drinking and blasphemy and their tendency to swarm like ants and erode the earth – he had sold up and moved out on to the veldt. Kimberley, he grunted, had become a town of sin and degradation, its downward path marked since the de Beer brothers had been forced to sell their land, outside the town, when the first dry mines – diamondiferous 'pipes' leading down into the earth – had been established on it. Five years ago, ten thousand diggers had moved into Kimberley itself and begun working a patchwork of small diggings each only thirty-one feet square. Some of them had gone down a hundred feet, leaving only narrow tracks on the surface to act as roads. The farmer believed that God had shown his disapproval by allowing many of these to cave in, killing the blacks and whites working below. Only He knew how many mines and diggers there were there now, further corrupting the town and its people. Local farmers wouldn't go near the place, except to buy basic necessities once a month.

Then they were into and out of the town within an hour.

Simon had been told of the original rough community along the river beds, of tents under the willow trees lit by candles, where food was taken quickly – even a glance away from the ceaselessly rocking cradle sieves, the diggers' 'babies', might mean the loss of a diamond. Of how when the second rush came in, lured by the promise of the 'dry' mining, the prospectors had been met by a hurricane with hail and wind that had torn through the tents and smashed the sieves. And of how they had all begun again, building a hotel made of mud, and even organising a ball for President Pretorius of the Transvaal, where the music was an accordion, a fiddle and a bass drum and the costumes ranged from tails to overalls.

Then the indigenous Griquas had tried to reclaim their land and been met by the rifles of the diggers and the support of the Transvaal administration, so that they appealed to the British, who set up a board of enquiry – 'Typical,' spat the Boer – which decided that the Griquas did indeed own the land and promptly bought it for them. Now, Simon was warned, the British Government at the Cape was in the process of annexing Griqualand West and administered the diamond fields, but it was only concerned with making money on custom duty and there was little law and order. The diamond rush was over – but the place remained a den of iniquity.

Hearing all this, Simon had become even more concerned about Nandi's safety. What sort of hell's kitchen had she stumbled into? How could this gentle creature, conditioned by the ordered environment of a family home, have survived in such a barbaric environment? He and Jenkins exchanged anxious glances, but they had no choice but to contain their frustration and dig in their spurs to hurry on – now to the south-west – as fast as their tired horses could take them.

Chapter 4

At last, after their days in the saddle crossing the dreary plain, they topped a rise and looked down on the beginnings of surprisingly orderly rows of shacks which formed the outskirts of Kimberley. Before them were spread single-storeyed box-homes of timber and corrugated iron, with sad veranda *stoeps* and overhanging roofs held up by slender poles, stretching out in disciplined rows with, here and there, a few red-brick constructions standing out by virtue of their second storeys. The dirt roads seemed wide and virtually empty, although dust rose in the hazy distance from what appeared to be the centre of the town.

'Phew.' Jenkins blew out his cheeks. 'Quite a big place, look you.'

'Hmm. Bigger than I expected.'

They urged their horses down the incline and began to amble along the track ahead of them. In these suburbs, Kimberley appeared to be quiet and bourgeois – almost disappointing. They passed a church, shops and, later, even a two-storeyed theatre. The white people now strolling by on the narrow wooden sidewalks seemed to be formally dressed, mainly in black. As they approached the centre of the town, however, its character changed. Simon realised that many of the shops were, in fact, bars and gaming saloons advertising baccarat and chemin de fer. He

92

counted five bars with evocative names: The Digger's Rest, The Hard Times, The Scarlet Bar, The Old Cock, and The Perfect Cure. The keen eye of Jenkins noted that, on their windows and sometimes on boards hanging by the swing doors, were advertised their wares: Cape Brandy at 7s. 6d. a gallon, 17s. 6d. for a dozen quarter-bottles of Bass Ale, one glass of beer for 6d.

'Bloody 'ell,' he murmured. 'They're not exactly givin' it away, are they?'

And there was hardly a woman to be seen on the sidewalks. Instead, the passage of the two travellers was observed by loafers who leaned back against the wooden walls, their thumbs hitched into their trouser belts, their eyes narrow beneath their slouch hats. Shoeless black men in tattered overalls loped along, their heads down, on journeys that seemed to carry no urgency. Then, as the pair passed a dance hall, they caught a glimpse of gaudily dressed women and heard the artificial tinkle of a pianola. Next door a 'private bar' offered its services.

'Lively, then, isn't it,' observed Jenkins, his tongue moistening his lips. 'I'd love a beer,' he ventured, 'but I think we ought to find Nandi right away, don't you?'

Simon nodded. 'No question about it. We've come too far to waste time now.' He asked directions for Currey Street, and within five minutes they were discreetly inspecting, from the other side of the street, a simple wooden building, detached and set between two alleyways – a house that seemed no different from the others in this quiet, though broad, side street. From behind a tree set at forty-five degrees to the house they examined the building more closely. The single door remained closed and the windows shuttered. There was no sign of life, or, indeed, any indication that the place was occupied at all.

'Strange,' muttered Simon. 'It's a damned warm day but all the windows are closed.'

'Gone away, then. Oh bugger it. What do we do now?'

'There must be a back door.' Simon pushed back his broad-brimmed hat and wiped his forehead. 'We can't be sure it's empty. Look. I don't want to put Nandi in more danger than she's in already, so we should make a proper reconnaissance of the place before we decide how or when to intervene. You stay here and I will see if I can find a back entrance. Don't reveal yourself or make yourself conspicuous while I'm gone. Right?'

'Right.'

Simon walked back the way they had come and took the first turning to his left and then left again, counting his paces to where he estimated he was level with the Currey Street house. Another house confronted him, one with children playing in the front yard. It obviously backed on to the silent house – and there was an alleyway to the side. Simon did not wish to appear conspicuous, so he waited a few moments until someone turned into the alley and then followed a few paces behind. Sure enough, number 5 Currey Street did have a back entrance but it was hidden behind a rough fence. The windows at the back of the house were open, although cheap cotton

94

curtains prevented him from seeing inside. With only a sidelong glance or two from under his hat brim, he walked back and, circuitously, rejoined Jenkins.

'Well?' The little Welshman was sweating profusely and frowning. The waiting game was not for him.

'I believe that the house is occupied. There are open windows at the back, and no one would go away and leave windows open in this place. And the fact that everything is shut up facing the street in heat like this is suspicious.'

'So what's the plan?'

'We ought to mount a watch on the place.' Simon frowned and looked down the street to where they had tethered their horses to a rail. 'But we can't leave the horses for much longer in this sun and I am inclined to try just one careful frontal approach. After all, if Nandi and this Big Man have left, then we mustn't waste time here.' He made up his mind. 'You stay here and I will go calling. But keep out of sight because I don't want to reveal that there are two of us.'

Jenkins nodded, but his sweat-streaked face looked anxious. 'Careful, then, bach sir. I'll be watchin'. If you go in and nothin's 'appened after a quarter of an hour, then I'll come in after you, see.'

Simon crossed the road and approached the house openly, carefully looking at each number as though he was a stranger. Then he knocked loudly at number 5. Surprisingly, it was opened straight away. Had they been observed from the interior? He doubted it, for they had been very

95

careful. From the darkness within a huge man emerged. He was all of six foot four inches tall, so that he stooped under the lintel, and was so wide that his shoulders almost touched the door frames either side of him. His clothes were those of a working Afrikaner but his face was unlike those of the Boer farmers Simon had met. It was seamed and sullen in expression and pock-marked and almost yellow in colour. His long black hair was tightly waved, as though curling irons had been applied. The eyes were black and they regarded Simon without expression.

'Ja?'

'Sorry to disturb, mate,' said Simon, doing his best to sound working class. 'Do yer speak English?'

The big man did not speak but nodded his head in affirmation.

'Aw right. I'm lookin' for an old mucker o' mine. Bloke called John Dunn. Thought 'e could 'elp me get work 'ere. Last I 'eard 'e was livin' at this address.'

'No.' The man swung the door to close it but Simon inserted his foot.

''Alf a mo', mate. John's missus back in Natal told me 'e was 'ere. Do yer know where 'e's gone to?'

For a moment a flash of something – recognition, awareness, even fear? – came into the man's eyes. Then he shook his head again. 'No. Nod 'ere. Mus' be some mistake.' He spoke with the guttural accent of the Boer but with a strange inflexion that Simon could not place. Then he swung the door to with a firmness that removed

Simon's foot. A bolt scraped home.

Simon stood looking at the door for a moment and then shrugged his shoulders and walked away, turning a corner before slipping back to rejoin Jenkins. He related what had happened.

'So,' asked the Welshman, 'is 'e tellin' the truth then?'

'No. Nandi wrote about a big man. He's the biggest I've seen for years and it's too much of a coincidence that he's living there. When I mentioned John Dunn he looked shifty and he was in too much of a hurry to get rid of me. No. We've found where she was all right.' He pulled on his lip. 'But is she still in there?'

Jenkins's face darkened. 'Look, if they've done anything to that little girl, I'll personally take that big dark bugger apart, see if I don't.'

Simon regarded his indignant friend with affection. After a moment he said, '352, you really *do* care for Nandi, don't you?'

The Welshman dropped his gaze and looked at the floor. 'Ah no, bach sir. Not like that, see. It's just that...' He shifted his weight from one foot to the other and looked around, as though seeking some way out of his embarrassment. 'After what she did for us in that Zululand place we owe 'er, now don't we?' He looked up again at Simon, almost pleadingly.

'Of course we do.'

'Right then. You go knockin' again, see, and keep 'im talkin' on the doorstep, and I'll go round the back and break in while you've got 'im at the front.'

Simon sighed. 'No. It won't do. Firstly, he will

97

probably not open the door this time; secondly, there could be a crowd of them, and if they're all as big as that fellow then even you could have difficulty. And thirdly,' he frowned, 'they could harm Nandi if they've got her in there and we try the rough stuff. No, we've come a long way. We've got to get things right. I need to think this through. Let's find somewhere to stay and put the horses, and I might even buy you a beer.'

They took their horses into a stable yard behind a wooden hotel off the market square in the centre of Kimberley, left them in the care of a Kaffir ostler and found the foyer bustling with activity. Simon heard French, Dutch and German mixing with the *taal* of the Afrikaner as he waited to catch the eye of the hotel receptionist. For the first time, he gathered an impression of a thriving business centre – a frontier town certainly, but one with a core of international commerce. Despite its unpretentious exterior, the hotel was obviously a crossroads for merchants and dealers from London's Hatton Garden, New York, Antwerp, Berlin and even Bombay. The sparkle of diamonds had given life to Kimberley, but, from the state of its buildings, it seemed as though the town itself had not had time to catch up with the demand for its product.

Simon eventually booked two rooms at a breathtakingly high price, twice the cost of their hotel in Bombay, and made a resolution to look around for somewhere cheaper the next morning. The price of beer, too, was horrendous, so they walked back a little towards Currey Street. A bar was not difficult to find and they took the only two chairs left at a table in the crowded room. Immediately, a grizzled, elderly man in dirty overalls sitting at the table turned and spoke. His tone was friendly and his cadences were those of London's East End. 'You're new, I fink. You lads lookin' for work in the diggin's, then?'

'Not exactly,' said Simon.

'Ah.' The man took in Simon's own very different accent and the set of his shoulders. 'Want to invest, p'raps, then. Eh?'

'Could be. We're looking for an old friend who has got some sort of a business here in diamonds. Name of John Dunn, from Natal. Would you perhaps know him?'

The man shook his head. 'Nah. Big place now, Kimberley. Not like the old days. You need to talk to young CJ. He knows everything that goes on 'ere.'

Simon exchanged glances with Jenkins. 'CJ?'

'Yus. Bright as a button, 'e is. Bought me out an' now 'e's company secretary or somethin' of de Beers, biggish operation, though not as big as old Barney's. You must 'ave 'eard of CJ.'

Simon shook his head. 'Sorry.'

'Blimey. Where 'ave you bin? CJ. Young Cecil John. Cecil John Rhodes. You'll find 'im in the de Beers office, at the eastern end of Main Street, orf the square. Approachable chap. If your bloke's around, 'e'll know abaht 'im, I promise yer.'

'That's very kind of you. Will you have a beer?'

'Don't mind if I do. Ta very much.'

Twenty minutes later, Simon and Jenkins found their way back to the market square, a huge crossroads in the centre of Kimberley, big enough to take outspanned oxen from ten or so teams and, obviously, the central meeting place for the town. The square was thronged, and an auctioneer was doing a thriving trade, selling everything it seemed from carts and oxen to household goods and clothing. Here, Simon paused.

'Look,' he said to Jenkins, 'it's pointless both of us going to see this man. We are wasting time. Go back to Currey Street, to the house. Make sure that you are not seen, but keep watch on it. I want to know exactly who goes in and out. Can you find the place again?'

'O' course.'

'Sure?'

'It's near the pub. I can certainly find that.'

Simon smiled. 'Very well. Now – whatever happens, don't get involved. Just keep watch. I'll come to you as soon as I've seen this Rhodes fellow.'

With a nod, Jenkins was gone and Simon strode around the square until he found Main Street. The de Beers headquarters was an unpretentious low wooden building with a corrugated iron roof, like virtually every other construction in Kimberley, it seemed. The door was open and a slim, pale young man sat inside at a desk, his head down over a ledger. On enquiry, Simon was told that Mr Rhodes was out of town but was expected back within two days. Simon left his name and, his brow furrowed in thought, wandered back into the market square. Hands deep in his pockets, he stood at the back of the crowd, unaware of the activity around him, and considered what to do next. There were two obvious courses of action: to check if Dunn was registered as the owner of a claim, and then visit it and see who was working it; and to keep watch on the house – at least until Rhodes returned and could, perhaps, throw some light on what had happened to Nandi's father. He was sure of one thing: there was little to be served by crashing into the house at this stage.

The auctioneer in the square had now finished his business and was packing up the few artefacts for which there were no bidders. Simon asked him if there was a registrar of claims, and was directed to a simple house on the other side of the square which bore a newly golden coat of arms of the Cape Colony on its door. Inside, a clerk ran his thumb down a ledger and found the name Dunn. He looked up.

'Initial J?'

Simon nodded.

'Here he is. Claim number 427. Registered also in the name of Joachim Mendoza. Their address is given as 5 Currey Street. The claim is part of the thirty-one separate mines in Kimberley Mine.' He nodded to the west. 'That's the big hole about ten minutes' walk that way.'

'These two own the mine, then?'

The clerk nodded. 'Yes, such as it is.' He turned back to the ledger. 'They've not done well. The place has hardly turned out any stones for two or three months now. Must be a yeller diggin'.'

'A what?'

'Yeller diggin'. You know...? Ah, new around 'ere then?'

Simon nodded again.

'Yeller diggin' means it's a small mine an'

101

probably an old one, more or less worked out by now. The yeller ground is found only down to about six to twelve feet or so. The blue ground is deeper, an' that's where the good stones are found now. But you need 'eavy machinery to get the blue ground out – steam engines, over'ead pulleys an' such. Yeller diggin's a thing of the past now, mate.'

Simon thanked him and, deep in thought, walked back to find Jenkins. When he reached Currey Street there was no sign of the Welshman. As before, the windows of the house were shuttered and the door appeared to be locked and bolted. Simon set himself to keep watch on the place from behind a tree some hundred yards away so as to remain unobserved, but it was with increasing impatience that he kept his vigil. After half an hour, he became concerned. Where was Jenkins? Was he lost? Or had something violent happened? The house remained seemingly desolate, so, with a sigh, Simon walked down the street and looked into the bar where, little more than an hour before, they had taken a beer together. It was full, of course, but of Jenkins there was no trace. The old Cockney to whom they had spoken remained at the same table but he confessed no knowledge of the Welshman.

With increasing concern, Simon continued on down the street, peering briefly into each bar. Surely Jenkins – even disoriented Jenkins – could not have become lost in the few hundred yards between the market square and the house on Currey Street? He walked on, constantly looking behind him and down each side road. On impulse, he turned into one of them and the sound of cheering and applause made him hurry to a single-storey wooden building which was no different from the others on the street except that it bore a wooden notice announcing that it was 'Barney Barnato's Boxing Academy'. He pushed through the swing doors.

The building contained one wood-panelled room, which was smoke-filled and crowded with a colourful mixture of men: some in smartly cut morning clothes and top hats, others in dunga-rees, as though they had just come from the mines. Their attention was directed to the far end of the room, where Simon, peering through the crowd, could just make out a makeshift ring marked out by a single strand of rope, and two contestants standing in opposite corners of the arena, obviously prepared to fight. Simon's eye was immediately drawn to the man in the left-hand corner, who was wearing a red sash round his trouser top and displaying a massive bare chest. He was huge – perhaps six foot three inches – and wore his black hair long. At first Simon thought it was the same man who had answered the door in Currey Street, but a closer look revealed that his skin was darker, probably burned by the sun, and that his complexion was smooth and bore no trace of smallpox. From his looks, he seemed to be a Boer, and his features were open and not unpleasant.

Facing him, in the other corner, stood Jenkins. Also stripped to the waist, the Welshman carried a blue sash round his midriff and his naked torso looked almost effeminately white compared to

103

that of the Afrikaner. Incongruously, he still wore his riding boots, and his breeches bore the dusty traces of their long ride. At first sight it appeared to be an incongruous mismatch. Jenkins stood only as high as the other man's shoulder, and his reach would be consequently disadvantaged. But the Welshman's chest was as broad and as well muscled as the Boer's and his waist showed no signs of the incipient paunch that marred the other man's otherwise fine figure. Both contestants wore soft gloves, as recently introduced to the boxing ring under the Marquess of Queensberry's rules, and they regarded each other stoically as a referee stood in the centre of the ring and studied a paper in his hand.

Simon's jaw dropped as he saw Jenkins. What the hell was he doing here? He opened his mouth to protest, but the English referee had begun to speak – or rather to shout, for the crowd was noisy.

'Gentlemen. Silence, please. This is a challenge bout which will take place under the Marquess of Queensberry's rules.' This brought a bout of good-natured booing from the crowd. Disregarding the interruption, the referee turned his head and addressed both men in turn. 'This means that there will be no holding and hitting, no tripping or throwing, no gouging or biting and no pushing and pulling–'

'An' no fun, neither,' shouted a wag in the crowd.

'Gentlemen, please. It means straight hitting to body and head. When a man goes down he has ten seconds to get up, and the fight will be broken into three-minute rounds with a thirty-second break between each. The fight will continue until a man cannot get up within the ten seconds or cannot come to the mark,' he indicated what Simon presumed was a line drawn across the ring, 'after the inter-round break.

'Now then,' he looked down at his paper. 'The match is between our champion here in Kimberley, Faan de Witt, and ... ah ... Mr Jenkins, who has accepted the challenge of fighting Faan for a purse of twenty guineas–'

Simon filled his lungs. 'Oh no he hasn't,' he cried. Every head turned towards him as, with difficulty, he pushed his way through the crowd to the ringside. 'This man is in my employ and he does not have my permission to fight anybody.'

Jenkins's jaw had dropped at seeing Simon and he had the grace to look embarrassed for a moment. ''Ang on, bach sir,' he hissed, 'it's all right. I can explain in a minnit. Just let me get on with this. It won't take long.'

'Won't take long!' shouted Simon. 'This man is twice your size, and we've got work to do, or have you forgotten?'

'No, no, this is all part of it, y'see...'

Jenkins's voice was drowned in a roar of derision from the crowd, and Simon felt himself being jostled. The referee once more held up his hand for silence.

'Now then, young man,' he said, addressing Simon, 'I don't know where you've come from, but it sounds like the old country. You should know that the old ways don't go down well here. This man has accepted the standing challenge of a bout with our champion, and out here in the diggings, a man has a right to do what he likes. The challenge has been accepted and the bout will take place, whether he works for you or God Almighty Himself.'

His statement was greeted with a roar of approval by the crowd, and Simon felt a sharp push in the back which propelled him forward.

The referee continued. 'But your man has no second, so if you want to help in his corner you may do so. Either that or leave this establishment.'

Another push, and Simon found himself outside the ring by Jenkins's blue corner. The Welshman gave him a grin. 'Fan me when I've knocked the bugger down,' he said.

'Fan you ... I'll sack you. That's what I'll do–'

But Simon was interrupted by the clang of a bell, and both men walked towards the line painted across the middle of the ring. There they faced up to each other, where immediately the disparity in size was evident. Jenkins was dwarfed by the giant Boer, and at about twelve stone, he was giving away some sixty pounds in weight. Simon had seen Jenkins fight, but it had been a free-for-all, not conducted within the new strictures of the Queensberry Rules, and he doubted whether even the Welshman's ingenuity and strength could overcome the disadvantages he was facing in reach and weight – and what did he know about clean punching and boxing anyway? The answer seemed to be not much, for immediately the Boer landed an extravagantly swung right hand to Jenkins's head, which sent the Welshman staggering across the ring.

106

Fortunately, because of the difference in height, it was a downward swing and lacked the force of an uppercut or hook. Jenkins blinked, shook his head and walked forward again, his hands held loosely at his sides, contrasting with the orthodox stance of de Witt, who kept his arms bent, forearms upright and clenched fists before his face.

The Welshman sucked in his top lip, in a familiar gesture which spread his black moustache across his face, but he did not move. He stood quite still, hands still at his sides, looking up at the Afrikaner. For a moment, neither man moved, so that a shout of 'Get on with it!' came from the back of the crowd. Then the Boer swung that great right hand again. This time Jenkins just moved his head back a fraction so that the blow whistled harmlessly by his nose, but he made no attempt to retaliate, merely standing motionless, a frown of concentration on his face, looking into the eyes of his opponent. Again the Boer swung, and again Jenkins swayed away, not moving his feet but slipping his head out of range of the glove.

So it continued throughout the three minutes of the round, with de Witt launching heavy punches which all missed their mark, thanks to the adroit timing of Jenkins, who now moved his feet to match the ducking and bobbing of his head. Only towards the end of the round did the Boer land a blow on Jenkins's body, and this was partly deflected by the little man's elbow. The round ended amid howls of derision from the crowd and with the Afrikaner perspiring and blowing but Jenkins quite composed.

Simon ran a superfluous towel round his man's face and hissed, 'Aren't you going to hit him back? He'll murder you if you don't.'

'No, bach sir. Let 'im be for the minnit. I'll get 'im later.'

'But for God's sake, man, why are you fighting him anyway?'

Jenkins looked puzzled. 'Why? 'Cos 'e's the bloke – the big Boer – from the 'ouse, that's why. The bastard who's keepin' our little girl. I'm goin' to give 'im the 'idin' of 'is life an' 'e won't know why, 'cos 'e don't know me from Adam, see.'

'But he's not the man from the house.'

'What?'

'That fellow is even bigger and he has a pock-marked face and hair that's very wavy. Except in build, he's not like this chap at all.'

Jenkins's mouth dropped and he turned and looked at his opponent. 'But ... but 'e seemed to be comin' from the 'ouse when I got there and I followed 'im to 'ere, where 'e immediately stripped off an' challenged all corners. It seemed, look you, like a good chance to 'ave a go at 'im.'

'Well, it wasn't and it isn't. So you had better call off this fight right here and now before you get really hurt.'

An air of sheepishness engulfed Jenkins. 'Aw, I'm sorry, bach sir, that I am. Look, let me ask 'im where 'e lives, just to make sure, eh?'

'Don't be so stupid. Just you go and–'

But Simon was interrupted by the bell and Jenkins, frowning hard, walked to the mark to meet the big man again. As they faced each other, Jenkins whispered, 'Eh, where d'yer live, then, Fritz, eh?' The Boer answered by swinging a blow that caught Jenkins on the shoulder and sent him spinning. The Welshman immediately ducked under his opponent's arm and fell into a clinch. 'No, come on.' His voice was quite desperate now from under the big man's armpit. 'Come on, tell me. D'yer live in, whatsit, whatchermacall it, Currey Street? Eh, do yer?'

'Hell, man. Why do you want my address when we're in the middle of a fight?' He pushed Jenkins away and swung a desperate right hand, which the other avoided easily.

'No, no, come on. Where d'yer live? Tell me like a good chap, and I'll let you 'it me. Honest.'

'What?' The Boer stood still for a moment in the middle of the ring, his breast heaving. 'Why do you want to know, for goodness' sake, man? Are you crazy or something?'

The crowd, sensing that some sort of conversation was going on between the boxers, was now hooting and hissing wildly, but Jenkins paid no attention. 'I just want to know if you live in this Currey Street place, that's all. Tell me and I'll give you a good shot at the jaw, honest.'

The Boer tried a straight left this time, but Jenkins merely inclined his head and let it brush past his ear. 'Ach, if you must know, not Currey Street. In Dutoitspan,' and he swung again, also abortively.

Jenkins stood still. 'Oh shit, bach, I'm sorry,' he said gloomily. 'I've buggered things up. 'Ere, boyo, 'ave a go then.' And he remained quite still, his eyes closed, and offered up his jaw.

The catcalls from the crowd slowly died away and silence fell on the room as everyone looked at the incongruous sight of the little Welshman standing in the centre of the ring inviting his huge opponent to hit him. The referee moved round to get a better view of Jenkins and then also stood still, uncertain about whether to intervene. The Boer turned to the crowd and shrugged as though appealing for advice.

'Go on, slam 'im one.' The cry from the back was taken up until the whole crowd was now shouting and stamping. Simon put his hand to his mouth in apprehension as the big Afrikaner turned back to Jenkins. Even then he was reluctant to hit his defenceless opponent, and it was only as the referee took a step forward, as though to intervene, that he unleashed a fierce right hook. It took Jenkins on the side of the jaw and sent him crashing to the ground. Simon immediately made to throw the towel into the ring, as a sign of submission, but it slipped backwards from his hand, over his shoulder.

The referee sprang to the side of the fallen man and immediately began to count to ten – to Simon's ears, desperately slowly. On six, Jenkins crawled on to his hands and knees and shook his head. On eight he was erect, and at nine, as the referee waved the fight on, he blinked and immediately fell into a crouch, his head weaving. The shower of blows that was rained on him he now took on his gloves, his shoulders and his back as he bobbed and swayed. The crowd was shouting for the kill, frustrated at the strangeness

110

of the contest and wishing for its fulfilment. They had come for a knockout, not an exhibition of defence.

Somehow Jenkins lasted the round and walked back to his corner where he stood – there was no stool – as Simon gently applied a cold sponge to his head and jaw.

'My dear old 352,' said Simon, 'are you all right?'

'Right as rain, thanks,' replied Jenkins, though his jaw was swelling where the blow had landed. "E muffed it up, yer know. 'E didn't 'it me cleanly. 'E 'ad the chance of breakin' me jaw. Look, bach sir. I got this bloke wrong. But I can't walk out now, so I think I'd better finish 'im quickly before he does land a proper one on me. It's my time now, anyway, 'cos 'e's gettin' puffed, I can tell.'

'Puffed! But you haven't landed a punch on him! Call it off now, before you get hurt further.'

Jenkins's eyes widened in indignation. 'What? And let this lot think this chap's better'n me? No bloody fear, beggin' yer pardon, sir. Anyway, there's that twenty guineas to think about. We could do with that, couldn't we? This place is a bit expensive, like.'

At the bell, de Witt moved forward aggressively, but to everyone's amazement, so did Jenkins. The little man suddenly began to swarm around the Boer, using his feet and moving his head, as before, to avoid the ponderous blows rained down on him, but this time he retaliated. Moving inside a wild right swing, Jenkins ducked his left shoulder and hooked his right hand into the big

111

man's midriff. In a flash, he swung his left in, just under the ribs, and danced away, only to feint to the body with his left hand and then deliver a crisp right hook to de Witt's cheek. The big man was strong, so he did not go down, but he stood swaying for a moment. As he did so, Jenkins came in again, attacking that suspicious bulge just above the red sash, hammering fierce blows to the body. The exertions of the first two rounds had already tired the Boer, but he bravely attempted to fight back. Now his height was a disadvantage, for Jenkins's lower centre of gravity enabled him to work to the body from under de Witt's guard. As the Afrikaner dropped his hands to protect his winded stomach, Jenkins stood back and swung a perfect left hook to the man's unguarded jaw. De Witt went down and lay crumpled as the count tolled over his head.

At the end of the count, Jenkins immediately bent down to cradle his opponent's head in his arm. 'Get 'im some water,' he called. 'I think 'e's all right, but you never can tell.'

Simon ran to de Witt's aid – the Boer seemed to have no second of his own – and sponged his face as Jenkins poured a little water between the big man's lips. In a second he opened his eyes, and smiled at Jenkins. 'Man, what a punch!' he murmured. The crowd was still baying and the referee was attempting to take Jenkins's hand to declare him the new Kimberley champion, but the little man stayed by the side of his erstwhile opponent, administering sips of water. Eventually he and Simon helped the Afrikaner to his feet, where he stood fingering his jaw. 'Ach, what a punch,' he said once again. 'You hit hard for a little man. God, you must be champion of all Africa.'

Jenkins looked almost bashful. 'Oh no,' he said. 'Only the 24th Regiment of Foot – an' that was some time ago, before they put me in the Glass'ouse. Let's find somewhere to sit you down, then I'm goin' to buy you a drink from my winnin's, 'cos I think I owe you that.'

Half an hour later, the three men sat down at the pub round the corner, each clutching a quart of Bass – Simon because they had nothing smaller, the others because they both vowed they needed them. Jenkins asked if de Witt worked in the mines. He replied that he used to do so but now – and here his open face clouded for a moment (was he dissembling? wondered Simon) – he made his way by prize fighting. Without mentioning Nandi or the reason for their interest, Simon explained to Faan de Witt how Jenkins had confused him with the big man from Currey Street.

'Ach, so you don't like him, then?'

'Oh ... we want to know more about him.'

'Well, he is not the nicest man in Kimberley, I can tell you that.' The Boer flicked a bead of perspiration from his brow. 'His name is Joachim Mendoza and he is quarter Dutch and three quarters Portuguese. He comes from the Portuguese territory to the east, at Lorenzo Marques, in Mozambique. He went into partnership on a yellow mine at Kimberley with a man from Natal but Mendoza is working the mine on his own now, with some Kaffirs.'

'What happened to the man from Natal?'

'I don't know. He hasn't been seen for some time. If you want to know, ask Rhodes, he knows everything that goes on here. He has probably tried to buy the mine – he's trying to buy everything.'

'He's away, but I shall see him in two days' time. Why does Mendoza have a bad reputation?'

'We think he used to sell guns to the blacks. Now he seems to be in the diamond business but I have hardly seen him here. He is a big bully of a man who is not afraid to use violence when it serves his purpose. Most of us stay away from him. Why are you interested in him, and why,' he smiled at Jenkins, 'is the mighty atom here wanting to give him a beating?'

Simon and Jenkins exchanged glances and each gave a small nod. Simon then explained the reason for their mission to Kimberley. The Boer listened carefully and sighed. 'This Mendoza once tried to rape my sister where she was farming up near the northern Drakensbergs. He has a place near there. We could prove nothing because he had an alibi, and anyway, there is no law up there. He is always surrounded by a gang of Portuguese and blacks so I could never get to him.'

The word rape brought consternation to the faces of his listeners. The Boer held up his hand. 'If he is holding your Zulu friend it will be for a reason. Normally, he would not respect a half-caste girl. He would have had his way with her and thrown her out.' He frowned. 'There must be something that she has over him which makes him keep her – and I doubt if he would harm her.

114

Can you see that?'

'Perhaps,' said Simon. 'But we must find out soon.'

De Witt nodded. 'Of course.' The Boer looked deeply into his beer for a moment, then seemed to come to a decision. 'Look. I have a grudge against this man, my friends. You will need someone like me, because you are new to this town and this territory. I know most of the land between here and the Lulu Mountains to the east, where he has a farm. Let me help you find this lady. Why not? Isn't it time the British and the Boers started working together in this land?' He grinned, but the smile did not reach his eyes.

An answering beam immediately lit up Jenkins's bruised features. 'Good idea, matey.' He turned to Simon. 'We could do with a good fighter like old Fanny 'ere, bach sir, isn't it? An' 'elpin' us find our way about an' that, eh?'

Simon smiled as his brain raced. Was this offer just a little too immediate? He quickly ran his eye over the big man's clothing. He was dressed just like a Boer farmer; there were no signs of opulence or high earnings. How could he just agree to throw in his lot with two strangers? Didn't he have a living to earn? But Jenkins was right. They would need someone to act as guide in this strange, wild territory. And it seemed that they had common cause. He let his smile grow wider. 'Good idea,' he said.

The Afrikaner nodded and they all exchanged handshakes, then Jenkins fumbled in his leather purse, the prize he had won.

'Right. Let's 'ave just another one to celebrate

the partnership.' He held up his jug to the barman and then suddenly stiffened as he looked over the shoulders of the other two. Simon turned and saw a handful of men – he quickly counted up to six – push their way through the swing doors and slowly, menacingly, make their way towards the table where he and his two companions were sitting. He recognised a couple from the front rank of the crowd at the boxing match: big men, roughly dressed and unshaven. The other four, although less tall, were broad and equally unkempt, and three of them were wearing diggers' overalls, clay on their boots. As they reached the table they spread out to surround it, pushing aside empty chairs from surrounding tables. A hush fell over the bar room and chairs were scraped back as men got up to leave.

The silence was palpable and Simon felt the hairs on his neck prickle as he regarded the circle of enmity that surrounded them. The eyes of the newcomers were cold, and every seamed, unshaven face reflected survival from a hundred fights and brawls in bars and gutters around the world. It was clear that these men, living in a culture of violence, unrestricted by conventional rules of law, were aggrieved and were bent on revenge.

The stillness was broken by Jenkins, his beer mug still raised, as he gave them his beaming smile. 'Good day, boyos,' he said, turning his head to include them all in his greeting. 'Come to buy the fighters a drink, is it?'

'You cocky little bastard,' said one of the two tall men. He spoke with what Simon recognised as an Australian accent and he put his hands on his hips as he looked down at Jenkins and then at the other two. 'You won't be able to drink by the time we've finished with you lot. There's a name for people who fix fights and cause punters like us to lose their shirts. In fact there's two names – fuckin' cheats. Look.' He nodded at the leather purse on the table containing Jenkins's winnings. 'We've caught 'em at it, sharin' the proceeds. I think we'll just take that little lot.'

'Ah no.' Simon stood up. 'I can understand why you think that, but it is not like that at all, I can assure you–'

He got no further, for the Australian caught him with a right swing that sent him reeling. Luckily, he had seen the punch coming and partly ducked so that the blow hit him on top of the head. But it was hard enough to send him staggering into the table behind him, which collapsed under his weight and sent him crashing on to the floor. As he lay amidst the debris, the big Australian made to come after him, but Jenkins, moving fast and low, delivered a left hook into the man's genitals and then, as he jack-knifed with a howl, swung his glass tankard upwards into his jaw. From somewhere, Simon heard a high-pitched voice – the barman's? – crying, 'Gentlemen, gentlemen, please!' but nothing now could stop the scene at the little table from degenerating into a raw, slugging brawl.

Simon's head was still spinning as he lay on the floor, so he watched the fight for a second or two as though observing a play performed in stylised slow motion. He saw de Witt pick up the round

117

table as though it were a toy and, using it as a battering ram, thrust it against two of the men who had, fatally, hesitated for a moment before joining the fray. He forced them backwards through a mixture of chairs and tables until he had pinned them against the wall, only to be sent reeling himself as a chair was broken over his head and broad shoulders from behind by a third man. Jenkins, looking incongruous enough already with his swollen jaw, had shattered the glass of his tankard and was now presenting it, as a jagged, frightful weapon, to the two remaining assailants, who, knives in hand now and showing no fear, were stalking him through the debris.

Around the perimeter of the bar room, those drinkers who had not slipped away at the first sign of trouble were now standing flattened against the walls, some of them carefully nursing the drinks in their hands but all of them grinning and watching the entertainment with wide eyes, as though they had seen it all before. Not one of them, of course, made any attempt to part the fighters. This was all too good to miss, even though – particularly now that knives had been produced – death might result.

The sight of the knives cleared Simon's head and, rising to his feet, he launched himself in a flying rugby tackle at the nearest of Jenkins's attackers. He caught the man at the bend of the knees and together they sprawled across the wooden floor, coming up against a thin screen of legs at the edge of the room, where spectators nimbly leapt over them, cheering wildly. Simon, attacking from behind, had the advantage, and he grabbed his opponent by the hair and crashed his head into the wainscoting until he felt him go limp. Gasping for breath on his hands and knees, he turned and saw the giant de Witt, blood now running down his face, whirling around him in an arc by its remaining two legs what was left of their table, keeping at bay the two men whom he had pushed against the wall. A third, presumably he who had brought the chair crashing on to his back, was lying face down, seemingly unconscious.

Simon had time to note that Jenkins had discarded his broken tankard, had somehow disarmed his last opponent and was punching him vigorously to the body, when a boot caught him in the stomach as he crouched and made him fold up in pain. As he lay on the floor in the foetus position, sucking in his breath, with his nose in a mixture of beer and sawdust, the boot came crashing in again to his ribs and Simon caught a glimpse of the big Australian looming above him, his leg bent back to kick again. This time forewarned, however, he was able to grasp the boot as it came thudding in and twist it with all his breathless strength. The pressure unbalanced the Australian, whose other foot slipped on the sawdust mess and sent him crashing to the floor, face down. Simon launched himself on to the man's back and, dimly remembering what he had been taught at school about all-in wrestling, slipped his hands under the momentarily stunned man's armpits and then threaded his fingers together at the back of his neck into a 'half-nelson' lock. The big man attempted to roll, but Simon spread his knees on either side of his opponent's body and tightened the lock, hanging on as the Australian began bucking and kicking in frustration. It was as though he was mounted on a frenzied horse, and he was jerked violently as the man arched his back in a desperate attempt to throw him off. But Simon gritted his teeth and, despite the pain in his ribs, clung on, recalling his gymnasium instructor's maxim: 'a half-nelson, once locked, can never be broken', and desperately hoping that the old saw had reached Australia. Every time the big man arched his back, Simon sent the Australian's forehead crashing on to the wooden floor.

After what seemed like minutes, but was probably only a few seconds, the big man suddenly became inert and began moaning softly as a trickle of blood came from his mouth and stained the sawdust on the floor. Had the terrible blow that Jenkins had delivered with the tankard broken his jaw? Simon dared not loosen his grip, however, and maintained his hold while he twisted his head to check the progress of the mêlée.

Amazingly, it seemed almost over. As Simon watched, Jenkins delivered one last crushing left hook to his assailant's stomach and the man slowly sank to the floor. The two men facing de Witt's flailing tabletop now exchanged a quick glance, ducked, and ran towards and out of the door, accompanied by derisory cheers from the spectators fringing the walls. Jenkins caught Simon's eye, winked, and gave as near to a grin as his bruised jaw allowed. Three men of the original attackers now lay on the floor, and the battle had lasted no longer than three minutes.

De Witt, a grin breaking through the bloody mask that was his face, lowered his now splintered table and walked towards Simon. Jenkins did the same, and they looked down at the strange pair lying before them, Simon still astride the Australian, who remained locked into the half-nelson.

'Well, bach sir,' said Jenkins, amiably spitting blood, 'are you enjoyin' yourself down there or would you like to be gettin' up?'

'Don't be so bloody smug,' gasped Simon. 'He's twice my size and it's the only way I can hold him. If I let go, he could start trouble again.'

'No, English,' grunted de Witt. 'He's out. Look. You did well.'

Gradually Simon relaxed his grip and tottered to his feet. The Australian lay where he had fallen, softly moaning, his forehead resting in the bloodied sawdust.

'Are you both all right?' asked Simon, looking in consternation at the still bleeding de Witt and the face of Jenkins, whose jaw had now swollen considerably. But there was no time for him to hear the replies, for his legs were suddenly swept from under him as the Australian sprang to his feet, amazingly agile for one who had already sustained such punishment in the fight. The big man caught Jenkins a blow to the stomach, but it was his last act of defiance. De Witt brought the tabletop crashing down on to his head and the Australian slowly subsided, like a brick tower folding from a dynamite charge, until, once again, he measured his length on the floor.

'Bloody 'ell,' gasped Jenkins, holding his stomach. 'Don't these lads ever give up?'

'I think they have now,' grunted de Witt, prodding the Australian with his boot. He looked up and then around at the faces staring at the victors. 'I think,' he added quietly, 'we had better get out of here before we are asked to pay for this damage.'

In a strange silence, the three men picked their way through the debris to the swing doors. No one attempted to bar their exit or intervene in any way.

Jenkins turned back at the doorway and addressed the room. 'Right, gentlemen,' he said, bestowing his grin on the silent, watching faces, 'thank you for your ready assistance, now, when we was so unfairly attacked. We bid you good mornin' and suggest you clear up this bleedin' mess.'

'Oh do shut up,' said Simon, pulling him away. 'Let's get back to the hotel and clean up. We have work to do.'

Chapter 5

Alice Griffith had been expecting the summons, but now that it had come, she could not suppress a moment of trepidation. She had always known that she walked a fine line here in the Transvaal: reporting on the activities of an undoubtedly jingoistic general for a readership composed mainly of imperialistic Tories while at the same time attempting to convey her own liberal disdain at the whole damned enterprise. She had managed to balance on this tightrope throughout the Zulu campaign and while reporting on the grand and much-lauded success of General Roberts in Afghanistan – until right at the end, that is. Then, however, she had evaded the General's strict censorship and criticised his hanging of the Afghans who had led the attack on the Residency in Kabul. Only Simon's help had saved her from deportation back to England and allowed her to report on Roberts's final triumphant battle at Kandahar.

She looked at the note: *Sir Garnet Wolseley would be obliged if Miss Alice Griffith could call upon him at his headquarters this afternoon at 3 p.m.* Crisp and to the point. It was, of course, a summons to appear in the headmaster's study; not quite for a caning, perhaps, but certainly for the sternest of reprimands. Would he demand her recall? She pursed her lips. Just let him try! She knew that Cornford, her editor, would support her, and the

123

Morning Post certainly had clout in Westminster. She knew too that Willie Russell, late of the *Times* and now of the *Telegraph*, and arguably the most influential journalist in the world, would back her because he had told her so over a chaste cup of tea in his hotel here in Pretoria. Nevertheless... She frowned, crumpled the note and decided that she had better wear a hat.

In fact, Alice dressed with unusual care for the appointment. She selected the better of the two dresses she had with her, slipped on a pair of high-heeled pumps and wound round her shoulders a shawl of fine silk, whose colour matched the band around her small straw hat. She observed her complexion in her little compact and decided that just a touch of face powder and rouge would not come amiss. She did not know Wolseley at all well – they had hardly exchanged a word on the long journey to Pretoria from Durban and she had seen him but twice since the column had arrived in the Transvaal's capital – but she had an instinct about the man. Although there was no hint of impropriety attached to his name, it was known that he liked the company of elegant women, and she had noticed that his protuberant eye had dwelt on her just a touch longer than was justified by mere curiosity when they had first met in Durban. Alice had long ago realised that she was attractive to the opposite sex, and equally long ago, she had coolly taken the decision to use this attraction to get what she wanted in the very masculine world in which she moved. She was certainly not above a touch of delicate flirting, then, when the occasion demanded; in fact, she quite enjoyed it. Perhaps the occasion demanded it now. She would see.

She had hired a pony and trap and was therefore spared the discomfort of walking through the dusty streets of the Boer capital to the fine house in which the General had established his headquarters. The sentry saluted her as she daintily lifted her skirts and stepped down from the trap, the black boy with the reins not having the training, of course, to hand her down. Once inside, she accepted a seat in an anteroom and covertly observed (and enjoyed) the frisson her presence evoked from the young subalterns who bustled about the place. There was no echo of this, however, from the General when she was finally ushered into his presence.

'Now then, Miss Griffith,' said Wolseley, as he gestured to the chair facing his desk, 'you will be aware, of course, why I asked to see you?'

Alice summoned her most winning smile. 'I am sorry, Sir Garnet, but I am afraid that I don't have the faintest idea.' She crossed her legs and exposed a silken ankle. Wolseley's eye followed the movement.

'Oh, I find that very hard to believe, my dear young lady.' The General's tone was brusque, but Alice noticed that his good eye had lingered on her ankle and seemed to have difficulty in tearing itself away to engage her own gaze. 'Humph, ah, yes. You will know well enough that the tone of your last article in the *Post* will not have furthered the cause of Her Majesty's Government here in the Transvaal, and nor has it pleased my masters back home.'

'Really, General. And why would that be, pray?'

Wolseley was dressed in the uniform of a full general in the British Army – a temporary rank granted him to carry out his extensive duties in South Africa – and he now inserted a finger at his throat to ease the tight blue collar which set off the magnificent red serge of the tunic. 'Well, you insinuated – no, plainly stated – that my intentions to attack the bePedi tribesmen in the north-east are nothing more than an expensive diversion to impress the Boers of the Transvaal with our, ahem, military might, so to speak, so that they will reconsider whatever intentions they might have of attempting to withdraw from British annexation.'

'Ah, but General, I did not say that.'

Wolseley slammed the table. 'Dammit all, young woman, you certainly did. I have the contents of your article here.' He waved the cable in his hand and half stood before sitting down again, an expression of contrition on his face. 'I beg your pardon, madam, for my language. You must excuse a soldier.'

Alice gave him one of her best smiles, revealing her even white teeth. 'Oh please don't apologise, Sir Garnet. I am used to soldierly talk. You forget, I am a brigadier's daughter and I *have* covered two overseas campaigns already, you know. No,' she leant forward in emphasis, 'I meant that *I* did not express those opinions. I only reported them. You must know that this is what the Boer leaders here in Pretoria are saying about your motives for this punitive expedition you are planning against King Sekukuni and his people.'

Wolseley's frown returned. 'They have certainly

not expressed those opinions to me.'

'Well, I don't suppose they would, would they? But they are saying that to everyone else here in Pretoria.'

'Even so, there is no need – no need at all – to report it. It is just tittle-tattle.'

Alice made a small gesture with her hands, lifting them from her lap as though in supplication. 'With respect, sir, I don't believe it is tittle-tattle. The Boer leaders are expressing this view in all sincerity to the German press who are represented here. It is my job – it is my duty – to report it also.' She smiled again, with just a touch of helplessness in her expression, as though she would dearly have liked to have acted otherwise but, alas, was unable so to do.

Wolseley was silent for a moment. This interview was not going at all as he had planned. The scenario of rebuke, some half-baked sort of explanation, followed by reasoned rebuttal from him and then an apology from this fascinating young woman was not being followed. Superb as he was in fighting his corner at the Horse Guards – particularly with his political enemies in the Duke of Cambridge's camp – he was unused to arguing with subordinates, particularly those who wore sky-blue cotton under the sweetest hat he had seen since his arrival in the Cape. He cleared his throat.

'My dear Miss Griffith, I must tell you that you must not continue to report matters which might harm my purpose here. I understand that you have duties to your newspaper – to your employer – but my duty, I must insist, is of a higher

127

level, and that is to my country. You must allow me to be the judge of what could be harmful in your dispatches.'

Alice opened her eyes wide. 'Oh, but surely, General you don't propose to impose censorship on the correspondents here, do you? After all, you are not campaigning yet and no one is in danger. Such censorship would amount to muzzling the press's reporting on purely political issues. Goodness, I hate to think what Mr Russell would write about that.'

Wolseley blinked. Strange as it seemed, Russell and he had much in common. The journalist had won world fame for his coverage of the Crimean War, and his writings and the campaigning of the nurse Florence Nightingale had led to widespread reforms in the British Army. Sir Garnet had a hard-won reputation as a reformer himself. The thought of being portrayed as a reactionary, a restrictor of the press's rights to report freely, was abhorrent to him.

He attempted to regroup. 'I must point out to you, dear lady,' he said, 'that you have earned a reputation within the army, and, indeed, at Whitehall, as something of a rebel. Why,' he leaned forward again and smiled at her in gentle rebuke, 'I understand that General Roberts ordered your removal from Afghanistan at one time. I am sure that you would not wish to do anything here to reinforce that, ahem, no doubt unfounded reputation which has grown up around you.'

Alice smiled in return. 'Oh, but Sir Garnet. That was, indeed, terribly unfounded. You will know, of course, that Sir Frederick Roberts was a

128

comparatively inexperienced leader when he took over the Kurran Field Force for the invasion of Afghanistan. He was India's Quartermaster General and had never commanded a force in the field before that expedition.'

She lowered her lashes for a moment and then looked up at Wolseley through them. 'He was, in fact, as unlike you as any senior officer could be. General Roberts was, let us say, unsure of how to handle correspondents in the field. No fault of his, of course. He simply had not had the experience. Therefore I am afraid that he was, by common consent, a little heavy-handed with us all. Now you, of course, have fought so many campaigns all over the world, and with such great success. I do not think for a moment that you will fall into that trap.' Her grey eyes widened and gave an air of complete innocence to her face.

Wolseley's jaw dropped for just one moment. Then he regained his composure. His good eye twinkled and he said, 'Miss Griffith, that is the most blatant attempt at flattery that I have ever experienced. And I have to tell you that it has completely succeeded.'

They both laughed – Alice with some relief, for she knew that she had gambled and won. This ploy, this attempt to tease a man who had complete power here and could have sent her home, had succeeded. It would never have worked with someone like General Roberts, the dour little engineer who had spent most of his life with leather-faced memsahibs in India. Wolseley, however, was a man of the world; a soldier who was as much at home exchanging badinage in the

129

sophisticated soirées of London and Paris as he was roughing it in the field. Her last card had not been trumped.

'However,' continued the General, 'I must tell you that as soon as my operations commence I will be forced to insist that all of the dispatches which you people send home will have to be vetted by me, or by my appointed censor, before they are allowed to go on to the telegraph wire.'

Alice's mind raced. Could she push him further? 'But why, Sir Garnet? Please tell me why.'

Wolseley's eyebrows shot up and he sat back in his chair. 'Well, I would have thought that the reasons were obvious. I cannot have my movements bruited around the world for the enemy to read and to make his dispositions accordingly. You must see that.'

'But my dear General, you are surely not telling me that King Sekukuni, in his mud hut somewhere on the slopes of the Lulu Mountains, will have his spies in the clubs of London, reading the *Morning Post* and relaying whatever snippets of information I have been able to gather back to him in time for him to react to your disadvantage. You will not exactly be fighting the Prussians, now, will you?'

Wolseley frowned. Once again this conversation was not going according to plan. 'That is not the point, young lady. We have people in Pretoria, as well you know, who are not kindly disposed to us and who are quite capable of transmitting sensitive information to the enemy.'

'I am sure that is true, sir. But the anti-British elements here are observing your every move anyway and will easily assess the strength of your force and the date on which you move against the King, without being told these sorts of facts by myself or my colleagues writing in our respective newspapers.' Alice gave her radiant smile, slowly crossed her legs again and smoothed the folds of her dress.

Wolseley rose from his chair and walked to the front of his desk, perching on its edge. 'Miss Griffith,' he said, and this time his smile was a trifle forced, 'I would hate you to think that I am not enjoying fencing with you in this delightful fashion, but I really do have some rather pressing work to do. I shall impose whatever restrictions on press reportage that I think fit and when I believe the time is right. That is my prerogative and my duty – and I always do my duty. Now, thank you for visiting me, but I really must ask you to leave.'

Alice nodded her head. 'Thank you, Sir Garnet,' she said. 'I really do appreciate your indulgence in listening to me and, of course, I appreciate all that you say. Please be assured that I would not wish to say or write anything which would harm your...' she quickly corrected herself, 'our cause. Thank you for your time.'

The General inclined his head and Alice rose. Then she paused. 'However, General,' she said, 'there is one question which I feel I must put to you.'

Wolseley lifted his eyebrows.

'As you well know, the Afrikaners are not at all well disposed towards the British administration here. You have told the farmers of Middelburg

131

that they will be unable to buy further ammunition – which they need, of course, to maintain their way of life – until they have paid their taxes. You were forced to send a troop of cavalry from Heidelberg to put down an incipient revolt.'

Wolseley listened without comment, but the scar under his blind eye stood out white as his cheek reddened.

Alice continued, betraying no recognition of the General's displeasure. 'Now, these people are not going to wish you well in your punitive expedition against Sekukuni. In fact, they have a grudging respect for this black chieftain who has already defeated forces sent against him by both the Boers and the British. They call him "The Devious". What is more, they don't believe that you have the force available to beat him. After all,' Alice tilted her head to one side and raised her eyebrows, 'you are operating some five hundred miles from your base in Durban and you brought very few regular soldiers with you from there. How can we correspondents reassure the British public that what you propose to do is achievable?'

'Stuff and nonsense,' exploded Wolseley. 'I am in the process of raising the Transvaal Field Force, consisting of fourteen hundred infantry of the line, with some four hundred colonial horse and nearly ten thousand natives. Eight thousand of those will be Swazis, the sworn enemy of the bePedi, whom I intend shall bear the brunt of the attack. We shall have artillery too. This will be more than enough to turn over this bees' nest and stop them marauding the border farms. You will see, young lady, you will see.'

132

Alice inclined her head and smiled. 'I am sure I shall, Sir Garnet,' she said. 'Thank you again. I shall bother you no further.' At the door she turned and smiled again.

Wolseley held up a hand as an afterthought to detain her for a moment. 'To be frank,' he said, 'and this is no great weakness, I do need reliable scouts who are able to ride ahead of my column and sniff out exactly where Sekukuni is and how he will defend his township. I think I know, but I want to be certain. Don't want to use Boers for obvious reasons and I can't really rely on native sources.' He walked towards Alice and lowered his voice. 'Those two British ex-soldiers who sailed with you from India: I believe you know them, yes?'

Alice frowned for a moment. 'Yes, I do, Sir Garnet. Why do you ask?'

'I know that they are damned – ah, excuse me again – jolly good scouts. I believe that they are somewhere Kimberley way. Miss Griffith, I could use those two. If you do see them, I would consider it a great service if you could somehow ... er ... put it to them or even ... well ... persuade 'em that it is their duty to serve with me. Do you think you could do this?' And his face, hitherto so authoritarian, now broke into a boyish grin of entreaty. Alice realised why he was popular with women.

She smiled back. 'I cannot promise anything, Sir Garnet, but I will do my best.'

'I am sure you will, dear lady.' He seized her hand, briefly raised it to his lips and returned to his desk.

Once outside, and in her carriage, Alice directed her driver to take her around the corner and stop. There she sat for a moment, drawing into her lungs satisfyingly deep breaths of this invigorating veldt air, so much more healthy than the humidity of Natal and the hot sun and fierce night cold of Afghanistan. She felt her cheeks glowing and realised that she was grinning. Then she slipped a notebook from her small bag and quickly wrote down the facts she had been memorising: *1,400 regulars, 400 col. horse, 10,000 blacks (8,000 Swazis). Difficulty with scouts.* She allowed herself a quick, triumphant nod. Russell and the rest had been trying for days to obtain some idea of the strength and composition of the field force now being raised in the Transvaal to fight the bePedis (and, of course, impress the Boers). She had succeeded where they had failed. She replaced the notebook with a smile and requested that she be taken back to her hotel, which was so conveniently situated next to the telegraph office.

Within her room she quickly wrote 750 words about Wolseley's preparations for the campaign. Sucking the end of her pencil, she grudgingly decided that she owed Wolseley *something* – his grin *was* infectious – and added that the sheer professionalism of the force, whipped together quickly so far away from base, was bound to impress the Boers of the Transvaal. Then she hurried away to file her copy at the telegraph office.

Back in her room – the hotel had given her a tiny sitting room leading from the bedroom, and she treasured this small luxury – Alice ordered tea, took off her shoes, lay back in her chair and allowed her mind to wander. It turned, as it increasingly did since her arrival in Pretoria, to Simon. She frowned. Alice had always regarded her contemporary from the green hills of Brecon as a friend – a good and dear friend – but nothing more. The very fact that her parents and his had made it clear years ago that a match between them would be more than acceptable had made the very idea anathema to her. She was not to be steered into a conventional marriage to please *anyone*. Events had pushed them together, of course, and Simon had rescued her career by taking her to Kandahar. She shook her head. But that was what friends were *supposed* to do: to help each other in moments of trial. It didn't imply love.

Yet was this good, dear friend turning into something more? Had the tribulations they had suffered together – the fighting, the killing, the deaths of those close to them – had all these horrific intrusions into her life drawn her closer, in fact, to this boyish – and yes, almost heroic – figure? Could she deny that her platonic feelings for him had metamorphosed into something warmer and deeper?

Alice stood and moved to sit before the small dressing table. The mirror reflected an attractive face, one that certainly would have been regarded as beautiful if it were not for the strong and even masculine jaw-line. She flicked the ends of her hair upwards with an impatient finger but her mind retained little of the reflected image. Instead the mirror showed a dark, hawk-like face with a

135

hooked nose whose savagery was more than offset by sad brown eyes. She smiled. He really was quite handsome, this person of contradictions, this young man whose acute sensitivity made him doubt his own courage and yet who could fight like a lion when cornered; this genuine gallant who couldn't dance or exchange small talk; this patriotic soldier who hated the army. His body was slim and scarred and once more she felt something stir as she thought of him. She shook her head to remove the memory.

Did he love her? Alice pursed her lips and put her head to one side as she considered the question. She had sensed that he was going to propose to her in Kandahar when she had interrupted him to tell him of her betrothal to Ralph Covington, the tall, commanding man she had met on her first posting to Africa and to whom she had felt attracted – and, indeed, to whom she had willingly lost her virginity. She had accepted his offer of marriage, and that, of course, was that. She frowned again. She had no right to let her thoughts dwell on Simon Fonthill. Once her work was done in the Transvaal she would resign once again from the *Morning Post* and take passage home to prepare for her wedding to Covington, the man she kept telling herself she loved. Covington, with his faint aroma of cigar smoke and shaving soap, his bristling moustache, his acres of land in Gloucestershire, his desire for children... Damn! She put her hands to her face and kicked back the stool.

As she did so, there was a tap on the door.

She composed herself. 'Yes?'

'Visitor downstairs to see you, missee.'

'Do you have his name?'

'He give me the card, missee.'

Sighing, Alice opened the door and took the visiting card from the cupped hands of the black boy. In italic script it bore the name *Piet F. Joubert*. She turned it over and read the message carefully inked on the reverse: *I feel it would be mutually beneficial if you could spare me a moment.*

Joubert! It must be the Boer who, for a short time, had been president of the Transvaal and who now was the leader of the strong faction within the Afrikaner community arguing – and threatening to fight – for independence. Alice had met some of his subordinates but not this intransigent militant who had a reputation as a shrewd commando leader and fighter. He tended to shun the limelight, but it was rumoured that he had threatened Wolseley with insurrection if the annexation was not reversed. Alice tapped the card on her thumbnail. 'Please show him up,' she said, and quickly dashed back to the dressing table to make sure that the pins holding up her hair were firmly in place.

Two minutes later a stronger tap on the door ushered in a thickset man of middle height, dressed in conventional formal day-wear and carrying a top hat. Only a lined face, a long, black beard and penetrating eyes that seemed to see far beyond the walls of the little room betrayed that he was a Boer, a man of the high veldt.

'It is good of you to see me, Miss Griffith,' he said. 'I apologise for what must seem like an intrusion.'

137

The graceful note pleased Alice, who had met little of this sort of courtesy so far from the gruff, straight-talking Boers of the Transvaal. 'It is an honour, Mr President,' she said.

He smiled and held up his hand. 'President no more, madam. Just a humble citizen.'

Alice returned the smile. 'That is not what I have heard, Mr Joubert. Won't you have a seat? Here, let me take your hat.'

The two looked at each other for a moment. Then Joubert put both hands upon his knees and leaned forward. 'Miss Griffith, my colleagues and I have been reading your dispatches from Pretoria with great interest.'

Alice inclined her head but remained silent.

'Yes.' Joubert allowed himself a flicker of a smile. His features seemed to imply that this was a rare indulgence. 'It has been most unusual for us to see in the columns of the *Morning Post* even the merest trace of understanding of the Boer position here in the Transvaal, and you have perhaps gone rather further than that.'

Alice raised her eyebrows. 'Oh, but sir. I have only tried to be balanced in what I have reported. And that word "reported" is important. I am not a leader writer. I pass on the views and actions of others. The leaders, of course, represent the opinions of my newspaper.'

'Ah yes. And certainly those have not altered. The editorials of your newspaper certainly seem to reflect what I am afraid I must call the jingoistic views of the Tory party.' He held up his hand as Alice made to interrupt. 'And until your arrival, the reporting of events here – particularly

138

of my earlier meetings with Sir Bartle Frere – has been less than accurate, I must confess. We have always been painted as insurrectionists, as stubborn, unworldly farmers who are unreasonable in wishing to go back on our so-called agreement with the British. You, on the other hand, have been able to suggest that yes, just conceivably, we might be patriots too.' This time he allowed his smile to spread.

Alice resisted the temptation to smile back at this seemingly gentle man. She could be on dangerous ground here, with one battle pending and, possibly, a new war waiting behind it. She *must* preserve her status of impartiality.

'Thank you, Mr Joubert,' she said. 'But, you know, I am not sure that I can accept that as a compliment. To repeat: I do not wish to be less than detached and impartial in my coverage of the political situation here, and if what might appear to be certain personal sympathies are perceived to be creeping into my reports, then I regret that.'

'Please do not, my dear miss.' The rather awkward form of address reminded Alice that this man was, after all, only a farmer and not a statesman, although by all accounts he was a good soldier, too. 'And this is the point of my visit to you.' He leaned forward again. 'In fact, there are two reasons why I came. Firstly, I wished to thank you for the balanced way you have been reporting the scene here. As I say, we are not exactly used to being portrayed so ... ah ... accurately in the British press.'

'Thank you, sir. And the second reason?'

'To ask you to preserve whatever flickering sparks of sympathy you may have for our cause – and I know from reading the *Post* editorials that sometimes you may well have come under pressure from your employers, and, perhaps, elsewhere, to snuff out those tiny flames. If you can manage to preserve your sympathy, then I can offer you co-operation at a level which, perhaps, we may well have to deny to your colleagues here.'

'What sort of co-operation have you in mind, Mr Joubert?'

He sat back and the wintry smile returned. He spread his arms and opened his palms towards her in an almost Semitic fashion. 'Ah, who can tell what will happen over the next few months? I fear I cannot be precise and, obviously, I could not inform you of something that might harm our cause. But whatever the conditions, you would have access to me personally at all times. I promise you that.'

Alice looked hard at the man opposite. She could be playing with fire here, she realised, particularly after the warning she had received from Wolseley. There was no way that she could allow herself to be perceived as a mouthpiece for the Boer cause. She well knew that it was only the patronage she received from her editor that prevented the more reactionary elements of the *Post*'s Board – and, indeed, other senior editorial staff on the newspaper – from having her dismissed as a dangerous liberal. Knowing just how far to go was a talent she worked hard at nurturing. And yet the journalist within her was fascinated by the opportunity that now presented itself.

'Thank you, Mr Joubert,' she said. 'I cannot enter into any kind of relationship with you and your colleagues that could prejudice my independence, you must understand that.'

Joubert nodded, albeit a little sadly.

'However, I can promise you that I will continue to report on Boer affairs as fairly as I possibly can, given that I am subject to the editing of my bulletins back in Fleet Street.' Alice decided to chance her arm. 'But while you are here, may I put one or two points to you so that I can better understand your position?'

'Of course.'

Alison retrieved her notebook and pencil. 'As I understand it, the annexation of the Transvaal three years or so ago was entered into with the full agreement of the then government of the Transvaal. And was it not surely an act which virtually saved your country from bankruptcy?'

Joubert shook his head slowly, an air of resignation on his hard features, but his eyes were glowing. 'There is some truth in that, my dear miss, but it is a distorted view, of course. It is true that the fiscal affairs of the Transvaal were in some difficulty. We are, after all, a small nation of farmers. We do not possess the resources of financial acumen that you British can call on from the City of London, for instance. In addition, please remember that we were not able to take any benefit from the discovery of the diamond mines in Kimberley, a territory which your government virtually took from us once it was clear that the mines were viable.' Joubert's eyes were now quite cold.

141

Alice held up her hand. 'But Mr Joubert, surely Kimberley is sited on land which was native owned, by the Griquas, and the British Government actually bought it from the tribe?'

'Not quite. We had administered the land for years on behalf of the Griquas, with their agreement. Naturally, they would sell their birthright for bags of gold – and the British had far more gold than we had. As for your point about the annexation being approved by our government at the time, I can only say that it was certainly not with the support of the full population of the state. You must realise, Miss Griffith, that we were a young, rather divided, and struggling nation.'

'And now?'

'And now, Miss Griffith, we have gained somewhat in confidence and completely in determination and unity. Our fathers and grandfathers trekked across thousands of miles to get away from British domination. It seems as though your people have doggedly followed us here to take our country away from us once more. Well, we will not run away again. This is our state, our country, and we want it back.'

Alice looked up from her note-taking. 'Mr Joubert, will you fight?'

Joubert smiled, although his eyes remained cold. 'I hope it will not come to that, Miss Griffith, and perhaps in your reports you can even help to dissuade the British Government from doing something so foolish as allowing its troops to attack us. We *do* have resources. As you know, the Kaiser is very sympathetic to us, and,' here an enigmatic smile spread across his face,

142

'Kimberley and its diamonds are not so very far from Pretoria.'

Alice glanced up from her notebook with raised eyebrows, but the Boer raised his hand and stood, as though he had already said too much. 'I have taken up a great deal of your valuable time, Miss Griffith,' he said. He picked up his top hat and, almost absentmindedly, ran the cuff of his coat around its base before walking to the door. 'Once again, our thanks for your sympathy. Please remember: we are patriots, not revolutionaries. Good day to you.'

Alice closed the door behind him and raised a pensive finger to her brow. What a strange encounter! But what good copy. At last she could quote directly the leader of the anti-annexation party in the Transvaal, who hitherto had not spoken directly to the British press. An exclusive, indeed, even though he had not said anything particularly new. Or had he? She bit the end of her pencil. Why on earth would Joubert point out that Kimberley and its diamonds was not so far from the Transvaal capital? As far as she knew, the poor state of Transvaal owned none of the diggings there. Was he planning to invade and take the town and its precious resources? Unlikely, for the Boers were defensive fighters and not aggressors. Anyway, she had no proof and it would be impossible to draw that inference without it. Nevertheless, she had the basis of a good feature article here.

Deep in thought, she wandered to the window and looked down into the dusty street below. Joubert was replacing his hat and beginning to cross the road. As she watched, a tall figure strode towards him and stopped him halfway across so that they could engage in conversation. The other man was hatless – unusual in itself in Pretoria – and seemed to be middle-aged. He had rather unkempt grey-flecked hair that clearly had felt no scissors' edge for months, and his beard was similarly untended. His legs were long and slightly bowed, as from years in the saddle, and his stride towards Joubert had been purposeful and rangy. Obviously a man of the outdoors, but somehow he did not look like a farmer, and his dress – riding boots, once-elegant jodhpurs, red shirt with unbuttoned waistcoat over it – showed none of the clerical conformity of the Boer. He was broad-shouldered and carried himself well, but he was clearly concerned about something, for his manner of address to Joubert was forceful and agitated.

As she watched, Joubert looked around with seeming perturbation and then beckoned the man back to the sidewalk. Together they disappeared from Alice's view.

The encounter had no obvious significance for Alice, except perhaps that Joubert seemed concerned to be seen to be in discussion in mid-street with such a man. But then he was a politician and a schemer. He must have many such assignations.

Alice settled down at her small desk, pulled copy paper towards her and slowly began to write. Yet the words did not flow. There was something about Joubert's meeting with the man in the street that disturbed her concentration, something about the stranger and his stride, his

144

lowering of the head and the earnest manner with which he engaged the Boer. She had seen that same intensity somewhere before. In fact, she had seen the man himself somewhere before. But where and when? Who was he?

Absently, she walked back to the window and pulled aside the curtain to look down into the street again. There was no inspiration there. A British cavalry officer trotted down the middle of the road, his upright, pennanted spear, fixed into a leather base by his gleaming boot, showing that he was a Lancer... Her mind immediately flew back to the Battle of Ulundi, where, from within the safety of the British square, she had watched the Lancers form up within the hollow before setting out to spear the Zulus as they fled, defeated, from the fire of the British Martini-Henrys and Maxims. Her lip curled as she recalled the glee on the faces of the horsemen as they revelled in the prospect of sport – man-sticking this time instead of pig-sticking or tent-peg-splitting. What fun! Her mind's eye recalled the gleaming ranks of the cavalry, their uniforms so far unsullied by any direct contact with the enemy. She saw once again a tall figure striding towards the Lancers' commander. A man dressed in civilian clothing and clearly a scout, for he pointed to where the horsemen should attack once the square had been opened for them to exit. A tall, rangy man...

Of course. That was *him*. John Dunn, the father of Nandi!

Chapter 6

Simon, Jenkins and de Witt limped away from the wrecked bar as quickly as their bruised legs could take them, for Simon was anxious not to be involved in further trouble. De Witt left for his own lodgings, having arranged to meet with the others the following day, and Simon and Jenkins slipped as discreetly as they could into their hotel. There they bathed their bruises – nothing had been broken – and Simon, anxious that time was passing, left Jenkins clutching a cold compress to his jaw and made for the mine which contained the Dunn/Mendoza holding, stopping on the way only to find more modest and inexpensive lodgings for the next day at a boarding house near Currey Street.

The site was a huge crater, perhaps some six acres in area and about 350 feet deep at its lowest point. It had once been a kopje, but thousands of shovels had turned it into a hole, though one with little symmetry to it. It was as if a huge meteorite had hit the earth at this point, shattering on impact and creating thin molars of rock standing vertically like stalagmites at various depths down the crater where the diggings had been sunk between them, and looking vertiginously dangerous to the men working like termites far below at their bases. Set back from the rim of the hole on the surface were huge drums and gantries from

146

which a bewildering network of ropes stretched down to the bottom of the diggings, enabling the diamondiferous ground to be hauled to the top for washing and sorting. At the bottom, where the buckets were being filled, scores of what seemed like white mushrooms could be seen scattered about – mushrooms which, on closer inspection, turned out to be the tops of umbrellas carefully arranged over the heads of the seated white overseers who supervised the labour of the Kaffirs working in each section. It was the largest man-made excavation in the world, and to Simon, watching the activity under the hot sun, the place looked almost Satanic.

He was directed to claim number 427. It was near the surface and on the periphery of the hole: a 'yellow digging'. No one was working there, and indeed, it looked as though the surface soil had not been disturbed for days. A neighbouring overseer, seemingly in charge of a group of ropes which disappeared into the depths, confirmed that the owners of the mine had not been seen on the site for some days now and that he had no idea if the holding was still being worked.

Simon walked away, his brow furrowed. Why had Dunn and Mendoza stopped working the mine? To Simon's untutored eye, it seemed that there was still surface digging to be done on their patch. Other 'yellow diggings' nearby on the edge of the crater were still being worked. But why had Dunn seemingly walked out on his partner? And why had Mendoza gone to earth in number 5 Currey Street – if, that is, he was still there?

That evening, they took it in turns to keep watch on the house, but there were no visitors and the place remained shuttered. Faan de Witt was added to the watch rota for the following day, but again the vigil proved abortive. It was as though the house had been locked and bolted many years before and not lived in since. As he stared at it during his watch from behind the tree, Simon began to feel that the building itself exuded malevolence, some strange essence of evil, as though the sun-scorched timbers, which could only have been thrown together less than a decade before, had witnessed years of misery. The feeling was confirmed by Jenkins, who confessed to Simon that he had disobeyed instructions not to break cover and, during the afternoon, driven by extreme boredom in the heat, had crept down the alleyway at the side to check on the rear entrance and had found nothing – except a terrible smell.

'What sort of smell?' asked Simon.

'Well...' For once, Jenkins looked embarrassed. 'A bit like ... you know ... a bit like...'

'No, I don't bloody well know. What sort of smell?'

The Welshman put a finger in his ear. 'It's a bit difficult to describe in polite company, look you. Not very nice at all.'

'What on earth are you talking about?' Then Simon had a moment of horror. 'It wasn't ... it couldn't be ... a decomposed body, could it?'

Jenkins wrinkled his nose. 'Aw, no. Not like a battlefield an' all that. I know that smell. More like a shithouse, actually.'

'Good lord!'

'Yes, well. I told you it wasn't very nice.'

'It's probably just dogs, in the alleyway.'

'No. That's quite clean. Seems to be coming from the house.' He frowned. 'Look, bach sir. I don't think we should 'ang about much longer. I think we should break in and 'ave it out with the people inside, see.'

Simon nodded slowly. 'I'm inclined to agree. But I think I should see this Rhodes chap first. He is back tomorrow. Maybe he can point us in the right direction, or give us some guidance on Mendoza. He may even have seen Nandi. Tonight, though, I think we had better keep watch through the night.'

They did so, but no chink of light gleamed through the shutters in the darkness and no one went to or from the house. It was with some frustration, then – and meeting with some surliness from his companions – that Simon set the guard rota for the morning and strode off to see Cecil J. Rhodes.

After a brief wait in an anteroom, Simon was ushered into a large room overlooking the de Beers mine, containing the longest table he had ever seen. At its end, a tall, broad-shouldered man in his late twenties, perhaps two years older than Simon, rose to greet him. He had thick wavy hair and rather bulbous eyes, and his rumpled cotton jacket and white flannel trousers did nothing to conceal the fact that he was running to corpulence. He walked quickly towards Simon – he had some way to come – with outstretched hand. As they shook, Simon realised that Rhodes

149

did so with the third and little finger of his hand curled inside his palm. Some sort of Masonic ritualistic signal, or was he concealing an injury?

'Fonthill,' said Rhodes in a surprisingly high and even squeaky voice. 'What's your game, eh? Do sit down. What's your game, then, eh?'

'I beg your pardon.' Simon was taken aback.

'What's your game? Want to sell me a holding? Can't buy everything, you know, but I've always got an open door. What can I do? What can I do?'

'Well, I don't have a game, as you put it, Mr Rhodes, nor do I have a property to sell you. But I am hoping that you can assist me in finding someone who has asked for my help.'

The bulbous eyes stared unblinkingly at Simon. 'Are you an Oxford man, Fonthill? University, I mean, eh?'

'Er, no. Actually, I went to Sandhurst.'

Rhodes's face lit up. 'An army man, then. Still serving, or what?'

'No, I resigned my commission in Afghanistan.'

'Been around the Empire, then. Splendid. I'm an Oxford man myself, you know. Still studying, as a matter of fact. Can't slog through the terms in the conventional way, don't you know, because of my health. Have to come out here regularly and clear me lungs, so to speak, do a bit of business and then go back to the university. But it's a good thing. This is the place to make money and, more importantly, build empires.'

Listening to the squeaky voice, Simon had an impression of great energy emanating from this unconventional young man. He noticed with relief that the little finger of Rhodes's right hand was completely bent at the knuckle, so that there had been no ritual in the handshake. Simon disliked secret societies. He drew breath to speak, but Rhodes went on.

'Been here long?'

'Kimberley? No. Two days. That's all. I just–'

'Look here, Fonthill. I will be quite honest. I like the look of you. Just the sort of fine young Englishman this place can do with.' The tall young man rose to his feet and began to pace around the long table, his hands buried deep in the crumpled cotton jacket.

'We have come a long way with this business in a very short time. We are not the largest concern in the diamonds business here – Barney Barnato is bigger at the moment – but we will be. Diamonds can no longer be mined with pick and shovel, yer know. Getting 'em out of the blue ground, further down where the diamond pipes are, is a matter for capital investment and heavy machinery. That means big companies, and that means buying and selling, merging, you know?'

Simon, fascinated with the flow despite himself, nodded.

'I shall be the biggest within a few years, maybe sooner. Fancy coming in? I can find work for you. Young chap like you, fit and knocked around the Empire a bit, can make your name and your fortune within a couple of years.'

Simon opened his mouth to speak, but again Rhodes lifted his hand and intervened.

'Fonthill,' he went on, 'I've got a dream. I've got a dream and, I'll make no bones about it, I intend to make it a reality. I know we've only just

151

met but I feel I can confide in you. May I?'

The large eyes bored into Simon's as though they could see right through him. It was a strangely appealing intensity and Simon found himself shifting on his chair. 'Well,' he said, 'yes, of course. But I really came to–'

'Splendid. You know, Fonthill, Englishmen are the finest race in the world, and the more of the world we inhabit the better it is for the human race. Mankind has suffered because the English nation is only increasing in numbers at half its capacity. We must extend the Empire. Just fancy, those parts that are at present inhabited by the most despicable specimens of human beings: what an alteration there would be if they were brought under Anglo-Saxon influence! I contend that every acre added to our territory means, in the future, birth to some more of the English race who otherwise would not be brought into existence–'

Simon tried once more to speak.

'No, no, Fonthill. Think of it. The unification of the greater part of the world under British control would mean an end to all wars. British domination would lead to the establishment of peace throughout the world. Africa awaits us still, and it is our duty to seize every opportunity of acquiring more territory – and more territory,' he leaned forward, the bulbous eyes now seeming to be starting from the head, and pointed his finger in emphasis, 'simply means more of the Anglo-Saxon race, more of the best, the most human, most honourable traits the world possesses. We can't leave this to politicians, whose lives have been spent in the accumulation of money. We can learn from a study of the Romish Church, from the Jacobites, even from the single-minded dedication of the members of the Masonic Order. Think of the power these people hold.'

Simon tore his gaze away and looked around the gloomy, dark-panelled room. Was the man mad? 'But how,' he asked hesitantly, 'how ... er ... would you do all this?' He realised that such a question sounded pathetically plebeian in the middle of all this rhetoric.

'Ah.' Rhodes stood and began pacing again, his head back and his words now addressed to the low ceiling. 'Let us form a church for the extension of the British Empire, a society which would operate in every part of the Empire, working with one object. Its members would be placed in our universities and our schools, and would watch the English youth passing through their hands and being sent by the society to that part of the Empire where it was felt they were needed. What d'you think, Fonthill, eh, eh?'

Simon gulped. 'Well, I ... ah ... I confess you make a good case, Rhodes. But...'

'Good. Well, why don't you come aboard and help me make it a reality? Make it a reality, eh? A reality, yes?' Rhodes seemed like a retriever dog in his eagerness.

'No.' Simon took a deep breath. 'I am afraid, sir, that I don't quite share your view of the superiority of the British. I have seen something of our behaviour in war which convinces me that our race, while basically honourable, can make mistakes born of arrogance which can lead us...' he stirred uncomfortably on his chair while he

153

sought for the right words to placate the strange man opposite, 'which can lead us into committing acts of folly – sometimes criminal folly.'

Simon expected an outburst, but the big man merely blinked his eyes and raised his brows. 'Really,' he said, and it seemed as though a shutter came down over his face. 'Well, Fonthill, we are both busy men and I certainly don't want to waste your time or mine in further debate on matters of philosophy. Now,' he resumed his seat, 'you came to see me. How can I be of service to you?'

'Thank you. I am grateful to you for receiving me and for sharing your views with me, which, I would like to emphasise, I have found extremely interesting.'

Rhodes inclined his head, but his eyes now began to wander round the room as though he found Simon of no further interest.

'I am told,' Simon continued, 'that you know virtually everything that happens in Kimberley.'

'Not quite true, but I keep my ear to the ground, certainly.'

'Do you know a man named John Dunn?'

Rhodes's head went back for a moment in contemplation. 'Yes, yes. Heard of him back in Natal, a few years ago. Didn't know him personally, though. Why do you ask?'

Simon decided not to confide completely in this strange, possibly dangerous man. 'I understood that he came here, under a year ago, and went into partnership with a man called Mendoza. And that his daughter came out to join him. She wrote to me, from here, asking for my help. But I cannot find her.'

Rhodes frowned. 'I haven't encountered Dunn here, though I do know of Mendoza. Understand that he can be a nasty piece of work, but nothing has been proved.' He leaned forward. 'You know, Fonthill, I waxed a bit lyrical about this place a moment or so ago. But I was looking ahead – at the potential. At the moment it is a mess that urgently needs sorting out. I shall be going into local politics next year to take a lead. It's no use just talking. People must actually get up and *do*.'

Simon gave a half-smile. He could well believe that Rhodes was not cut out to sit on the sidelines. Despite his growing anxiety to get away, now that it was obvious that Rhodes could be of no help, he could not resist asking, 'What's the main problem, then?'

'Oh, we've lots of them. Lots of shortages: shortage of water to drive the steam engines, shortage of capital to fund expansion, and shortage of price stability in the international diamond market. But I suppose the most pressing problem is IDB.'

'IDB?'

'Illegal diamond buying. It's something we are all looking at now as a matter of great urgency. We are talking about the Kaffir and Hottentot workers stealing diamonds in their raw state from the diggings, smuggling them out and then selling them to unauthorised buyers. All the mine owners are losing vast sums of money in this way, and these crooked dealers are making fortunes because, of course, they buy low – the natives have no idea of the worth of the stones – and sell high. Then they're smuggled out, sometimes down to the Cape, sometimes across to Portuguese East

155

Africa and from there, of course, to Antwerp or London.'

'But surely you can search these workers when they leave the mines?'

Rhodes threw back his head and gave a girlish chuckle. 'Oh, we do that all right. But the devils are now getting very inventive. We've found stones stuffed into cartridges, in the cut-out heels of their leather sandals, and even in their mouths. Now they're on to something new – and quite disgusting.'

'What's that?'

'They swallow the stones and then retrieve them later after they have passed through the stomach and out of the body in the ... er conventional way.'

'Ugh! How disgusting.'

'Quite. But to them it's worth the risk of ruining their digestive systems. They can make a year's wages by selling just one stone.'

Simon fell silent for a moment as he remembered Jenkins's disgust at the smell at the back of number 5 Currey Street. 'Could it be,' he asked Rhodes, 'that this man Mendoza is an illegal diamond buyer?'

'I wouldn't know. Have you any evidence?'

'Not at the moment, but it does not seem that his holding is being worked now, yet the man remains living in Kimberley.'

'Hmm. Suspicious – and I understand that he has a bad reputation. Bring us proof and we will nail him. But I am afraid that I can't help you with the whereabouts of John Dunn or his daughter. I am sorry.'

Simon stood. 'You have helped more than you

know. I am most grateful to you, Rhodes. Good luck with your ... er ... ambitions.'

The two shook hands, with Rhodes grasping Simon's hand perhaps a second or two longer than was necessary. Then Simon was gone, making almost indecent haste from the room and back to the observation point in Currey Street. There he met de Witt and, without explanation, took him back to their boarding house to pick up Jenkins – and the brace of Colt pistols.

As the three gathered together in Simon's room, Simon explained what Rhodes had told him – although he omitted the lecture on the superiority of the British race. 'Don't you see?' he said as the others wrinkled their brows. 'The awful smell. Number five must be the place where the thieves go straight from the diggings. There they ... er ... relieve themselves and Mendoza buys the diamonds and smuggles them away, probably across the border to Portuguese East Africa.'

'Where he has a farm,' said de Witt.

'Exactly.'

Jenkins's nose was still wrinkled in disgust. 'Ooh,' he said. 'I wouldn't fancy buying any of *them* after where they've been.'

'Well obviously the diamonds are washed,' said Simon. 'They'll still be in their raw state and will have to be thoroughly cleaned and perhaps even polished anyway before they are sold, and I guess this could be done at somewhere like Lorenzo Marques. That means that there must be a smuggler's route running to the north-east from here.' He handed one pistol to Jenkins and kept the other. 'Do you have a gun, Faan?'

'No.' The Boer grunted. 'But I can use my hands.'

'Right. Let's go and rescue Nandi.'

The three walked now with a sense of purpose towards the wooden house. At the broad tree they paused. 'You two go to the back,' said Simon. 'You will need to get over the fence. I will knock on the front door while you break through from the back. Try not to make too much noise because we don't want neighbours interfering. No shooting if you can possibly help it. We don't want blood on our hands. Use the pistol to threaten. Right. Now go.'

After waiting until the others had made their way down the side alley, Simon tucked his Colt into his belt and banged on the front door. Nothing stirred within the house. He waited a moment and then tried again. Nothing. He looked up and down the street, but the sun was at its highest and no one was to be seen. He ducked down the side alley and climbed the wooden fence to join the others waiting in the little back yard, by a narrow door. Jenkins was right. The smell was overpowering. The three held handkerchiefs to their noses and de Witt put his shoulder to the wooden door. It resisted for only three massive blows before it splintered and the Boer was able to reach inside and turn a key left conveniently in the lock.

They pushed open the remnants of the door and found themselves inside a narrow vestibule. To the right was a primitive toilet consisting of a wooden seat set over a large bucket, across the top of which rested a crude metal grill. The grill was filthy, and the bucket had not been emptied. 'Bloody 'ell,' muttered Jenkins, and they hurried through into the house, handkerchiefs still at their noses and mouths.

It took less than a minute to see that the building was empty. There were four bedrooms on the upper floor, three of them quite large and each containing three beds, the blankets and sheets of which had been roughly thrown aside, as though the occupants had recently left. The fourth was tiny, with room for only a small single bed, neatly made, and a washstand with jug and bowl. On its edge stood a tiny glass vase from which a wan veldt flower sagged.

Simon and Jenkins exchanged glances. 'It's 'er room,' whispered Jenkins. 'The bastards. What 'ave they done with 'er...?'

A quick search of the rooms on the ground floor proved equally unproductive. The remains of a meal had been left on a table; it was as though the occupants had left in a hurry.

'Right,' said Simon. 'Let's see if we can find when they left and if anyone knows how many lived here and where they might have gone. Faan, you go to the right and knock on doors and find out as much as you can. 352, you do the same to the left – oh, damn it all, man, that's that way,' and he pointed. 'I'll ransack this place to see if I can find any clues at all.'

Simon began his systematic search upstairs. Apart from soiled towels in two of the rooms, and the bedclothes, no personal effects had been left. All drawers were empty, as were the rough cupboards. There were no curtains at the windows, but shutters had been bolted across them from the inside. Only dust lay under the beds. Simon's

159

sole company during the search was flies – and they were everywhere.

The rooms downstairs provided little more. The kitchen was comparatively well stocked with cutlery, crockery and pots and pans, but the other rooms were sparsely furnished. A few old bush hats and one or two items of harness hung from hooks in the dark vestibule at the front of the house, leading to the locked front door, but a sideboard, a bookcase and one further cupboard yielded nothing except old newspapers printed in Afrikaans and what appeared to be a Portuguese Bible. It was an empty house and one exuding masculinity. If Nandi had lived here, the only trace she had left was that dead flower in the smallest bedroom.

Simon returned to it in the hope that, somewhere, she had managed to leave a note. He tore out the newspapers lining the drawers under the washstand and examined them, and the wood of the drawers, with great care. But he found only spiders. He unfolded the layers of blankets on her bed and shook them out, repeating the exercise with her pillow and then the old sagging mattress. Nothing.

With a sigh, Simon sat on the bed and buried his head in his hands. The thought of that sweet young girl being forced to live in this foul place filled him with horror and then impotent rage. Why would diamond smugglers – and he was sure that was what they were – keep a young half-caste Zulu girl a semi-prisoner in this place? They could get housekeepers easily enough. As a sex slave? He breathed deeply and tried to rationalise. There were plenty of brothels in Kimberley, and de Witt thought there was a deeper motive. But what was it? And where the hell had they taken her?

He went down the creaky stairs and began his search anew, this time pulling back the worn scraps of cotton rugs to examine the floorboards for trap-doors or other cavities. Taking a deep breath, he even subjected the loathsome lavatory to a cursory but fruitless search. The house gave forth nothing. It was an empty shell.

A bang on the front door and a muted call from de Witt outside prompted him to stride to the forward vestibule, but there was no key on the inside of the lock this time. 'Go round to the back,' he shouted through the door. Then, as he looked again at the harness and the hats hanging from the hooks, he realised that one of the hats, a cracked and greasy typical Boer 'wideawaker', had been thrown on top of another. He snatched off the old hat and his heart missed a beat when he saw what lay beneath. It was headgear of a similar type to the others, although of better quality, and unusually for a Boer hat, it had leather thongs hanging down and tied in a loop so that the hat could be swung back to dangle down the wearer's back. He was sure he had seen the thing before. He remembered a big man riding across the Zulu plain and, reining in, throwing back his hat as he talked to a party of Zulus.

But it was not the hat that excited him. Wrapped around the bottom of its crown was a bright orange bandanna. Surely this had been worn in that sun-dappled glade, and, indeed, in the courtroom where, on the last day of his court

161

martial, Simon had been saved from the firing squad by the evidence of its wearer. Nandi's scarf, of course – and wrapped around her father's hat!

Carefully, as he heard de Witt and Jenkins enter the house from the back, he unwrapped the scarf and, momentarily, put it to his lips. As he did so, a scrap of paper folded within it fell to the ground. He picked it up and read, in that now-familiar schoolgirl handwriting: *Simon. Steelport. Nandi.* The scrap of paper was still quite crisp and not faded.

Containing his excitement, he went to meet the others. 'What news?' he asked.

Jenkins shook his head and made a wry face. 'Nothing from me, bach sir. Nobody in for two doors, look you, and then, when I did find somebody, he only spoke this African lingo, see. But old Fanny 'ere 'as done better.'

De Witt nodded. 'Five men and one girl lived here. Kept to themselves and the girl was hardly ever seen. But they left two nights ago – the day we all met. They went after dark in three Scotch carts but pulled by horses, not oxen, so that they could travel faster.'

'Damn. My fault. I must have frightened them away. Where did they go?'

'Don't know, man. These men did not talk to anyone. Nobody really knew them.'

'Was the big man with them?'

The Boer shrugged. 'Hard to tell. It was dark.'

'Anything else?'

'Ja. This place was often visited by Kaffirs. They would come in, probably straight from the mines because they were covered with dust and soil,

162

and leave after about ten minutes.'

'Of course.' Jenkins's beam lit up the gloomy room. 'They came to spend a penny and left with ten quid.'

'More like fifty.' Simon was able to smile. 'Look.' He showed them the slip of paper. 'This is from Nandi. She must have seen me when I came calling and left this as they cleared out on the same night. This means she's still alive – or was. But where's this Steelport place, Faan? Is it a town on the coast?'

'No. It's a river. Up in the north-east. It's at the foot of the Lulu Mountains, which are really the end of the northern Drakensbergs. It fits together because that is where this bloody man has his farm.'

'Do you know exactly where?'

'Ach, no. That's the problem. I never did know. It's big territory up there, wild and mountainous. There are not many farms, so that's one good thing. But there is one big problem.'

'What's that?'

De Witt gave his slow smile. 'It's bePedi country, man. They are a handful, I can tell you. They are always raiding the Boer farms in that territory and they are good fighters. They've got guts and, what's more, they've got guns. It's not the sort of territory anybody can just wander into right now.'

Jenkins's huge grin cracked his face again and he directed it at the other two in turn. 'That's nice then, boyos,' he said. 'Couldn't be better, could it? When do we start?'

'Right now,' said Simon. 'Come on, let's get out of this dung heap.'

Chapter 7

Pretoria was now strangely quiet, for Wolseley had decided to move his headquarters to Middelburg, some seventy-five miles to the east of the Transvaal capital, where he was building his Transvaal Field Force for the advance against Sekukuni. Alice had decided not to travel with her press colleagues in the wake of the General, at least not for the moment. She had persuaded herself that it was better to stay for a while where Joubert could reach her easily, in case the Boer leader felt able to reveal more of his intentions. There would be little hard news at Wolseley's HQ, only colour pieces, and she had done enough of those and could afford to dally a little in Pretoria. Now, however, on the third day, she grew restive and faced up to the reality that her real reason for remaining behind was to collect news of John Dunn.

Alice's first thought was to tell Simon that Dunn was in Pretoria, but how to find Simon? Where would he be on his quest to find Nandi – a search whose dedication raised a faint feeling of irritation in Alice? She recognised and felt ashamed of that feeling, for there could not possibly be any feeling of jealousy within her. After all, she did not love Simon and she was genuinely fond of Nandi. Dunn's strange appearance in Pretoria could prove a key to solving the puzzle. Why had he abandoned his daughter and why had he turned up in the Boer capital? The man was obviously near to hand – but how to pin him down?

On realising the identity of the stranger who had accosted Joubert, she had rushed down to the street, but both the Boer and the Natalian had disappeared. Alice had then retraced her steps back to the hotel and beckoned to her new friend Charlie, the black concierge, pressing a crisp white five-pound note into his hand. Like all good journalists, Alice had developed on her travels a nose for sniffing out locals who could help her in a new environment. In Pretoria, Charlie had proved to be a revelation. It was he who had first told Alice of Wolseley's threat to deprive the Middelburg farmers of ammunition, and he who had warned her of the imminent departure of the cavalry troop to Heidelberg. It was amazing how Charlie, who never seemed to leave his desk in the hotel, knew exactly what was happening – and about to happen – in Pretoria. So it was to Charlie that she had given the simple task, 'Find John Dunn,' and she knew that if anyone could locate the tall, bluff Natalian in this surly, teeming town it would be the little man with the Zambesi-wide smile and crinkled white hair. Yet she had been waiting now for two days for Charlie to deliver. She could not afford to delay too long. Sir Garnet had a reputation for speed. He would begin his advance any day now and she must not miss that, for all the Dunns in the world.

It was with relief, then, that, sitting in her

165

bedroom, she saw a note pushed under her door. It contained only two lines: a name and an address in one of the Pretorian suburbs. She rang and gave instructions to have pony and trap waiting at the hotel entrance and dressed hurriedly in what she regarded as her working dress: cotton blouse, jodhpurs and riding boots. This interview might be difficult and she wanted to appear as professional as possible.

Within twenty minutes she was standing before a small wooden boarding house so near the edge of the town that she could see the brown flatness of the veldt stretching away from the end of the street. The woman who answered the door was careworn and harassed – taking in boarders was obviously her lifeline, and she looked in consternation at the trim figure before her: polished boots, crisp blouse and fair hair tied back with a soft bow. Alice seemed like an apparition blown into her leaden world from another, golden planet.

Alice quickly stole a look at the name on her scrap of paper. 'May I see Mr John Robinson, please?' she enquired.

''E's in 'is room.' The accent was nasal Essex.

'Oh good. I will go on up, then. What number is it?'

'We don't 'ave numbers. First on right at top o' the stairs.'

'Thank you.'

Alice climbed up the stairs and, taking a deep breath, knocked on the first door on the narrow landing. Lord, she hoped Charlie had got it right!

Her eyes brightened, then, when the figure she

166

had seen from her bedroom window opened the door. Dunn had aged since the last time she had seen him closely, drinking a gourd of Zulu beer after the victory at Ulundi. She had been surprised to see, looking down on him three days ago, how unkempt this fine man's appearance had become. Face to face now, however, she looked into eyes that were tired and a mouth, once firm, that was now dragged down with care. Yet there was something more: from above his right ear a half-healed, jagged wound crept into the tousled hair, there were signs of old contusions on his face, and he held his right arm stiffly across his chest, the thumb hooked into his shirt opening as though for support.

'Hello, Mr Dunn,' she said.

Dunn stood looking at her, frowning. Then, 'You've got the wrong man,' he said. 'Name's Robinson.'

'No it isn't, you're John Dunn, formerly Chief of Intelligence for the Eshowe column in Zululand, and, more important to me at the moment, Nandi's father.'

Dunn's eyebrows went up, and at the mention of Nandi's name, a look of intense apprehension came into his sad eyes.

'What do you mean? Who are you? What's my daughter got to do with you?'

Alice gave him the benefit of one of her most appealing smiles. 'My name is Alice Griffith, Mr Dunn, of the London *Morning Post*, and we have met before, albeit briefly.'

Dunn's frown returned. 'I can't talk to any newspaper people,' he said, and began to close

167

the door.

Alice inserted a boot. 'Mr Dunn, I am not here professionally, but as a friend. I believe that Nandi is in danger and I want to help if I can.'

Again that hunted look came into his eyes. 'You'd better come in.'

He limped as he led her into the room, which matched his own dishevelment. The narrow bed was unmade and dirty water remained in the washbowl on its stand. The only chair, stuffing protruding from its back, sat under a window which had not been cleaned for weeks. Alice remembered with an inward sigh how Simon had described the forceful character of Dunn and the high style – champagne, running hot water for showers, fine linen – in which he had lived as one of Cetswayo's *indunas* in Zululand. She sat gingerly on the edge of the chair while Dunn perched on the bed.

'I don't know you,' he said, 'but if you have news of Nandi I want to hear it.'

A touch of truculence had now crept into his tone, and Alice noted the large revolver and belt of cartridges that hung behind the door. How much to tell him? This would have to be a trade-off of information. But to what extent was he to be trusted? She decided to be open with the man. Simon had always said that he had integrity.

'I am sorry to walk in on you like this, Mr Dunn,' she said. 'I have to say that you don't look well. Have you been hurt?'

He shook his head. 'It's nothing.'

'We met after Ulundi. I am a friend – an old friend – of Simon Fonthill, and I got to know your daughter well at Simon's court martial.'

Recognition dawned in Dunn's eyes. He relaxed perceptibly.

'Ah yes, Miss Griffith. Now I know who you are. Nandi spoke highly of you. And of course I remember Fonthill. We served together scouting for the Eshowe column during the Zulu War after his ... trouble. Good man. Any friend of his is a friend of mine.' He looked round the room sadly. 'I am sorry I cannot offer you refreshment, but as you see, I am temporarily living rather rough.'

'Oh, please do not concern yourself about that.'

The big man leaned forward, wincing as he did so. 'I am worried out of my mind about Nandi. What do you know of her?'

'Mr Dunn, if I tell you all I know about your daughter – and, I fear, it is not a great deal – will you reciprocate by telling me what has happened to you? Together, perhaps, we can help Nandi – and Simon.'

Dunn looked up sharply at the name. 'How is he involved here? I thought he was in Afghanistan.'

'He was. Now listen.' Alice relayed all that she knew: of Nandi's letter, the diversion to South Africa of Simon and Jenkins, and of how the two of them had set off from Durban across country to find Nandi.

Her story did not take long, and Dunn did not take his eyes off her for a moment as she told it. 'Have you heard from Fonthill and Jenkins?' His tone was urgent. 'When would they have arrived in Kimberley?'

'I've heard nothing.' Alice shook her head. 'But

169

they would have reached Kimberley perhaps a week ago. They had an address to go to.'

'Hellfire!' Dunn threw back his head in anguish. 'If they've gone blundering into that damned hole, they could have caused all sorts of trouble. They don't know what kind of people they are dealing with. Ach ... she could be dead by now.' He bowed his head and put a hand to his eyes.

Alice rose immediately and laid her hand on his shoulder. 'No, Mr Dunn, I think you are under-estimating Simon. He would never blunder blindly into anything.'

The big man held up his head and she could see tears in his eyes, but there was a half-smile on his mouth. 'Well, the fool – the brave fool – walked into Cetswayo's kraal on his own on the eve of the war. He wasn't too clever about that. Oh God! What the hell should I do now?'

Alice resumed her seat. 'I think, Mr Dunn, that you had better tell me everything.'

Dunn regarded her from under lowered brows. 'Very well,' he said, 'but you must keep what I tell you to yourself. I want your word. I have been a bit of an ass and I could end up in a British jail – mind you, I don't care much about that if I can get my daughter back.'

'You have my word.'

'Very well.' He took a deep breath. 'After the Zulu war, I went back into Zululand to try and rebuild my life on my farm. But the new general – Wolseley, the one that's up here now – took over and promptly broke up the whole damned structure of the country. He divided the kingdom into petty little chieftainships, so that there could

170

be no unity in the country and no more Zulu army. No more threat from the assegais, he said.' Dunn's face grew hard. 'There was never any threat in the first place. It was the bloody red-necks – the British – who caused the war by invading. But that's by the by.'

He swept a fly off his beard. 'The trouble is that my farm, my land, got divided too, and I lost all my best grazing. I was left with patches of veldt that a mountain goat couldn't live on. All of this after I had helped the blasted British to beat the King.' He looked hard at Alice. 'There's injustice for you.'

Alice lowered her gaze. 'I am sorry,' she said. 'I really am.'

'Not your fault, miss. Anyway, I had to do something to rebuild. So I left Catherine and the few of my other wives who had stayed with me and decided to take a chance and push off to the new diamond fields up at Kimberley to see if I could get lucky. Once there, I found a room to rent cheaply and looked around to see where I could start digging, so to speak. But it wasn't as easy as that. I soon realised that the days when you could stake a claim for tuppence-halfpenny had long since gone. I was about to give up and return home when I met this man – a Portu-guese-Mozambiquan, name of Mendoza – in a bar. We got talking and the whisky flowed. Maybe he had done this before, I don't know, but it wasn't long before he offered to let me have a half-share in his own mine on the edge of the Big Hole in Kimberley.'

Dunn pulled on his beard. 'I wasn't that much

of a fool that I was going to part with my money then and there over the glasses, so I went to look the place over with him the next day. It seemed reasonable: a patch right on the edge of the hole, not deep at all, but he had two Kaffirs working on it, digging away. He explained that he paid the Kaffirs but he rarely worked on the mine himself, only overseeing it, so to speak, because he had other business interests in the town. He said if I would work on the diggin' and pay his price for my share he would continue to pay the Kaffirs. He showed me a few diamonds that he said had come from the claim in the last week and promised me half of what was to come. The money he wanted would clean me out, but I liked the look of the stones he showed me and I fell for it.'

Dunn stood up and walked to the window, looking through the dirty panes with unseeing eyes. 'Trouble is, Miss Griffith,' he continued in a low voice, 'my pride was on the line. I didn't want to limp back home to Natal with nothing to show for my long journey, and I couldn't see any other chance on the horizon. Mendoza could see I was hovering, so he offered me a room in his place in Currey Street, where, he said, he lived with some "associates".' Dunn emphasised the word heavily. 'He said I could live there rent free, as part of the deal. However, he also said that he used the place for business and there would be no room for me there during the daytime. Bed and breakfast, so to speak. I could only return at the end of the working shift.

'It seemed a bit strange,' he looked across at

Alice with a half-smile, 'but I decided to take it. Until I earned money, I had nothing with which to pay rent anyway – and, Miss Griffith,' the sad smile widened, 'I was thinking of those diamonds.' His eyes lit up at the mention of the stones. 'They do get to a man, you know.'

Alice nodded. 'So I've heard.'

'The next day I moved into this place in Currey Street and I decided to send for Nandi to keep me company.' His voice grew tender and almost apologetic. 'Y'see, I had been accustomed to having her around for so long and, well, I suppose I missed her.' He shot Alice a quick glance. 'Shouldn't have done it, but I did. I was lonely and I thought she could keep house for us, so to speak, and the place stank to high heaven and obviously needed a good clean and a woman's touch generally.'

'Why didn't you send for Catherine, your ... er ... number one wife?'

'She had to stay to keep what was left of the family together. Anyway, I sent the letter off and then I told Mendoza, never thinking for a moment that he would object, because I knew that there was a little room in the house where she could sleep and she could earn her keep by looking after us. But he grew very angry and I then saw the dirty side of him.'

'What happened?'

'He told me that I had no right to get anyone else in; that it was his house and it would not be possible for her to stay there during the day, and so on. He worked himself into a right rage and told me to write to her cancelling my original

173

instruction... It was all very strange. Anyway, I sent off another letter to Nandi telling her not to come and started work on the mine, shovelling with the Kaffirs. I didn't have much idea of what I was doing, but at least I was working again. We found no diamonds that day, nor the next, but on the third, one or two little stones came up on my shovel. Not much and not very valuable, but enough to encourage me to keep digging.'

'Where was Mendoza during this time?'

'I did not see him during the day-time at all, but he took the couple of diamonds from me and, later, showed me a receipt for them from a buying agent. We got forty pounds for them and he gave me twenty – my first earnings for quite some months. So that encouraged me to keep going for a time, but nothing else turned up on our little ledge – and the Kaffirs had stopped turning up also. I was told that they were temporarily working at another mine but I started to smell a rat, particularly as Mendoza was now virtually ignoring me at the house in the evenings and his associates had turned out to be big bruisers who treated me with a kind of contempt.'

'How awful.'

'Well, I'm not exactly a blushing veldt rose, but it was all getting me down, particularly as I began to feel that our patch contained as many dia-monds as there are tigers in the Transvaal. There was also this strange, foul smell about the house. Then I began thinking about why I was not allowed into the place during the day-time and wondering what was going on there. So one afternoon I slipped back to Currey Street and watched the place for a while.'

Dunn paused at this point, and his eyes puckered as he recalled the memory. The silence hung heavily in the room and was eventually broken by the woman below slamming a bucket down. The big man seemed to jerk back into the present, but stayed silent.

'What happened?' demanded Alice. 'What was going on there?'

Dunn turned and sat again. 'While I watched,' he said slowly, 'a succession of black workers from the mines arrived throughout the afternoon. They would stay for a quarter of an hour or so and then leave. About five of 'em came and went in a couple of hours. They went in and out of the front door, so while the last one was inside, I slipped down the alleyway at the side of the house, climbed the fence and looked through a window. I was able to make out Mendoza and one of his hard men washing something in a bowl on the table. They were quite excited, so they didn't see me peering in. They were washing diamonds – and God knows what the stones were covered in, but the smell was awful. Then a black feller came in from the passageway, slinging up his trousers, and I realised what they were up to.'

Alice was frowning. 'I am sorry, Mr Dunn, but I don't quite follow.'

'The details don't matter, miss. But these Kaffirs were not our chaps. They were from the deep diggings – the mines that were turning up diamonds in the soil like currants in a cake – and they were stealing stones, smuggling them out of

175

the mines past the security people and selling them to Mendoza. No wonder he didn't want me in the house during the day.'

'But why would he want you to be involved at all?'

'I've thought about that and I am still not quite sure. But first of all there was the money I paid him. He's a crook and couldn't resist the temptation of picking up an easy profit. Then I suppose he wanted some poor fool to continue working the mine to give him cover, because, you see, the big owners are getting very jumpy about stolen diamonds and suspicious of people who hang about the place without visible means of support, so to speak. With him still owning a mine which was being worked, it took the spotlight off him for a while, so that, while I was digging for him, he could operate his racket in Currey Street.'

'Go on.' Alice was by now hanging on his every word.

'The Kaffir left – by the front door, luckily – and then they put the little pile of diamonds that, presumably, they had collected that day into a small hessian sack, pulled up a floorboard and deposited the sack there. I decided I had seen enough so I did a silly thing.' Dunn shook his head and looked at Alice with reproachful eyes. 'I resolved to have it out with Mendoza then and there and went straight to the back door and banged on it. They let me in and I strode in and said, "Right. What the hell's going on?"'

'I remember angry words and Mendoza losing his temper but not much more because someone hit me over the head with a very hard object.' He fingered his scalp. 'Just here, see?'

Alice drew in her breath. 'That could have fractured your skull.'

'Damn near did. Anyway, I went out like a light and only came to in the cold air. I must have been out for about three hours because it was pitch black as well as cold. I realised that I was being trundled along in a cart and that, strangely, I stank to high heaven of whisky.'

'Whisky? Had you been drinking?'

'Not a drop since I had started working on the mine. No, it was on my shirt, which had been saturated by the stuff. Then suddenly I was seized and carried out of the cart, and for the first time I realised where I was.' He paused, as if for effect.

'Yes, yes,' said Alice, her eyes wide, 'where were you?'

'At the mine and being carried to the edge of the Big Hole. I knew what they were going to do and I tried to struggle but I was still muzzy and didn't have much strength. Before I knew it, I was flying through the air, legs flailing, down towards the bottom of that infernal drop.'

Alice put her hand to her mouth. 'Oh my goodness. How far did you fall?'

'Well, it's about three hundred and fifty feet all the way – and if I had gone all the way, I wouldn't be here talking to you now. But, of course, I didn't. I suppose me kicking my legs must have saved my life for I caught one of the devils on the shoulder as he was heaving me and, presumably, he wasn't able to put his full weight into the throw. Anyway, I hit the side of the hole and just

177

bounced down into the blackness until...'

'Yes?'

'Some sort of bush, stunted but sturdy, saved me. I don't know how far I fell but perhaps it wasn't all that far because I hadn't gathered sufficient momentum to crash through that bit of bush. Anyway, it brought me up with a jerk and there I stayed, bent round it like a hairpin.'

Alice had meant to take notes of Dunn's story but it had been so dramatic that she had forgotten to produce pencil and notebook. She remained looking at Dunn, her eyes wide. 'So they tried to kill you, to murder you in cold blood?'

'Oh yes. As I lay there, with – as I found out later – a broken arm, two broken ribs and a head which had been hit very hard many times ... as I lay there, miss, in a lot of pain, I realised what the plot was. They had doused me with whisky and thrown me to the bottom, as they thought, with the idea that I would be found and buried as just another drunken old digger who had slipped over the edge of his plot. That had happened before. Luckily, it was dark and they couldn't see I hadn't gone all the way down.'

'I see. How were you found?'

Dunn smiled ruefully. 'I've no idea. I obviously slipped back into unconsciousness because the next thing I knew it was daylight and I was being gradually winched to the top, lashed into an earth bucket and dangling from one of the hawsers that link up to the diggings at the bottom. That hurt a fair bit too, I can tell you, and the pain knocked me out again. When I came round, I was in some sort of makeshift hospital, under canvas, at the mine. My arm was in splints and my head bound up and I had bandages round my ribs, but,' he smiled again, 'I was not getting much respect. They thought I was an old drunkard.

'Anyway, my main thought was to get out of there because I feared that the news might get back to Mendoza and Co. that they hadn't quite got rid of me and they would come round again to finish me off. So I hobbled out of the little compound which had been set up as a first-aid post. Nobody stopped me and I somehow found my way back to the place where I had stayed on first arrival. Those so-and-so's had not emptied my pockets and I still had some of that twenty quid on me, so the dear old biddy in my lodgings was happy to put me up there and keep quiet about it. What was left of the rest of my money was back in Currey Street. I lay up for a while, trying to get my strength back and thinking what to do next. It didn't take me long to make up my mind.'

Alice frowned. 'Surely you went to the authorities?'

'What authorities? The army is the only real force, but the nearest contingents were here, in Pretoria. Anyway, I had a better idea.'

For the first time since he had begun his story, Dunn looked uncomfortable. 'Now, I'm not exactly proud of this next bit, miss,' he said, his eyes not quite meeting Alice's, 'because I have always been a law-abiding man. But I was pretty desperate by this time, y'see – and also pretty damned angry. These people had tricked me, stolen what little money I had, tried to kill me

179

and left me for dead. As I lay there I decided that I wasn't having that, not at all.'

'So...?'

'So, after about a week, when I felt a bit better, I spent what was left of the money I had in buying a pistol and then, in the middle of the night, I crept out of my digs and paid a visit to Currey Street. I must confess that I was scared as hell, because I knew that if I met up with Mendoza and his gang I was in no position to fight and would have to shoot to kill, but I decided to take the risk. I managed to get over that fence again – God knows how I did it with busted ribs, but I did – and prised open the padlock on the back door to the house. The wood round it was pretty rotten and I was able to cut into it with hardly a sound. I crept into that back room and ... found what I was looking for.'

Alice sucked in her breath. 'The diamonds?'

Dunn nodded. 'The floorboard lifted easily and there was the sack. It must have been just before Mendoza was due to sell 'em on, because that sack was pretty full.' He gave a wan smile. 'I was out of there like a greased lizard and back in my little boarding house without disturbing a soul. The next day I left town, reckoning that Mendoza would soon work out who had taken the stones, because he would have heard by now that the Big Hole had coughed up an old sozzler who'd then walked away from the hospital tent. I figured that it wouldn't take him long to track me down, so I bought some ammo for my pistol and a horse with one of the stones – and rode away as quickly as I could.'

'Where did you go?'

'On the way over from Natal, I had stayed in a farm about twenty miles out on the veldt, with a Boer chap I had known in 'Maritzburg. He could see I was still in bad shape but he didn't ask any questions and put me up. Trouble was, I didn't have any cash left, only the diamonds, so I decided I would have to sell one or two of them pretty quickly so that I could pay my way until I could set off home again.' Dunn pulled at his beard. 'Problem was, I didn't want to take any risks by going to a respectable diamond buyer. He might want to see proof of origin and that sort of stuff. So I needed a kopje walloper.'

'A what?'

'Ach, sorry. They're unofficial diamond buyers. Usually they trade in stolen diamonds and buy from the Kaffirs. They kill you on price because they usually pay the blacks in what's called "Cape smoke" – uniforms, old watches, even mouth organs – but of course they don't ask questions. My Boer farmer knew one, and as soon as I was able I rode into town to meet him. He looked at what I offered him and said that he would buy but didn't have the cash with him and would have to meet me next day to finalise the deal. I didn't like the sound of that but I had no option. So I arranged to meet him on the edge of town – I didn't want to be trapped in no office.'

Alice realised that she had been sitting in the gloomy bedroom for almost an hour. She had still not taken a note but that mattered little, for every twist of Dunn's story was now stored away in her mind. She nodded for him to continue.

181

'I rode back next day; it was very early in the morning, just after dawn, because this feller didn't want to be seen with me. I took my pistol and approached this barn where we were to meet with great caution. He was inside all right and seemed to be completely alone. He handed over the money as right as rain and took the three diamonds I gave him. Then he said that he would buy the rest and offered me a very good price for them.

'I might have realised something was wrong, because the price seemed too good – and he also offered to come to the farm the next morning to save me the trouble of riding into town. He asked me where I was staying and,' Dunn shook his head, 'I was fool enough to tell him. Then I saw a movement behind a hay bale and realised that it was an ambush. I grabbed the walloper round the throat, stuck my pistol in his ear and shouted, "Come closer and I'll kill him!" What an idiot!' A grin creased his face. 'They didn't care a toss whether I killed him or not now that they knew where I was keeping the rest of the diamonds, and they let off with their own pistols. Luckily, I was protected by the walloper and he took a slug in the chest. I shot back and made 'em duck behind the hay bales, which gave me just enough time to drop the walloper and get out of the barn, slamming the door behind me and slipping the bar into the padlock. Then I ran as best I could to my horse and rode off.'

Alice's mouth remained open for a moment as her imagination recreated the scene. 'Did they follow you?'

'No. Couldn't think why at first, though I knew it would take 'em a minute or two to get out of the barn. Then I realised that they probably hadn't picked up the name of the farm and that either they had killed the walloper or he was too badly injured to talk and tell them where I was staying. But I soon found out...'

'Yes?'

'I decided to leave the farm as soon as I could because I knew it would only be a matter of time before Mendoza came calling, but Van der Watt – he's the farmer, splendid chap – told me I was still too cut up to ride far and that it was unlikely the Portuguese would attack the farm openly. So I stayed put waiting and worrying but they didn't show up.'

The Natalian paused for a moment and rubbed his good hand across his face, kneading his eyes with thick fingers. Alice sat thinking. Eventually she asked, 'But where does Nandi fit into all this?'

Dunn blinked. 'Funny you should ask that,' he said, 'because she fits in more or less about now in the story.'

'How?'

'Well, I had written to her about three weeks before telling her not to come and I presumed that I had caught her before she set off, because there would have been things she had to do before leaving Catherine. But I didn't. She must have been almost waiting for me to call her, and set off virtually as soon as she received the letter. She arrived, of course, after I left the damned house.'

'How do you know?'

'After I had been sitting in the farm, my pistol in me lap, for about three days, a black boy arrives – I recognised him because he was one of the Kaffirs digging with me on our mine. He'd brought a letter from Mendoza. It was just a note which said, "We've got your daughter. Bring the diamonds and you can have her."'

'How did you know they weren't bluffing?'

'Good point. In the envelope was one of the little scarves she used to wear. I would know it anywhere. I questioned the Kaffir and it was clear that Nandi had arrived just after I'd pinched the diamonds. They must have realised, of course, that it was me, so they kept her to bargain with me. So – what to do? Of course, I had to get Nandi out of there but I knew that they wouldn't let me stay alive after I had given them the diamonds because I knew too much. I am not fool enough to think that Mendoza would do a fair swap. Once they had the diamonds they would kill both Nandi and me. So I sort of compromised. I wrote to him saying that I would do the deal – provided that Nandi was unharmed in every way – but only in a public place, like the big square in the middle of the town, where we could all be seen. But he wasn't having any. Two days later he sent me back a note saying that would be too dangerous and that he stood the risk of having the diamonds confiscated by the mine security people, who were always on the lookout for stones passing from hand to hand in this sort of way. No. I had to come to the house.'

'And did you?'

'No. It would have been signing a death warrant for both of us. I was not strong enough – in every sort of way – to ride in, risk everything and storm the house on my own, so I asked Van der Watt if he and his boys would come with me. But he refused. Can't blame him. He's got his farm and his wife and kids to think about, and it wasn't his fight. He had stuck his neck out far enough as it was in giving me protection. No. There had to be another way. So I played for time, sent a note saying I was too ill to move for the moment, and made my way up here.'

Alice frowned. 'What? Just ran away, do you mean?'

'Oh no. I heard from Van der Watt that Commandant Joubert, here in Pretoria, was desperately seeking diamonds he could use to buy guns and ammunition from the Germans so that he could rise up against the British in the Transvaal. So I felt that if I could see him I could do a deal with him.'

Alice made a mental note and then asked, 'What sort of a deal?'

Dunn sighed. There was now an air of hopelessness about him. 'I had an idea,' he said, 'that if I gave Joubert the diamonds he would lend me some men to attack the house and set Nandi free. Not a bloody commando, but just enough to do the job that I couldn't do on my own.'

'What did he say?'

'Said he'd think it over. Kept me waiting a fair time and then I met him in the street and he said no. Firstly, he said he had his own source of diamonds from Kimberley, and secondly he could not risk starting an armed confrontation on British territory which could prejudice what he was hoping to do later.'

Alice's eyes widened as she mentally recorded these facts, but the big man was continuing.

'And anyway, I'm not sure he believed a word I was saying. He probably thought I was mad.' He smiled at Alice sheepishly. 'It must sound like a tall story to you.'

Alice shook her head. 'Oh no, Mr Dunn. Anyway, I know of Nandi's letter to Simon.'

The air of despair returned to Dunn's face. 'Yes, I know. That's what's worrying me even more now. Fonthill and Jenkins – and that Welshman is a fiery little devil – could have gone in all guns blazin' and ruined everything.' He looked at Alice and held out his good hand as though in supplication. 'What on earth am I going to do now, Miss Griffith? What am I going to do? I've wasted so much time.'

The two sat looking at each other in silence. Eventually Alice spoke. 'To be frank, Mr Dunn,' she said, 'I don't know.' She stood now and paced the little room.

'It seems to me,' she said eventually, 'that you have two alternatives. You could ride back to Kimberley to find Simon and Jenkins, which would be difficult in a town that size. Or you could come with me to General Wolseley, explain the position, and ask him to help you. I am sure I could get him to see you, and, after all, he is High Commissioner for South-East Africa as well as Commander in Chief of the Armed Forces, and, as such, responsible for law and order here. He

186

must be able to do something about this bunch of diamond thieves, surely?'

Dunn shook his head. 'No, miss. I just don't trust that man. He broke up my country, and anyway, he would look upon me as a jewel thief myself. After all, I am sitting on stolen diamonds.'

Having rationalised a course of action, Alice now espoused it vigorously. She spoke with conviction. 'No. You must say that you have brought the stolen property back to the authorities and hand the stones over to the General. Then appeal to him to help you regain your daughter.' She smiled. 'I suspect that he's a bit of a gallant at heart and the task might appeal to him, even though,' and now she frowned at the thought, 'he is about to fight a campaign against the bePedi.'

Dunn sat deep in thought, running his fingers through his beard. 'All right,' he said at last. 'You are probably right. Even if I went back to Kimberley I might be too late to help Fonthill. And if I turn up with the British Army, that should daunt even bloody Mendoza.'

'That's the spirit,' said Alice. 'Now, come on. Get your things together. I will collect you tomorrow at seven o'clock and we can ride directly from here to find Wolseley at Middelburg. It's time I was there anyway.'

Alice grabbed Dunn's hand and gave it a firm shake, then ran down the stairs, giving the gaunt landlady a cheery wave as she went past her, and climbed into the trap.

187

Chapter 8

Despite their determination to leave the disgusting house in Currey Street and to hurry after Nandi as soon as possible, it was not until just after dawn the next morning that Simon and his two companions set off to the north-east to find the Steelport River. Firstly there was a horse to be found for de Witt. Simon's funds were now beginning to run low and he decided to allocate him their third, relief mount. The horses had all been rested well enough since their arrival in Kimberley, and although the journey to the Lulu Mountains seemed long and, even with the help of their map, almost immeasurable, Simon felt that they could manage with only three mounts. Then he insisted that a rifle had to be bought for the Boer and it took a little while to find a decent Snider at the right price. Lastly, de Witt proposed that he should revisit Currey Street and make a detailed search of the house – just, he said, to make sure there was nothing left there which could help them find the farm. Reluctantly, Simon agreed that he should do so, although he thought the request was strange. With all the delays, then, and despite their anxiety to be on the road, there would have been little to be gained by setting out on their long journey across the veldt just before nightfall.

As the first hint of sun lit the sky the next day,

they met up and mounted. Predictably, de Witt reported that he had found nothing in Currey Street that could help them, so they set out across the reddish sandy veldt along a trail which would take them, estimated Simon, well to the east of Pretoria in the general direction of the new goldfields that had been found at Lydenburg, from which they must head due north to find the Steelport. It was a journey, said de Witt, of over 250 miles, and given that they could not afford the luxury of taking their time, it would not be comfortable. Simon gave an inward groan, for he was still uneasy on horseback. This information had quietly been conveyed to de Witt by Jenkins, and behind Simon's back, these two exchanged a quick grin.

Their route lay through the northern edge of the Orange Free State into the Transvaal and enabled them to stay well away from the dangerous rocky fastness of Basutoland. In fact, said de Witt, their long trek should be free of danger until they reached the land of the bePedi tribe, near the end of their journey.

The boxing match had forged a bond of sorts between Jenkins and de Witt and the two rode side by side chatting – or with Jenkins, at least, happily making the conversation, while de Witt responded monosyllabically, although with gentle good humour. Simon dropped behind a little on that first morning and regarded the big Boer from the rear with puzzled interest. It was vital that they were able to rely on de Witt if they ran into trouble. Studying him from the back, Simon could see that he was at home in the saddle: he rose gently to match the horse's pace and his hands were soft on the reins. But that was to be expected of a Boer, for these men seemed to have been born on horseback. Yet it was strange that he seemed to have no visible means of support and that he possessed no rifle. It was time to discover a little more about the man's past, so Simon urged his horse forward and drew level with the other two.

'I know you worked in the mines once, Faan,' he said, 'but did you come to Kimberley at the beginning of the diggings?'

The Boer nodded. 'Ja. I was there in the early days, the good old days, when the fields were part of the Free State.' He smiled ruefully. 'Before you *roijneks* came in and tried to bring some kind of damned European order to the place.'

'What was it like, then?'

'Well, I'm talking about '73, '74, when the rush began.' He eased forward in the saddle and smiled for a moment at the recollection. 'If there are about five thousand whites in Kimberley now, there were some twenty-five thousand in those early days. We had the dry sortings then, man, and used ordinary buckets and not the big tubs. The roads went through the mines and we just went on digging by their side. You know the tall, thin towers of earth that are in the Big Hole now? Well, they're all that's left of those roads. We took the oxen down seventy feet or more at the sides and men were always getting killed one way or the other, with the earth collapsing or a tin bucket falling on a man's head.'

'Hey, Fanny,' asked Jenkins, 'did you find

diamonds yourself, then?'

'Ach, many, my friend.' He became almost loquacious. 'I would be sifting one morning and find some big diamonds and say to my mates, "Hey, come and have some champagne" – it was five shillings a bottle then – and we would go and get drunk and leave the sorting to the Kaffirs. Most of them were honest in those days and they would bring us in the evening the diamonds they had found and I would say, "Boy, go and have a spree and here is five pounds." Maybe a poor fellow would come in with nothing and I would say, "Go into my claim for the afternoon and take what you can get and just give me a share. It will set you up." Yes, man, those were the days! Sometimes I would clear three thousand pounds a week on my claim. Ach, yes.'

'Blimey!' exclaimed Jenkins. 'What happened to all the money, then?'

'Drink and gambling. The usual thing, you know. Now I have nothing. But I don't regret any of it, except,' the disingenuous grin gradually left his face, 'the British coming in and taking over. That was not right, you know.'

'Well,' said Simon, 'I'm afraid I know nothing about the politics. But how did you get into boxing?'

'Barnato set up what he called his boxing academy before he really hit it rich. I was down and out but managed to pull myself together and get off the drink, so I began to box a bit there, just to get fit again. Then they began this champion nonsense and I found that no one could beat me, so I started earning money at it. Until, that is,' the rueful smile came back, 'this big man here knocked me out. Then I realised that I couldn't fight – well, not properly.'

Jenkins blew out his cheeks. 'There's nonsense, look you,' he said. 'You 'it very well considerin' you're out of condition, see. Anyway, what do these diamond things look like, when they come out of the ground?'

'Well, they're coated with grease usually, with earth stuck to them of course. But colour is important; the brown and darker ones are worth far less, of course, than the clearer stones, though yellow diamonds can be valuable. They're all shapes and sizes, too. But they're hard, damned hard, that's for sure.'

'Hardest substance known to man,' interjected Simon. 'The word comes from the Greek *adamas*, meaning unconquerable. They're made of pure carbon, about a hundred and forty times stronger than any other mineral.'

'Well I'll be blowed,' said Jenkins. 'You don't get that sort of interestin' stuff in your Army Certificate, now do you?'

They rode on, pushing the horses as much as they dared. The veldt was flat and uninteresting, rolling gently to a horizon that seemed continents away. It also appeared lifeless, although on the second day a harsh croaking cry drew their eyes to a sandy patch where a black-trousered secretary bird, its wings open, was prancing around a snake and kicking it to death with powerful feet. If the terrain was uninteresting, however, the sky was not. Bulging grey dumplings of cloud marched overhead, with their bases cut off uniformly clean,

192

as though with a knife, and to the south, a long purple smudge extended from east to west, often keeping them distant company throughout the day but never closing to threaten them at first hand.

Until, that is, the evening of the third day, when they had just pitched their three tiny tents and hobbled the horses. They owed it to the Boer that they fared no worse. It was he who pointed to the pelmet of purple cloud that hung over that southerly horizon but which was now fringed at the bottom by a black line which seemed to meet the earth and was nearing by the second. 'Quick,' shouted de Witt, 'dig a channel round the tents.' They fell to with a will but had no time to finish before the storm hit them. The rain was presaged by a red dust storm that raged down on them with a hissing sound. It knocked over the tents and carried away the kitchen utensils, bowling them away before the wind as though they were blossom tops and making the men hunch over, backs to the storm and handkerchiefs to their mouths. Cracks of thunder deafened them and lightning played all around; not forked and white, as in England, but like red-hot pieces of iron waving about in the darkness. The rain fell in heavy sheets and, kneeling before the blast, they laboured to complete the trench to channel the water away and so prevent their campsite from becoming completely flooded.

The tempest passed away as soon as it had come and the drenched trio were left to recover their tent and their equipment and soothe the trembling horses as best they could. 'Ach,' growled de Witt. 'Veldt storm. They get lots of them around here. Sometimes there are hailstones as big as pigeon eggs that can kill a sheep. If you get caught when riding, the only thing to do is to dismount, take off the saddle and kneel with it over your head. This bit of a storm wasn't much, really.'

As the journey progressed, the Boer's value became more apparent. It was he who showed them how to skin a dead sheep and then keep the meat from rotting in heavy, thunderous weather by laying the skin, wool downwards, in a hollow and adding salt, water and pieces of flesh overnight, so preserving it. They bought food and some fodder from the Boer farms that were now becoming increasingly rare as they penetrated deeper into the high veldt of the Transvaal. Often the farmers, remote in their rectangular stone buildings, would be resentful of the travellers' request for shelter and sustenance, but they always complied. De Witt explained that, under Roman Dutch law, Afrikaners had an obligation to provide food and shelter for travellers, as long as the supplicants could pay. Simon then understood the surly acceptance with which he and Jenkins had been met when they requested hospitality on their journey through the Free State.

The pace they set, although perforce not fast, was hard on the horses, and by the second week, they were forced to lead them for part of each day to give them some respite. Simon now wished that they had bought a couple of the ubiquitous Scotch carts that formed the main means of carriage in the Transvaal. It was possible that better progress could have been made with this form of transport. He had given up all thought of overtaking Mendoza's party, and the chance of meeting them on this vast plain was remote anyway, but he was anxious to be hard on their heels so that if they decided to stay awhile at Mendoza's farm before heading on to the Mozambique border, he would be able to catch them there, off their guard – if, that is, they could find the farm and the bePedi did not intervene.

Sometimes they were able to find shelter in a small inn. At a mean little town some 120 miles to the east of Pretoria, they found rooms in the Hotel Burgers and were able to buy oranges at twelve to the shilling. But vermin careered over tables, chairs and beds and they were glad to be out on the veldt again, heading towards the town of Lydenburg, although with some trepidation on Simon's part now. He remembered that Wolseley had said he would move his invading force out to there, presumably as a springboard for his final advance. Would he have done so by now? He had no intention of being sucked into the General's scouting force, and in any case, the Steelport River lay further to the north, so he set a course to by-pass the town.

In doing so, the little party now entered into very different country. Here, as they climbed higher, the veldt was greener, and wooded hills appeared with occasional small lakes shimmering in the sun. Soon, however, they began climbing, and once more were riding across a high plateau, where the air was cooler. For the first time they saw signs that this was no longer peaceful country. Farms were fewer, and as they penetrated further north-west, many of them had been burned out and left desolate as a result of the recent depredations of the bePedi. De Witt explained that the farmers, tired after repelling constant attacks, had departed for the nearest towns, leaving their homesteads to be burned by the tribesmen. As dusk approached and they had not camped, it was obvious that the Boer was becoming increasingly uneasy.

Simon noted this and asked, 'Do you think the bePedi are still marauding this far west, Faan?'

The big man stirred in his saddle. 'Ach, no. It's lions I'm worried about.'

'What?' Jenkins's eyes stood out above his moustache. 'Lions, bach! Bloody 'ell. I don't like the sound of that.' He turned, almost accusingly, to Simon. 'But them black chaps a few weeks ago said that we were miles away from bloody lions.'

'We were much further south then. But I didn't realise this was lion country, Faan.'

'Ja. This territory never used to be – oh, the odd one or two maybe, but not too many. They stayed up north or in Mozambique, where game is plentiful. Now, though, there has been a drought in the north and over the border, with rinderpest killing cattle, and they have been coming down here. It's dry, hot and sandy, but with plenty of low cover and a bit of game here and there. Ideal for lions.'

'But I have always understood that lions don't attack humans.'

The Boer's face broke into the familiar half-smile that never reached his eyes. 'Ja. That's what

196

you *roijneks* and city people always say. We Afrikaners know better.'

'Yes, but,' Simon frowned as he tried to remember what he had read, 'those lions that do attack people, aren't they usually just a very few, who have been injured in some way so that they can't catch game in the normal way?'

'Ja, that is true. But it's a bit different around here.'

'Why?'

De Witt jerked his head backwards. 'That last burned-out farm we passed. Did you see anything strange about it?'

'No.'

'Ach, you people don't have eyes in your head. There were skeletons out in the bush, four or five of them.'

'Blimey, Fanny.' Jenkins's face now wore an expression of extreme disquiet. 'I saw 'em. They were sheep or cattle, weren't they?'

'No. They were human remains. BePedi, I should think, who were shot while attacking the farm. The farmers probably didn't have time to bury them when they left, or...' he gave his mirthless smile again, 'just didn't bother. The lions had them.'

'Could have been vultures, surely,' said Simon.

'Vultures pick quite delicately. These limbs were torn apart and were quite scattered.'

'Hyenas?'

'One or two of the spotted variety round here, but not many. Man, those were lions, I could tell. It's not generally realised that lions scavenge, too. The trouble is, once they get the taste for human

197

meat, it stays with them, particularly, as you say, if they can't outrun game. This war with the bePedi has left many bodies – and a lot of wounded men. Back there they ate carrion. But once they have attacked a live human they lose their fear and will do so again.'

They rode on in silence for a while, and Simon noticed that Jenkins was now looking around him with great care and fingering the stock of his rifle in its saddle holster. The two of them had faced many dangers, and so far two things only had produced fear in the little Welshman: the sea and heights. Now, it was clear, a third had been added to the list.

After a while Jenkins spoke. 'Hey, Fanny, I can't spot any signs of these lions, see. Are you sure you're right about them?'

The Boer silently pointed to a sandy patch of soil to their right. The imprint of large pug marks was clearly defined, each showing indentations for the four claw digits and one for the heel of the pad. De Witt drew his rifle and pointed to them but did not dismount. 'They're quite fresh,' he said. 'He was probably watching us as we approached.'

'Oh bloody 'ell,' exclaimed Jenkins.

De Witt gazed about him keenly. 'Pity we didn't camp back at that farm,' he mused, 'but it was too early.' He turned to Simon. 'We are losing the light and it is not safe to ride on. I think we camp here. But make big fire, eh?'

'Very well,' said Simon

They had only one tent, a low bivouac just big enough for Simon and Jenkins. De Witt slept in the open. Simon and the Boer foraged for dry wood while Jenkins stood watch with his rifle, and then the three men, all strangely silent, ate their rations by the side of the fire they had kindled. De Witt pulled his sleeping bag close to the fire, his rifle by his side.

'I think we should have a watch system,' said Simon.

'Not necessary,' said de Witt. 'This fire will keep the big cats away.' He slipped into his sleeping bag. 'Good night, English.'

Simon and Jenkins exchanged glances and then shrugged shoulders and crept underneath the flimsy protection of their canvas.

'It don't seem right, bach sir, old Fanny sleepin' out there with them lions about,' said Jenkins, his eyes wide.

'I agree, though this tent isn't much protection if they do decide to come sniffing around. But look, I'll lie awake for the first couple of hours or so and then wake you. We can keep watch that way.'

Simon awoke with a start perhaps some two hours later, cursing that he had dropped off to sleep. The comfort of the sleeping bag and the long hours in the saddle had inevitably prevented him from staying awake. He looked at his watch, which showed just after midnight. He had no idea what had woken him but a glance proved that Jenkins was wide awake also.

'What was it?' whispered Simon.

'Don't know. I've just woken up. Some sort of noise, I suppose.'

'I'll just take a look. It's probably nothing. You stay here.' Simon crawled out of his sleeping bag, pulled on his boots, picked up his rifle and undid the strings of the tent opening. Poking his head through, he noted the sleeping form of de Witt and the fire guttering dangerously low. The sky was richly patterned with stars and the night was still, unusually still, as though the darkness that surrounded them was holding its breath, waiting for something to happen. Simon lay there for a moment, half in and half out of the tent, resting on his elbows, his rifle by his side, listening and looking. The silence slipped around him like a heavy cloak, resting on him oppressively. He felt the hairs stand up on the back of his neck.

'It's out there.' De Witt's whisper was so low it could hardly be heard, but it made Simon start. The Boer's tone was unemotional and betrayed no fear. 'It's somewhere to my right. I can hear it breathing. Don't want to slip out of my bag in case that prompts it to spring, but I've got my rifle. Can you reach to throw a log on the fire? Move slowly. A sudden movement might make it attack. The fire's the answer, but the damned thing's nearly out.'

Slowly, his eyes wide in an attempt to penetrate the darkness, Simon picked up his rifle, cocked it, and then began to crawl on his elbows through the tent opening towards where they had left a small pile of kindling wood near the fire. His feet free, he inched his way nearer to the pile, his belly pressed close to the ground, his eyes desperately trying to focus into the blackness that lay beyond the flickering pool of light cast by the fire. Was it his imagination, or could he smell a strange, musky odour in the velvet stillness? Either way, he knew he was frightened, very frightened.

When it came, the attack was blindingly quick in its action and frightening in its ferocity. The lion sprang from the edge of the small clearing, exactly where de Witt had indicated, its shape just a blur at first by the light of the fire's embers. Then Simon had a momentary impression of a huge, fully maned head and staring amber eyes. But if the lion was quick, de Witt was quicker. Still in his sleeping bag, he rolled to one side and fired his rifle into the living mass that landed across his legs and feet. Furious at missing its prey, and half blinded by the flash of the rifle, the lion turned its head and Simon glimpsed the yellow fangs of the beast as they sought the throat of the Afrikaner. On one knee, Simon raised his rifle instinctively and fired into the great head a few paces from him. The bullet penetrated the brain and the beast convulsed for a second and then lay still, half across de Witt.

'Quick,' gasped the Boer, 'reload. My gun's underneath the lion and I can't get it. These animals come in pairs. There's another one out there. Behind you, I think. Quickly now.'

As though on cue, a deep-throated growl came from out of the blackness. In less than a second, it had swollen into a roar of frightening proportions – the most terrifying sound that Simon had ever heard. It came, as de Witt had predicted, from the edge of the bush immediately behind Simon, and from very near. Simon had just half a second to appreciate the beasts' cleverness in planning their attack from different directions – and at exactly that moment, he realised that he had no more ammunition. His cartridge belt lay, with his Colt revolver, by the side of his bedroll. Both he and de Witt, the latter still trapped underneath the first lion, were defenceless.

Immediately, Simon plunged for the tent opening. The move undoubtedly saved his life, for the second lion chose exactly that moment to launch itself at the half-erect being so near to it. In midair the beast realised that its prey had moved and it twisted round so that it skidded as it hit the ground, paws clawing into the sand to change direction for another attack. As its head swung round, Jenkins's bullet crashed into the lion's shoulder, the .45 calibre Boxer slug spreading on impact to smash bone and sinew.

Even then, however, the animal was not finished. Paws scrabbling, it raised its head to launch another spring, and Simon, hunched in the tent's opening, caught a glimpse of a snarling, wide-open mouth. Looking straight into the lion's eyes, he saw the malevolence there, framed by the magnificent mane. Man and beast regarded each other for perhaps two seconds – long enough for Simon to realise that he was as good as dead but just time enough for Jenkins to slip another round into the breech and fire again, at point-blank range. The second shot took the lion exactly between the eyes. Slowly – incredibly slowly, it seemed to Simon as he watched – the beast's head sank to the ground, the terrible eyes still open, glaring defiance.

A strange silence returned to the clearing,

suddenly broken by a crackle from the fire as a last brand settled into the red ashes. Simon realised that his body was trembling as he knelt at the tent opening. Jenkins lay at his side, his rifle poking under the skirt of the tent, his sweat-streaked head resting on one side across the rifle stock and his eyes closed. Eventually the Welshman spoke. 'I'd rather fight the savage Zulus *an'* the Pathans all at the same time than face these wild beasts again, I'll tell you,' he whispered.

'Thanks, 352,' said Simon. 'You're a bloody marvel, you really are.' He realised that his voice was hoarse and wavering.

'Will somebody get this bloody animal off me,' growled de Witt. 'It's crushing my legs.'

'Sorry, Faan.' Simon, still trembling, got to his feet, and he and a bootless Jenkins, together using their rifles, were eventually able to lever the lion off the Boer.

'You hurt?' queried Simon.

'No. Lucky he fell across my legs, mainly with his hind quarters.' The big man slowly stood erect and immediately slipped another round into his rifle. 'My pride's a bit wounded, though. I should have realised that these two weren't going to let a dying fire stop them from hunting.' He looked across at Simon and held out his hand. 'I'm grateful to you, English. You kept your nerve and shot true when you had to. As did 352 here. Thank you.'

'Oh, think nothing of it, boyo,' said Jenkins, smoothing his moustache. 'I always shoot lions on a Tuesday.' He looked out into the surrounding darkness. 'Any more like this out there then, is there, Fanny?'

'No. Almost certainly not. But let's build this fire up anyway. It's my fault for letting it go out. They would never have attacked if it was blazing away.' They all set to and threw more wood on the still-hot ashes, so that the fire immediately blazed up and illuminated the clearing. De Witt then turned and knelt down by the lion that had nearly killed him, before examining the other. 'Look,' he said. 'They are badly out of condition.' He pointed with the toe of his boot to where the ribs of the animals were clearly defined. 'And look here. This one's got a badly deformed leg, probably broken in a fight and not healed properly, and the other one has this hind leg clearly shorter than the other. They could not have hunted. That's why they turned to man-slaying. They would have finished off those bePedi skeletons we saw back there. Shame really.'

'Oh yes,' said Jenkins. 'Me 'eart is fair breakin'.'

The three were now far too wide awake to try for sleep in what was left of the darkness, so they sat drinking tea and whisky around the fire. De Witt explained that the two lions were young males, probably brothers, who would have been expelled by their pride and who had sustained their injuries before they had had time to found families of their own. Forced to live alone on the plain, with no lioness to hunt for them, and unable to run down fleet-footed prey themselves, they had become man-eating outcasts.

'Should we try to bury the carcasses?' asked Simon.

'No. Vultures and other scavengers will clean

their bones pretty damn soon.'

'Good. I don't want to waste time. Let's get on before sun-up.'

They had not reached the Steelport River at the end of the next day, although de Witt said they could not be far from it, when they rode up to a farm which was still inhabited, although it looked more like a fortress. The sun was sinking and a group of men were herding cattle into a large pen enclosed by a thick stone wall. One side of the pen was formed by the farmhouse itself. The windows of the house had been bricked up, with apertures left as rifle slits. The little homestead housed fourteen men, and the leader, a grim, bearded patriarch, was glad to hear that the lions were dead. They had been standing guard each night to protect their cattle against them. He explained that all the women had been sent into Lydenburg while they defended their property against the bePedi, who had been ravaging the surrounding country.

'We fought them off, thanks be to God,' he said, 'but they will come again.' He nodded to Simon. 'Your General thinks he can defeat them, but no one can. We just farm here as best we can and defend our homes when they attack. Others have gone, but we shall never leave because it is our land, but it is becoming more and more difficult.'

The visitors enquired after Mendoza's farm, but the patriarch had not heard of him, although he thought there were several farmers of Portuguese extraction from Mozambique who were trying to scratch a living in the face of the bePedi further up the Steelport Valley. The river itself, he explained, was now only two miles or so away. Simon also asked if there was news of Wolseley's advance: had he reached Lydenburg yet, or even penetrated further? But the Boers had no information.

As they rode on the next day, Simon jerked his head back to the farm and asked de Witt, 'Is it, in fact, their land?'

The big man looked surprised. 'Of course,' he said.

'But weren't the bePedi here first?'

'Ach, yes, I suppose so. There was a king called Thulare who set up his capital in the valley up ahead in about 1800 and his regiments raided all over the place: south to the Vaal, west to the Magaliesberg and north to the Soutpansberg. They built up a thriving trade in ivory, horn, skins and even metal goods but they also fought with the Swazis, who are a bit further east from here. They became traditional foes, but the Zulu impis also raided up here from time to time.' He gave his grim smile. 'Man, this has never been a quiet place. Then we, the Boers, trekked up here in the middle of the century and established a community around about Lydenburg.' He gestured to the low green hills which now billowed up from the plateau. 'It's good farming country around here. You can see that–'

He was interrupted by Jenkins, who reined in and lifted his hand. 'Listen.'

Nothing at first, then, in the distance, the faint but unmistakable sound of gunfire, coming from ahead of them and slightly to the left, over the gentle wave of hills.

'Is it the General?' asked Jenkins.

'I think not.' Simon shook his head. 'It's too far away to be certain, but that doesn't sound like Martini-Henry firing to me. And there's no cannon. Could be just a skirmish, though. Let's find out.'

They kicked their horses into a canter and rode towards the distant spluttering of musketry, taking care, as they neared its source, not to be silhouetted against the sky. Eventually they reached a copse of stunted trees which gave cover for their horses and allowed them to crawl through the underbrush and look down on a small valley, which cradled a farmhouse and a stretch of the silver Steelport that wound round the building to disappear behind another hill. The farm had a small stone enclosure extending from its walls, rather like the property where the three men had spent the night. Behind the walls a handful of men were maintaining a steady fire on their attackers, who were firing from the vantage points of rocks which climbed the hill. Simon had invested in an old pair of field glasses before he left Kimberley, and he now focused them on the scene below.

'Looks as though they could be bePedi attacking,' he murmured. He turned to de Witt. 'Do they look like Zulus – stripped down and with cow tails tied to their calves?'

'Ja. Exactly like that. Here. Let me see.'

Simon handed him the binoculars.

'Ja. They are bePedi all right. And, of course,

they've got guns. They're trying to get the cattle.'

There were a handful of beasts corralled within the enclosure, but more – although perhaps only forty or so – had already been captured by the attackers, for they were being looked after by a couple of tribesmen higher up the hill, on the edge of another copse of trees.

Simon took back the binoculars and concentrated on the defenders. There were only six of them, not enough to man all of the walls sufficiently well, and as they watched, they could clearly see the bePedi crawling from rock to rock and getting nearer to the enclosure. It would not be long before they were close enough to rush the defenders and overwhelm them. He could see assegais glittering down below.

He turned to his companions.

'How many are attacking, would you say?'

'Forty or fifty maybe,' said Jenkins.

The Boer nodded in agreement. 'Man, it's a hell of a lot for us to take on,' he said. 'These blacks are good fighters – as good as the Zulus. Three against fifty in the open are not good odds, particularly as they've got rifles.'

Simon frowned behind the lenses. 'Yes, but are they good shots? It doesn't look as though they've hit anything yet.'

'Beggin' your pardon, bach sir, that's not true.' Jenkins was pointing to the far corner of the enclosure, where a figure could be seen, obviously tending to another lying on the ground.

Simon swung the glasses round. 'You say this is good farming land, Faan?'

'Ja. Of course.'

'Then why isn't any of the land cultivated around the farm? And why haven't they got more cattle? There can't be more than fifty beasts in that herd altogether. It seems very strange.'

'Well, bach sir,' said Jenkins, wiping his moustache with the back of his hand, 'strange or not, if we don't get down there and start a bit of shootin', like, there isn't goin' to be any of them chaps left in the farmyard to 'erd the bleedin' cattle anyway.'

'He's right, man,' grunted the Boer. 'If we have to go at all, let's mount and ride down among the Kaffirs now. At least we should be able to scatter them and get behind the wall and add our guns to the others down there.'

Simon lowered the glasses and shook his head. 'No. I'm not sure that three of us would make all that much difference. I think we would do better if we could get down there among the cattle and—'

'No.' De Witt began to get to his feet. 'We should ride down now.'

''Alf a minnit, Fanny.' Jenkins put his hand on the Afrikaner's shoulder. 'Listen to the Captain. 'E's good at this sort of stuff. Soldiers' work, look you.'

De Witt scowled, but lowered himself to the ground again.

'Here's what we do,' said Simon. '352, you and Faan slip down this hill, keeping under cover, until you are within fairly good rifle range. Don't be seen, now, and don't open fire until you hear me shoot.'

'An' where the 'ell are you going to be, then?'

Simon pointed behind and to the right. 'I am going to ride down behind this ridge here until it falls away and meets the top edge of that group of trees – the one where the cattle are being mustered at its bottom edge. Then I shall slip through the trees, get rid of those two natives down there and stampede the cattle so that they run right into the bePedi as they are massing to charge the enclosure.'

'With respect, it won't work, bach sir.'

'What do you mean? Of course it will.'

'Well it's a sound plan, but it needs a good horseman and a crack shot to ride down there, kill them black fellers and then start the herd and run with 'em. With great respect, sir, you'd fall off.'

'Oh, to hell with you, Jenkins. Very well. You go and we'll cover you. Don't shoot until you are near enough to kill. And 352...'

'Yessir?'

'Don't lose the damned way. Keep just below this ridge here and you will come to the trees. Even you shouldn't get lost.'

'Oh, thank you very much, I'm sure.'

The little man squirmed back into the cover of the trees, mounted his horse and galloped away, down the reverse of the ridge towards where the distant copse crept up to its crest.

Simon grinned at de Witt. 'Thank God he's gone in the right direction, anyway.'

Slowly the Boer grinned back. 'I shall never understand the English,' he said. 'You are funny people – in all kinds of ways.'

'Umm. Particularly when you throw the Welsh

210

into the equation. Come on. Let's get down this hill.' He pointed. 'If we can reach that outcrop of rocks there, we should be in good range. When Jenkins lets the cattle loose, fire off about half a dozen rounds and then come back up here and get the horses while I double down and help Jenkins.'

De Witt looked at Simon with narrowed eyes. Then, slowly, he nodded his head. 'You seem to know what you're doing, Englishman,' he said. 'I will do what you tell me.'

Slowly, the two men, bent double, flitted from rock to rock down the hillside until they had reached a stone outcrop that formed a little ridge some 250 yards from the bottom of the slope. They were unseen by the attacking tribesmen, who were all facing the farm, firing and then squirming forward to position themselves for the final attack on the walls. The bePedi herdsmen, on the edge of the other copse and roughly level on the hillside with Simon and de Witt, were also unaware of their approach, for they had their hands full with the cattle, who were becoming increasingly restive at the sound of gunfire.

Settling on to his stomach, Simon rested his rifle on the top of the rock and cocked the lever behind the trigger guard. The natives below were now only about fifty yards from the walls of the enclosure, but there was little further cover for them and it was clear that they were about to make that last charge, which, given their great advantage in numbers, must surely overwhelm the defenders. Simon looked to the cattle on his right. There was no sign of Jenkins. What on

211

earth could have happened to him? He should have been in position long ago.

'I don't think we can wait any longer, Faan,' he said. 'Pick your target and fire quickly.'

As soon as he had spoken, two loud reports came from the edge of the copse to their right. The two herdsmen dropped immediately as a loud yell issued from the wood and Jenkins emerged, waving his rifle, his heels drumming on the sides of his horse. He drove the animal straight into the herd of steers, which rolled their eyes, flattened their ears, and began lumbering down the hill, ever faster as the horseman pursued them, scurrying round their rear like a Welsh sheepdog, harassing and steering the little herd towards the men grouped at the bottom of the hill.

At the same moment, Simon and de Witt began firing. At that range it was difficult to miss, and six of the attackers fell immediately. The others scattered, wide-eyed and not knowing which way to run. Their problem was acute. The defenders were now standing and pouring in fire from the walls; rapid fire was also coming from their rear above them, and the stampeding cattle were bearing down on them. There seemed no escape.

'Right, Faan,' called Simon. 'Fetch the horses before they get round us up the hill.' The big Afrikaner got to his feet and ran back up the hill towards the clump of trees that harboured their mounts.

Some of the bePedi sprinted past the farm, plunged into the Steelport and were quickly carried downstream by the current. Others ran for their lives and disappeared round the slope of the hill that ran down to the river. The cattle had now caught some of the more indecisive of the warriors and their screams rose above the thunder of hoofs as they were hit by the herd and then disappeared in the plunging mass of horns and heads. Four warriors, however, avoided the beasts and headed directly up the hill towards Simon. For a brief moment he had time to admire their courage in singling him out in the middle of the carnage and then attacking him across open ground.

He brought the leader down quickly enough, but the others fanned out to present a more difficult target. Nevertheless, he was able to put a bullet into the thigh of a second man (damn, the rifle was firing low!), so that he too fell. The remaining pair were now within a hundred yards of him and he could see the perspiration pouring down their faces and hear their gasps of indrawn breath as they ran up the hill. To speed reloading, Simon had spread cartridges from his pouch along the top of the rock. Now, in his haste to select a round, he knocked all but one of them on to the ground. With fingers that seemed all thumbs, he thrust the remaining cartridge into the breech, fired it into the breast of the nearest attacker and struggled to his feet to meet the survivor, who was now some ten feet away.

The tribesman halted at that point, his chest heaving as he regained his breath. He was a big man and he carried a short stabbing assegai, which he held underhand, his other hand extended towards Simon, as though to balance himself. Slowly he approached, his face and massive chest streaming with perspiration, and his eyes wide, the yellow eyeballs giving a demonic cast to his features. Simon realised that there was no time to grope for the cartridges in the grass, so he gripped the empty Martini-Henry and presented it to the bePedi as though there was a bayonet at the end. He had no other weapon, for his Colt revolver had been left in his saddlebag.

At first the black man looked at the rifle apprehensively, then, as he realised that no shot was forthcoming, his features relaxed into a grin and he made a dismissive gesture with his free hand. Simon now knew fear. His mouth was quite dry and he could feel his heart thumping. He remembered only too well the pain made by an assegai thrust, and the old wound in his shoulder seemed to throb, as though to prompt that memory. Where was Jenkins – and how long would it take de Witt to return with the horses? He dared not turn to look for them. What was it Jenkins always said? Watch their eyes, that was it. Never let your gaze wander. Always keep your eyes on those of your opponent. That way, you had a chance of seeing what they were going to do a split second before they did it.

And it worked. The warrior's gaze flickered for a second to Simon's stomach. Then he feinted to Simon's head before quickly moving his feet and swinging the assegai low and hard to the belly. Forewarned, Simon did not move his head but brought the long barrel of the rifle down to parry the thrust, swung the butt of the gun over the blade of the spear and hit the bePedi hard in the face. The man staggered, and blood sprang from his nose. Immediately, Simon jabbed the barrel of his gun into his assailant's stomach and brought his knee up into the man's face as he doubled up. He swung the butt back again, on to the head, and the warrior collapsed on the ground with a grunt, to lie unconscious.

'Well, look you. I've never seen anything so pretty in all me life.'

Simon looked up, his breast heaving and sweat oozing down into his eyes. Jenkins was sitting on his horse, rifle in hand, beaming down on him.

'Where the hell were you when I needed you?'

'I was farmin', like, just as you told me to. Now I can't do *everythin'*, can I?'

Simon realised that he was trembling, but he looked around. The bePedi seemed to have disappeared, and de Witt was riding down the slope, leading Simon's horse. But on closer examination, he realised that the fight was not over. Not all of the attackers had run. To escape the stampeding cattle, a small group – perhaps a dozen – had braved the fire of the riflemen at the walls and leapt over the enclosure, where they were now engaged in hand-to-hand fighting with the farmers inside, who seemed to be outnumbered by two to one.

'Come on!' shouted Simon and, clumsily climbing into the saddle – he realised that his damned legs were still trembling – he urged the horse down the hill and directly at the low stone wall. Somehow, at full gallop, his mount picked his way between the fallen bodies left by the stampede

215

and then, at some twenty yards from the enclosure, Simon's heart came into his mouth. He realised that he had left it too late to change direction. There was nothing for it; there was no time to pull up or veer to left or right. *He would have to jump the wall!* He felt the horse tense itself for the jump, and, in a split second, he tried to remember the rules about jumping: something about gripping tight with your knees, going forward as the horse took off and leaning back as it landed...

The horse took the wall beautifully but, seeing the milling figures around it in the enclosure, shied away on landing, tossing Simon through the air to land on the back of a bePedi warrior, who was in the act of spearing one of the defenders. The collision completely winded the tribesman, sending him sprawling on the ground, his assegai knocked from his grasp to skitter along the beaten earth of the enclosure. It also severely jolted Simon, but it saved him from injury and, shaking his head, he was able to scramble to his feet within seconds. It was then he realised that he had arrived in the middle of a vicious hand-to-hand fight without a weapon of any kind. His horse saved his life. The excitement of the gallop, the jump and the violence all around it caused it now to rear and kick, its eyes rolling. The enclosure was not large and it already contained some ten cattle, which, alarmed at the gunfire, took further fright at the arrival of the bucking animal in their midst and now themselves began to mill around the little courtyard, bellowing, their heads down and their horns tossing from side to side.

It was all too much for what was left of the attackers. As one man, they leapt over the wall and ran for the river without a backward glance, hugging its banks and disappearing around the bend of the hill. After three attempts, Simon was able to grasp the bridle of his horse and quieten it. The four defenders who remained standing instinctively spread out and began to soothe the cattle, helped now by Jenkins and de Witt, who had pushed open the gate to the enclosure and ridden in on horseback.

Jenkins looked down on Simon with a slightly shamefaced smile. 'Sorry, bach sir,' he said. 'You went off like a bat out of hell, look you, and I couldn't keep up. Mind you, you took that jump beautifully. Pity about the landin', though, wasn't it?'

'Bloody horse.' Simon wiped the mud off his face. 'Had a mind of its own. Have the bePedi gone?'

Before Jenkins could answer, one of the farmers approached them and addressed Simon in Afrikaans.

Simon shook his head. 'Sorry,' he said. 'I only speak English.'

'Ah.' The man nodded and then spoke in heavily accented English. 'Now I see. A Dutchman would take that jump easy.'

Simon, aware that Jenkins was listening with interest, frowned. 'Well,' he said, 'there was a bloody fight going on, and there wasn't much room for a graceful sort of landing, now was there? But you said Dutchman. You are not a

217

Boer, then?'

The man, tall, heavily bearded and with closely set eyes that reflected no amusement, shook his head. 'No. Part Portuguese – from Mozambique. But tank you for coming. It was going bad when you arrive.'

Simon nodded and exchanged a quick glance with Jenkins. De Witt seemed to have disappeared. 'Mozambique, eh? We must be near the frontier, then?'

'Ja. About two hundred kilometres there.' He pointed to the east.

The other defenders had now gathered around. They were all big men, dressed like Boers in scruffy corduroy and broad-brimmed black hats. Simon gave them a quick glance. Like their spokesman, they had a lighter tinge to their skin than that of the ordinary Afrikaner; a sallow, almost almond colour. They wore their hair long, greasily curling over their collars from behind their big hats, and some of them carried revolvers in holsters on their hips – something rarely seen on the veldt. They seemed more interested in Simon and Jenkins than in their two wounded colleagues propped up against the wall.

Simon nodded towards the wounded. 'Are they badly hurt?'

The spokesman turned, regarded the slumped men and spoke without emotion. 'One dead. One not so bad.'

'Oh, I am sorry.'

'We will bury him. The bePedi will not be back.' He gestured with his head over the wall. 'They have lost warriors. More than they tink. It will be

218

some time before they come to this farm again.'

'Is it your farm?'

The Mozambiquan shook his head. 'No, it belongs to ... to ... my friend.'

'Ah, I see. Who is that, then?'

'Why you want to know?' A hint of suspicion appeared in the big man's eyes. After the initial expression of gratitude there had been little friendliness in his manner. Nor did the other men looking on seem to convey any appreciation of the fact that the arrival of Simon and the others had probably saved their lives. The attitude was one of sullen curiosity.

'No real reason.' Simon became aware that he was suddenly very tired. The tension of the duel with the bePedi warrior – the nearness of death represented by that gleaming, sharp-as-a-razor assegai aimed at his stomach – had left him, he realised, as weak as a baby. The bloodbath in the enclosure and the killing on the hillside now brought back to him the disgust he felt about the slaughter of war. Why did it always affect him so and not others? He stole a quick glance at Jenkins and then de Witt, who had silently joined the party and was standing at the back. Their faces betrayed no disquiet. Damn the army and its ritual of violence! He turned back to the Portuguese, whose face now seemed to exude malevolence. He decided that truculence could be a two-way street. 'Is it a secret, then? Why are you worried? Did you steal the bloody farm?'

The big man was taken aback for a moment, 'Ach no. Owner is Joachim Mendoza. Important man. He live in Kimberley.'

Simon heard Jenkins draw in his breath sharply but he did not look at him. Holding the gaze of the Portuguese, he said, 'Well, I don't know him. I am from England, you see, and am unfamiliar with these parts. Is Mr Mendoza here?'

'No. He left for Kimberley last night. Important business.'

'Good lord. Travelling alone in bePedi country? That's dangerous, surely?'

The other smiled, for the first time. 'Mr Mendoza, he know the bePedi,' he said. 'They don't touch him.'

'I see. But why did they attack his farm, then?'

The smile disappeared and was replaced with a frown. 'You ask many questions. Could be that these bePedi not from King Sekukuni's people. Could be Swazis. We don't know why they attack.'

An uneasy silence fell on the little group. Jenkins broke up the awkwardness.

'Well,' he said, leaning forward in the saddle and favouring the Portuguese with one of his face-splitting grins, 'now that we've got rid of them buggers, is there any chance of a nice cuppa tea? Or p'raps even somethin' a big stronger, eh?'

Simon shot a grateful glance at the Welshman. They had to get inside the house somehow to see if Nandi was hidden there – or had she been taken back to Kimberley by Mendoza? He felt his mouth dry again at the thought that they might be near the end of their quest. But the big man opposite was showing no sign of extending hospitality in the Boer fashion.

He glowered at Jenkins and said, 'We don't

have tea.'

Jenkins allowed the smile to slip from his face. He leaned forward and down so that he was almost on a level with the big man's eyes. 'Then, boyo,' he said softly, 'we'll just 'ave to 'ave coffee, won't we?'

For a moment the two men looked at each other without blinking. Then the Portuguese turned and asked a question in Afrikaans of one of his comrades. The man shrugged his shoulders, cast a quick look towards the house, and replied. It seemed to satisfy the leader, for he said, 'Come inside. We give you food and you sleep here tonight if you want. In the barn on hay. No other room.'

'Thank you very much.'

The group broke up. Two of the defenders went to their injured comrade, who had a bullet wound in his arm but seemed otherwise unharmed, and took him into the house. Another gestured to the three travellers and they followed him, leading the horses to a barn that extended from the farmhouse. He pointed to where they could feed and house the horses and then left them to it.

Simon quickly turned to de Witt. 'What did the big man ask the other one?'

'He asked, "Is the girl still locked away?" and was told, "Yes." This is good, I think, yes?'

'Good?' Jenkins almost shouted. 'It's bloody marvellous, boy. We've found 'er at last. We've done it.'

Simon turned from unbuckling his horse's saddle girth. 'Look,' he said, keeping his voice down, 'we must handle this with great care.

221

Firstly, there's a chance that this girl may not be Nandi, although I am sure she is. I can't see why Mendoza would bring her all the way here and then take her back again to Kimberley. It's more likely that, having deposited her here, he has gone back to Currey Street to get another shipment of diamonds to smuggle across the frontier, or,' a further thought struck him, 'perhaps he's gone to see the King to tell him of Wolseley's advance. If he's close to the bePedi, he could be feeding the King information about the coming attack.'

Jenkins sniffed. 'Well, as you said, if 'e's in 'is back pocket, so to speak, why did these Bapedo fellers attack 'is farm? It don't make sense.'

'What do you think, Faan?' asked Simon.

The Boer shrugged. 'It could be that, as that Portuguese said, these Kaffirs came from the far side of Sekukuni's land, probably by the Swazis, and they wanted the cattle to trade with the Swazis. I don't think they *were* Swazis, though. That's why they left so quickly. They had a long way to go back home and they knew that there was a British army nearby. But there's another thing.'

'Yes?'

'Rifles. Look.' De Witt turned and Simon realised that there were two rifles propped against the stable wall by the Boer's horse. De Witt picked up one of them. 'See.' He turned the butt of the gun over by the trigger guard. 'That is a Mozambique stamp. This Mendoza is selling guns to the bePedi as well as smuggling diamonds. This rifle was dropped by one of the Kaffirs. That's why he

222

has ... what you call it ... safe passage through this land.'

Simon nodded. 'It makes sense.' Then he shot a sharp glance at the Boer. 'Where did you disappear to when we first arrived after the fighting? Did you go into the house?'

The Boer dropped his gaze for a moment. 'Ja. I just had a look around. But I couldn't see anything.'

'Very well. Now both of you listen. We will go in and have supper with them. It may be that Nandi will be allowed out to cook – they probably locked her away in a bedroom when the bePedis first attacked. Now, 352, if we see her, you must show no recognition and I will do the same. I will try to indicate to Nandi that she must show no sign of knowing us. None of us has been seen by this gang before today – except me, when Mendoza opened the door to me. And he, thank goodness, is not here.'

The Boer growled. 'What do we do then?'

'Damned if I know. Obviously, we must get her out of here.' He thought for a moment. 'The best time will be just before dawn when, hopefully, the whole house will be asleep. If they need Nandi to cook for us all, I should be able to slip a message to her, warning her. Then, while you two saddle up, I will steal into the house and bring her out. We shall need another horse: 352, sniff around these stables and pick out a good one that we can take. I wouldn't want to have to outrun this gang – or the bePedis, for that matter – with Nandi on my lap.'

Jenkins tugged at his moustache. 'What if they

don't let her out, like? Or...' depression descended on him, 'what if it isn't Nandi at all locked up in there? We'll be a bit buggered then, look you.'

Simon nodded. 'We will indeed. But I sense it is our Nandi. Why else lock her away? For some reason, she is precious to them, that's obvious. Come on. Let's just see what we find.'

They finished feeding and bedding down the horses and Simon tore a page from his pocket diary and, with a scrap of pencil, wrote a message for Nandi. He folded it tightly into the size of a postage stamp and put it in his shirt. Then all helped to dig a grave for the member of the defending band who had been killed. Simon insisted that they also bury the fifteen bePedi warriors who had died, but the Portuguese said that they had the cattle to retrieve, and it was left to Jenkins, de Witt and Simon to dig out a shallow grave and lower the bodies into it.

''Eathens,' spat Jenkins. 'An' I mean that lot,' he pointed to the farmhouse, 'not these.'

It was not until just before dusk that the work was finished. The three washed in the river – they had been offered no other facilities – and walked into the farmhouse. As an afterthought, Simon took with him an empty water bottle. The house was typically Boer: wooden walls and floors, rough timber furniture and no decoration of any kind. But the table had been laid, Simon noted with a lift to his heart, with care, and precisely in the centre a veldt rose nestled softly in a small earthenware pot. It surely was – it must be –

Nandi's touch. Simon and Jenkins exchanged a glance.

The four defenders of the farmhouse were standing around a rustic stone fireplace, and the fifth, wounded man, sat nursing a bandaged shoulder. All were drinking what seemed like native beer from gourds, although none was offered to Simon and his companions. The five did not acknowledge the others' entrance, but continued their low conversation in Afrikaans. From behind a closed door came cooking smells.

Jenkins gave the room the benefit of one of his smiles. 'Evenin' all,' he said. 'Nice day for it, then, wasn't it?'

Five blank faces regarded him briefly and then they returned to their conversation. Simon held up his water bottle.

'Can I get water from in there?' He gestured towards the closed door. No one replied. 'Oh good. I need to refill my bottle.'

Before he could be prevented, he strode to the door, thrust it open and casually swung it closed behind him. There, bent over an open fire, was Nandi.

It had been eighteen months since he had last seen the girl. Then, at a camp fire by the Buffalo River in Natal with Alice, they had drunk champagne, eaten well and laughed. They had been a little sad, too, because Nandi had mourned the coming reinvasion of Zululand and the killing they all knew was to come; yet there had been much merriment between the three young people and Simon remembered how pretty she had looked, dressed in a simple shift that was

225

perfectly complemented by one of her brightly coloured scarves tucked around her throat. Her hair then, tied back in a tail like a young pony's, had been black as a raven's wing, with a sheen to it from constant brushing. Her eyes, within that elfin oval face, shone and danced in amusement at the good company.

Now the face that turned towards him, though flushed from the flames of the fire, was sullen and lifeless, like that of a London East End drudge. Her hair hung lifeless and unkempt and her simple blouse and skirt were stained. She was shoeless, her feet were dirty, and a large bruise like a ripe plum glistened on her high cheekbone. Simon could not help recalling from a childhood nursery book a painting of Cinderella in her kitchen, a picture of despair. Yet the face that he saw now was transformed immediately. First, a look of astonishment swept across it, then one of huge relief and, lastly, great joy. She opened her mouth to speak, but Simon quickly bent his leg behind him to keep the door shut for a second while he put his finger to his lips in a plea for silence.

'May I have water, miss?' he asked loudly. As he did so, the leader of the Portuguese party flung the door open, but all he saw was a once-again-passive Nandi silently gesturing towards the water pump in the corner of the room.

The man curtly demanded something of her in Afrikaans. She shook her head, pointed mutely to the pump and returned to stirring a concoction in the giant stewpot which hung above the open fire. The Portuguese stood silently in the doorway, watching as Simon pumped water into his bottle. When the task was done, Simon replaced the stopper and made to walk past Nandi at the fire. But he stumbled and dropped the bottle. Immediately she stooped, picked it up and gave it to Simon, who took it from her, quickly slipping the stamp-sized note into her hand as he did so.

'Thank you, miss,' he said. Then, to the big man, 'I don't mind water, but it would be kind if you could spare us a little beer, don't you think? After all, we have been of service to you.'

The man scowled – was he born with that expression? wondered Simon – and held the door ajar so that Simon could leave the kitchen. 'Three beer,' he demanded of Nandi, and then followed the Englishman.

Jenkins was sitting at the table and Simon put a hand on his shoulder as he passed and squeezed it hard. It was a warning to the little man, but, even so, it was hard for Jenkins to suppress his feelings as Nandi entered with three gourds of beer. After a first glance, the Welshman lowered his gaze, but Simon hoped that no one had seen the fleeting look, first of joy and then of anger, that swept across his face. As Nandi offered the beer to them, carefully keeping her back to the others, Simon observed that tears were beginning to pour down her cheeks. Hurriedly, he held the kitchen door open for her.

'Smells good, whatever it is you're cooking,' he said. She nodded, and hurried back into the kitchen.

The leader of the Portuguese was about to

follow her when Simon stopped him. 'Look,' he said, 'we will be off before dawn tomorrow. We were journeying to Lorenzo Marques but we somehow lost our way. Can you give me a bearing for it on this compass?' He snapped open the cover and offered the instrument.

The man looked at the compass in puzzlement. 'Don't know those things,' he said. 'But you are long way from Lorenzo trail. Come. I show you.'

Together they went to the door, where the setting sun was reflecting dazzlingly from the waters of the Steelport. The man gestured to the east. 'You go that way,' he said. 'Keep sun on your left shoulder and climb all time to Drakensbergs. You will hit trail,' a humourless grin broke his features, 'but you probably hit bePedis also. What would an Englishman want in Lorenzo?'

Simon smiled back. A mischievous thought had occurred to him. 'Diamonds,' he said. 'We want to buy diamonds.'

The face opposite his remained expressionless but he thought he caught a quick gleam in the eye. Silently, they went back into the house.

The meal was equally silent. The Portuguese ate their soup with both hands, dipping in spoon and bread, but they exchanged no word with each other. It was clear that Jenkins was desperately trying to keep his eyes off Nandi, who served them demurely, but it was equally clear that the little man was seething within. Once, as Nandi leaned over him to ladle soup into his bowl, Simon saw him brush her hand momentarily with his and what was almost a smile appeared on the girl's lips, but the gesture went unnoticed as far as

228

he could see. He allowed himself one look at Nandi as she backed through the kitchen door – clearly she did not eat with the men – and their gazes met. Her eyes immediately moistened but this time they were glowing. Then she was gone.

Simon wasted no time with pleasantries once the meal was finished. He stood, nodded and led his companions out into the barn.

'Did you see that bloody bruise on 'er face?' demanded Jenkins. 'Did you see it? The swine 'ave been 'ittin' 'er.'

Simon put a hand on his arm. 'It looks like it. But we must not get upset. Our priority is to get Nandi out of here. There are five men in there and I don't want to have to fight them all to get to her.' He gestured to the newly dug grave outside the enclosure. 'There has been enough killing here for one day.' He turned to the Boer. 'Faan, you went into the house while we were talking to the Portuguese out here; did you see any sign of Nandi then?'

'No. But I think that they had locked her in that one little room with the ladder leading to it. In what you would call the loft, I think.'

'Yes, I noticed that too. The others must all sleep downstairs, which makes it awkward for getting Nandi out.'

The Boer nodded. 'What is your plan then?'

'Let's just go in there with our rifles and take 'er, that's what I say.' Jenkins's face was still flushed, but he looked imploringly at Simon. 'Come on, bach sir. It's the simplest and easiest way.'

Simon sighed. 'Then what do we do – kill them

229

all in cold blood, or tie them up and hope that they don't break free and follow us? No. Let's try my way. We can get violent afterwards if we have to. This is what we do. We rest here until an hour before dawn, which is when most people sleep the heaviest. Then you, 352, will saddle our horses, including one for Nandi – but you must be very, very quiet.'

The little man opened his mouth to protest, but Simon held up his hand. 'Faan and I will enter the house–'

'How?' growled the Boer. 'It will be locked.'

'No it won't.' Simon reached into his pocket and showed them a key. 'I palmed this when we went outside to be shown the trail to the border. And there is no bolt.'

'Well I'll be blowed,' said Jenkins. 'You're get-tin' to be less of an officer and more of a barrack-room fiddler every day.'

'The problem is that they might realise I've taken it, but we have to risk that. In any case, they will probably have a guard on watch – to look out for the bePedi, if not for us. Faan, we will have to deal with him somehow – but I don't want him killed unless we really have to. We must be quiet.'

De Witt nodded, but Jenkins was still unhappy. 'Look, bach sir,' he said. 'Let Faan look after the horses an' I'll come in with you. I won't make a fuss, I promise.'

'Sorry, old chap, we can't take that risk. You're just itching to clump someone, I can see that. Besides, you're good with horses. Come on now. I will take the first watch. You two get some sleep.'

De Witt and a still-reluctant Jenkins spread their

blankets out on the straw while Simon, rifle crooked in his arm, leaned in the shadows just inside the door of the barn. The others were soon asleep. After about an hour, the door to the house opened and a tall figure emerged, also carrying a rifle. He picked his way between the cattle which had been herded into the enclosure to the edge of the wall and scanned the hills around before turning and strolling towards the barn. Simon silently crept to the straw, lay down and pulled a blanket over him, with his cocked rifle hidden beneath it but pointed towards the doorway. He placed his hat over his face, low enough to conceal his features but positioned so that he could observe the doorway from under the brim. The Portuguese loomed into the opening and Simon braced himself to shoot. But the man merely inspected the inert figures, appeared satisfied and walked away.

The rest of the night passed without further incident, and at about four a.m., the trio slipped out of the barn. As Jenkins tiptoed to the stables, Simon laid a hand on de Witt's arm.

'Do the bePedi have night calls to communicate before they make a surprise attack?' he asked.

The Boer pulled a lugubrious face. 'Perhaps, but I don't know them.'

'What about a nervous cow? Can you imitate that?'

De Witt grinned. 'Oh, ja. I think I can do cows.'

'Good. We need the guard to come outside. We will stand either side of the door and, when he pokes his gun out to investigate – as I hope to

God he will – I will pull him out, you hit him hard on the head and I will break his fall. The point is to make very little noise. Understand?'

The Boer nodded.

'We will need rope to tie him. There's bound to be some in the barn.'

Within a few minutes, de Witt returned with a length of rope. The two men tiptoed to the house and stood either side of the door. Simon nodded, and the Boer took a deep breath and made a very passable imitation of a steer in discomfort. Nothing happened. Simon mouthed, 'Again,' and the big man cupped his hands and lowed, directing the sound away from the house. Its verisimilitude was sufficient to set the herd moving restlessly, and within seconds, the door latch was lifted and, first, a rifle barrel and then a head appeared. Simon, flattened against the wall, sprang forward and, forgetting the plan, crashed the butt end of his Colt into the man's face. The guard staggered against the door post and Simon was only just able to catch the rifle before it clattered on to the wooden floor. He thrust the muzzle of the revolver into the man's bleeding face and, finger to his lips, motioned him outside. Once beyond the opened door, de Witt sprang forward and hit the guard on the head with the butt of his rifle. Simon caught him, and as the man lay senseless, they stuffed his own kerchief into his mouth, gagged him with Simon's handkerchief and then bound him with the rope.

Breathless, the two men crouched, but whatever noise they had made was covered by the restless movement of the cattle and no one within the house stirred. Simon beckoned, and he and de Witt moved stealthily into the house. Six doors led off from the big living room, including that for the kitchen, but all were closed. A rough stairway rose up to a single door high up on the wall. Simon nodded towards it and de Witt gave a confirmatory nod.

Simon leaned close to the Boer. 'Stay down here and cover each doorway,' he whispered. 'I will go up and get her. We can only gamble that it is her room – and that the bastards haven't locked her in. Don't shoot unless you have to, but if you have to, shoot to kill.'

De Witt nodded and, pistol in hand, Simon ascended the stairway, testing each step before putting his weight on it to avoid creaks. At last he reached the little platform at the head of the stairs. He looked down, but the Boer had disappeared. What the hell...? Simon craned his head, but de Witt was nowhere to be seen. Perhaps he was directly underneath the platform. Too late to go back now, anyway. With bated breath, Simon put his hand on the latch and gently pushed it upwards. It lifted and he was able to push the door open. Inside, all was dark and Simon realised that either the room had no window or that it was shuttered. Was she inside? His question was answered within a second when two arms were thrust around his neck and he felt tears on his cheek as his ear was roundly kissed.

He shushed her and untangled himself. 'Are you ready?' he whispered into her ear.

Nandi choked a sob and he felt her nod her head.

'No shoes,' he said.

'I don't have them any more, Simon,' she whispered back.

'Bastards. Now, down the stairs very quietly, on your toes. Hold my hand and follow me.'

Together, in the light cast by the moon through the unshuttered windows, they crept down the stairway. As they did so, de Witt loomed out of the open kitchen door. The two men exchanged glances and de Witt allowed Simon and Nandi to tiptoe through the front door, while he stayed behind for a moment, rifle in hand, to cover their exit. Simon took a precious moment to lock the door behind him and throw the key as far as he could beyond the enclosure wall. Then all three ran for the stables, where a very anxious Welshman was waiting for them, holding the reins of four saddled horses.

Nandi immediately leapt into Jenkins's arms and he buried his moustache under her left ear and lifted her off the ground, swinging her round as though she was a doll. Then, almost in the same movement, the broad little man swung her into the saddle of the smallest horse, where she immediately hooked her big toes into the stirrups, in the Basutho style which Simon remembered so well from those days in Zululand when they had ridden together. He smiled at the thought but put his finger to his lips in warning again. He looked back at the house, but all seemed silent and the guard they had knocked senseless still lay where he had fallen. Then he led the little posse at a walk through the cattle and the gateway, out of the enclosure, on to the open hillside. There, Simon paused while he took a compass bearing roughly towards Lydenburg. Then, pointing the way for the others, he pulled on the reins, kicked in his heels and the little party was off at the gallop.

They crested the hill well away from the farm and met a breeze that brought stimulation and exhilaration as they thundered along in the moonlight. Simon turned in the saddle, grinned at the small figure bent low over her mount's head immediately behind him and permitted himself a whoop of triumph. They had rescued Nandi!

Chapter 9

Alice and Dunn rode into Middelburg with some apprehension. As they neared the outskirts, Alice's fear that she had lost precious days and that Wolseley would have begun his advance became more intense. From the stern visage presented by Dunn as he rode beside her, it was obvious that the Natalian harboured his own concerns – had he done the right thing by throwing in his lot with this young woman? Was this the way to free his daughter? It was in silence, then, that they let their tired mounts pick their way along the rutted outer suburbs of this small farming town.

But as they neared the centre, it became clear that Alice's concern at least was unfounded. The army's presence was obvious: waggons and limbers being loaded with tents, cooking utensils and boxes of ammunition; platoons of British troops in scarlet serge and white helmets marching 'at ease' towards the centre; mounted colonials in brown serge with carbines in their saddle holsters trotting to and fro; and, everywhere, black levies carrying spears and, sometimes, rifles being drilled by pink-faced British non-commissioned officers, who screamed in frustration at the incompetence of their charges.

'Gawd,' murmured Dunn.

'What?'

'Your General has got himself a motley crew here, all right.' He eased himself forward in the saddle and gestured towards the black troops. 'He's got all sorts. Look: there's Swazis, Knobnoses, Mapock's Kaffirs, blacks from Zoutpansberg... He must have promised 'em all the cattle and women in the Transvaal to get 'em to come and fight for him. Hasn't he got enough redcoats of his own?'

Alice shrugged. 'It's the great colonial trick, Mr Dunn. We are a small country with a big empire. We don't like big standing armies and we don't have enough troops to go round. The idea is to get the people of the country you've colonised to soldier for you – to be indigenous policemen, if you like. The Romans started it, of course, and we have developed it to a fine art in India.' She could not keep a note of disapproval from her voice, and Dunn shot her a sharp glance.

They reached what was obviously a central square, and Alice stopped a young subaltern to ask the way to the Commander-in-Chief's headquarters.

He gave her a puzzled but approving smile. 'Just opposite you, ma'am,' and gestured with his cane towards a two-storeyed building on the edge of the square. A pennant fluttered from a flagstaff at its door.

'Of course,' smiled Alice. 'How stupid of me. I see Sir Garnet's standard now. Thank you.'

The officer was about to stride away when Alice leaned down from her saddle and put a hand on his shoulder. 'Do tell me,' she said, 'what on earth are you wearing on your cap?' She gestured

237

to a small piece of animal fur attached to the front of his headwear.

'Ah, that.' The young man looked a trifle sheepish. 'That, ma'am, is a meerkat's tail. All of the officers on this campaign are wearing it. We call it Sekukuni's Button. I think it's the General's idea.'

'Pah!' Dunn's disapproval was made clear.

Alice gave the young man one of her most dazzling smiles in compensation. 'How fascinating. Thank you so much.'

They dismounted and tied their horses to the hitching rail in front of the headquarters, and on presenting her credentials, Alice and Dunn were allowed to enter. They sat in the hallway on a hard bench while an orderly hurried away carrying Alice's card and a request for a few moments of the General's time. The request was rejected. The C-in-C, it seemed, was too busy. Alice sighed. Obviously the piece she had cabled giving the details of the invading force had met with disapproval. She scribbled a note hoping that an appointment the following day would be convenient and they left.

'Never mind, Mr Dunn,' she said. 'Tomorrow will do. Now let us find somewhere to stay and I must catch up with my colleagues – the competition here, you know – to find out when the advance is likely to begin.'

They found rooms in a modest hotel and, leaving Dunn to rest after their journey – he was far from being fully recovered from his injuries – Alice sought out the small house which had been requisitioned for use by the press corps. This had grown considerably since she, Willie Russell and one other had constituted it in Pretoria. Now there were twelve journalists, including representatives of the main news agencies, accompanying Wolseley on his expedition and Alice found herself once again admiring the sagacity of Cornwell, her editor, in sensing that this little conflagration in a corner of the Transvaal could provide a good news story. She was relieved to find that the great-bearded Russell was in town, for his absence would have meant that this most enterprising of journalists had sniffed out some development that could have left her high, dry and scooped. She was delighted when he expressed the same sentiments about her arrival.

'I've been worried,' he said, bowing over her hand. 'Have you been up to something?'

'Ah no, Willie. I promise. Just trying to help a friend. Do we know when the General will advance?'

'Any day now, probably. I think he is a touch apprehensive about moving into the rough country to the north. He needs better information about water and fodder for the horses than he has now. He has a scouting party out there, probing, but it's hard desert country and local knowledge is virtually impossible to get, I hear. He can't leave it too long, though, or the Boers will start to say he is funking it.'

Alice thanked him and then retreated to the hotel to gain a little rest and put her thoughts in order. As she lay on her lumpen bed, with its horsehair mattress, she attempted to concentrate on the campaign ahead and to marshal her arguments if and when Wolseley attempted to deny her permission to travel with the rest of the press party to report the attack on Sekukuni. But her thoughts kept returning to Dunn. Had she done the right thing in insisting he come to Middelburg to see the General when perhaps it would have been better for everyone had he joined forces with Simon? Simon. Ah Simon! Why had he now begun to dominate her moments of introspection: smiling that sad smile of his, with his gentle brown eyes, his quiet air of resolution, that slim, firm body... Damn! She pulled the pillow over her head.

A note came back from the General that evening, intimating that he would see her at eight the following morning – but only for a few minutes. She hurried to tell Dunn and they set off early the next day. On this occasion Alice eschewed the temptation to enlist femininity to her cause and chose to appear professional in her jodhpurs and riding boots. Dunn, she was glad to see, had found a clean shirt from somewhere. They were received, with some surprise and a faint air of annoyance, by Wolseley.

'I expected you to be alone, Miss Griffith,' he said. Sir Garnet was wearing his blues, with a Sam Browne belt and his revolver in a buckled holster. There was a sense of purpose about him, very different from the gently bantering gallant Alice had last met.

'My apologies, General, but I do think it important that you see Mr Dunn.' She effected the introductions and Wolseley gestured for them to sit.

'Dunn, yes,' he said. 'I remember. You did good work with the Eshowe column, I hear, when Chelmsford went in to Zululand again from the south.'

'Thank you, sir.'

'Well, you're a long way from home. You'd better tell me why.'

Hesitantly at first, with many a glance at Alice, Dunn told his story, in level, matter-of-fact tones, but gaining in confidence and authority until he mentioned his daughter, when his voice broke for a second. At the end, he reached into a capacious pocket in his riding coat and pulled out a small hessian sack, knotted at the top, which he put on the desk before Wolseley.

'The diamonds?' queried the General.

Dunn nodded. 'Twenty-three of them, Sir Garnet. I have come to hand them in to you as the Commander-in-Chief here. But on the condition that you help me.'

Wolseley's good eye remained quite cold. 'So you want me to detach a platoon of my men to go back with you to Kimberley to free your daughter from her captors?'

'That's about it, General.'

'And, in return, you will give me the diamonds?'

'Er, yes, sir.'

Alice realised that this interview was going quite the wrong way.

'Sir Garnet,' she began.

The little man held up his hand. 'Thank you, Miss Griffith, but I think I have grasped the

241

situation.' He leaned forward. 'Now listen to me, Dunn. Many would regard your story as being a complete cock-and-bull confection. But I happen to have had confirmation of some of it, at least, from young Fonthill in Durban. So I realise that you are telling the truth and, of course, I sympathise with you about the plight of your daughter. But you must realise that I am about to embark upon a remarkably difficult military exercise, on the success of which hangs important issues. As Miss Griffith knows,' he shot a quick and not exactly approving glance at Alice, 'I have precious few British soldiers of the line available to me here and I have to place great reliance upon colonial troops and black levies. Under these circumstances, I could not even begin to consider detaching some of my more reliable men to help you. Can you not go to the police?'

Dunn's face was black. 'They hardly exist in Kimberley. Do you know the place?'

'Whether I know it or not is immaterial. I am in the middle of a military campaign and about to fight a most dangerous enemy force, in the midst of a country whose white population is antagonistic towards us. Apart from my inability to spare men, I cannot afford to risk provoking that population further, which could happen if I send soldiers to Kimberley. Now, if you can wait until I have beaten Sekukuni, then I may be able to help you. But not until then.'

Dunn scowled and slowly rose to his feet. 'Then I will take my diamonds and go elsewhere, General.'

Wolseley also rose. 'Oh no you won't, Mr Dunn.' As he spoke, that telltale scar under his blind eye glowed whitely again. 'Those diamonds are not your property. They have been stolen and it is my duty to take possession of them and see that they are returned to their rightful owners.' He picked up the little bag, slid open a drawer in his desk and dropped the diamonds into it. 'There can be no question of these stones being used as a kind of bargaining counter. I have no idea of their value, but I am quite sure that, in the wrong hands, they could be used to the detriment of Her Majesty's Government here in the Transvaal. I cannot afford to take that risk. I will see that you have a receipt for them, but they must remain with me.'

The two men confronted each other across the desk, the diminutive General, resolute as a bantam cock and exuding command from every inch, and the tall Natalian, clenching and unclenching his fists, his face now consumed with anger.

'Look,' said Dunn, making an obvious attempt to control his voice, 'I came here in good faith because this lady said it was the right thing to do. If you take those diamonds, I have nothing I can use as a negotiating tool to get my daughter back. I am prepared to give them up, but only in return for help. For God's sake, man, you must see that.'

Wolseley's back seemed to become even straighter as he looked up into the face of the big man opposite. 'Now look here, Dunn. I have not the desire, the time or the authority to negotiate with you. You have admitted that you stole those diamonds from the diamond thieves themselves

243

and you did not wish, at the time, to use them as a bargaining counter. Your intention was, as I understand it, to keep them for yourself. I could, therefore, throw you in jail–'

Alice rose, her face flushed. 'But General–' she said.

Once again Wolseley cut in, his voice sharp and cold. 'Please be silent, Miss Griffith. This matter does not concern you. If you believe, Dunn, that your daughter remains in some sort of captivity and that there is insufficient constabulary strength in Kimberley to help you, then you must go to Pretoria and make your case to the civil authorities there. I repeat that I will do what I can to help you after the successful conclusion of my campaign against Sekukuni, but for the moment, I regret that I cannot be of assistance to you and I must ask you to leave.'

The two men continued to confront each other in silence for perhaps thirty seconds. Then, slowly, keeping his gaze on Wolseley, Dunn moved to his left to get round the desk. 'I want those diamonds back,' he growled.

'No, no, Mr Dunn,' Alice called and reached out to put a restraining hand on Dunn's arm, but Wolseley was quicker.

He banged the desk hard. 'Sergeant!' he shouted. 'Orderlies...'

Immediately, the door was flung open and a young red-coated infantryman, rifle and bayonet fixed, entered.

'Arrest this man,' ordered the General, 'and put him in the guardhouse. If he attempts to resist or run away, shoot him.'

Dunn stood for a moment, glowering at Wolseley. 'Bastard,' he said. Then, with a quick look at Alice – expressing a mixture of both appeal and resentment – he allowed himself to be led away by the orderly, now joined by a moustached sergeant.

Slowly, as though to get her breath back, Alice resumed her seat. So too did Wolseley. 'Sir Garnet,' said Alice, 'I am so sorry that that happened. But you can see that the man is clearly at his wits' end.'

'I quite see that.' The General was perfectly composed. It was as though he had just brushed away a too-frisky puppy. 'But he was threatening, and frankly, Miss Griffith, at this point in this campaign I just can't afford to let myself be roughed up by some malcontent. I have far more important things to do. And there was no way I could allow those diamonds – whatever their worth – to be made available to Boer elements who could use them to buy weapons for their revolutionary purposes. You must see that.'

'Yes, I do. But may I beg you to be lenient with him. Perhaps just a couple of nights in a cell before releasing him...?'

'Very well. Perhaps I was a little harsh. But it must be my decision as to how I deploy my men. And you know very well that I have few enough for the job in hand as it is...' He frowned and looked away for a moment, gazing out of the window as though Sekukuni's Fighting Kopje was looming there. 'It is undoubtedly going to be a rather tougher task than I at first envisaged. Although,' he hurried on, returning his gaze to

Alice, 'we shall prevail, of course. Now, as far as this man is concerned, I shall let him cool down in the guardhouse for a day or two, but not press any charges against him. If you have influence over him, then do try and persuade him to return to Pretoria and lay charges with the constabulary there. Now, young lady, I wish to talk to you – for a few moments only, I am afraid, for I have many urgent tasks to perform.'

Ah, thought Alice, here comes the verdict and the sentence. She steeled herself for an argument. 'Of course, Sir Garnet,' she murmured. 'I am sorry that this matter has taken up so much of your time.'

He waved his hand. 'When we first met, I warned you that I would not allow you to go forward with my column in the final stages of the attack on Sekukuni's stronghold. Well, I am informed by my superiors back home – rather surprisingly, I must say – that I must not discriminate against you because of your gender.' He pronounced it, with some emphasis, as 'gendah', and as though the word in itself was rather offensive. 'Therefore I am prepared to allow you to accompany the other members of the press contingent,' again, he stressed the last two words as though they represented something strange, new and rather reprehensible, 'on the advance towards our final attack. However,' he paused, lowered his chin and looked grimly upwards at her as a headmaster would warn a difficult pupil, 'under no circumstances will you approach the firing line – whatever your colleagues do. Is that understood? Do you accept these conditions?'

Alice smiled inwardly. Good for Cornford. He must have anticipated her problem and lobbied extensively on her behalf. What the hell! She would give any pledge that was necessary to get near the action. But once the firing began, she would be her own woman. She shared her smile with Wolseley. 'Of course, Sir Garnet. That sounds eminently reasonable.'

The General's eyebrows shot up. He was clearly relieved not to have to cross swords in argument again with this young woman. 'Good. Splendid. Now, there is something else. Once we advance, we shall – we must – impose a system of security clearance upon the writings of, ah, you people. Not exactly censorship, you understand. But our cabling facilities will be under great strain on the advance and we must ensure that the use of them by the press is, er, to the point and, er, so on. I am sure you understand?'

Alice gave him another smile. 'Of course, General.' She would fight this battle on her own terms when she had to. But now was certainly not the time.

Wolseley, clearly relieved, stood up. 'Splendid. Well, now I am afraid you must excuse me, Miss Griffith. Oh, by the way,' he bestowed on her his boyish grin, 'I well knew that you would report on the details of the breakdown of my force that I mentioned to you when last we met, but I am glad that you were able to express the view that you felt our Boer friends would be impressed by the preparations I was making.'

'Ah, but General, you are once again falling under the misapprehension that I express my

247

own views in my copy. That was not *my* view, but that of the Afrikaner leaders who were observing your preparations in Pretoria.'

Wolseley shrugged his shoulders. 'Well, whatever. You clearly have good contacts among them, dear lady.' And he shot her a hooded-eyed smile. 'Ah, one more thing.' The smile broadened. 'I understand that you will be getting a visitor this afternoon. A most welcome one, I would think. But no more of that now, for you really must excuse me.'

Alice frowned. A visitor? But she returned the smile, gave a courteous nod of the head and left the little General to his plans. As she walked back across the square to her hotel – only five minutes away and therefore not worth taking a carriage, even if one were to be found in this unsophisticated town – she pondered. Could it be Simon? Her heart leapt. Had he, somehow, freed Nandi, found that her father was here in Middelburg and brought her to join him? Would she see Simon this very day? Then the exaltation disappeared. Of course not. If Wolseley knew this, he would have told Dunn immediately and there would have been no need for that frightful confrontation. The thought of Dunn saddened her mood. In the end, she had done nothing to relieve his plight. True, she had successfully pleaded for leniency from Wolseley, but Dunn was in jail because of her. Was she not just an interfering busybody?

Glumly, she turned on her heel and walked back to Wolseley's HQ. She enquired as to the whereabouts of the guardhouse from the rather startled sentry, and found it – a very large converted shed – at the end of the garden. She was denied access to Dunn, but the guard sergeant, a grizzled veteran with a pepper-and-salt beard, succumbed to Alice's smile and a folded one-pound bill and promised to deliver to the prisoner the note she hurriedly scribbled. She could offer only a little comfort to Dunn: *W says that you will be in jail only for a couple of days, until he advances. Then you will be out without charges. DO NOT cause trouble! I will try and see you tomorrow. AG.*

Back in the hotel she was able to procure a cheese sandwich and a glass of milk for lunch and lay on her bed munching while she began drafting a colour piece to keep the *Post* happy until she was able to file harder copy. She wrote of the amazing mixture of black levies Wolseley had been able to assemble, and of the last-minute – and probably abortive – attempts to give them some kind of barrack-square discipline; of the still desperate need for scouts; and of the barren nature of the country that the British column would have to traverse to reach Sekukuni's stronghold. She became so engrossed in the task that all thoughts of her visitor had slipped her mind. The brisk knock on her door, therefore, startled her and, forgetting to brush crumbs from her blouse and to push back a stray lock of hair, she rushed to open the door.

There, beaming down on her, was her fiancé, Colonel Ralph Covington CB, resplendent in scarlet jacket, gleaming jackboots and sword. He encircled her waist in one movement and swept her to him, burying her mouth in his sweeping moustache.

She broke free. 'Ralph! What are you doing here? I thought you were still in Afghanistan. Why didn't you cable or something...?' She tailed away, suddenly realising that she was not evincing perhaps the right amount of enthusiasm that an engaged woman should display to her future husband.

Covington did not seem to notice. He strode in, looked about the little room with some distaste, and then, theatrically, held up his hand. 'Deuce it! Knew I would forget something.' He walked back into the corridor and reappeared carrying a rather scrawny bouquet of thorny mimosa and wild jessamine, together with a bottle of champagne. Without ceremony he threw out the half-dead wisps of bush blossom that protruded from the only vase, tossed the discoloured water out of the window, poured new water into the vase from the washing jug and thrust his flowers into it. He picked up the mug from which Alice had drunk her milk and looked around with a frown.

'No glasses! Good lord, Alice, you should live better than this.'

Alice sighed. She hated to be rebuked. 'I *am* on campaign, Ralph.'

He gave her his great smile that almost, but not quite, lit up the china-blue eyes, yet did curve upwards to the great moustaches that bent around his face until they met his long sideburns. Covington was a handsome man. At forty-two, he was beginning to lose the hair at his forehead, but his brow and cheeks (those, at least, that

250

could be seen around his whiskers) were smooth, and he was tall and broad-shouldered. The early signs of a middle-aged paunch were mitigated by excellent tailoring and his fine military bearing.

'My darling, we are *all* on campaign out here,' he said. 'Never mind. I will find two glasses. Now, don't you move an inch. We must talk.'

Champagne bottle in hand, he marched to the door and she heard him crashing down the uncarpeted stairs (he must have *tiptoed* to her room!) and calling, 'Boy, boy!' She took the opportunity to smooth her skirt and hurriedly brush her hair, throwing cold water from what was left in the jug on to her face. He came back within a minute holding two wine glasses.

'Not for champagne, but they will have to do. After all,' he smiled impishly, holding them up, 'we *are* on campaign, you know.'

Despite her irritation – her fiancé was the last person she wanted to see at this time and in this place – she smiled back. 'But why *are* you here, and why *didn't* you telegraph or cable?'

'Wanted to surprise you.' He twisted the cork and then used his thumbs to prise it out. The subsequent explosion gave childish pleasure to them both. 'And I am here to fight – and keep an eye on you.'

'I don't need a nanny, thank you.'

'I am not so sure about that, my girl.' His face became stern for a moment. 'Shortly after you left Kandahar, word came back that there had been some sort of fuss in Bombay and that that bounder Fonthill and his damned Welshman had probably been involved in it. And that he had cut and run for South Africa – your destination, of course.'

Alice blushed. 'What sort of fuss? I know nothing about that.'

'I don't know the details, but it's typical of the man that he should leg it on to the nearest steamer. But I was not at all happy that it should be one bound for Durban and probably with you on board as well.' He handed her one of the glasses and began to pour the biscuit-coloured wine into it. Keeping his eyes on the task he asked softly, 'Did you know he was sailing to Durban, and on your vessel?'

'Certainly not. I met them – Simon and Jenkins – on board the ship for the first time when I boarded it. Their destination was nothing to do with me. They were as surprised as I when we met on the deck.' Alice's indignation began to grow as she realised that her cheeks were burning and that these veiled accusations now had some foundation. Untypically, she felt the need to bluster. 'Look here, Ralph, I will not be questioned like this. There is no point in continuing our engagement unless we trust each other.'

He held up his glass to her and said, 'And, darling Alice, *do* you wish to continue our engagement?' His eyes, levelled at her from just above the rim of the glass, were clear and cold. Ah, the moment of truth! The confrontation she had been dreading. Did she love Covington? Did she *really* want to shed this present fascinating lifestyle for the security of marriage, wealth and the very different challenge of motherhood? And, most probing of all, wasn't it now Simon whom she loved? Was that love strong enough to make her go back on her word, an act which she had always considered to be dishonourable and the characteristic of a weak, shallow person?

She gulped and forced a smile. 'Of ... of course.'

If Covington had been aware of that momentary hesitation, he gave no sign. 'Good,' he said. 'Then we shall say no more about blasted Fonthill. Let us, my dear, drink to us.' He lifted his glass in a toast and, after a brief moment, Alice lifted hers in reply.

'To us,' she whispered.

'Now.' Covington dabbed his whiskers with the back of his forefinger in that familiar movement, sat on the bed and patted the mattress in invitation. 'You asked me what I was doing here.' He lifted her hand and pressed it to his moustache. 'Of course, in replying that I wanted to keep an eye on you, I was telling the truth, in that I know how headstrong you can be, my darling, though I also admire your guts, you know that. I am well aware that, whatever Wolseley says, somehow you will get to the fighting, and I want to be there to make sure that you don't court danger unnecessarily. Now, I shall have my own responsibilities once we attack, so I can't exactly watch over you, but I stand more chance of being of some use to you here than stuck back in Afghanistan.'

He chuckled, and Alice began to warm once again to this strange mixture of a man: the bully and the sensitive carer, the stereotypical career officer and the admirer of rebellion. Sitting at his side on the lumpy bed, she became aware of the strange, musky smell of the man; a combination perhaps of tobacco, horseflesh and ... what? Downright animal magnetism? She stirred uncomfortably, aware of the conflict which had so recently disturbed her, but Covington was continuing.

'I also said that I had come to fight, and that is equally true. Once you had gone, I realised how empty things were in Kandahar. Old Bobs, the General, had completely destroyed what was left of Pathan resistance and I felt that there was nothing really left for me to do there. I knew that Wolseley was planning this campaign and I itched to be with him.' He smiled at her, almost in apology. 'I'm a Wolseley man, yer know, fought with him in Ashanti, and I suppose I'm regarded as being one of the Ashanti Ring. So I cabled him and asked if I could join. He wired back saying that I would be welcome if Roberts would let me go. Bobs didn't think much of it, I imagine – you know that he and Wolseley are fierce rivals now – but he really couldn't stop me, so here I am.'

Alice stood and refilled her glass and his. 'What are you going to do on the campaign?'

'Oh, I shall have a line command of some sort. Haven't been told exactly what yet. I gather that Sir Garnet is in a bit of a stew about exactly how to attack this damned heathen's hill fortress, because there's no reliable information about it. He's got no decent scouts – none that he can trust, anyhow – and those he has got are afraid to penetrate too deeply into the Sekukuni territory, which I gather is pretty rough and wild. As a result, he doesn't know the lie of the land and is

254

in a bit of a quandary about how to launch an attack. But all this will be sorted out when we near our objective, I am sure. I gather we move tomorrow.'

'What?'

'Oh yes. The little man is fed up with hanging around here. He will leave with the vanguard tomorrow, and I shall go with him. The rest of the army will come on in stages. The General will set up an advance base north of Lydenburg. He calls it Fort Weeber. Weather looks bad, though.'

Alice frowned. 'Forgive me, then, Ralph. I must file a story today and also make my own preparations for the move. I shall go with the van, of course.'

Covington's eyebrows rose. 'Don't know whether the press johnnies are going with the forward party or not...'

'Oh yes, they will. Now, Ralph, please excuse me, for I have much to do.'

The tall man rose. 'Of course, my dear.' He put down his glass and enfolded her in his arms. She did not resist. He murmured into her hair, 'Now this will be your last campaign, my love. You really must get used to the idea.' He gently pushed her away and held her by the shoulders at arm's length, looking into her eyes. 'You must, you know.'

Alice nodded, trying to keep the tears back. 'Yes, I know,' she said.

'Very well.' He kissed her lightly on the mouth and was gone.

Alice slumped on to the bed and buried her face in the pillow. Then, almost immediately, she

255

sat up, blew her nose, walked to the wash stand and sponged her face. As she dried herself, she scrutinised her features in the wall mirror. Well, she told her reflection, that was that. If she was not committed before, she was now. Better make the most of it and get on with her life. No more thoughts of Simon Fonthill. She threw down the towel, tied her hair back and slipped on her riding jacket.

At the General's HQ, she receive reluctant confirmation that the advance guard would be marching out at dawn the following day to march north-eastwards, and that the press contingent would be allowed to accompany the column. Alice gained details of the make-up of the party, then wandered the square and surrounding area to gain further colour details for her story.

She cabled it that evening and then gave notice to her hotel of her early departure. She took care, however, to pay for John Dunn's room for the next three days, and then hurriedly penned a note to Dunn, explaining that she would be unable to see him because of the advance, urging him to return to Pretoria to seek help there, and, as an afterthought, enclosing £50. She felt guilty and frustrated that she could do little more to help Nandi, but prayed in her heart that Simon had been successful or that Dunn would swallow his fears and go to the authorities in Pretoria. The grizzled sergeant took the note this time with no thought of payment and confided that he had instructions to release Dunn in two days' time. Alice felt better at this news and returned to her room to pack. She had a job to do – yes, and when it was finished? She would prepare for her new life, of course. Her jaw was set as she pushed her carefully folded garments into her battered bag, but her eyes were moist.

The next morning, shortly after dawn, Alice mounted her horse and joined the long column that wound out of Middelburg. Ranged out ahead of it rode a distant screen of colonial cavalry, while in the van of the infantry marched the soldiers of the 21st Regiment of Foot, under their white cork helmets, known as 'Wolseley topis', their pipe-clayed belts and crossed bandoliers standing out brilliantly from their red coats. Immediately behind the first company, Sir Garnet Wolseley and his staff, dressed in sombre blue, walked their horses as they chatted. At the rear of the infantry, just ahead of where the cannon of the field artillery bumped and jingled along the bush veldt track, rode Alice and her colleagues – ahead of the artillery to avoid the dust clouds which the latter produced. Behind the guns, the black levies loped along in noisy disarray, bulging out wider than the regimented lines of the column, as though a python had swallowed a warthog and not yet digested it. Then came the commissariat, with its waggons and carts piled high with camping gear and cooking utensils. A detachment of the 94th brought up the rear, forming the narrow tail of the snake and marching in glum discomfort as the dust enfolded them. Far out on either flank, brown-uniformed cavalry pickets patrolled, to protect the column from surprise.

Riding out on that fine morning, with a crispness in the air reminding her that they were some four thousand feet above sea level, Alice felt excited to be with the army again. Ahead, above the bobbing pith helmets of the 21st, she could just make out the broad shoulders and ramrod back of Covington, engaged in conversation with the General. Whatever the future held, it was good to be on the march again.

Chapter 10

Simon and his companions rode as fast as they could for the first two miles and then slowed to rest their horses. As the reborn sun gave welcome warmth to the riders and their mounts, the four bunched together companionably and, for the first time, began talking – all, that is, except for de Witt, who stayed silently in the rear.

'You've had a bad time by the look of it, Nandi,' said Simon.

'Bloody awful I'd say, look you,' Jenkins chimed in.

She smiled at them both, tears appearing again in her eyes. 'Oh yes. But I am much better now. I am so grateful to you and I can never begin to thank you all for getting me away from those awful men.'

'What I don't understand, see–' began Jenkins.

'No.' Simon held up his hand. 'Not now, 352. We can hear Nandi's story when we stop. I just want to make sure that we are not being followed.' He looked behind them and pulled his horse's head round so that he could climb a small mound that gave some distance, at least, to his view. In the growing light he scanned the landscape behind them with his binoculars. 'I can see nothing,' he called down, 'but I don't think it safe to stop yet. Can you keep going for a while, Nandi?'

She nodded acceptance and they set off again in single file, travelling at as fast a pace as their horses could take, until they came to a small kopje that provided some shade and the chance to establish a lookout post. There they dismounted and broke out some of the meagre provisions they had saved. While de Witt climbed the kopje to keep watch, Simon and Jenkins heard Nandi's story.

Her letter to Simon had been a forlorn gesture because she harboured little hope of the letter reaching him, so vague was the address. Yet she could think of no one else she could turn to as the days went by and her father did not return. Police seemed nonexistent and her mother in distant Natal was too frail to help. Mendoza and his companions had made her a virtual prisoner from the start, only allowing her to leave the house accompanied in the first two days and then afterwards denying her access to the outside world completely. She had escaped once, only long enough to post her letter, before they found her and brought her back. That was the first time they had beaten her, but it happened often after that.

Here a grim-faced Jenkins interrupted. 'Did they, did they ... you know ... did they ever...?'

Nandi sat cross-legged, gnawing a piece of biltong, her bare, dirty toes burrowing into the coarse veldt grass. She looked up at the Welshman with eyes that hid a wealth of misery in their dark depths. 'I would rather not talk about that, please,' she said, and looked down, into her lap.

'Swines,' said Jenkins. 'Bastards. Look, let's go

260

back and–'

Simon laid a restraining hand on his arm. 'It's important we hear everything, 352,' he said. 'Go on, Nandi.' But his face, too, had gone white under its tan.

'Well,' she continued in a low voice, 'it seems so long – a lifetime, perhaps – and yet little happened, in fact. For a long time I had no idea what they were doing, what sort of business they were in, because, although I did all the cooking, I was not allowed to eat with them. But I started to listen at doors. Sometimes they spoke in Portuguese, but often they spoke in Afrikaans, and I realised that they were buying diamonds from the native workers and selling them on at big profits. They do not sell them in Kimberley, oh no. The prices there would be too low because of the competition. So they take them over the mountains to Mozambique, where they have connections with Lisbon.' She looked at them both with that wide-eyed wonder that Simon remembered so well. 'They make a lot of money, you see.'

'What about your father?' Simon asked.

She put her hand to her eyes. 'I think he must be dead. He did not come back from his business trip and it must have been a long while ago when he set off. Whenever I asked about him, the big man, Mendoza, said that he would be back but they did not know when. He said – with a nasty smile – that they would be waiting for him when he did.'

Simon frowned. 'Yes, but Nandi, why do you think they kept you there?'

'Oh, I wish I knew.' Tears came into her eyes

261

again and she lowered her gaze. 'I suppose I was useful because I worked for them there for no pay and because, because of the other thing...'

Jenkins seized her hand. 'Now, dear Nandi, don't you get thinkin' about that, look you. That's all in the past an' it's all over. Nothin' like that is goin' to 'appen to you again. You can take my word for that, see. We're lookin' after you now. An' they're goin' to suffer for it, you see if they don't.' Simon felt that he had never heard the little Welshman speak with such intensity.

They fell silent for a moment, then Simon said, 'I don't believe your father is dead, Nandi. I think these thieves know that he is alive and they desperately want him for something, though I don't know what. I feel that they were holding you as some sort of bargaining counter to get him to come back. And perhaps he knew this and was trying to find a way to get you out of there without harm.'

Nandi's eyes widened and she looked at them both with new hope. 'Oh, do you think so? Yes, perhaps that would make sense, wouldn't it? Otherwise why should they bring me all these miles out here to the farmhouse. I had never been there before.'

'Yes.' Simon nodded. 'Tell us about that.'

'Well, I was feeling very miserable before you came to Kimberley. In fact, I was thinking that I must ... you know ... kill myself, because I had no hope.'

'Aach!' Jenkins turned his head away.

'And then, that wonderful day...' Nandi's eyes regained their brilliance at the thought. 'I was upstairs when I thought I heard your voice, Simon, at the front door, though you spoke strangely. They always had the shutters down on my window and the others, but by peeping through a crack at the corner, I was just in time to see you walk away. Then, later on, I caught a brief glimpse of dear Mr Jenkins, and I knew that you had not gone away for ever. Oh, Simon, I was full of hope again.'

Jenkins gripped her hand tighter. 'Now, Nandi, you must call me 352, like the others do.'

'Oh!' She smiled, showing small white teeth. 'I couldn't do that. It's so very ... very ... army, that's what it is. And I don't like your army. Tell me then, what is your first name?'

Jenkins coloured immediately. 'Oh no, 352 will do.'

'No, go on.' Simon's face was perfectly straight. 'Tell Nandi your first name, 352. She would like to know.'

'No. I've ... er... forgotten it. 352 will do nicely, thank you. If you don't mind.'

Simon cupped his hand to Nandi's ear and whispered loudly, 'Actually, it's Cyril, but don't tell anybody. He doesn't like it.' They both grinned, and Jenkins, his mouth completely disappeared into his moustache, looked away. 'Now,' continued Simon, his face serious again, 'to go back, they left immediately because we had called?'

'I think so. I was just told to put things together and we departed the evening after you had knocked on the door. I was just able to tie a scarf round Daddy's hat and put my message in it for you. I did not know where we were going, but I heard Steelport mentioned. Oh, Simon, I was so glad, so *very, very* glad when you walked into the kitchen and then I saw dear 352 again.' The tears came back into her eyes and both men stirred uncomfortably.

'Tell me, Nandi,' said Simon eventually. 'Where is Mendoza, and when did he leave?'

'Ah, that terrible man. I am very, very frightened of him, Simon, and so must you both be.'

'No, no,' said Jenkins, and he patted her knee gently as he would a child. 'That gentleman does not frighten us. I shall personally present both his ... er ... kneecaps to you, when I have finished with him.'

'No, but he is big and cruel and very–'

'It doesn't matter,' interrupted Simon. 'He was not at the farm. Do you know where he is now?'

'Yes, he left almost as soon as we arrived and I heard them saying that he would go to see King Sekukuni to warn him that the British were going to attack him. He seems to be close to the bePedi.'

'Ah. I wonder, then, why the bePedi attacked the farm.'

'Oh, they were not bePedi. I caught a glimpse of them. They were Swazis. They were quite a long way from their homeland but they were obviously desperate for cattle. The bePedis are their enemy so they were wearing the Pedi ... what do you say ... regalia, yes, so that the blame for the attack would go to them.' She sniffed. 'It is not something that the Zulus would do.'

Simon exchanged a grin with Jenkins. 'Of course not. Well, that explains that.'

Nandi gave them both a rather knowing smile in return. 'By the way,' she said, 'it is a pity that we had to leave the farm so quickly. We could have taken the diamonds.'

'What? There were diamonds in the house?'

'Oh yes. Those thieves thought I did not know, but I did. They had a hiding place for them under the floorboards in the kitchen. I suppose they put them there before going on to sell them at Lorenzo Marques.'

'Well I'll be blowed,' said Jenkins. 'We could 'ave been millionaires.'

Simon shrugged. 'Not our property. Anyway, too late now—'

He was interrupted by a call from de Witt on top of the kopje. 'Hey, I see something. Can you come here?'

Simon and Jenkins scrambled to their feet and joined the Boer. The big man pointed to the south-east. 'There, can you see?'

Simon focused his binoculars. The veldt stretched away from him in a sombre brown vista, broken by low hills and, here and there, a few conical kopjes, like their present vantage point. Then a flash came, just below the horizon, followed by another, then a third where the sun illuminated the distant plain. What – a spear point, harness, the steel of a bayonet?

'Your eyes are better than mine.' Simon handed de Witt the glasses. 'What do you make of it?'

The Boer grunted. 'These reflections go all along. It's a column, I think.' He handed back the binoculars. 'Your people. The *roijneks*. The bloody army, man.'

265

'Are you sure it's not the bePedi army?'

'No. They wouldn't be out here in force on the veldt marching to meet the British. That's not their style. They will wait back in their country in that stronghold of theirs and challenge your General to get them out. That's what they've always done in the past – and they're damned good at it.' It was quite a long statement for de Witt, and, as though tired, he turned and ambled down the kopje, leaving Simon and Jenkins alone on the top.

'What do you think?' Simon passed the glasses to Jenkins.

'Can't see much,' murmured the Welshman. 'He's probably right, you know, bach sir. He knows this country well, an' these Bopiddlers an' all.' He lowered the glasses. 'Is this the way our blokes would be comin', then?'

'I think so. We have been heading south-east towards Lydenburg, although I told those damned dagos that we would be heading east straight to the border, to put them off the scent if they tried to follow us. These troops look further to the east, so perhaps they have left Lydenburg. Without a good map I can't be sure. But if we can meet up with this British column, so much the better. At least we can deliver Nandi into safe hands.'

'And get landed with a bit of scoutin', an' all?'

Simon shrugged. 'Well, if we have to, then we must. We owe Wolseley something for helping us in the first place. But our priority is to make Nandi safe. Then,' and his face hardened, 'we have some unfinished business with Mr Men-

266

doza. Come on, let's move on towards the army, although,' he squinted up at the sun, 'we won't be able to reach them by nightfall. We will make as much ground as we can, camp, and then catch up with them early tomorrow. A column like that can't move fast.'

They scrambled down the kopje and the little party mounted and set off to the east-south-east, with the sun on their backs. It was warm enough, despite their height above sea level, but Simon noticed that Nandi was showing signs of discomfort. She remained silent but he realised that she had begun to shiver and that two spots of colour had appeared high on her cheekbones, one shining through that horrible bruise. He took off his coat and slipped it over her shoulders, and she smiled but did not protest. By the time the sun had begun to dip, it was clear that the girl had developed some kind of fever.

They found a camping site of sorts in a dried-up watercourse and Simon decided that they must risk lighting a fire, for Nandi was now shaking and hunched under his coat, her eyes unnaturally bright. They boiled water and brewed tea, holding the mug from which she sipped. She refused food but nodded gratefully as they wrapped her in two blankets, and within a second she was asleep.

As she lay, Jenkins gently bathed her forehead with a handkerchief he had soaked from his water bottle. He looked up at Simon with anxious eyes, his moustache sucked under his lower lip. 'Do you think she'll be all right?' he asked.

'I don't know, but it looks to me as though she will not be able to ride tomorrow. We must keep

267

her warm and make sure that she does not develop pneumonia. She can have my other blanket.'

'No. She can have another of mine.'

'All right. Can you take the first watch? I want a word with Faan.'

'O' course.'

Simon walked to where the Boer, sitting separately as usual, was munching a hard biscuit. He sat beside him. 'Faan, how much riding would you say we have to do tomorrow before we catch the column?'

'Don't know. Did you set a course to cut them off?'

'Yes, but I don't know how fast they were travelling or how far they were from us. The problem is, I don't think Nandi will be fit to ride tomorrow, and if we stay here we may lose the column completely.'

'Ja. Then keep the girl here and you two go to find the army and bring back a doctor.'

'I don't like leaving her here with just one of us.'

'Better that way. We are hidden here and should be all right. But just one man riding on this open veldt is not good. In this country you have to watch your back. The Pedi army will not be out, but they could have patrols watching the British. Two would stand a better chance of fighting them off. I will stay with the girl. You two go. You know your own people. She will be safe with me.'

'I am sure she will. But I hate to leave just one man guarding her. Do you think there is any chance of those people in the farmhouse picking up our tracks and following them to us here?'

De Witt shook his head. 'No. It's difficult to track on the veldt when it is dry like this, and anyway, only Kaffirs can do it, and not many of them. I would say we were safe enough here.'

'Good.' Simon sighed. 'We'll just have to see how Nandi is in the morning. She may be able to ride.'

Daybreak brought some relief in Nandi's condition, but it was only a marginal improvement. She drank a little warm coffee and then insisted on standing, but her legs collapsed under her and it was clear that the fever had not run its course and that she would not be able to ride until it had done so.

Simon scrambled to the top of the donga and scanned the southern horizon with his binoculars, but there was no sign of the British column. In fact the veldt seemed empty at all points of the compass. He called the other two men to join him.

'Nandi can't travel,' he said, 'but if we all stay here we might lose the column completely. Faan will stay with Nandi and you and I, 352, will ride as hard as we can to catch up with the column and bring a doctor back here.'

'Oh no, bach sir.' Jenkins's face was set. 'I'll stay here with Nandi. I'll look after her. You two go.'

Simon sighed. 'No, that will not do. If something happens to us out there then I believe that de Witt, with his knowledge of this country, is the best man to get Nandi back into care. You can't do it because you can't handle a compass, and I must go to explain things to the column

269

commander. Faan believes – and I agree – that it would be too dangerous for just one man to go. So that's that. Now let's mount up.'

Jenkins sought for words to argue but realised that he could not change Simon's opinion. Nandi had once again lapsed into sleep, so he knelt by her side for a moment, bent as though to kiss her, thought better of it and lightly brushed the back of her hand with his palm. Then he stood and bundled up his bedroll, but it was clear that he remained unhappy. The two gave a share of their food rations and ammunition to de Witt and then, with a backward glance at Nandi, they rode off, on a course which Simon set, hopefully to catch up with the British column.

Their journey was uneventful, for the veldt seemed empty and endless, with no trails or signs of wildlife or habitation to break up the khaki expanse of dried grass and rock. The further they rode, in fact, the more desert-like the conditions became, and Simon wondered if they were now well and truly into bePedi country, for they had passed no farms of cultivated land since they had left the farmhouse the previous morning.

Eventually, however, they hit a well-worn trail which Simon presumed was the main route between Lydenburg and the mountain passes which travellers would have to traverse to reach Mozambique. It was clear that the army column had passed that way, for there were signs of beaten grass and fresh waggon ruts. They turned left and urged their horses on. Almost immediately, the column had departed from the trail and forked sharply north. Ahead now was a low mountain range that rose sharply from the surrounding plain like a row of giant ant heaps, blue in the rays of the setting sun.

'Must be the Lulus,' said Simon, breaking a long silence between them. 'The column must have formed an advanced camp somewhere up ahead because the map shows nothing at all in this area – not that it's been much good anyway.' He folded it and thrust it into his saddle bag. 'Come on, we must find them before dark.'

They did so, just before the troops had bivouacked for the night. They were challenged by a weary picket of colonial cavalry, sombre in their slouched hats and brown bandoliers, who had formed the rearguard on the march. To Simon's surprise, for the column was quite small and numbered only perhaps eight hundred men, he was informed that General Wolseley himself was commanding the force, and he was taken to him.

Sir Garnet's tent was being erected and the little man was sitting at a folding table nearby, busily writing and seemingly impervious to the cold. He looked up with surprise.

'Good lord, Fonthill.' He rose and offered his hand. 'Well done. Come to keep your promise and to help me, eh? Splendid. You are just what I need now.'

'Good evening, sir.' This was not the welcome he wanted. 'This is my colleague, Jenkins.' Wolseley gave the Welshman a nod. Jenkins managed a tired grin in return. 'General, I am sorry but we cannot join you just at the moment, although we will as soon as possible. But I need your help.'

Wolseley frowned. 'Damn it all – I need *your* help. I am desperate for a couple of good scouts to reconnoitre the ground ahead. Surely you can do that for me? I can give you some locals to help you – they're Ndebeles and know the territory – but I need someone to interpret it militarily on the spot, so to speak.'

'Sorry, General. We will happily help you, but first I need a doctor and two days of his time.'

'What? You'd better tell me your story. You look all in, anyway.' Wolseley turned and lifted his voice. 'Orderly!' A blue-coated servant came running. 'We need a fire lit right away and two other camp chairs. Oh, and bring some tea and brandy and get someone to look after these horses.' He turned back to them. 'We've got a base camp up ahead about ten miles or so, called Fort Weeber. Can't reach it tonight, of course, but I can't advance further than that until I know the lie of the land.' He gestured to the lowering sky. 'This weather is going to get worse, they tell me, so I can't go much further anyway. Now, sit down and tell me what the hell this is all about.'

Gratefully accepting the tea, while Jenkins even more gratefully drank a brandy, Simon told Wolseley their story, omitting nothing. The General listened without interrupting. Eventually he spoke.

'I know something about this already,' he said. And he relayed his encounter with Alice and John Dunn.

Simon's eyes widened. So Dunn was alive! And Alice... 'Is ... is ... Miss Griffith here with you in the column?' he asked.

272

'No. The press johnnies are still back at Lydenburg, itching to get up here, of course, but I don't want 'em yet. Look, yours is a strange story, and if I didn't have the other elements to fit in, frankly, I would doubt it. But the activities of these men are disgusting and must be stopped. I can't spare anybody long enough to go down and sort out this damned farmhouse and arrest this Mendoza man, not while this campaign is on at least.' He held up his hand as Simon began to protest. 'But in the morning I will give you a sergeant and ten men and a doctor to go and fetch this young lady of yours. We will send a Scotch cart, too, so that she should be able to travel. But, mind you, I want 'em all back quickly. And you most of all – to start work for me.' The one bulbous eye stared directly at Simon. 'Agreed?'

'Agreed.' The two shook hands.

'Agreed,' chimed in Jenkins, who, to the General's consternation, also rose from his chair and warmly shook Wolseley's hand. 'Very good of you, General bach,' he said.

'Er ... yes. Very well. Set off early in the morning and return to me at Fort Weeber. Now go and get some rest.'

Simon and Jenkins were up before dawn, and were joined by a sleepy young army surgeon who would have looked perhaps twelve years old without his fair, swept-back moustache. The party was completed by a black-bearded sergeant and ten men of the 21st Regiment. The surgeon sat by the driver in the Scotch cart and the party set off, Simon anxiously consulting his compass, for the veldt seemed characterless and, with Nandi's life at stake, the last thing he wanted was to lose his way in this semi-desert.

It was with huge relief, then, that after a day's ride, slowed by the pace of the bumping, bouncing cart, they located the sunken water course. The cart followed the lip of the donga round as it curled sinuously, while the horsemen carefully negotiated the stony banks down to the dry river bed. Simon stood in the stirrups and hallooed as they picked their way between the stones. 'Faan!' he shouted again. Only a startled secretary bird fluttered up to acknowledge the call.

'Hey, something's up,' cried Jenkins, spurring his horse on around the bend of the river bed. Simon dug in his heels and followed close behind.

They pulled up in horror as they came upon the campsite. The ashes of the fire had been scattered and the blankets and the meagre belongings of de Witt and Nandi were strewn up the sides of the donga, slashed and torn as though in a fit of vindictiveness. The Boer lay prone in a pool of blood, one arm outstretched, the other folded across his chest. Of the horses and of Nandi there was no sign.

'Doctor,' called Simon as the cart appeared on the edge of the donga, 'get down here quickly and see to this man. Sergeant, spread your men out and look for a young lady. She might be further down the donga or out on the veldt. Quickly, now.'

Though he wore no insignia of rank, Simon's

274

air of command was enough for the sergeant, and he and his men galloped away. Yet Simon realised how abortive would be the search. The look of the camp – the tattered cloth, the cold ashes and the congealed blood in which de Witt lay – all were evidence that the attack had taken place some time before, probably the previous day as he and Jenkins were riding to find Wolseley.

A low moan made him spin round. Jenkins was on his knees, holding a torn fragment of Nandi's dress. The Welshman looked up at Simon with deep fear in his black eyes. "Ave they killed 'er, d'yer think?' he asked. 'Or 'ave they taken 'er again?'

'I don't know, old chap. Come on, we must help them look. Perhaps they have left her nearby.'

The two men joined the soldiers who had fanned out around the site. There was evidence enough of a fight, for spent cartridge cases lined the bottom of the donga and the walls of the bed were broken and marked where horsemen had forced their way down. But there was no trace of the girl they sought.

Simon, out on the veldt, was alerted by a cry from the doctor. 'Mr Fonthill,' the young man shouted, 'this man is still alive.'

Simon ran back to the river bed with Jenkins on his heels. The doctor – now looking much more mature – was forcing a little water between the lips of de Witt as he cradled the Afrikaner's head. 'Here,' he called to Simon, 'take this and see if he can drink, while I see if I can dress this wound.' The young man tore away de Witt's blood-

275

stained shirt to reveal a crusted black hole on the right side of the Boer's breast. An assegai had torn a terrible cut in his shoulder, there was another stab wound under his ribs on the left side, and it was clear that he had been steadily bleeding, although the big man had stuffed a handkerchief in the breast wound to staunch the blood. Bending over him, Simon could hear a low rattle as the wounded man fought for breath.

The doctor spoke as he gently probed the wound. 'I'm afraid this has gone downwards through the lung,' he said. He looked up. 'Whoever did this must have shot him as he lay on the ground. He must have been down and almost out with these spear wounds anyway. Then they came along and shot him as he lay.' His face wrinkled into a frown. 'Doesn't seem like the work of natives. Who are the people who would do this?'

Simon, tipping the water bottle to release a little more liquid, saw de Witt's mouth twitch and he began to swallow. 'Mozambique Portuguese, I think,' he said. 'He's beginning to swallow. What hope, do you think, Doctor...?'

The young man grimaced and spoke almost in a whisper so that the wounded man could not hear. 'None, I'm afraid. The gunshot has shattered his lungs and he has lost so much blood. It is amazing that he has survived the night.'

As though to refute the statement, de Witt opened his eyes. His lips worked for a moment without sound and then he said, 'Ach, English. So you've come then. Too late, I think, though.' He began to cough, and blood trickled down his chin on to his beard.

'Faan,' said Simon, 'can you tell us what happened?'

'And where Nandi is.' Unnoticed, Jenkins had crept up.

The Boer's eyes flickered open again and he spoke in a voice so low that Simon had to hold his ear near to the man's lips to hear him.

'They came about three hours after you had gone. Mendoza and maybe twenty bePedi. I got a couple but they were too much for me. Mendoza shot me after I had been speared. Thought I was dead.'

'What about Nandi?'

'They took her.'

The Boer's eyes closed. Simon bent closer. 'Faan, do you know where? It's important.'

It was all of thirty seconds before de Witt's eyes fluttered open again. 'I heard them say Sekukuni's place. To report on the *roijneks'* approach. English,' his eyes were now wide open, 'I don't think they kill her. They keep her for something... I don't know what.'

The eyes closed again and the Boer's breath was now coming in shallower bursts, his face contorted in pain.

'Can you hold his head?' asked the doctor. 'I have some morphine in the cart. Stupid of me to have left it. It will ease his pain. I won't be long.' The young man got to his feet and scrambled up the side of the donga.

As though he had waited for the doctor's absence, de Witt opened his eyes again and his lips curved into some resemblance of a smile. 'I cheated them, though,' he murmured. 'They

277

didn't get the diamonds.'

'Diamonds? What diamonds?'

'Ach, you didn't think I had come with you for a ride in the country, did you? No. I wanted those diamonds. The house in Kimberley was empty. Knew they had taken them. So while you were talking to the dagoes in the farmyard, I went into the house. Saw they were buried under the floorboards in the kitchen. Took them while you were upstairs getting the girl...'

He burst out coughing again, and Simon said, 'It doesn't matter, Faan. Don't talk.'

'They're buried by the fire here. Big stone. Underneath it.'

'What do you want us to do with them?'

The dying man gave his wan smile. 'They were meant for Commandant Joubert in Pretoria. That was my job in Kimberley. Get diamonds to provide money for the fight against the English. I don't suppose you will give them to him for me now, eh?'

Simon smiled in return. 'Sorry, Faan. Can't quite do that.'

'No. Thought not. All right. Give them to the girl when you find her. She deserves them... She's a good...' His voice died away and his head fell to one side.

''As he gone?' asked Jenkins. 'I couldn't 'ear what 'e was sayin', see. There's no sign of Nandi. Does 'e know if they took 'er?' His eyes were wide, and perspiration was trickling down his face.

Simon bent his ear close to de Witt's lips. 'He is just about breathing, but I don't think he will last long. He says he thinks Mendoza has taken Nandi to the bePedi capital.'

'Oh no!' Jenkins buried his face in his hands. 'That bastard has got 'er again.' When he took his hands away, his face was contorted with anger. 'Look. We can't waste no more time 'ere. We've got to go after 'er.'

Simon sighed, still cradling de Witt's head. 'No. The attack took place yesterday, and they had horses. We would never catch them, even if we knew exactly which way they were heading. But look, 352, we will get her back, I promise you that.' His voice took on a harder edge. 'It's my fault, because we should never have left them alone, but we came to this God-forsaken place to rescue Nandi and we will not leave it until we have done so. I promise. I just need time to think.'

The two men looked into each other's eyes without speaking, and then Jenkins's angry glare softened. 'It's not your fault, bach sir. You did what you did for the best, as you always do. O' course we'll get 'er back. O' course we will.'

Simon looked beyond Jenkins. The doctor had not returned and the soldiers were still searching the bush. 'Look,' he said. 'Just round that bend, by the ashes of the fire, there's a big stone. I noticed it when we came in. Underneath it will be a small package – probably more like a little sack. Can you take it and hide it without anyone knowing?'

Jenkins gave a puzzled nod.

'Right. Go now, but don't let anyone see you.'

As he spoke, the doctor came glissading down the side of the donga in a shower of stones, small bottle and gauze pad in hand. 'Is he still...?'

'Just about, I think.'

'Right.' The young man took up de Witt's wrist and felt for the pulse. Then he put his ear to the Boer's chest. Eventually he sat up, his face wearing that look of disappointment and self-admonishment that only doctors know. 'Ah, he's gone,' he said. 'Sorry.'

'Not your fault, Doctor. You did all you could.'

'Not enough, I fear.' The young man tugged at his moustache and looked up at Simon. 'Who was he, anyhow?'

'Ah.' Simon thought for a second. 'He was a ... patriot.'

'What? A ... er ... patriot, you say? Oh, I see. Well, I don't actually, but never mind. I suppose we had better bury him.'

The sergeant appeared at the lip of the donga. He addressed the doctor, as befitted one service-man talking to another in the presence of a civilian. 'Found two bodies, sir. In freshly dug graves. Both of 'em Kaffirs, sir. Spears an' all. But nuffink else.'

'Right, Sergeant.' The doctor looked down at de Witt, almost apologetically. 'Well, I'm afraid that we have another one to bury now. Can you see to it, please? There are shovels in the cart.'

'Very good, sir.'

At that point Jenkins reappeared, a small bulge in the pocket of his jacket. His eyes asked a question of Simon.

'For Nandi,' said Simon.

'Ah, right. O' course. When we find 'er, that is. Good idea, bach sir.' He looked down at de Witt.

280

''As 'e gone, then?'

'Afraid so.'

Jenkins blew through his moustache. 'Pity, that, isn't it? 'E was a good chap, old Fanny. Funny feller, though, in 'is way. But pity. I could've taught 'im to fight, see. With 'is build an' all, 'e could 'ave been a champion, look you. But not now. Not now. Pity.'

As they spoke, four soldiers scrambled down the side of the donga and, with some difficulty, picked up the big man.

'Wait a moment,' said Simon. 'I must go through his pockets to see if there is someone we should tell of his death.' He quickly searched the dead man, but found nothing except a couple of pound notes and a handful of change. It was as though de Witt belonged to no one and had passed through life without putting down even the greenest of roots.

Simon stood up and nodded to the sergeant, then handed him the notes and the change. 'You and your chaps might as well have this,' he said.

The little party camped that night in the sad donga, taking care to pitch their tents away from the scene of the fighting. Before sun-up the next day, they set off back to find Wolseley's forward post at Fort Weeber. Simon and Jenkins rode side by side, the former deep in thought, and Jenkins knew well enough not to interrupt.

'Look,' Simon said at last. 'We know that they have taken her back to Sekukuni's township, for a while at least, while they decide exactly what to do with her. It seems they want to trade her for

281

the diamonds that John Dunn is supposed to have. And Dunn won't know that she is at Sekukuni, so it might seem pointless to keep her there. Pointless, that is, unless...'

Jenkins, his brows pulled down as he tried to follow Simon's reasoning, pulled at his moustache. 'Pointless, yes, what?'

'Pointless,' said Simon, his face lighting up, 'unless we somehow send a message to Mendoza at Sekukuni, saying that *we*, not Dunn, will come and trade for Nandi. Give him the diamonds that de Witt stole in exchange for her freedom. What about that, then?'

Jenkins turned a lugubrious face towards Simon. 'Oh yes, fine, absolutely fine, look you. And 'e lets us ride into this Secooni place, drop 'im the bag of sparklers and then ride out again with Nandi. Oh, very plausible, I'd say.'

'So would I. I'm glad you agree, 352. That's what we'll do, then.' And Simon urged his horse forward in a canter to pass the trundling Scotch cart.

Chapter 11

They found Fort Weeber with little difficulty, for it was easy to follow the trail left by the column across the virgin veldt. The fort was just that: an artificial town, or large village, constructed simply to serve the army as a holding post in hostile territory. There were no wooden ramparts built to keep out attackers, not least because there was insufficient timber available, but also because Wolseley, in his arrogance, did not expect to be attacked. *He* was the aggressor on this campaign. Sekukuni's stronghold was some twenty miles distant, along the Steelport River valley, and although occasional small parties of bePedi patrols had been sighted, keeping the column under observation, the General was confident that the native chieftain would sit behind his impressive fortifications, waiting to repulse the aggressors, as he had so many times before. Fort Weeber, therefore, was a temporary army camp, the springboard for the final assault.

In fact, as Simon and his small party approached it, it was clear that Sir Garnet was not yet prepared to attack, for his force was by no means concentrated. They passed some contingents of red-coated British infantrymen, plodding along under field service marching order packs and accoutrements, but the main elements of the long, straggling column that now stretched back

283

to Lydenburg were local units hurriedly gathered by Wolseley. Simon recognised elements of Ferreira's Horse, a colonial regiment which had distinguished itself under Buller in the Zulu War; the unusual sight of 150 coloured men of the Transvaal Mounted Rifles; and even a handful of Hlubi's men of the Natal Native Horse, whom he remembered from the war as the 'Basuto Horse'. There were many others he did not recognise, all riding or marching north to clear out once and for all the hornets' nest of King Sekukuni. It was obvious to Simon that the General had scoured the territory to build his force for this campaign – an eclectic mix. Would it meld together into an effective and homogenous fighting unit?

Simon thanked the doctor and the sergeant, who peeled away to find their units, and he and Jenkins rode towards the centre of the bustling little metropolis, where they could see the Commander-in-Chief's standard fluttering. As they did so, there, striding towards them, the sun glinting off her fair hair, was Alice.

She stood still for a moment, her eyes wide. Then she threw up her arms and came running towards them, her smile removing any doubt that an onlooker might have of her feelings of warmth towards these two dusty travellers. 'Simon, Simon!' she shouted, and then, half apologetically, '352. Wonderful! You have come through. Wonderful! Thank God...' She put her hands on the stirrups of the two men and stood between them, her face looking at each in turn, flushed at the exertion and at her pleasure in seeing them. 'Oh,' she said, 'I am so glad. So glad. I have been so worried. I thought you might have–' She stopped suddenly, realising that her display of emotion was not, perhaps, seemly, gulped and regained her composure. 'Sorry,' she said, looking up at Simon and taking in his tired, worn face, burned by the sun to a dark mahogany colour. 'Sorry, it's just that I am so glad and relieved to see you ... both.' She turned to Jenkins, almost as an afterthought.

Startled, surprised and yet, despite his reserve, delighted by her welcome, Simon slipped from his horse, went to embrace her, thought better of it and seized her hand to bring it to his lips. She flung it aside and put her arms around his neck, and hung there for a moment before, blushing now, she stepped away.

'Alice,' gulped Simon. 'I am ... er ... very glad to see you. How have you been?'

'Oh, *I* have been fine. But what about you, and where...? Did you find Nandi?'

Jenkins leaned down from his saddle. 'Yes we did, miss,' he said, his face set hard, 'but we lost 'er again, so to speak, like.'

Very quickly, Simon recounted the story of Currey Street, the farm and the attack in the donga, and also what Wolseley had told them about John Dunn.

Alice frowned as the enormity of it sank in. 'I know about Dunn, but not the rest. Where do you think she is now?'

'I should say that Mendoza is keeping her in Sekukuni's township for the moment. It would be difficult to smuggle her out now, anyway. And we intend to go there and get her out.'

'What?' Alice's face lit up with incredulity. 'You

can't do that! No white man can get in there and out again. It would be difficult enough, from what I hear, in normal times, but not now, when Wolseley is preparing to attack the place. You will be killed as soon as you enter that valley.'

Simon smiled. 'Yes, well, we have to go there anyway. I promised Sir Garnet that we would go and scout the territory for him, to help him make his plans for the attack. Once there, I think we can find some way of getting in.'

'Rubbish! Look, my dear, I ... I ... don't want you to do this. Do you understand? You must not risk your life in this way. I could not stand it if you were...' She gulped and took a deep breath. 'Look, it would be suicide. There must be another way.'

'Well, if there is, I can't think of one.' Simon fought hard to maintain his composure. Her concern had caused his heart to soar. Had she, could she have ... changed her mind about him? His eyes dropped to her left hand. Of course not. She was engaged to this other man. He coughed. 'Alice, you must excuse us for we have to report to the General. Perhaps we can meet later?'

Alice breathed deeply. 'Yes, of course. I am sorry. By all means.'

Both men touched their hats to her, and Simon mounted and they moved away. Alice stood in the middle of the track, amidst the bustle of an army preparing for war, looking after them with tears in her eyes.

The two men rode in silence for a while. 'Well,' said Jenkins eventually, 'I will only say two things, bach sir. One, she loves you, and two, she's talkin' sense about goin' into this place on our own.'

'Don't be ridiculous. Look, here's the HQ. Now,' his face was stern, 'don't say a damned thing to the General about rescuing Nandi. We are just going there to scout the territory and report back. Right?'

'Oh, very good, sir.'

Wolseley saw them immediately and gave them his full attention. At the end of their story he said, 'Right. Well, if the girl is in Sekukuni's town we will get her out right enough when we go in, don't worry about that. Now, when can you go up the valley and take a look at the lie of the land for me? I am now urgently in need of information because I want to attack soon.'

'Crack of dawn tomorrow, sir.'

'Good. Now listen. We don't have maps that are really any good for my purposes – taking in exactly where the township is and where this damned stronghold of his is. I understand that he has created a trench system in quite a sophisticated way. You may not be able to get close enough to see this...' Simon and Jenkins exchanged glances, 'but find out what you can and the best way in. Look here.' He spread out the map. 'Ideally, I would want to make a frontal attack from the west, here, coming up the valley by the river. It's the easiest way to go. But it looks a bit too easy. Have a good look at it and report on the options.'

Wolseley looked up at them sharply. 'Now I

know you know the veldt country well enough, but the ground rises quite a bit between here and the township, and from what I hear, the valley is a sort of flat desert with these mountains rising either side. Better, then, to keep to the hills. I have two good Ndebele trackers to give you who know the territory – and the bePedis – well. The Pedis are their traditional enemies and they hate them. They speak reasonable English and I will give them enough money to set themselves up for life to go in with you. What they don't have, of course, is an appreciation of an army's needs. But they are brave and should be loyal enough.'

The little man eased the collar of his tunic. 'I shall have enough men here to move up within about ten days or so. I would like you back in five. Think you can do it?'

'I should think so, sir.'

'Good. Pick up your trackers here first thing. Oh, and get yourselves two fresh horses, and provisions and plenty of ammunition from the QM.' He scribbled. 'Here's a note. Still got your Martini-Henrys?'

Simon nodded.

'Very well. Start as soon as you can. I will not be here in the morning – have to go back to Lydenburg for a day.' He looked up sharply. 'No heroics about the girl when you're there. Just observe and leave.' He held out his hand. 'Good luck to you both, and may God go with you.'

It was still dark when the two men collected their Ndebele guides, Ophrus and Ntanga. They were both good-looking tribesmen from their homeland at Erholweni, bordering the bePedi territory to the south-west; each standing six foot tall, wrapped in shawls against the cold of the dawn, and leading serviceable ponies. They had been issued with Snider rifles, which they carried with pride, and they greeted Simon and Jenkins with wide smiles, flashing white in the semi-darkness. They all shook hands, mounted and set off.

A few yards from Wolseley's headquarters a tall figure loomed up and a familiar voice cut through the darkness. 'Well now, Fonthill, I hear you have once again failed in whatever so-called mission you have just been undertaking. You remain predictable, I must say.'

Simon's heart sank as his eyes adjusted to the gloom and he recognised his old adversary. Although the hour was early, Covington was impeccably dressed in field blues, with boots and Sam Browne belt polished so that they reflected the light from nearby lanterns as he stepped forward. Ignoring Jenkins, he regarded Simon with a faint smile.

Simon drew in a breath and restrained himself. 'Thank you for your good wishes,' he returned, in a voice as cold as the morning. 'Now kindly stand aside, for we have work to do.'

Covington gave an ironic half-bow and made way for them. As the horsemen moved away he called after them. 'I gather that you left the half-caste girl out on the veldt while you scuttled back to get help from the General. Some things never change. Well, if you run away from *this* job, I shall be waiting for you, mark my–' His last words were lost as they pulled away.

They rode on in silence and then Jenkins said, 'Nice of 'im to get up early to see us off, isn't it? And to wish us well like that.'

Simon smiled, but inwardly he was seething at Covington's taunts. Where had he suddenly appeared from? Afghanistan? And how did he know about Nandi? Could Alice have told him? No, surely not. It could have been Wolseley, of course, the doctor or even the sergeant. Probably the whole damned column knew about it now. Although he desired to see Alice more than ever, he was glad he had not kept his half-promise to visit her the previous evening. She was, after all, engaged to be married to the man he disliked most in the whole world. The man who was now here, in Africa, by her side. And there was nothing, nothing at all he could do about it. They rode on in silence.

Two days later, the four men hunched among the scrub and low mogwagwatha cactus trees of the Lulu hills and looked down at the sandy floor of the flat-bottomed valley that housed King Seku-kuni's capital. The journey had been difficult because, as Wolseley had predicted, the valley leading to the township was quite level and open, providing no cover for their approach. They had therefore been forced to climb the hills and go via the wooded slopes by a circuitous route, sleeping under thorn bushes, not daring to light a fire and supplementing their rations by plucking figs from the mogo trees that, luckily, were plentiful. Now, after leaving their horses tethered on the reverse

290

slope of the mountain, they had found a vantage point from which to study Thaba Mosega, the native name for the bePedi capital.

Below them, huts were spread along the barren floor of the valley and up towards them on the steep hillside. Stone walls ringed the edges of the town. Countless numbers of men and women were going about their business, many carrying rifles. They were obviously expecting to be attacked. Ophrus nudged Simon and pointed down to a small stony kopje directly below them.

'Baas,' he said. 'That Mosega mountain. Storage place for the town. It full of holes, caves and tunnels, and when people attack, the bePedis drive their cattle in there. Very safe.'

'Good lord,' said Simon, focusing his glasses. It seemed a perfectly ordinary kopje, barren and rocky, with no obvious entries to caves and certainly no paths for cattle to climb. He felt a nudge from Ophrus, who was now pointing to the east, where, about half a mile away, a sharply pointed and higher kopje rose like an ant hill from the flat desert floor of the valley, right in the middle of the town.

'That is Ntswaneng, what white people call the Fighting Kopje. The bePedi people very clever. They have lot of holes in that mountain, too, and they built stone walls and trenches all up the sides. They stay in there and fire on people who attack. No one gets them out from there, baas.'

Simon studied the kopje with interest. It was about 350 feet high at its sharply pointed tip, and it seemed to rise steeply from the valley floor on all sides, so that any force attacking would not

291

only have little cover in approach but would have to climb at an acute angle and haul itself up among rough scree and boulders. Entrenched defenders up above would be able to fire directly down on the climbers. It seemed an unassailable position. Had Wolseley, cocky, confident Wolseley, bitten off more than he could chew here?

Ophrus nudged him again. 'And bees too, baas.'

'Bees, for God's sake!'

The black man nodded, his grin revealing teeth like ivory tombstones. 'Yes, bees. They all up that little mountain. When people attack, the bePedis tip up the hives and push them down the mountain. Bees swarm and sting. Very painful.'

'Bloody 'ell,' breathed Jenkins. 'I don't call that fightin' fair. I don't at all.'

'Neither do I.' Simon turned his binoculars to study the lower slopes of the hills on the other side of the valley. He pursed his lips. 'It looks as though they have made emplacements of sorts on that side of the valley, too,' he murmured, focusing the lens. 'Yes, stone walls and, probably, trenches too. They know what they're doing. Anybody advancing up this valley would be subjected to a cross-fire from both sides. Damned lucky they don't have cannon.'

Jenkins sniffed. 'Yes, but with respect, bach sir, what about Nandi?'

'No. I haven't forgotten.' He turned to Ophrus. 'Does the chief have a royal residence, the biggest hut, or something like that?'

'Yes, baas. That one.' He pointed to a larger hut that nestled in the V where two slopes of the hills met the sandy floor, almost directly beneath them.

Simon focused. 'I doubt if she would be in there. But she could be in either of those two.' He indicated two other large huts that flanked the King's. 'They look as though they might be what you would call "grace and favour" residences – you know, for distinguished visitors like Mendoza. But first, we have to see if the Portuguese are there.' He put down the glasses. 'You three go and get some rest. I will watch for a while to see if any white men appear.'

The two Ndebeles turned away to where their sleeping mats lay. 'I'll stay with you,' said Jenkins.

Their watch was rewarded within an hour. Through the glasses Simon saw a tall man wearing a slouch hat and European clothes emerge from the smaller of the three huts. He was followed by two others, similarly dressed. 'It's Mendoza, I'm sure,' said Simon. 'Here, see what you think.'

Jenkins nodded slowly. He passed the binoculars back and his eyes were cold. 'And them other two, see, were back at the farm. Let's just slip down an' shoot the buggers while we've got the chance, eh?'

'And what happens to Nandi then? No, we've got to do better than that.' Simon's mind raced. The first need was to establish that Nandi was indeed alive. He could not share his apprehensions with Jenkins, but it could well be that she was now dead. Although her fever was undoubtedly better when he and Jenkins had left the donga, she was still very weak. The circumstances of her capture and de Witt's death could well have brought back her high temperature and the threat of pneumonia. Even if she had recovered, her captors might have given up the idea that Dunn would return and simply cut their losses and killed her to rid themselves of a burden. If they could establish that the girl was alive, and where they were keeping her, then perhaps...

'I think I have an idea.' He handed Jenkins the binoculars. 'Stay here and keep focused on those three huts. Let me know who comes in and out. I'll be back in five minutes.'

He crawled back to where they had tethered the horses – it was not riding country, and they had had to lead their mounts for the last mile or so up the other side of the mountain. From his saddle pack he took a sheet of notepaper and a pencil and scribbled a message. Then he covertly took out the little parcel of diamonds, selected the smallest one, and placed it with the notepaper in an envelope. He addressed the envelope simply 'Mendoza' and scrambled back to where the two trackers were sleeping. Waking Ophrus, he whispered to him intensely. Wide-eyed, the black man listened, frowning, but in the end nodded his head, took the envelope and thrust it into his loincloth. Then he lay back and within thirty seconds was asleep again.

Simon crawled back to where Jenkins was lying, observing the township. 'Anything?' he asked.

'A bit of movement, like. The big bastard 'as gone back into the first 'ut an' the other two walked across to the other place, not the King's palace, whatever, the 'ut there on the right, see?'

294

He pointed.

Simon nodded. 'So far, so good,' he mused. 'There are three of the Portuguese that we have seen, but there could be others inside.'

Jenkins turned anxious eyes on him. 'There's no sign of Nandi, though. D'you think she's down there?'

'Yes, I do. It stands to reason that they wouldn't let her just walk about the place. But we should know soon.' He explained his plan to Jenkins. Just before dawn, the two Ndebeles would slip down to Sekukuni and wait their opportunity in the half-light to capture a woman from a hut on the edge of the town – Ophrus had confirmed that they were usually up and about before the men. The woman would be told to take the envelope to Mendoza and warned that she would be watched from the mountainside and shot from there if she did not do so. The diamond would give proof to the Portuguese that the stones were available as barter for Nandi. But first he had to bring the girl out and show that she was alive and well. Then he would receive further instructions about how the exchange would take place.

'Blimey!' said Jenkins. 'But won't they just all come chargin' up 'ere and track us down?'

'They might,' nodded Simon. 'If they do, then at least we shall have plenty of time to withdraw with our horses and escape, or even cut round the side of this hill while they are up here looking for us, and charge in on horseback down the valley, go straight to Sekukuni's hut, put a gun to his head and exchange him for Nandi.' He smiled at the expression on Jenkins's face. 'Look, I know

295

it's a gamble, but this is the only way to see if Nandi is still alive, and, secondly, find out where they are keeping her. We can't just wander about down there, peering into every hut.'

Jenkins still showed disbelief. 'So bloody Mendoozi brings Nandi out. Then what?'

'I have told him to bring her to the centre of the valley, facing the other side – those hills there – at noon. I hope that he might believe that we are, in fact, hiding over there. We watch, then, where he takes her back.'

'But we'd be daft to go down there and trust 'im to 'and 'er over. They could kill us and take the diamonds anyway.'

'I have explained in the note that Sir Garnet Wolseley is poised just outside the valley to begin his attack, and that if we don't come back he will put a death sentence on Mendoza's head. But if we do come back with Nandi, then he will be spared and given free passage to Mozambique with his gang.'

Jenkins slowly nodded his head. 'Ingenious, bach sir. But does old Sir Garbage know about this?'

Simon gave a mirthless smile. 'Of course not. And we're not going down there to hand over the diamonds anyway. Once we see where they take Nandi back, we will wait until nightfall, then slip down this hill, go to the hut and take her out. It looks as though the bush goes quite near the edge of those three huts.' He frowned. 'But it's not going to be easy, because we can't use our rifles unless we are rumbled. We know that the bePedi have their scouts out up the valley, because we saw them on the way in. That is probably true of the other approach routes as well. Yet they don't seem to have guards around the town – manning those walled defences. They will know that they will have plenty of warning of the advance of a heavy British column, with its artillery, marching troops and such like. They will have time to get to their trenches and up that kopje, so that's why they're not guarding the town itself. They won't be worrying about a night raid from up here, so I doubt if we will meet anyone just before dawn.' He shrugged. 'Anyway, it's our only hope. We can't afford to wait and try and get Nandi out under cover of Wolseley's attack on the town. Once they see the redcoats they would probably cut her throat. Sorry, but that's how I see it.'

Jenkins sank his head on to his chest. Then, quietly, he asked, 'And if they don't take Nandi out, what do we do then?'

'Back to that damned farm. But my guess is that she's here and that Mendoza will be curious to know if we really will come down into the valley and trade. Don't forget, he wants those diamonds – and I've told him that we've got the cache that Dunn stole, too. His thumbs will itch at the thought of those stones.'

'I see that. But if we 'ave to go to the farm, we won't be back with the General in time for 'is advance. You could be court-martialled again – an' me too, this time.'

Simon's eyes narrowed. 'Can't do that – we are not soldiers now. But to hell with the army anyway. We came here to get Nandi. If we can do so *and* help Wolseley as well, then fine. But whatever happens, Nandi comes first.'

For the first time since Nandi's capture from the donga, Jenkins's face broke into one of his great grins. 'Well spoken, bach sir. To the slaughter'ouse, then, eh?'

'To the slaughterhouse.'

They spent the rest of a desultory day keeping watch on the township. The bePedis seemed remarkably sanguine about the danger of attack. Although the tiny figures seen down below sauntering between the huts and out into the valley often carried rifles, there was no sign of patrols combing the hills flanking the valley. The life of the bePedi capital seemed to continue as normal, with women cooking on open fires and, further away, washing garments in a little stream that threaded its way across the desert floor from the Steelport on the far side of the valley. If riflemen were manning the ramparts on the far hillside, they gave no evidence of their presence.

The four observers, now cramped and uncomfortable in their hiding place among the low trees, curled up early in their blankets as the temperature dropped sharply at dusk. They rose well before dawn. Simon crouched down by the two Ndebeles to repeat his instructions. They smelt of oil and stale perspiration but their senses were alert and their eyes were sharp in the darkness. 'Take the woman from the eastern edge of the village, away from us.' He pointed. 'Take her into the trees,' he said, 'and make sure she makes no sound. But don't hurt her. Tell her that the white soldiers are all around watching her and that she will be shot if she does not go directly to the big Portuguese and give him the letter. Now go. Good luck, boys.'

Simon and Jenkins breakfasted meagrely on biltong, hard biscuits and figs and returned to their observation post as dawn sent exploratory fingerposts of sunlight down the valley. They watched, with growing anxiety, as the township came to life, and waited, their hearts in their mouths, for a shout, a shot, from the eastern end of the huts that would show that the plan had failed. But all seemed quiet and normal. Then Jenkins, who was watching through the field glasses, stiffened. ''Ere,' he said. 'She's come. It must be.'

He handed the binoculars to Simon, who focused on a small female figure, running through the huts, her head turning up to search the hillside as she went. She made her way to the second largest hut, that from which Mendoza had emerged, and disappeared inside.

'Good,' muttered Simon. 'So far, so good.'

After three minutes or so, the unmistakable figure of the big Portuguese emerged. Simon concentrated hard on him, through the lenses. Mendoza walked out tucking his shirt into his trousers, hatless and his long hair dishevelled, but Simon's notepaper in his hand. His pock-marked face came into clear focus as Simon rotated the lens wheel, and he was scowling as he scanned the hills on the far side of the valley and then turned to look immediately above him to where the two men lay. Instinctively, Simon and Jenkins ducked their heads but, hidden as they were in the foliage, it would have been impossible to detect them from so far away.

'I think I could pot 'im at this distance,' murmured Jenkins. 'It might save us a lot of time and trouble.'

'No,' said Simon. 'Good as you are, you might miss and that would reveal our position. No. Let the plan run. The vital thing is to see if he has Nandi. We will just have to wait until noon, unless he tries to move her before then. But, then, where would he take her?'

The Ndebeles returned, happy at the success of their mission and bringing news that gave huge relief to Simon and Jenkins. The woman had been taken easily and she had confirmed that there were four Portuguese Mozambiques living in the town, and that, indeed, they had a young woman with them, a woman who was kept in their hut and not allowed to leave. Noon brought further confirmation. Mendoza's door was opened and the big Portuguese emerged, holding by the arm a slim, girlish figure. Simon focused on her quickly and the sad face of Nandi sprang into view, so clear from the magnification that he felt he could put a hand out to touch her. Even at that distance, it was clear that her face was sunken. She was shrouded in the blanket that Jenkins had given her at the donga and, as before, her feet were bare.

'Yes, that's 'er all right.' Jenkins's voice was hoarse. 'Let me see.' Simon handed him the binoculars. The Welshman's sigh was a mixture of relief and anger. 'Thank God for that,' he murmured. 'Poor little thing. She's not well, look you. You can see.' He lowered the glasses. 'That man will pay for what he's done, see if he won't.'

The girl was taken to the centre of the valley by Mendoza, turned to face the far hillside, as instructed, and then brought back to the hut and thrust inside.

'It looks as though it's worked,' said Simon. 'Now we'll let him stew for a while, waiting for our next message.'

That afternoon, while Jenkins kept watch with the binoculars, Simon, Ophrus and Ntanga cautiously reconnoitred a route down the steep hillside to where the town began. It did so, in fact, way above the valley floor and Simon realised that to reach their destination they would have to pick their way through, firstly, a surprisingly elaborate defensive network of trenches and stone walls erected in rows along the hill about two hundred feet from the bottom, and then more than a score of wooden shacks which straggled down the hillside. The trenches and walls were not manned although there were plenty of tribesmen and women in evidence among the huts. As a result, the three could descend no further in daylight and the crouching Simon concentrated on the hut in which Nandi was imprisoned. Its door was made of wood and, although it had no obvious padlock, it looked quite substantial. It was roofed in what appeared to be reed and it huddled up to the hillside against a large rock. Thoughtfully, Simon led the retreat back to where Jenkins was waiting.

Darkness was falling as Simon told the others

301

of his plan. 'We wait until the hour before dawn,' he said, 'when, hopefully, the town will be in its deepest sleep. As I have said, the bePedi know that they cannot be taken by surprise by a large force, so they will not have guards posted on the periphery of the town.'

'Where's that?' Jenkins gave Simon his most impatient frown.

'The edge, dammit. Now, if we wake anyone we are as good as dead, so we must creep silently through those shacks at the bottom there. We must all wear blankets, so that, if we are seen, at a quick glance we will look like bePedis – no boots for us, 352, I fear. We cannot make a frontal attack on the hut, so we will go in through the roof, from that big rock which is roughly level with the top of the hut. Ophrus tells me that it should be possible to cut through the reeds quietly with a couple of sharp knives, so he and Ntanga will do that. Then we will all drop through – it's only about eight feet or so. Now comes the hard part.' He smiled. 'We must leave our rifles on the rock because they will hinder us on the roof. So it will be knives for Ophrus and Ntanga and bayonets for us two, 352, once we are inside the hut.'

Jenkins's teeth flashed in the dark. 'Then we kill the buggers inside, yes?'

'Yes.' Simon made an effort to keep his voice level and unemotional. 'This is a huge risk because we don't know how many people will be sleeping inside, we will not be sure if they *are* sleeping, of course, and we can't afford to make a loud noise. I have looked carefully and, thank God, I have seen no dogs in this corner of the

302

town. So ... 352, you will drop in first and take out immediately the guard, if they have one, and if they haven't, go for the man nearest the door. I will follow and single out Nandi–'

'Can't I do that?' asked Jenkins.

'No. You're a better ... killer than I. You two boys drop in quickly and stab the others. I will help as soon as I have found Nandi and pushed her out of the way. Look, this is going to be very difficult. Our success depends upon silence, speed and ferocity. We must kill these men as they sleep, if possible.' He shook his head as if in disbelief. 'I know it sounds terrible, but we have no choice. Once a hole is cut in the roof, you, Ophrus, should be able to look inside and tell us by signs how many men are there and roughly where they are sleeping. Is this understood?'

The two black men nodded, no smiles now on their faces, for the danger inherent in the attack was obvious. 'How do we get away, once we've done the business?' asked Jenkins.

'Ideally, the way we came, back up on to the rock, through the bush and over the top to our horses – which, by the way, we will tether a little higher up the hillside. If we are discovered, there are about seven bePedi ponies tied past the huts on the left, facing the valley. We must get our rifles and fight our way through to them and escape that way.'

Jenkins gave a grim smile. 'I know what you're going to say,' sighed Simon before the Welshman could speak. 'They won't be bridled or saddled. Well, you will just have to tie me on.' Everyone grinned.

'Right. Any questions?' Three heads shook in unison. 'We must get some rest now. You, 352, will take the first watch. I will do the last one, until three hours before dawn. I estimate that it will take us about an hour to find our way *quietly* down the hillside, which leaves us two hours to carry out our work and be back up here well before daylight. Sleep now.'

But sleep did not come easily for Simon. He lay under his blanket, his eyes closed but his brain racing. Success for his plan, he realised only too well, demanded outrageous luck. Everything must fall into place perfectly, like the easiest of jigsaw puzzles. They must not be heard on their approach past the stone walls, the trenches and the shacks; they must cut through those reeds so quietly that no one sleeping below would be disturbed; they must drop eight feet or so without injury, and then kill silently and ruthlessly – all without disturbing man or dog, and who had heard of an African village without a regiment of dogs keeping watch through the night? Then they must make good their escape, avoiding the bePedi patrols that would be guarding the approaches to the valley. Simon's thoughts turned to the killing and he felt a small rivulet of cold perspiration creep down his face. He *had* killed with cold steel: with the bayonet at Isandlwana and Rorke's Drift and yet again in Afghanistan, and he trembled at the memory and brutality of it all. But that was in the heat of battle. Here, this would have to be brutal assassination, cold-blooded killings of men emerging from sleep and desperately struggling to their feet. Could he do it? He frowned and

304

thought of Nandi, innocent, childlike Nandi being brutalised. Oh yes, he could do it all right! Eventually, he drifted off to sleep.

He woke the others at the end of his watch and without a word they checked their rifles, knives and bayonets, pulled their rough homespun blankets tightly around them – as much for protection from the cold at this altitude as for disguise – and, with Ophrus at their head, made their way in single file down the hillside. Some two hundred feet down, they stopped and Simon and Jenkins removed their boots. The moon was shrouded with sullen cloud, visibility was poor and Simon blessed the sure-footed presence of the two trackers, who seemed to pick their way through the shrub and scree with the nimbleness of mountain goats. The problem, however, lay with the scree, for it seemed impossible, in the stillness of the night, to place one foot in front of the other without causing a small cascade of stones. To Simon's sensitive ears, the four sounded like a battalion on the march. The worry about noise was compounded by the pain from the sharp stones which made the two white men, in their socks, hop and silently curse, as though they were walking on pin cushions.

And then the luck that the audacity of the plan demanded came along – it began to rain. At first the fall was soft and gentle, but then thunder rumbled and the rain fell more steadily and heavily. The noise became a hiss as the heavy drops bounced off the rocks, and their footing was further hindered as the narrow track they were following became a rivulet. The blankets wrapped around the four men became sodden and heavy. But Simon, his hair plastered to his head and streams of rain coursing down his cheeks, exchanged a grin with Jenkins in the semi-darkness. Their discomfort did not matter. The storm relieved them of the need for silence, and down below, dogs began to howl their distress to the moon.

They picked their way through the network of stone walls and rough trenches and then, heads down, rifles concealed beneath their sodden blankets, trod even more warily between the shacks. No one challenged their progress and it seemed as though the whole of the population of Sekukuni was huddled indoors, sleeping through the downpour. At the flat rock, the four men laid down their rifles and covered them with their blankets. Simon gestured to the others to lie prone and he crawled to the edge to look out over the rooftops of the town. No one was stirring and even the dogs, it seemed, had given up their protests. The rain was drumming a muted tattoo on the reed roof immediately below him, so noise should not be a problem, unless the downpour was keeping the occupants of the hut awake. But would the seemingly fragile roof take Ophrus's weight? He beckoned the Ndebele forward.

'Be careful,' he hissed. 'Spread your weight out and cut quietly and quickly.'

The big man put his long knife between his teeth and lowered himself on to the edge of the reeds, where they met the wooden wall of the hut. Then, with infinite care, he knelt down, gradually transferred his weight on to his hands and then lowered his stomach to the reeds so that he was spread-eagled across the roof. The reeds sagged a little but did not collapse. Ophrus edged his way forward until he was within arm's reach of the ridgepole and began cutting, carefully removing each handful of reed and distributing it around him. Eventually he had made an opening about three feet square. He lowered his head inside and kept it there until his eyes were accustomed to the gloom within. Then he pulled out and began crawling back to the rock, clambering up to sit beside Simon, his body glistening in the rain. The others gathered round.

'How many?' asked Simon.

'Four, baas, including the lady.'

'Where are they sleeping?'

'Lady is here, by the rock. The others are like this.' And he pointed to the three corners of the hut.

'Right. In you go, 352. Make sure the reeds can take your weight. As soon as you go down, we will follow quickly.' He held out his hand to the Welshman, his face anxious against the wind and the rain. 'Good luck, old chap.'

The two men shook hands and then Jenkins edged his way out along to the opening. His bayonet between his teeth, he wriggled his feet into the opening and disappeared. Simon followed him, crawling along the reeds on hands and knees without caution, until he too thrust his feet down and, not stopping to look, launched himself down into the blackness below.

He fell with a soft thud on to a floor of beaten

earth. Aware that Ophrus would be following him, he immediately rolled away, gained his feet and transferred bayonet from mouth to hand. It was dark but strangely quiet. Then he became conscious that figures were rising from the corners of the hut. Looking above him to the square of lighter darkness in the roof to orientate himself, he fumbled his way to where, he hoped, Nandi was lying. His hand touched something soft beneath a rough blanket.

'Nandi?' he whispered.

'What? What?' The voice was weak but unmistakable. 'Simon, is it you?'

'Yes. Pull yourself to the wall of the hut and lie still.'

He heard a grunt and the sound of a scuffle from the other side of the hut, and then a sigh. As he swung round, a dark figure cried out and launched itself at him in the half-light. Simon jabbed out his left hand, his arm held stiff, and caught his crouching assailant on the top of the head. But the charge was only deflected and the man's head crashed into Simon's midriff, winding him and sending them both sprawling so that they slammed into a low bed from which a third man was rising. He was knocked over in the mêlée and the three men began a desperate tussle on the floor of the hut, Simon trying to find room to free his bayonet, the other two impeding each other in their attempts to rise and face whatever had materialised to attack them in the darkness of the hut – all as the thunder crashed and rolled above them.

Then Ophrus's knife flashed and the third man

groaned and fell, but Simon was unaware of this because his original assailant had now clasped both hands around his throat and was pressing hard. Blackness was descending and a loud pounding developed in his ears, but the Mozambiquan's double-handed attack enabled Simon to free his bayonet at last and thrust it into the man's side, feebly but effectively, for the pressure on his throat relaxed immediately. Once again Ophrus's knife swept down and Simon was dimly aware that hot blood was pouring over his face as he lost consciousness.

He must have come to almost immediately, for he was dimly aware of Jenkins's voice hissing, 'No more. We've got all of the bastards.' Then the familiar face appeared above him, the eyes full of concern above the bedraggled moustache. 'God, the blood!' said Jenkins. 'Where've you been 'urt, then, bach?'

Simon struggled to speak but no sound came from his aching throat. He shook his head, blinking hard to see through the blood, and was eventually able to croak, 'I'm all right. It's his blood. Half throttled. Help me up.'

The Welshman spat on his handkerchief and was about to wipe Simon's face when he was thrust aside by Nandi, who knelt down and, with the edge of her shift, began to clean away the blood with infinite tenderness. 'Thank you,' gasped Simon. 'Must get up.' Together the two helped him to stand and, still sucking in air, Simon looked around the interior of the hut.

The three Portuguese lay dead on the beaten earth, one bayoneted by Jenkins and the other two killed by Ophrus's knife. The fight – no, the massacre – had taken no more than forty-five seconds. All was suddenly still and quiet in the hut, except for the gasps of the raiding party. The surprise had been complete. Ntanga, who had dropped into the hut last of all, had not been needed in the affray.

Simon put a hand to his bruised throat and swallowed with difficulty. He nodded to Jenkins. 'Help Nandi get her things together,' he croaked. 'I'll look outside. Stay quiet.'

The last injunction was hardly necessary, for as Simon eased the door of the hut open, the rain was still falling with a hiss and the black sky was booming with thunder. A flash of lightning lit up the surroundings for a second, but no one stirred among the shacks. Amazingly, Sekukuni remained comatose under the deluge. Gratefully Simon held up his face for a moment and allowed the rain to wash away the blood, his face smarting under the sharp pinpricks.

Re-entering the hut, he saw Jenkins wrapping a blanket around Nandi, who was clutching a pathetically small bundle of possessions. The two Ndebeles were searching through the clothing of the hut's other occupants.

'Enough of that,' said Simon. 'We must leave. Push this table underneath the hole. We will go back the way we came in. 352?'

'Yes, bach sir.'

'Is Nandi able to stand?'

'Yes, Simon.' The girl's voice was little more than a whisper. 'But they bound my legs and I don't walk very well.'

310

'Don't worry, lass,' said Jenkins. 'I'll carry you. Now, love,' he said. 'Lean on me. Offy, you get up on to that straw stuff on the roof and I'll hand the lass up to you. Be careful now.' He turned back to Nandi. 'Put this other blanket around you, see, because it's a wee bit wet outside and we don't want you catchin' your death o' cold out there, now do we?'

Nandi's smile was weak, but strong enough to light up that corner of the hut, now that everyone's eyes were accustomed to the darkness.

Ophrus climbed on to the table and then, with a spring and a kick of his legs, he had wriggled through the hole back on to the roof. He stretched his arms down and seized Nandi round the waist as Jenkins lifted her up from the table. In a second she was outside, on the roof.

'Take her under cover,' hissed Simon to Ophrus. Then, to Ntanga, 'You next.'

As the second tracker disappeared through the roof, Simon felt Jenkins's hand gripping his arm. 'There's only one problem,' said the Welshman.

'What's that?'

'Mendoozi's not 'ere.'

'I know. He is sleeping in the other hut, obviously. Well, never mind.'

Jenkins climbed up on to the table and bent down, making a cradle of his hands. 'Come on, then, I can toss you up there, just like mountin' a bloomin' 'orse. Always the perfect groom, see. You go on, bach sir, and look after the lass. I'll come on after you. I'll only be a minnit, look you.'

Simon drew in a sharp breath. 'Oh no you don't, 352. If you go in that other hut after him,

311

you will be pushing our luck just too far. You could bring the whole bePedi nation around our ears. No. Leave him. We must get away while we can.'

Jenkins shook his head, his moustache jutting out truculently. 'No. I'll be quiet and I'll be careful.'

'There's no question of it. That's an order.' Simon looked up. Ntanga was looking down through the hole in the roof, his hands hanging down. 'Get up there. I'm not asking you. I'm telling you.'

Slowly, and with a scowl, the Welshman raised his hands and was hauled up. Standing on the table, Simon took a last look around the hut, now a scene of carnage, with blood spreading into congealing pools beside the bodies of the three men. The place had a distinct and unpleasant smell about it of ... what? Death, evil, or just dampness? Shaking his head, Simon felt momentarily nauseous. He had killed in cold blood, brutally. Was he becoming a monster? He shook his head again, as though to fling off the thought, and looked up into the face of a glowering Jenkins. Then he allowed himself to be pulled up.

Regaining their blankets and their rifles, they began the long climb back through huts and trenches and walls, their journey this time made the more arduous because it was upwards and the rain had added mud to the hazards of slippery stones and clinging thorn bushes. But they regained their boots and, half carrying Nandi, crossed the summit, reaching the little clearing where their horses were tethered just as the rain stopped and dawn began to lighten the eastward sky. There they all mounted.

Simon consulted his compass and then shot a worried look at Nandi. The girl sat behind Jenkins, her arms around his waist and her head lying on his broad back. She looked frail, soaked and exhausted, but there was a faint smile on her face. 'Are you all right, Nandi?' he called.

She kept her cheek pressed against Jenkins's back and whispered, 'Oh yes, Simon. Oh yes. Now that I am back with you two, I know that I am all right. But please, don't leave me again.'

Jenkins snorted. 'No question of that. No question at all.'

They rode for four days, taking a circuitous route. Nandi hardly spoke during the journey, half sleeping as she rode behind either Jenkins or Simon, for she could not sit on a horse on her own. They did not discuss her captivity but Simon did explain that her father was alive and told her a little of Dunn's efforts to rescue her. At this, her eyes lit up and then filled with tears. She smiled and shook her head, as though she could not believe that her bad luck had turned and her misery was over. She was clearly exhausted, mentally and physically, and Simon decided that they would not intrude further on her recovery.

Two miles from Fort Weeber they met a British patrol. Inevitably, it was commanded by Colonel Ralph Covington, late of the 21st Regiment of Foot and now of the general staff, the last man that Simon wished to encounter.

The elegant horseman rode a little ahead of his

patrol towards the bedraggled party. 'Ah, it's you, Fonthill,' he called 'Thought you'd run away again. You're a day late reporting, dammit. Typical. What the hell...!' As Simon's horse half turned he had seen the slim figure of Nandi, now mounted behind him. The handsome face, already florid, turned a darker shade. 'Ah! Now I understand. You haven't been scouting for the General at all. You have been neglecting your duty to go off to find this damned half-breed. While we've bin waitin' here, kicking our heels to start the advance, you've been gallivanting about the bloody countryside, pursuing your own agenda, no doubt to gratify your damned cock.' He turned and shouted behind him. 'Sergeant, bring up a section and arrest these two men. Sharply now!'

'You're making a mistake, Covington,' said Simon. 'You're going to look a fool again. This girl needs treatment as soon–'

'Be quiet. Take their weapons, Sergeant.'

Six troopers surrounded Simon and Jenkins as the Ndebeles looked on, their frowns reflecting their puzzlement. The sergeant, his moustache almost as resplendent as Covington's, slipped Simon's Martini-Henry from its holster and his Colt from his belt and turned to do the same to Jenkins – only to find himself looking down the muzzle of the Welshman's rifle.

'Get your 'ands away from my 'orse, arsehole,' growled the Welshman. 'And don't go anywhere near that lady there, or I'll blow your belly open.'

Covington's voice rose loud and clear. 'If he has not lowered that rifle within five seconds, shoot

314

him,' he called. 'I will begin counting now. One, two...'

Simon reached across and gently pulled Jenkins's rifle from his hands, and handed it to the sergeant. 'Steady on, Sergeant,' he said. 'This man fought at Isandlwana.'

'I don't care where he fought.' The NCO's face was as red as Covington's. 'He called me an arsehole!'

'Yes,' said Simon, 'but there's no need to act like one, now, is there?'

'Surround them,' called Covington, 'and follow me to the fort.'

Simon could sense Nandi's distress behind him. 'Simon,' she whispered, 'are we all in trouble now? Don't let them hurt 352. It's all because of me, isn't it?'

'No, no,' he whispered back. 'This is just the army behaving badly. You remember you said you didn't like our army. Well, do you know, I find that I rather agree with you.'

As the sad little party trotted back towards the fort, the sky darkened and rain began to fall again.

Chapter 12

At the fort, Simon helped Nandi to dismount and said to Covington, 'Colonel, whatever you do to us, this lady needs urgent medical attention, food and a warm bed.'

Covington nodded curtly. 'I will see to that,' he said. Simon and Jenkins then kissed Nandi, shook hands with the two Ndebeles and were led away to the guardhouse – a larger than usual tent – where they joined three native levies, still reeking of cheap beer, and a happy Welsh private of the 24th, whom Simon vaguely recognised. The latter rose unsteadily to his feet, peered closely at the visitors, allowed his jaw to drop and promptly fell over.

Jenkins bent and hauled him to his feet. 'Now, Jones 389,' he said, brushing him down, 'don't go fallin' over in the presence of an officer. Get yer 'eels together and say good mornin' to Mr Fonthill 'ere, there's a good lad.'

The young man blinked and smiled. 'Good morning, sir. Beggin' your pardon, sir, never thought to see you in the brig, isn't it. Nor you, Jenkins 352. What's bin goin' on, then?'

'Sit down, Jones, there's a good fellow,' said Simon. 'How on earth did you manage to get drunk out in this desert?'

'Goodness, sir. It was these lads here.' He indicated the three levies, who were regarding events

316

with lacklustre eyes. 'They'd brought along a jug or three and I was just 'elpin' out with 'em, see.'

Jenkins's eyes lit up. 'Blimey. Beer? None left, is there?'

'Not in 'ere, mate. Sorry.'

Further conversation was interrupted by the entry of the moustached sergeant, who scowled at them all. 'General wants to see you two 'mediately,' he growled. 'Step out smartly now. Can't keep Sir Garnet waiting. Outside now.' His voice rose to a scream. 'I SAID NOW! Right. Now. Lef' right, lef' right, lef' right...'

'Fer Chrissakes, bach,' said Jenkins. 'You're shoutin' at Captain Fonthill, late of the 24th Regiment of Foot and of Her Majesty's Royal Corps o' Guides, and Sergeant Jenkins of the same. But we're not in the army now, see. So we'll just walk to the General, if it's all the same to you. Right?'

The veins in the sergeant's forehead suddenly became prominent and his face once again began to change colour, but Simon intervened. 'It's all right, Sergeant,' he said. 'No disrespect intended. Just show us where to go and we will get there smartly, I promise.'

'What? Oh, er, very well, er, sir. Straight ahead then an' turn left at the end. But I'm right behind you, now.'

Simon and Jenkins were ushered into the large tent which formed the General's headquarters. The little man, dressed in his field khaki, was sitting at a trestle table on which several maps were spread. Behind him stood an array of

317

officers, with Covington prominent among them. They looked up as the sergeant slammed to attention, gave a huge salute and shouted, 'Prisoners on parade, sir.'

'Thank you, Sergeant. That will be all. Wait outside.' Wolseley's voice was measured but cold. Two chairs were placed in front of his table but he uttered no invitation to use them. His good eye ran over the two men standing before him, their clothes still dusty from the journey, their trousers and shirts crumpled and creased from the heavy rain and their faces grimed and seamed.

'Well, Fonthill,' he said eventually. 'I think you had better explain yourself.'

'In what way, General?' asked Simon pleasantly.

Wolseley slammed his hand on the table and rose to his feet. 'Damn your impertinence, young man,' he shouted. 'Don't you play games with me. I sent you off on a mission, and from what I hear, you have gone off on a chase after a young woman.' Once again the scar under the General's blind eye stood out vividly. 'Now, sir. As I said: explain yourself.'

Simon felt Jenkins stiffen beside him. 'I was on my way here to report to you,' he responded, 'when that man there,' he gestured towards Covington, 'arrested me and Jenkins here. Now, sir.' He kept his voice level but cold. 'I am happy to report to you, but – and you must understand this – I will *not* be shouted at. Neither of us is in the army and I would have thought that rules of civilised conduct should apply, wouldn't you agree?'

There was a massed intake of breath from the officers behind Wolseley, and Simon heard Covington say, 'Damn you, Fonthill.' The General regarded Simon steadily. When he spoke, his voice was as level as Simon's and equally cold.

'You will not be impertinent towards me, Fonthill,' he said. 'I have martial law powers here, which means that I can throw you into jail without specific charge and leave you there to rot, if I wish. I would have no qualms in doing so.'

Simon sighed. 'I don't wish to be disrespectful, sir, not least because, back in Durban, you were most understanding of what I was trying to do and, indeed, you helped me. But I do resent very much indeed being arrested and thrown into the guardhouse and then treated as some sort of miscreant. Now, General, you can do what you wish here. I understand that. So arrest me – arrest us both – by all means, but I think it would be better if I was allowed to make my report to you, as I intended, without being shouted down. You have a battle to fight. I can help you. The choice is yours.'

A silence fell. Simon ran his eye along the faces of the officers arrayed behind Wolseley. Covington's, of course, was suffused with anger but his features also demonstrated a kind of satisfaction that the man he clearly hated so much had gone too far this time. His eyes gleamed and his chin was thrust forward. The others displayed only one emotion: shock that anyone should talk to this revered general, the most feared and respected senior officer in the British Army, in this adversarial manner. It was not *lèse-majesté*. It

319

was worse than that. It was suicide.

Eventually, Wolseley spoke. 'Tell me what you know, Fonthill.'

'Very well, sir. May I?' Simon gestured to the maps on the table.

The General nodded.

Simon pulled the maps towards him. He discarded all but one, the largest. 'Right, sir,' he said. 'You are now camped roughly here. Your best plan of attack would seem to be – as you yourself intimated before we set off – a straightforward march to the north-east, along the old Boer track here, up the valley of the Steelport up to here, where the valley opens out and where Sekukuni has his capital. But I suggest that you would have trouble taking this route with the whole of your force.'

'Why?'

'There is very little fodder for the animals because the veldt quickly transforms into virtual desert country. From what I can gather, it is also pony-sickness country, which could affect your transport, although I don't know what causes it. But the main point is that there is almost no water so you would have to carry everything with you, which would be expensive and cumbersome and would slow you down considerably.'

'Rubbish.' Covington's voice cut in. 'We should be following the line of the Steelport. For God's sake, man, there is plenty of water along the river route.'

'How do you know? Have you been along there?'

'No, not exactly ... well, not all the way. But it

320

stands to reason that we can use the river for our horses and the rains should replenish it if it is dry. There will be plenty of water.'

'You have not been there but we have.' Simon's voice remained unemotional but it had a cutting edge when addressing Covington. 'The river goes underground, just about here.' He prodded the map with his finger. 'And it comes out around here. I gather it is one of the longest stretches of underground watercourse in the whole of Africa. You can't get at water at all while the river goes underground like that. You would have to carry it with you.'

'Go on, Fonthill.' The General's voice now displayed interest and involvement.

'The other reason for not making a single attack along this route is that, as the valley narrows here and then broadens out to where the town is situated, the bePedis have dug trenches and erected stone walls along the sides of the valley and around the town itself. I don't think they have artillery but they do have rifles, and they could make it hot for anyone who launches his main attack along this way.'

'Hmm. Are there other ways of approach?'

'In essence, sir, you are going to have to make two assaults. One on the township itself here, Thaba Masega, tucked in a cleft in the sides of the valley and spreading out across the valley floor. When they discover you are coming – and with a column of this size, the bePedi scouts will know when you move so there will be no chance of a surprise attack – the townspeople will put their cattle, women and children into this hill

321

here, by the side of the mountain, which is honeycombed with passages.'

'What, it can take cattle, too?'

'Oh yes, sir. The Ndebeles know all about this. In they will go and the tribesmen will then man the rifle pits and entrenchments that have been built around the town and the hill. These will command the approaches along the ground here, and coming down from the hills here.'

'What's the other attack you say I will have to make, then?'

'On Ntswaneng, here, the famous "Fighting Kopje". It stands in the middle of the town and rises straight out of the flat bed of the valley, like a sort of pyramid. It's their Gibraltar, really. The story goes that no one, ever, has been able to dislodge the bePedi when they take refuge there. Higher up it is ringed by trenches and stone walls and deep caves. Oh, and I am told it has beehives which the bePedi tip over on to their attackers as they try and climb the kopje. Not much fun, really.'

The General put his hand to his chin. 'Hmm. Why can't I surround the damned place and stop them running to it when I attack the town?'

'Well, you could, sir, but my guess is that it will be separately manned and defended. They will know you are coming and man it before you arrive. From what I have seen, studying the town for a while, they will have enough tribesmen – and they all seem to have rifles – to defend both places.'

'Very well. So what's the best approach to this blasted place?'

Simon swept his finger round to the east side of the Lulu range. 'I would take your main column up here, sir, along the valley of the Oliphant River where there is fodder and water. We rode back that way to avoid pursuit.' He shot a quick glance at Covington. 'That's why we were a trifle late getting back to you, and I wanted to scout the territory there anyway. You could then swing round the northern tip of the Lulus here, in a loop, so to speak, come down this little valley and attack the town here. Another column should follow the route of the first, but stop off halfway along the range, about here, and go over the mountains to take the town, down the hillside, from its south-eastern side. A two-pronged attack, in fact.'

Simon looked up into the General's cold blue eye. Was he being too presumptuous? The silence in the tent was palpable. He had the complete attention of the officers behind Wolseley. Even Covington was scowling at the map in concentration. He decided to continue anyway.

'From what I have heard, sir, the bePedis have always been attacked up the valley along the Steelport from the south-west. The approach I am recommending should take them by surprise and set them back on their heels, so to speak.'

He swung the map around, the better for the General to see. 'You will probably need to establish another two forward bases or forts, in addition to this one, where you can concentrate both attacking forces. It is wild marching country, Sir Garnet, and too far to launch the attacks from here at Fort Weeber.' He jabbed the map again

323

with his finger. 'The first should be for your larger column here, round the end of the Lulus. There is a ford there. The second should be this side of the hills, where the Oliphant starts to curl away to the north-east. As the crow flies, it is not far from Sekukuni's town, but it is a tough climb up and a scramble down again.'

'What about this Fighting Kopje place?'

'I don't think you will be able to attack everything at once. I suggest that you leave the defenders of the kopje to stew in their own juice while you take the town. But you must stop them, of course, from directing heavy fire down at you. You could do that, I would think, by using artillery to make 'em keep their heads down. It's very, very rocky and shells exploding there would send stone splinters everywhere and probably cause more damage than the explosives themselves. Then, when you have taken the town, you could turn your full attention to the fortress.'

Simon straightened his back and, for the first time, addressed the listening officers as well as the General. He was aware that Jenkins, at his side, was standing at the formal 'at ease' position, hands stretched down behind his back to form a V, the fingers of his right hand in the palm of his left. But his chin was thrust forward and his moustache bristled, as though daring anyone to contradict his captain. Simon swallowed a half-smile and continued. 'I have to say, gentlemen, that this will be no walkover. I understand that the bePedis are very tough fighters and these defences are strong. The whole exercise could take two or even three days, I would say, and I do not think success is guaranteed. This is a formidable position.'

The crowded tent was silent again, except for the buzzing of insects. It was hot within and Simon could feel perspiration trickling down his chest. This was as far as he could go, he felt. It was not his job to tell the best general in the British Empire how to do his job. Then he remembered one more thing.

'I understand, sir, that you intend to use Swazis?'

'Yes. Got about eight thousand of them. They form the main part of the column. I couldn't attack without them.'

'I see.' Simon frowned. 'I do not wish to tell you what to do, sir...'

Wolseley's eyebrows rose. He gave a distinct 'Harumph! Can't think why, you've bin doing it for the last ten minutes. Go on, man. Go on.'

'Well. You will probably know that the Boers also relied on the Swazis when they made their big attack on Sekukuni. But they depended on them too much, holding off themselves and sending the Swazis in first. The Swazis, I understand, hated this, and as a result will probably not attack if you send them in first.'

Covington interceded again. 'Hearsay. How do you know?'

'The Ndebeles will tell you. They told me. They know the Swazis well.'

The General remained silent for a moment as he studied the maps. 'Interesting challenge.' Then he looked up. 'Now, Fonthill. I think you owe it to us,' his tone took on a note of irony, 'if we ask you nicely, that is, to tell us about this lady who sent you her *cri de coeur*. Where was she, and how did you get her out?'

Briefly Simon gave his story.

Once again silence descended on the stuffy tent. Then, slowly, the General spoke. 'You mean to tell me that you slid down this damned hillside, found your way through the heavily guarded town, cut through the roof of this hut, killed everyone inside but the girl, and rode away again?'

'That's it, more or less, sir.'

Suddenly Jenkins snapped to attention. 'Every word true, General bach. The Captain 'ere knew exactly what 'e was doin', see.'

Wolseley blinked, directed a quick glance over his shoulder at Covington and then slowly extended his hand across the table to Simon. 'I think, Fonthill,' he said, 'that we all owe you an apology. You certainly have my thanks for your report, which I will consider very carefully and discuss with my staff here. Now go and get some rest.' They shook hands. 'Oh, one more thing. I cannot order you to come with us when we attack, but I would be very grateful if you did so – both of you. You would be invaluable in leading us in.'

Before Simon could reply, Jenkins had spoken. 'Delighted to, General bach. We've got to go back there anyway, see. We've got a man to kill, look you.'

The General's eyebrows shot up. 'What? Good lord. Oh well, I see. Yes. Quite.' He turned to a young officer. 'Bulmer, go with them and make

326

sure they get a good tent and kit and so forth. Oh, Fonthill, you will find your young lady in the sick bay. She is being looked after, I understand.'

'Thank you, sir. I am grateful.'

The two men turned and followed the young captain out of the tent. Once outside, he turned to Simon, a warm smile curving his fair moustache. 'By jove,' he said. 'You took your life in your hands when you answered back to the General like that. Never heard anything like it in all me life. Deuced brave thing to do. Mind you, he took it well, didn't he?'

Simon regarded the man for a moment and decided not to be contentious. 'Yes,' he said. 'Didn't he? Now, before we worry about tents and such like I would be grateful if you would show us where the sick bay is.'

'Right you are, old chap.' The captain pointed. 'Big tent along there, can't miss it. Got a red cross painted on the side. When you've finished, come to the guard room and we'll fix you up. Cheers!'

Simon nodded his thanks and they both watched as the young man marched away, red-coated back as rigid as a ramrod. Jenkins broke the silence.

'Well,' he said, 'bloody marvellous is what I'd call that performance in there, bach sir. Bloody marvellous.' His black eyes gleamed. 'Did you see old Covington's face when you told 'im about the water? That was nice, wasn't it? I didn't know you was noticin' so much as we was ridin', that I didn't.'

'Oh come on,' said Simon. 'Let's go and see

327

how our little girl is.'

Nandi was half asleep, tucked away like a brown cherub between stiff grey army sheets. They stood looking down at her for a moment, and were about to tiptoe away when she opened her eyes and smiled, lighting up a face which, in repose, had looked drawn and sad.

'Oh, there you are,' she said, reaching out a hand. Jenkins took it and knelt down awkwardly on the beaten earth. The smile widened and her knuckles showed white as she gripped the Welshman's thick fingers. 'I thought the big General might have shot you – and if *he* hadn't then the horrible Mr Covington would have done so.' She held out her other hand to Simon, who took it, bent down and kissed it. 'But tell me, are you being punished?'

'Goodness, no,' said Jenkins, his eyes suspiciously moist. 'The Captain 'ere told the General what to do with 'is bloody battle – 'scuse me, miss – an' they let us off. Colonel Covington was not best pleased, I'm thinkin'.'

'How are you feeling, Nandi?' asked Simon.

'Oh I am all right now, thank you. Just tired all the time.' She looked around the canvas room and blinked, as though trying to hold back tears, yet her eyes remained dry. 'I have been doing so much thinking. I must have led a very happy and sheltered life, you see, until the war. Now, in the last two years, I have seen so much unhappiness, with my country being invaded, Papa losing his land, my brothers dying and me being so badly treated by those...' her voice faltered for a moment, 'terrible men. I realise that the world is an awful place and I would not mind leaving it.'

'Oh, come now, lass.' Jenkins clasped her hand in both of his. 'You mustn't say that, look you. You must never say that.'

She turned her head towards him, withdrew her hand and ran her fingers through his thick, spiky hair. He smiled sheepishly. 'Oh, don't worry, dear 352. I have decided not to die. Not just yet anyway.' She turned back to Simon. 'Not while I have such good friends as you two. I owe you so much for rescuing me. I can never thank you enough.'

Simon shook his head, not quite sure what to say. But Nandi continued. 'Alice has been to see me, you know.'

'Alice?' Simon could not conceal his alarm. 'She is still here?'

'Oh yes.' Nandi gave him her slow smile. 'I thought you might be interested, Simon.'

Simon coughed. 'No. It's not that. I didn't realise that Wolseley would allow the press to stay so far forward. It's not really safe.'

'Well, she is here and she came to see me less than an hour ago. She must have heard right away. And Simon...'

'Yes.'

'She has sent a message to Pretoria telling my father where I am.'

'Good lord. But how does she know he's gone back to Pretoria?'

'I don't know. But she says that she has a friend called Charlie in Pretoria who knows everything and will find him and tell him to come here right

329

away. So I am very pleased...' He voice trailed away and her head slumped back on to the pillow, a vein on the right side of her temple standing out prominently.

Simon and Jenkins exchanged glances. 'I think we are tiring you, Nandi,' said Simon. 'We will leave you now. Try and get some sleep and we will come and see you again tomorrow. Goodbye, my dear.'

He leaned forward and kissed her on the cheek. After a moment's hesitation Jenkins did the same, and Nandi nodded. The two men crept out of the tent.

'Now,' said Simon once outside. 'Where's the damned doctor? I don't like the look of her.'

'Nor me, neither. What's wrong with 'er, do you think?'

Simon frowned. 'It could be anything, after what she's been through. But there's one thing we must check.'

They found the doctor in a separate tent, visiting a row of bed-bound soldiers. He was young – perhaps Simon's age – with ginger hair and freckles. 'Ah,' he said, 'the young mystery beauty. Was it you who brought her in?'

'Yes.' Simon's tone was abrupt. 'Can you tell us what's wrong with her? Is it ... is it anything serious?'

The doctor shrugged his shoulders. 'Haven't had time to examine her thoroughly. It was important to give her warmth and rest right away, and that's what we've done. She's weak all right but I don't think she has pneumonia, probably just a touch of fever, and, by George, she needs

330

feeding. Looks as though she hasn't had a proper meal in months. Where did you find her?'

'She had been taken prisoner by the bePedi. Look...' Simon coughed. 'We believe that she ... er ... she has been abused. Raped, in fact. Is there a chance she might be pregnant, do you think?'

Simon was aware that Jenkins, by his side, had stiffened. The doctor took the question in his stride. 'Wouldn't know, old chap. Oh dear. How terrible.' He frowned. 'I can take tests in the morning, once she's had a good night's sleep.'

'Thank you.' Simon held the young man's gaze. 'It is important that she does not know what you are trying to find out. We don't want to upset her, you understand.'

'Oh, absolutely. Don't worry. I'll be discreet.'

The two nodded their thanks and walked outside into the crisp sunshine of the late afternoon. They made their way to the guard room in silence. Eventually, Jenkins spoke. 'Never thought of that,' he said. 'Pregnant. Oh bloody 'ell.'

They were allocated a tent near the horse lines and both took the opportunity to have a bucket shower and rid themselves of the grime of more than a week of riding and sleeping rough. The guard commander had offered Simon the opportunity to mess with the officers of Ferreira's Horse, but no arrangement had been made for Jenkins, so Simon declined. That night the two men made their own meal over an open fire outside their tent. There was little conversation between them, for each was lost in his own thoughts, and they turned in early.

331

The next day, at mid-morning, Simon and Jenkins visited Nandi again, but she lay asleep. To their anxious eyes she looked somehow less frail. She was breathing regularly and easily and that vein at her temple seemed to have disappeared. They stood looking down at her for a moment and then left silently. The doctor, however, had seen them and hurried over.

'Made a quick examination this morning,' he said. 'As far as I can tell – short of asking her about her monthly ... you know ... she is not pregnant.'

'Thank God for that,' said Simon.

'Amen,' echoed Jenkins.

'Apart from sheer exhaustion,' the doctor continued, 'I can't be sure about what ails her. She has a temperature and slight fever but I think that what she needs is simply rest and care. I shall advance with the army when we march, of course, but I will see that she is left behind here in good hands.'

Simon and Jenkins exchanged grins of relief. 'Splendid,' said Simon. 'Thank you, Doctor. She has been through a terribly harrowing time and she does deserve care and sympathy now. She is a rather special girl and we are grateful.'

It was clear that the doctor was puzzled, but the two gave him no chance for further questions. They each grabbed and shook his hand and walked away.

'Now what?' asked Jenkins.

'Well, since you so graciously offered to go into the attack with the General, I supposed–'

He was interrupted by a young trooper. 'Mr ... Captain Fonthill?'

Simon nodded.

'The General would like to see you right away, sir.'

'Damn. What now, I wonder?' Simon turned to Jenkins. 'Better go back to the tent and sort things out – like a bit of washing. I think we might be on the move more quickly than we thought.'

Simon was relieved to find only one other person in the General's tent this time, and regarded him with interest. The stranger was dressed like a Boer: full beard, wide-brimmed hat, dark jacket and trousers tucked into riding boots. The face was seamed and sunburned, but under the beard, a clergyman's rather grubby white collar could be glimpsed.

'This is the Reverend Merensky,' said Wolseley. 'He knows more about the bePedi than any living European, having worked amongst 'em and ... er ... tried to convert 'em for years.'

The two men shook hands. Merensky's grip was like a vice.

'The Reverend,' Sir Garnet continued, 'has been telling me about the lay-out in the Sekukuni valley and about the bePedi tactics when they are attacked.' The suspicion of a smile crinkled the corners of his eyes. 'You will be glad to hear that he has confirmed everything you have said, Fonthill, and he recommends the two-pronged attack you have suggested.' The smile broadened and the General gave a friendly nod to the clergyman. 'Mr Merensky has a damned good grasp of military tactics for a padre.'

The clergyman spoke with a deep German accent. 'Every man in this country has to fight,

333

General,' he said. 'Even a man of the cloth.' He regarded Simon with a not unfriendly air. 'This young man, whom you tell me does not know this country very well, seems to have learned about it quite quickly.'

Simon nodded at the compliment.

'The most important thing in warfare,' continued Wolseley, 'is good reconnaissance. So I had to double-check. Now I need to see for myself. We will ride at dawn tomorrow, Fonthill. I want to study this town and its approaches, particularly this impregnable kopje. We will travel light – only a troop of cavalry–'

'Oh, I don't think so, sir,' interrupted Simon.

The General's sigh was almost histrionic. 'Young man,' he said, 'you seem intent on telling me my job at every turn. Now why, pray, would I not take a troop of cavalry as protection when reconnoitring unknown and damned unfriendly territory?'

'Too many, sir. Even though it has been raining, much of the way is high desert country and a troop will kick up dust that will be seen for miles. The bePedis will know now of my raid and they will know that you are camped here and preparing to advance against them. They will be on the qui vive for any further intrusions. Take a section, ten men at the most, sir. We should be able to slip through undetected, if we skirt wide. Though we may have to travel by night for the last few miles. And we shall need my two Ndebeles.'

Wolseley looked across at Merensky. The clergyman's expression of dour detachment did not change, but he nodded his head.

'Very well. A section it will be – and bring your extremely friendly Welshman, but tell him to stop calling me bach. Ah, one more thing, Fonthill. Colonel Covington will be coming with us. He will be needed to lead the attack over the hills to take the town from the east, so he must be part of the reconnaissance. Now, I want no trouble between you. He is a gallant officer whom I had the pleasure of decorating in the field on the Ashanti campaign. He will be treated with respect. Do you understand?'

Simon sighed. 'Very good, sir. As long as the respect is mutual.'

'I shall see to that. I have now had time to second you formally to the army as scouts – with pay starting a week ago. Report here at five a.m. tomorrow. That will be all.'

Simon found Jenkins laboriously washing shirts. '352, where are the diamonds?'

Jenkins looked up, his face lugubriously questioning. 'The what?'

'You know, man. The damned diamonds de Witt stole.'

'Good lord. You know, bach sir, I'd forgotten all about them. Funny I should do that after so many people 'ave died because of them, isn't it?'

'It won't be funny if you've lost them. Are they still in the saddle bag?'

'Blimey. 'Ope so.' The Welshman, his hands still covered in soap suds, rushed to a corner of their tent where the leather bag lay on the floor. Unbuckling it, he took out the small hessian sack, untied the string and looked inside. His

335

smile shone in the gloom of the tent. 'They're still 'ere,' he said. 'What are we goin' to do with them?'

'Well,' said Simon, 'We are off again in the morning and I don't fancy leaving them here.' He explained about his meeting with the General and the news that Covington would be riding with them.

'Blimey, bach sir. If 'e tries any of 'is funny stuff with us again – arrestin' us an' all that – then I shall just 'ave to shoot 'im. P'raps, look you, I should warn 'im before we go, what d'yer think?'

'You will do nothing of the kind. We shall just have to ignore him. I have given my word to the General that there will be no trouble from us. Now, about the diamonds. We obviously can't take them with us, so we should give them to Nandi. They will be hers anyway and they should be safe enough here with her, until we get back.'

'Good idea.'

'I will take them to her now.' Simon looked at Jenkins and had a better idea. 'No. You go. Tell her that these diamonds are for her and her father, to compensate for all the agonies they have been through. Tell her to keep them safe, and above all not to tell anyone she has them. Is that clear?'

A sudden, unfamiliar, hunted look came into Jenkins's eyes. 'Oh, I'd rather you went, bach sir. You know Nandi better 'n me, see. Should be you telling 'er this sort of stuff.'

'Nonsense. She would love to see you and I can't imagine anyone better than you to bring her this news.' Simon paused for a moment. 'She is very fond of you, you know.'

Jenkins looked at the floor and wiped his still-soapy hands on the back of his trousers. To see Jenkins embarrassed was something new for Simon. 'Well, I'm not sure of that at all now,' the Welshman muttered. 'But all right. I'll go.' Then he looked up in consternation. ''Ang on – what if she's asleep?'

'You will just have to wake her gently, won't you? But don't leave until she understands what's in the sack and decides where she will put it for safe keeping.'

'Very good, sir.'

Jenkins tucked the package into his shirt and, wiping his hands on his hair, trudged through the tent opening. Simon sat for a moment and smiled. Jenkins was in love, right enough. It didn't sit well on the little Welshman, for it made him gauche and unsure of himself – and self-confidence was something that Jenkins normally possessed in barrowloads. But in this new battle-field of the heart, the great warrior who feared no one was a novice. None of his normal weapons of courage, coolness and skill in fighting could help him now.

Simon lay back on the narrow camp bed, put his hands behind his head and grinned. He could not imagine a better pairing than the loyal, resourceful Jenkins and the brave, pretty Zulu girl. But did she – would she – reciprocate 352's feelings? He remembered the way she had taken the little man's hand and then rubbed her fingers through his stubbly hair with such tenderness. Ah yes, there must be something there! He recalled with affection how, back in Zululand, he

337

had been so tempted himself by Nandi's ingenuous but somehow innocent flirting. But that, of course, was before Alice... Once again, however, his immediate recall of that golden hair and those steady grey eyes was jerked to a halt, as though a steel door had thudded down to end his thought process. She was engaged to be married to Covington, and that, for God's sake, was very much the end of that.

'Simon...' The call from outside was low-pitched and tentative, as though the caller was half hoping that the tent would be empty. 'Simon.'

Simon sprang to his feet, ran a quick hand through his tousled hair, and ducked his head through the tent opening. She was standing, just as he had involuntarily recalled her a second or two ago, with the setting sun glinting in her hair, her grey eyes troubled, wearing the softest of white cotton shirts, a fawn riding skirt and those familiar boots. 'Alice,' he said, all his intention of retaining his distant manner swept aside as soon as he set eyes on her. 'How good to see you. Do come in.'

'Oh, I don't think I should, you know.'

'Goodness, don't be silly. There's no chaperone here at present, but old 352 will be back very soon. Come in. It's getting chilly.'

'Very well.' She ducked her head and followed him inside the tent.

'Sorry there's no chair,' said Simon, his brain reeling with the desire to throw his arms around her and bury his face in the bun into which she had wound her hair at the nape of her neck. 'Here. Sit on my bed. It's a bit less rumpled than

338

Jenkins's. He's gone to see Nandi.'

Alice's troubled face broke into a smile. 'Oh, Simon,' she said. 'That is why I came to see you. I am so proud of you ... er ... of you both. What you did in releasing that girl from her captivity was brave and bold in the extreme. The whole camp is buzzing with it. I just wanted to ... you know ... congratulate you.'

Simon gulped and scratched his nose. 'Oh, goodness. It was surprisingly easy in the end. But look here. I ... er ... we must thank you for going to see Nandi and for sending news to her father that she is safe. And, for that matter, for finding old Dunn.' He paused for a moment while they looked into each other's eyes. 'I say,' and he grinned, 'this sounds like a mutual appreciation society.'

She grinned back. 'Goodness. That would never do.' They sat smiling at each other, as the evening sounds of the camp – the low neighing from the horse lines, the crunch of the cavalrymen as they carried fodder to their mounts, the distant creaking of waggons – came from without the canvas walls. Eventually Simon broke his gaze and looked away, and they both sat silently.

'Alice...'

'Simon...'

They spoke together, breaking the impasse at exactly the same moment, and then each of them stopped, their mouths open, their eyes beseeching the other. Immediately Simon pushed forward from the low camp bed on to his knees before Alice and swept her into his arms. They embraced with a passion that only frustration and longing could produce.

'Alice, darling Alice,' he breathed into her hair. 'Don't – don't marry that man. I love you. I always have. Marry me. Please, please.'

'I know,' she responded. 'I know. I love you too. It's been awful, awful. I don't know why I said yes to him. I have been so miserable for so long. I didn't know what to do. But Simon, I do love you so.' She pushed him away, tears pouring down her face. 'What are we going to do?'

'Well, stop crying for a start. This is the happiest day of my life. Here, take my handkerchief. Sorry, it's not very clean. I think bloody Jenkins is in love as well, and he's not been looking after me properly.'

She smiled through her tears, wiped her cheeks, blew her nose and immediately kissed him, her tongue questing deep within his mouth, her hand clasping the back of his neck. He responded, and they stayed in their embrace, kneeling on the beaten-earth floor between the two trestle beds, as uncomfortable as hell but neither of them worried about that. Eventually Alice unwound her arms, gently pushed Simon away and sat back on her heels, smiling at him as she cupped his face between her hands and studied his features as though for the first time.

'You know,' she said, 'as I believe I told you once before, I think this broken nose rather suits you. Gives you a sort of predatory appearance, a bit hawk-like. Quite shivery, really.' She kissed his nose gently. 'God, my knees are killing me.'

'Oh, my dear, I am sorry.' He helped her to her feet and they sat together on his bed, hand in hand, smiling at each other.

That was where Jenkins found them. 'Blimey,' he exclaimed, and executed a smart about-turn and clumped away.

'There,' said Alice. 'Now what is dear old 352 going to make of all this?' And as if to show that she didn't give a damn really, she brought Simon's head down and kissed him again. Then she stood up. 'I wish I could stay, but I've got to go and file my story.'

Simon stood up and held her close to him. 'Yes, my love,' he spoke gently, 'but you also have something even more important to do that won't really wait.'

She gave him a sombre smile this time. 'I know, I know. Of course I shall tell him. I shall not enjoy doing so, but it must be done and, don't worry, I shall do it. But I've been thinking about it – all of the last twenty seconds. You see, Ralph Covington, as you well know, can be a very vindictive man, and I am about to upset him considerably. Now, I know that he is going with you and Wolseley on this reconnaissance tomorrow.' She paused, and a frown replaced the smile. 'This mission is going to be dangerous enough as it is, with you, my newly discovered love, retracing the steps you have just taken in fleeing from Sekukuni's capital. Going back into that valley will be like trying to tiptoe into a hornets' nest. If I had to tell Ralph before he leaves that I am not going to marry him but have chosen you instead, then I would worry that this would upset the balance of such a small party in such a dangerous place. No,' she shook her head, 'he is not a

341

dishonourable man, although I know just how much you dislike him. But he is very fond of me and this could affect his judgement in some way, out there, when danger threatens.'

She caressed Simon's cheek. 'And I am not going to take that risk. I shall tell him about us all right. Have no fear of that. I will not change my mind. But I shall tell him when you return – no, there is still the battle to come, in which you both could be involved. I shall tell him *after* that. At this point I do not wish to arouse what I know will be his fierce jealousy.'

Simon drew breath to protest, but Alice put a finger on his lips. 'No, Simon. This will be for the best. Please don't worry.' She put her head on one side and regarded him. 'I really do love you, my dear, and it just means that we must keep our secret for a little longer. I hope you understand.'

Glumly, he nodded.

'Good. Now I really must go.' She kissed him again and held him at arm's length. 'Please, please be careful on this mission tomorrow. I would hate to lose you just when I have found you.' Then she turned and was gone, leaving a very faint trace of perfume inside the little tent.

Chapter 13

The conditions could not have been more unpleasant when the small party rode out of Fort Weeber the next morning. A night of thunder and sheet lightning had given way to a surly dawn of heavy rain that bounced off the glistening capes of the horsemen. Merensky had declined to join them, pleading the adverse effect of the damp on his arthritic joints, so there were sixteen of them: Simon and Jenkins in the lead, with the two Ndebeles; followed by the General, cutting a hunched, diminutive figure on a large grey; Covington, riding erect at his side; and the moustached sergeant, the only Englishman in the ten-man section of Colonial Horse. The little troop looked disconsolate as it picked its way along the old Boer track towards Sekukuni. Heads were bowed against the driving rain and only Covington rode high, his back straight and his face seemingly impervious to the fierce storm.

At the head of the party, however, Simon and Jenkins were happy enough beneath their wide-brimmed hats. On Jenkins's return to the tent after Alice's departure, no mention had been made of her visit. Nor had Simon enquired after Nandi. Each man was busy with his thoughts. As the rain beat a tattoo on his hat brim, Simon only now asked, 'How was Nandi, then?'

Jenkins's teeth flashed under his moustache.

'Good, very good, bach sir. Perkin' up quite nicely, in fact see. She was eatin' when I saw 'er an' she was fair puttin' it away, that she was.'

'Good. And the diamonds?'

'Well, she was reluctant to take 'em at first. I think she felt they was dirty, like, or – what's the word – tainted, see. But I persuaded 'er, I think. Told 'er that we didn't know who their true owners might be an' that it was only fair that she an' her da should 'ave 'em, seein' that no one else could claim 'em. I think she felt that Mr Dunn might appreciate 'em, look you.'

'I am sure he would.'

They fell silent for a while and then Jenkins said, 'Beggin' your pardon, but I don't much like this job we're on now.'

'Neither do I. It's too bloody wet.'

'No, I don't meant that. I just think that we are pushin' our luck goin' straight back to this blasted place. We was a bit lucky, look you, to get away with it the first time, but surely they'll be lookin' out a bit better now?'

Simon nodded and sent a shower of water from his hat brim on to the mane of his horse. 'I'm inclined to agree. But we don't have much choice. Only we know the way in and out and the General wants to recce for himself. I would wish to do the same in his place.'

'Hmm. But there's the other thing.'

'What's that?'

Jenkins lowered his voice a fraction. 'Our old CO, Colonel Covington 'imself, is with us, and he don't like you much – and if he thinks of me at all, I should imagine he don't much fancy me either.'

'So?'

'So, I don't like the idea of goin' back to this Sookondi place with 'im protectin' me back, so to speak.'

Simon grunted. 'Rubbish. The man's a bastard, that's for sure, but he's an English officer and he wouldn't let us down in the field.'

'Well, if you say so. But when are we goin' to get this Mendoosi chap, then? I'm not leavin' this awful part o' the world without puttin' 'is evil bones to rest, that's for sure. Not after what he did to Nandi. We got rid of most of the rest of 'em; when are we goin' to see to 'im?'

Simon rode silently for a while before he replied. 'I've been thinking of that. Like you, I have no intention of letting the man get away. I doubt if he would have returned to Pretoria, knowing that John Dunn was still alive and that we were on to him and now had Nandi. He would be too vulnerable back there. He might have gone back to the farm, but after the visit of the Swazis and without the rest of most of his gang, he would feel vulnerable there too. My bet is that he is still with his great chum the King. Knowing that both the British and the Boers have failed so far to dislodge the old rascal, he would have no reason to think that this attempt will succeed. So he will stay and take his chance in the coming battle. And then, 352,' Simon's voice was low and cold, 'that's when we will get him.'

'Right. But, bach sir, one request.'

'Yes?'

'Leave the bugger to me.'

Simon nodded, and they rode on in silence.

345

They all camped on the open veldt that night in gloomy misery, putting up small bivouac tents in the pounding rain. Covington studiously avoided Simon and Jenkins, and there was precious little other conversation, Wolseley merely observing to Simon that he could have 'brought a whole bloody army along here without raising dust in this weather, let alone a cavalry troop'. They saddled up again at first light, and although the rain continued, it was now less heavy. The day was uneventful but they camped again that night with more care, pitching their tents and tethering the horses in a small patch of low stunted trees and scrub, sufficient to provide some cover at least.

On the third morning, still in persistent rain, they rode under the lee of the blue foothills of the Lulus and followed the swollen course of the Oliphant. Studying his compass and taking a bearing from a declivity in the jagged silhouette of the hills, Simon called a halt. 'This is where you should situate Colonel Covington's force, General,' he said. Then he pointed. 'They should go over the top through that cleft in the hills. The township lies directly below on the other side.'

Wolseley wiped the rain from his binoculars and focused on the hills. 'Hmm,' he murmured. 'Looks damned hard going. How difficult is it?'

'Not easy for fully equipped troops, sir, but it can be done. We came back that way.'

The General focused again. 'Looks like a job for the Swazis to me. Think you could take them up and over, Covington?'

The reply was unhesitating. 'Of course, sir. Just

give me a stiffening of our lads.'

'I could give you four companies of British infantry. All right?'

'Good enough, sir.'

Wolseley turned back to Simon. 'How many bePedis would be under arms, d'you think, Fonthill?'

Simon frowned. 'Well, I only know what the Ndebeles tell me and what I could see, looking down on the town, but I should guess that they could muster about three to four thousand warriors.'

'Hmm. Merensky says four thousand, so that's near enough. Could you see how well they were armed?'

'Assegais, of course, but a very large number of them were carrying what looked like modern rifles. Some muskets, certainly, but through the glasses most of them looked reasonably up to date: perhaps Sniders and certainly some Mausers.'

'Right. Well we can't hang about here if we are that close to the town itself. Can't understand why we haven't been spotted, as it is.' He gestured to Ophrus. 'You, my man. Why haven't the bePedis attacked us? Eh?'

The black man wrinkled his nose. 'Too wet, baas. They inside.'

'How very sensible. Right, Fonthill, take us round the northern end of these hills, where I can have a good look at the town from that end and at this damned Fighting Kopje which everyone seems so afraid of.'

So, in the ever-present rain, the little party rode on, leaving the Oliphant and hugging the edge of the wooded foothills of the Lulu range for cover and then veering round the end of the range to the west. There, with great caution and with the two Ndebeles riding out ahead as scouts, they approached the valley of Sekukuni. At last, the strange central kopje of the King's fortress came into distant view, its swelling mound rising sheer from the valley floor, ending from this view in a little sharp kink and then a point. The party led their horses up the side of the foothills, keeping under cover, until Wolseley was close enough to study the approach to the town at length. He sat for perhaps half an hour looking through the glasses and making rough sketches.

'Well, you and Merensky were right, Fonthill,' he said eventually. 'The whole damned place is well fortified. They've got the town ringed by walls and trenches – quite well done, as a matter of fact. Right, I've seen what I want to see from here. Now we must go back and take a closer look down at the town from where the Swazis will attack.'

Simon cleared his throat. 'Are you sure you need to do that, sir? We've probably chanced our arm enough already, and after the four of us went into the town that way just a few days ago, they will almost certainly have that route pretty well guarded now.'

'What's the matter, Fonthill? A trifle concerned about danger, are you?' Covington's tone was languid and icy.

'Now that will do, Ralph,' said Wolseley. 'Fonthill has made a very reasonable point.' He turned to Simon. 'I'm afraid I do need to take a

348

closer look from that side, young man,' he said. 'I would not dream of sending troops to attack a position I have not studied for myself. We must find a way through somehow.'

With equal caution the party retreated the way they had come, thankful, despite their discomfort – for the rain had long since penetrated their capes and soaked outerwear and underwear equally – that the weather and poor visibility continued to give them cover. Wolseley noted a crossing on the northern curve of the Oliphant, which the Ndebeles told him was called Mapashlela's Drift and which he felt would be ideal for the siting of the fort from which the main attack could be launched. In fact, despite the constant rain, the General was in high spirits when the party arrived back at the proposed site for the attack over the hills. 'We will go up and over ourselves first thing in the morning,' he announced.

Simon and Jenkins exchanged glances and the Ndebeles, when told that they were expected to lead the party over the mountain the next day, rolled their eyes and maintained a sullen silence while the camp was prepared.

The rain had stopped and a watery sun was struggling to penetrate the low, pewter-coloured clouds as the party set off the next day. As though in celebration of the better weather, small duiker antelopes bounced ahead of them as they made their way carefully up through the foliage and scrub of the hillside. Vervet monkeys chattered overhead and hoop-hoop birds gave their eponymous cries above and around them. The world seemed a better place after the persistent rain, but it was clear that the Ndebeles remained unhappy. They went on ahead on foot up the hillside, making their way with infinite care as they ducked under the low trees, carefully placing their bare feet so as to avoid causing a noisy cascade of loose shingle. But a glimpse of their yellow eyeballs as they constantly turned their heads to scan all around them showed that they were nervous. After half an hour it was necessary for the main party to dismount and lead the horses as the ascent became steeper and more difficult and, paradoxically, the scrub thicker.

'Can we get eight thousand Swazis up here?' demanded the General, his puce face reflecting the effort of the climb.

'As I understand it,' replied Simon, 'they live in mountainous country themselves and I doubt if this would be much of a climb for them. But with respect, sir, we are not far from the top now and I do think we should be quiet.'

Wolseley nodded and the party continued the climb in silence until Simon gestured that they had reached the little plateau and clearing where it was possible to leave the horses tethered. They did so under the care of three troopers and continued their climb even more cautiously now, for they were nearing the summit. The top itself was exposed rock, jagged on the skyline, but the approach was scrub so thick that Simon, in the lead, nearly bumped into the two Ndebeles, who were crouched down, peering through the bush.

'What is it?' mouthed Simon, holding up his

350

hand to stop the others approaching.

Ophrus turned. 'Two Pedis, up there.' He pointed.

'What are they doing?'

'They on guard, baas. They not move.'

'Let me see.' The Ndebeles moved aside and, cautiously, Simon crawled forward on his stomach. Parting the bushes he saw two tribes-men sitting just below the summit on a rock, holding rifles and looking completely bored. One, in fact, seemed to be asleep.

He returned. 'Are you sure there are no more?'

'Only two, so far.'

'Stay here.' Simon turned around and, on his bottom, levered himself down the hillside to where the others waited. 'There are two bePedi warriors guarding the track over the summit just up ahead,' he said.

'Damn,' swore Wolseley. 'Is there another way around?'

'There may be but I don't know where it is, and thirteen of us could make an awful lot of noise trying to find it.'

'Then we shall just have to remove them.' It was Covington who spoke.

'We can't shoot because that would rouse the whole township.'

'I am well aware of that,' said Covington. His voice was beautifully modulated, as though explaining an obvious truth to a difficult child. 'You will just have to take them out quietly, then, won't you? This is a job for scouts, skirmishers – what you're being paid for now, eh, Fonthill?'

Jenkins sniffed. 'Care to give us an 'and, then,

Colonel?' he enquired, his black button eyes as cold as Covington's.

'That will do, 352,' said Simon. He addressed Wolseley. 'I suggest you all stay here, sir. If you do hear a shot, then I'm afraid you will have lost your chance of a personal reconnaissance from this side of the town and you must go hell for leather for the horses. The bePedis won't have mounts this side of the hills so you should all be able to get away across the plain. But we shall try and do the job silently. Give us twenty minutes.'

'Very well, Fonthill. Good luck.'

Simon crawled back with Jenkins to where the two Ndebeles lay. There he stopped for a moment to catch his breath and to attempt to still the thumping of his heart. His mouth was dry and he realised that he was damned well frightened again. He cast a glance at Jenkins, who gave a reassuring beam, not even a bead of sweat on his forehead. Not for the first time, Simon deeply envied the Welshman's ability to remain cool in the face of danger and seemingly unaffected by it. He was the complete fighting machine – even when up against lions, which he confessed had terrified him. Simon shook his head and attempted to concentrate.

He beckoned the two natives closer. 'Look,' he whispered. 'I want you two to stay here and be very quiet until...' He looked at Ophrus, who always played the leader of the two. 'Can you count, Ophrus?'

The tall man nodded. 'Yes, baas, up to twenty – fingers and toes.'

'No, that won't do.' Simon looked around. The

sun had now made a welcome reappearance in a blue sky to the north-east. He did a quick calculation. 'When the sun touches that high peak,' he said, 'I want you to make a noise to attract the attention of the guards up there. Nothing much, for we don't want them to shoot at you. Maybe just send some stones falling down the slope, as though an animal has disturbed them. Just enough to distract them for a moment. Do you understand?'

Ophrus's eyes opened wide as he looked at the peak. He and Ntanga nodded. 'Yes, sir.'

'Good. When I call, I shall want you both to come up to the top and bring our rifles. But I will only call softly, in case there are other guards about, and you must come quietly. Yes?'

The two men nodded. 'Right,' said Simon, then, to Jenkins, 'Come on, then.'

Jenkins's face was a study in indignation. 'Come on to where, for God's sake – and with respect, bach sir. There's nowhere to go except up and bloody down, isn't it.'

Simon sighed. 'We will work along this patch of scrub to the right, where it looks as though we can climb over the summit and get down to the other side, the township side. Then I'm just hoping we can crawl along to the trail, climb up it and take the guards by surprise from the back when our two lads here divert their attention.'

'What – and then shoot 'em and 'ave the whole bloody town on our backs?'

'No.' Simon's face was set. 'We obviously can't do that, and I am glad that we can't because I am tired of killing men in cold blood. We shall threaten them with our revolvers and then tie them up and gag them so that they don't make a noise.'

Jenkins rolled his eyes. 'We'd better ask their permission first, look you.'

'Don't be bloody stupid. Come on.' With a nod to the Ndebeles, Simon began crawling with infinite care along the scrub line to the right, keeping an anxious eye on the position of the sun. Eventually they came to a break which he had noticed in the jagged line of the summit. It was not a trail, but a protruding buttress of rock hid them from the guards and they were able to crawl up the rock face to the top, ascertain that it was unguarded and then wriggle down the other side to where the bush line began, some ten feet down. As they did so, they could see that the township below presented a far more active sight than the last time they had viewed it from on high. People were swarming like ants between the huts and thronging the stone walls that linked the houses and ringed the town. It was a citadel preparing to defend itself, and even from that height, it looked a formidable fortress.

The two men, now on hands and knees, turned to their left and soon struck the trail that led down to Sekukuni below. It seemed to be unguarded; presumably the bePedis were banking on the two sentries on the crest being sufficient to give warning of an attack from over the mountain and the unlikely quarter of the Oliphant River.

Drawing their revolvers, Simon and Jenkins now began crawling carefully up the track towards the summit. Simon had lost all idea of whether the sun was touching the distant peak, and he could only hope that he still had a minute or two in hand before Ophrus created his diversion. They were now on the edge of the scrub line, and Simon began inching up the bare rock until he froze, his face pressed close to the rock face. He could just see the ends of the bePedis' headdresses waving gently in the soft breeze. This was the moment of truth, and he held his breath. If and when the two guards stood quickly, he should be able to see their heads looking away from him. If they looked down at him, he and Jenkins were lost and they would have to shoot. He levelled his revolver at the tip of the crest and waited, his heart in his mouth.

He had no idea how long they lay there. Perspiration was rolling down Simon's face as he concentrated his gaze along the length of his revolver on to those feather tips, dancing lightly above the brow of the summit, and he could feel Jenkins tense, lying by his left foot. Then, suddenly, the headdresses appeared full length, as also did the back of the heads of both of the sentinels as they stood, obviously alarmed at some happening on their side of the mountain. Simon immediately began crawling upwards, as fast as he could without making a noise. He could sense Jenkins now almost at his side and he waited, just below the crest, until the two of them were level. Both of the bePedis were now in view, staring down at the reverse side of the mountain, their backs innocently presented to the climbers but their rifles at the alert. Then, as Simon and Jenkins watched, the rifles drooped as no obvious sign of intruders presented itself to the guards. At that point, Simon gestured with his Colt for Jenkins to take the bePedi on the left, and springing to his feet he leapt over the ridge and rammed the nose of his revolver into the cheekbone of the guard on the right. Jenkins was a fraction late in following but the surprise was complete, for neither of the natives, turning with a start at the new noise behind them, had time to level their rifles.

Immediately they were disarmed, and Simon, his thumb on the cocked hammer of the Colt and his left forefinger to his lips in the universal command for silence, gestured to both men to lie face down on the rock.

'Now what?' asked Jenkins.

'Go and get Ophrus and Ntanga – but quietly, there may be other guards about.'

Within seconds, Jenkins had brought back the two Ndebeles and, using a combination of wrist-bands and ankle thongs, the two guards were bound and handkerchiefs thrust into their mouths and secured as gags. Simon then sat down and realised that he was shaking and that perspiration was soaking his shirt.

'You all right, bach sir?' As usual, Jenkins was unperturbed by the recent tension but was now solicitous.

Simon nodded and swallowed hard. 'I'm fine, 352. Well done. Very well done. Not a drop of spilt blood anywhere. That's shown the bloody army how to do it. Now, will you please go and get the others, but warn them to be quiet.'

Within five minutes the party was assembled, just below the ridge of the mountain. Covington regarded the pinioned bePedis with consternation but Wolseley hardly paid them a glance. 'First class, Fonthill,' he murmured. 'Now, is the bePedi township straight down the other side?'

'More or less, sir.'

'Capital. Now,' he turned to the sergeant, 'you stay here and keep guard on these prisoners with one man. Once over the top we will split into three parties. You, Ralph, take two men and one of the Ndebeles as guide and go as far as you can straight down to the town – but not too near, mark you – and plan your route for attacking it with your natives. I will go to the left with three men and note the approaches to the town from the south-west through the valley. That is probably where I will mount my headquarters. Now, Fonthill.'

'Sir?'

'You were at Sandhurst, were you not?'

'Yes, Sir Garnet.'

'Did they teach you topography and sketching there?'

'Yes, they did.'

'Good. Go to the right, with your man and the other Ndebele, and take a good look at the Fighting Kopje from as near as possible from this side. Sketch it as best you can and observe what would seem to be the best way to climb it. Here is some paper and a pencil. I have already done the same from the other side, but I like to be as well prepared as possible before I commit any man in an attack.'

'Yes, sir.' Simon marvelled at the attention to detail paid by this General. He had even thought of bringing a spare notebook and pencil! But Wolseley was continuing.

'It is clear that we have very little time here, and we cannot presume that there are no more warriors guarding the tops of these mountains. So we will each have no more than forty minutes. Within that time we must be back here and ready to return. And, gentlemen, no shooting unless you are in extreme danger. Obviously, if a shot is heard, everyone must double back to the horses. But if we are hotly pursued and the last party has not returned, we cannot afford to leave their horses as a gift to our pursuers. We must take them with us. Is that understood?'

Everyone nodded before scurrying over the rim of the mountain and going their different ways. Progress was not easy for Simon, Jenkins and Ophrus because it was difficult to keep their footing in the shale under the scrub, and there was no path. But Ophrus maintained a reasonable pace as they descended and they eventually found a little clearing from which they could look down on the north-eastern end of the town and on the kopje, the top of which was now roughly level with their position.

Simon observed it closely. From this point, he could clearly make out the terraced walls and trench systems, winding round the kopje from halfway up. The summit itself was formed of a large plateau on its northern side with the spiked pinnacle on the southern, nearer side. Dark openings, presumably caves, could be discerned in the sides of the hill, and also black boxes, which Simon guessed were beehives. Blocks of

358

dark brown granite were tumbled everywhere on the steep slopes, as though a giant had scattered pebbles. It would be damned difficult to climb and extremely dangerous under fire. Frowning, he began sketching.

Suddenly, the sound of a single gunshot came from the middle section, on their side of the mountain, above the town and roughly where Covington and his group would be. It echoed and rebounded, magnified from the other side of the valley as though it had been fired by a cannon and not some small arm.

'I knew it,' hissed Jenkins. 'That bastard of a colonel has let us in for it. We've got the furthest to go. We'll never get back. Look!' He pointed down and to the left. As though the shot was an expected and awaited signal, streams of warriors could be seen running between the stone walls and up the mountainside, the leaders already disappearing into the low trees.

Simon stuffed the notebook into his shirt and scrambled to his feet. 'Is there a quicker way back, Ophrus?'

The black man rolled his eyes. 'Don't know, baas.'

'Right. Then back the way we came, quick as we can. It will be a race against time to see who gets to the horses. We shan't be able to fight the whole damned nation.'

Stumbling and slipping through the shale and shingle, they hurried upwards and to their right, back to the main trail. Despite the fact that he had no footwear, Ophrus was easily the most sure-footed and he had made about one hundred yards on the others when Simon saw him suddenly stiffen and drop to the ground, waving downwards with his hand behind him as he did so. Immediately, the other two did the same, hugging the protection of a group of moshwana thorn bushes. They could not see what Ophrus could see, but they heard voices and grunts of exertion. It was obvious that they were too late. They were cut off.

Ophrus wriggled back. His eyes protruded as he spoke. 'Many bePedi, baas,' he said. 'Going up hill by our trail. We too late.'

'Oh shit,' said Jenkins. 'Now what do we do?'

'We go back,' said Simon. 'Come on.'

'Back? Where to?'

'Back down the mountain, towards the town. Just where they won't expect us to be.'

Jenkins's eyebrows nearly met his moustache. 'But 'ow do we get out of 'ere, then? What about the 'orses?'

'Remember what the General said. They will take all the horses with them if a party is cut off. So we will just have to do without them – unless we can steal some from the town itself.' Simon's mind raced. 'No. Impossible. There's no way we could disguise ourselves long enough to get through to their horse lines, even at night. We'll just have to walk. Come on, let's try to get to the northern end of the valley, where we were yesterday. They won't expect to find us there.'

'Oh lord lumme,' exclaimed Jenkins. 'That's marchin' away from 'ome, look you; even *I* know that.' But Simon had turned his back and was making his way northwards, away from the trail down to the town. Jenkins sighed and directed his beaming smile at Ophrus. 'Ah well, Offeous old sport,' he said. 'We're in for a bit of a stroll. An' you without a pair of boots to yer name. Shame that is, indeed it is.'

But the Ndebele was in no mood to smile back. His face was a lugubrious picture of anxiety as he followed the two white men down the mountainside, rifle at the ready. They strode and scrambled for two hours, always on the alert, until they had descended to about a hundred feet above the valley floor. There they stopped, well within the tree and scrub line, and saw that they had left the capital well behind them and were heading towards where the valley widened again and the northern end of the mountain range curved around to the east. Here, they sat together and Simon squinted up at the sky through the low foliage.

'It's about two hours before dusk,' he said. 'We will rest here until then, and we can break out into the open and make for the Oliphant under cover of night.'

'We goin' to walk all the way back to the fort, baas?' enquired Ophrus, his face a picture of apprehension.

Simon answered with a confidence he did not feel. 'We certainly are, Ophrus, but only at night. We will rest up during the day. There should be enough cover all the way along the river bank to hide us during daylight. We will take a wide loop and follow the Oliphant down until we are roughly level with Fort Weeber, then we will strike east across the veldt to the fort. We should

361

be safe that far south.'

'Do you think they will come lookin' for us?' asked Jenkins.

Simon wrinkled his nose. 'Perhaps. But I am banking that they won't know how many were in our party and that they will be more worried about the others that got away – as I am sure they did, because they were so much nearer to the horses than us. My guess is that they will go back to the citadel and pull up the drawbridge, so to speak, in preparation for Wolseley's attack.'

'What about that rifle shot, then?'

'Indeed. Actually, I am not all that sure it even came from a rifle. I just don't know. Maybe one of Covington's party stumbled upon a guard, or it could have been an accident if it was a rifle. The Martini-Henrys have been known to go off when there's a round up the snout. Anyway, we can find out from Ntanga when we get back.'

'Ah yes. When we get back. How long will that take, d'you reckon?'

Simon blew out his cheeks. 'Well, we're all fit, and a bit of marching won't kill us. I'd say we'd have about eighty to ninety miles to cover, going the long way, as we must. Say perhaps a week.'

'A week! What are we goin' to eat? I've got a few biscuits an' a bit of that dried meat rubbish. But that's not goin' to get us far, is it?'

'It's roughly what the Boers had when they set off on their Great Trek. We shall have to be careful, of course, but once out of gunshot we should be able to get a rabbit or two, or trout from the Oliphant. And there will be water from the river. We shall live like lords. Come on now.

362

Try and get an hour or two of sleep before we start the long march. I'll stand watch.'

Ophrus was soon asleep, happy to have no responsibility, and Jenkins, with his knack of being able to sleep whenever an opportunity occurred, was soon stretched out also. Simon was content to be alone with his thoughts as he leaned against a low tree, his rifle across his knees. They were in danger, there was no doubt about that. Without horses they could not run from attackers, and it would be a long, arduous trek back across the veldt, with little cover if a bePedi party did catch up with them. Travelling by night would have its own dangers because it would be difficult to take compass bearings and their progress would be slow, particularly if the rains returned. And yet his heart sang.

The pattern of existence that he and Jenkins had followed for the last three years had been lived right on the edge, and danger had been such a constant companion that he, at last, had come to accept it almost as an old friend (Jenkins, of course, had rubbed along with it since boyhood). The frisson so provided was now an essential part of life; the spice that gave a taste to this otherwise hard existence and which had long since replaced his old fear of cowardice, of being thought afraid. He still had his moments of fear, but they now seemed normal, something which sharpened the senses and made him more combative. But more important than all of that – much more important: Alice loved him! He smiled at the recent memory of her kisses and hugged to himself the recollection of her warm, ardent admission. With Alice in his heart – a loving, receptive Alice – there was nothing that he could not do. There was a spring in his step, then, as, with the sky darkening, he woke his companions and they set off on the long march back to Fort Weeber.

For all its hardship, it proved to be an uneventful journey. They found the muddy, hard-flowing Oliphant that same night and set off to follow its course south. Camping during the day under the low willows by its banks, they travelled by night, sometimes trudging on a compass bearing when the river looped too far away from their desired course and rejoining it in time to sleep. The nocturnal pattern of the journey suited them anyway because they had no blankets or sleeping bags and the nights were incredibly cold. So they put their heads down and marched sturdily by starlight, slapping their arms to their sides to create some warmth. After the second night, away from the Lulus, they were able to light fires to cook the trout which Jenkins, with skills learned in the very different gin-clear waters of Wales, was able to catch with his hands. They also shot a couple of small veldt bucks and ate meat which lasted for two days. The waters of the Oliphant were discoloured but drinkable and the air was clear and fresh. Although clouds rumbled threateningly, there were only small showers. Not once did they see another living soul on that vast plain until, having left the Oliphant on the sixth day, they trudged to the east and, in the heat of midday, encountered a picket of Colonial Horse and, the subject of great curiosity, were taken into Fort Weeber.

It was a different tented town from that which they had left a week and a half before. An air of bustle and urgency now characterised the place: all of the non-essential servicing tents were being struck, waggons loaded and cannons hitched to teams of horses. Bell tents stretched out across the veldt, and between them pyramids of rifles were leaning, ready to be snatched at a bugle call. It was clear that Wolseley had at last been able to bring his disjointed force together and that the attack on Sekukuni was about to be launched.

Simon and Jenkins exchanged handshakes with Ophrus and then left to find General Wolseley. Their welcome in the Commander-in-Chief's tent this time was much warmer than that which they had received nine days before. Wolseley sprang from his chair and shook them both by the hand. His gaze was direct, as always, but the smile was, perhaps, a little too wide and betrayed a touch of embarrassment.

'Welcome back, both of you,' he said. 'Never doubted for a moment that you would make it, but I am relieved to see you both back, I must stay. Sorry we had to leave you, but there were too many of those Kaffirs for us to have held them off until your return. But, as I say, I knew you would make it. Now tell me how you got back.'

He gestured to them to sit, and briefly and matter-of-factly Simon told their story. At the end he reached into his pocket and handed Wolseley a piece of paper.

'Eh? What's this then?'

'It's my sketch of the Fighting Kopje, sir,' explained Simon. 'I thought you wanted it.'

'Ah, yes, of course. Hmm. Very useful. I will study it later. Most useful, I should think, although I have, of course, made my plans for attack and given out my order of battle.'

'Yes, sir. Of course.' Simon felt Jenkins stir at his side. 'Can you tell us who fired the shot that alerted the bePedi to our presence on the mountain?'

'What? Ah.' This time the embarrassment on Wolseley's face was unmistakable. 'Very unfortunate, that. It was ... er ... Colonel Covington, as a matter of fact. I understand that he tripped on the mountainside and involuntarily discharged his revolver. It was very careless of him and, I must say, most unlike him. However, it had no serious repercussions, for he had completed most of his notes and so had I. My preparations were not affected.'

'Just a pity about us then, eh, General?' Simon's tone was impersonally cold and Jenkins's snort was quite audible.

'What?' Wolseley rose and leaned across the table, frowning, his chin thrust forward. 'That is quite unworthy of you, Fonthill. As I explained, we had no option but to ride away. The preparations for this battle could not be endangered. Let me make it perfectly clear that I will not tolerate either of you casting aspersions upon the character of a senior officer on my staff. I shall take action immediately if I receive any such reports. Is that quite clear?'

The two also rose to their feet, but Simon let a

silence hang for a moment in the tent before replying. 'Oh, quite clear, General, thank you.'

'Very well.' The frown remained on Wolseley's face but his tone lightened somewhat. 'Now, you did very good work in helping me to prepare my plan of attack, and I am grateful. I shall see that this is mentioned in my dispatches back to the Horse Guards. Now, you look as though you could both do with a good meal and some sleep. Tell the Quartermaster that I wish you to be well looked after.' His smile returned. 'He will be rather busy, because we march out tomorrow. I am following your advice, Fonthill, and attacking over the mountain with the Swazis to hit the rear of the town, so to speak, from above, while I make a frontal attack with my white troops and artillery down the valley from the north. Both columns set out tomorrow. I originally asked you to accompany the attack, but your preparatory scouting has been so successful that I will not need you to come with us. Your duties as scouts are finished and I wish you a well-earned rest. Now, if you will excuse me, I have much to do...'

Simon stiffened. 'Actually, General, we are both quite fit, despite our long trek, and would wish to go forward with the troops. I believe that we could be useful to you in the attack.'

Wolseley's eyebrows rose. 'Well, I am not so sure about that. But I ... ah ... admire your spirit and would be happy to have you with me.' He thought for a moment. 'But, Fonthill, I do not wish you to accompany Colonel Covington's column. You will be attached to my headquarters. Is that clear?'

'Quite clear, sir, thank you.'

Jenkins spoke for the first time. 'As a matter of fact, General bach,' he said in happy, conversational tones, 'we wouldn't want to be within pistol shot of the Colonel, if that's all the same to you, sir.' And he bestowed one of his face-splitting grins on the General.

'Eh?' Wolseley looked as though he was about to administer a rebuke and then thought better of it. 'Very well. We march at dawn. Good morning, er, gentlemen.'

Once outside, Jenkins blew out his cheeks. 'There you go, then, bach sir. What did I tell you? The bastard fired his popgun deliberately to leave us stranded, isn't it? He knew we were furthest away and wouldn't be able to get back. He left us for dead, as sure as God made little green apples.'

Simon frowned, staring away into the distance but seeing nothing. 'The man's a bastard, that's certain,' he said eventually, 'but I can't bring myself to believe that he would do that deliberately. He's a senior British officer, as Wolseley said, and they just don't do that sort of thing. It must have been an accident.'

'Saving your presence, bach sir, accident my arse. He 'ates you, and despite my charm, like, he doesn't think much o' me. Now, where do you think old Mendoozi will be in that 'eathen place?'

'Well, we know which hut he was using, but he won't be there. If he's got any guts – and, in fairness, he probably has – he will be in the firing line somewhere, so we will just have to look for him.'

'That we will, sir. That we will.'

The pair, bedraggled, dirty and dust-covered from their days and nights on the veldt, set off to find the Quartermaster. They learned that, predictably, their original tent had long since been dismantled, but they were allocated another, told where their horses were in the cavalry lines and given chits to eat with the infantrymen of the 21st Foot. It was quite clear from the Quartermaster's disapproving glance at Simon's appearance that he did not consider him a gentleman and worthy to eat in the officers' mess. But that caused Simon no concern, and, once installed in their tent and reunited with their modest belongings, the two men set off to visit Nandi.

She was still in the sick bay, but was now sitting on a camp stool at her bedside, and it was clear that she had made great progress, for her hair had regained some of its black sheen and her face and body had filled out in response to what had obviously been a healthy and regular diet. Her smile when she saw them was ingenuously warm, and she jumped to her feet and embraced each of them.

'Oh, I am so glad to see you back safely,' she said. 'I heard that you had gone missing and I have been so worried.' Tears now trickled down her cheeks. 'But I am happy again now.'

'Oh sit down, lass,' said Jenkins. 'You'll wear yourself out, jumpin' up like that.' He ushered her back to her chair and he and Simon sat on the bed, rather self-consciously.

'There was no need to worry about us, you know,' said Simon. 'You must know that bad pennies always turn up again.'

Nandi frowned, child-like. 'What do you mean, bad pennies...?'

'Oh, sorry. It's just a silly expression I remember from my school days. Now, tell us. How are you?'

She smiled again. 'Oh, I am much better, Simon, thank you. The doctor with the red hair has been, what shall I say...' She giggled. 'Very attentive.'

'I bet 'e 'as,' growled Jenkins.

'But, listen, best of all – Alice's man in Pretoria has been able to find my father, and he is on his way here!' She clapped her hands like a schoolgirl. 'Now what do you think of that?'

'Splendid, my dear,' acknowledged Simon.

Jenkins smiled politely, but not with his eyes. 'What ... er ... will you do then, lass?' he asked. 'After you and your da 'ave sort of got together, like, after all this time?'

Nandi's eyes widened. 'Oh, I don't know. I have not thought of that, you know. I expect we will go back to Zululand.' Then a happy thought struck her and the smile returned. 'Now that you have given us those...' her voice dropped, 'those things – you know?'

They both nodded.

'Papa should be able to buy more land and we can have a proper farm again – like we used to before the awful war. You know,' she continued, her face wearing that familiar earnest expression, 'I am – we are – so very grateful to you both. I would have died without you, and perhaps Papa would have also. We owe you everything.' And she

370

reached out and took a hand in each of hers.

Simon coughed to break the silence. 'I will ... er ... leave you two, if you don't mind,' he said, standing. 'I must ... er ... find someone.'

'Yes, of course,' said Nandi, lowering her eyes. 'She has been to see me every day, even though I know she has been so busy with her writing and all. She is in the press lines, Simon, on the left, not very far from here.'

'Ah, yes. Thank you. See you at the tent in half an hour, 352.'

It was not difficult to find Alice because, in reality, she found him. He was walking along the lines, looking for the press enclosure, when she burst out of it and ran towards him, dressed in crisp cream shirt, jodhpurs and riding boots, her hair tied back, her face radiant with joy – the very reincarnation, he thought, of an English spring day out here on the barren veldt of South Africa. She was running, but, realising the impropriety of that, she stopped and walked solemnly towards him, smiling.

They met but could not, of course, embrace. Instead she took his arm and walked him back companionably to her tent. 'The word has spread already. I heard that you had somehow walked back to the fort, seventy-five miles through bePedi country,' she whispered. 'You are so magnificent, Mr Fonthill. There is no other word for it.'

'Well, I don't know about that. Bloody lucky would be more appropriate, I would have thought.'

'No. No. When I heard that you had been left

371

behind I just did not know what to do. My love, I was so worried. But then I felt better when Ralph said that you would be all right–'

'He said what?'

'Oh.' Alice lowered her eyes. 'I had to ask him where you where, of course, when the General's party returned alone. He explained that the reconnaissance had been interrupted and that most of the party had been forced to flee, leaving you behind. However, he assured me that you were far away from the attack, well hidden, and that the General and everyone else were sure that you would find your way back.'

'Really? Without horses?'

'What? Ah, I see you are upset.' They had reached the group of tents marked 'Press Enclosure: No Admittance'. 'Come into the tent and tell me about it. You sound bitter, my love.'

The press enclosure seemed deserted, and they entered Alice's tent and immediately embraced. 'Ah, that's better,' said Alice, gently pulling away. 'Now I *know* that you are back. Come. Sit down and tell me the story.'

Simon did so, and after a moment Alice pulled out a pad and pencil and began making notes. She looked up. 'You don't mind, do you?' she asked.

'No. Having been left to rot out there by Wolseley and Covington I don't care a fig about them, Alice. You write what you like.'

'No, Simon,' explained Alice. 'I will not write about your adventures – although I am most anxious to know what happened to you – but it would help me if you can tell me about the

General's plan of attack. Covington won't give anything away, of course.'

'Ah,' smiled Simon. 'Good. Do write about it, because if there is a row afterwards, I am quite happy for Covington to get the blame. Now, where was I?'

When Simon related the story of the pistol shot alerting the bePedis, Alice laid down her pencil and listened with a frown. At the end, she knelt before him, put her arms around his neck and kissed him again, before returning to her seat on her camp chair.

'Look, my love,' she said. 'I do not believe for a moment that Ralph Covington would do such a thing deliberately. Whatever you think of him – and I must tell you that I remain fond of him, although I *do* love you, my dear – he is not dishonourable. It must have been an accident.' She regarded Simon intently, her eyes wide.

Simon ran his hands over his face. 'Alice,' he said, 'I am damned tired and perhaps I can't think straight any more. I must say that I didn't imagine Covington could do such a dastardly thing, but now I just don't know what to think.' He looked at her sharply. 'Have you told him yet about us?'

Alice held his gaze. 'No. I have not. As I said to you, I decided to leave doing so until after the battle for the reasons I explained, and … and … to be frank … to tell him that I loved you while you were missing would, I thought – I know this is stupid – but I thought it would tempt the fates and that you would not return.' She smiled. 'But now you are back I shall tell him immediately

373

that our engagement is ended. There is no further cause for delay. As a scout you have more than played your part, and will play no role in the attack.' She paused for a moment. 'That is ... I have presumed that. Surely your scouting work is done and they will not need you further?' She leaned forward with anxiety in her face.

Simon shook his head. 'It's not quite like that,' he said. 'Jenkins and I have work to do in Sekukuni, apart from which, I believe that the General wants me to help guide them in.' He looked away to hide his embarrassment at the falsehood.

Alice's eyes widened. 'What work? Oh, Simon, I don't like the sound of any of this. I don't want to lose you now that I have found you again.' She leaned forward and took his right hand in both of hers before continuing, speaking earnestly and quickly. 'Look, my love, I do not know what you have to do in that damned valley, but I do know that this attack will not be easy. Everyone says that even Wolseley is not so cocksure about it now that he has been able to make a proper reconnaissance of the place. Many of his horses have gone down with the sickness and a lot of his native drivers have deserted. He will have a hard time of it.' She paused and then continued, speaking now almost in a whisper. 'Simon, I have an awful premonition about all of this. I know you well enough to realise that I cannot stop you going if you feel you must. But please, please promise me that you will take great care – and don't move an inch without 352.'

At this they both laughed. 'Wouldn't think of

it,' said Simon. 'After all, someone has to look after the scoundrel.' They laughed again and then kissed once more, hungrily.

'Well,' said Alice eventually, whispering from under his right ear, 'that settles it. I shall certainly not tell Ralph before the battle. I just don't want to tempt the gods. But I promise that I will break off the engagement when you all return safely.' She stood. 'Now, my darling, you must go, for I have a dispatch to write and you look as though you could do with crawling into bed.' She giggled. 'Although I'm sorry I can't be with you.'

'So am I. But tell me. You are not being allowed to advance with the troops, are you?'

'Of course. We scribes will have a front-row seat, as far as I understand.'

'But you – not a woman, surely...?'

'Good God! *Of course.* Some time ago Wolseley huffed and puffed about me not going up, but no one has said a word since. I am a fully accredited correspondent, and even if they banned me specially – which they would not dare to – I should ignore them and make my own way. You know that, Simon.'

Simon sighed. 'Yes, I suppose so. But stay out of trouble, I beseech you. Do not go within rifleshot, please, Alice.'

'Have no fear for me, my love, I shall not be crossing swords personally with the fierce bePedi.' She smiled at him with moist eyes. 'Oh well, I suppose we will just have to worry about each other. Now, please, do go.' They kissed again and then he left.

Jenkins and Simon rose well before dawn the next morning, refreshed after some ten hours of sleep. They oiled their rifles and revolvers, saddled their horses, packed the little they needed in their saddle bags and reported to General Wolseley's headquarters. His tent was already being struck as they arrived and the first column of infantry was marching out of the camp. Wolseley nodded to them curtly, but there was no sign of Covington. Presumably he had gone ahead with his column. The dawn was hard to distinguish, for the sky remained a swollen black, and as soon as the General's party began to walk their horses forward a vast and blinding sheet of lightning sent the animals prancing and dancing, their eyes wide with fright. Then the rain began, hurtling down like a curtain of steel rods, forcing them all to don their capes. The advance on King Sekukuni's stronghold had begun.

Chapter 14

The similarity of the weather was the only element in common with Simon and Jenkins's ride to Sekukuni eleven days before. This time the pace was frustratingly slow, for Wolseley was moving forward some 1,400 British infantry, including contingents of the 21st, 94th and 80th Regiments of Foot, together with pipers; 400 colonial horse; four guns of the Transvaal artillery; a small detachment of Royal Engineers; and the commissariat. But the main portion of his army, of course, was the native levies, mostly 8,000 Swazis, intimidating and picturesque, even in the rain, in their headdresses of cranes' feathers, with leopardskins worn over their shoulders. They had been raised in Swaziland by Captain Norman Macleod of Macleod, the British agent there, and it was whispered that they had been promised most of the bePedi's cattle as reward for taking part in the campaign.

Simon found himself riding, head down against the driving rain, next to the chatty captain who had been present when he had first reported to Wolseley and who was a member of the General's staff. He learned from this source that Sir Garnet had been a whirlwind of activity since his return from the scouting trip. He had immediately forwarded strong parties to create two forts from which the assaults would be launched. The first,

377

on the eastern side of the Lulu Mountains, would be the base for Covington's column and had been christened Fort Burgers. The second, from which the main attack would stem, was called Fort Albert Edward and had been established on the Oliphant, north of Sekukuni, at Mapashlela's Drift. The main army was now marching towards Fort Burgers, where the Swazis, plus four companies of British regulars, would be left, while the remainder, the mainly white contingent, would march on northwards and concentrate at Fort Albert Edward.

'The General's had the deuce of a job with the logistics,' confided the captain, raindrops dripping off the end of his moustache. 'Given the attitude of the blasted Boers, it's bin like campaigning in hostile territory. Our nearest proper base, of course, is Durban, five hundred miles away, and we've not bin able to get supplies up here from within about a hundred miles – in fact, doncher know, the nearest farmhouse to this God-forsaken Sekukuni place is fifty miles away. All grain fields and tropical groves have bin abandoned for miles around.'

Simon tried to be sympathetic. 'So everything's had to be brought up from Durban and around Pretoria?'

'Yes. The supply line has stretched for miles – and it's had to be guarded all the way.'

'Good lord! Did the General really believe that the Boers would make an attack while the army was concentrated on the war with Sekukuni?'

'It was a possibility.' The captain grinned. 'In a way, I think that the old man rather hoped they

378

would. It would mean that he could settle this damned Transvaal business once and for all. But it hasn't materialised and I doubt if it will. After all, these Dutchmen want Sekukuni dealt with almost as much as they want their own independence, yer know.'

Simon nodded. 'Yes, I see that.' He pulled down his hat brim. 'But nothing's going to happen in this damned weather, anyway.'

In fact the weather became worse, if that was possible. Great claps of thunder rolled up at them from across the open veldt, and three men were killed by lightning before the long column camped for the night. The succeeding days were the same; mud was added to the problem, and streams sprang up from nowhere as the waggons struggled along the now lushly overgrown old Boer track. Horse sickness took its daily toll of the mounts of the officers and colonial cavalry. It was rumoured that Wolseley was in some personal distress with pain from an old leg injury, but he gave little evidence of that, riding round in the rain at the end of the day, ensuring that troops and natives alike were finding shelter for the night.

On one such expedition, he grinned at a wet and dishevelled Jenkins and observed, 'Nothing like a soldier's life, eh, bach?' before riding on.

Eventually, as the storms relented, the little army was able to split and concentrate on the two forts. Simon and Jenkins rode with the European column to Fort Albert Edward – another misnomer, of course, for it was nothing more than a tented encampment fifteen miles north of Sekukuni town. Nevertheless, Lieutenant Colonel Baker Russell, a trusted member of Wolseley's Ashanti's Ring whom the General had decided should have tactical command of the attack, had already set up an advance post, seven miles ahead, and had conducted a successful action the previous day at the kraal of Umkwane, one of King Sekukuni's chiefs, at the northern entrance to the valley. Wolseley decided that he would attack without further delay.

He called a meeting of his staff that evening. The sky was clear so the small group was able to sit around a camp fire under the stars, and Simon, having ridden with the staff, decided that there was no reason why he should not listen, so he quietly attached himself to the outer fringe of the group.

Wolseley, his stocky figure loosely wrapped in a large cavalry cloak, looked vaguely Napoleonic as he stood etching the outline of the mountains and the valley in the damp sand with his riding crop. In a few concise words he gave his orders. At two a.m. the troops would be roused (no bugle calls) and Baker Russell would take the column down the narrow valley that ran north-south parallel to the main valley of the township. At dawn, he would curl into the main valley and launch his attack on the town itself. Shortly afterwards, Covington's column would come over the top of the Lulu range and attack the town from above. Meanwhile, the artillery would bombard the Fighting Kopje and keep its defenders from playing a decisive part in the battle. Only after the town had been taken would all forces converge and attack the kopje.

Craning over the shoulder of the friendly captain on the edge of the circle, Simon allowed himself a smile. Just as he had recommended! He stole away to find Jenkins, who had erected their small bivouac tent and laid out their groundsheet and two sleeping bags.

The small man sniffed. 'P'raps they'll make you a general yet, then. Well, I'll tell you this, bach sir. You'd make a damned sight better one than most of 'em. Tell me, was Colonel Covington there?'

'No,' said Simon. 'He is obviously with his troops on the reverse side of the Sekukuni mountain. He must have been given his orders previously. There is no reason why we should see him because I intend to go in with the main attack, at ground level. This the best way to find our man, I think. Agreed?'

'Agreed. But won't the General 'ave a few jobs for us, like? We're supposed to be scouts out 'ere 'elpin' 'im, aren't we?'

'That's true, but our main job has been done, in the initial reconnaissance, that is. So far he has hardly noticed us, so I think there should be no problem in slipping away with Colonel Baker Russell. Which means we must be ready to march at two o'clock. Better get some sleep.'

They were noticed, however. Predictably, the rains returned as the column formed up, the troops miserable in a drenching darkness only relieved by the crashing flashes of sheet lightning. Wolseley, his cape glistening, rode up to Simon as he and Jenkins tried to make themselves inconspicuous on the edge of Baker Russell's small staff.

'Ah, Fonthill,' he called. 'There you are. Been looking for you. You and your man will accompany Colonel Baker Russell up front and help him find his way in this damned weather down this valley. Know it, don't you?'

Simon felt his heart sink. He had only glimpsed the narrow valley at its northern end, from which it had looked navigable but, with the need to deliver Nandi to safety, he had had no time then to reconnoitre it personally. The Ndebeles, however, had told him that it shadowed the larger, Sekukuni valley for most of its length and that a large force could traverse it. He nodded. 'More or less, sir. Should be fine.'

Wolseley gave him a sharp glance from under his dripping hat brim. 'I damn well hope so,' he said. 'You get them there in time to attack at dawn. Understood?'

'Very good, sir.'

The journey was a nightmare. There had originally been a hunting track down the centre of the valley but now it was overgrown with dense bush and the waggons made very heavy work of pushing through the foliage. Waggons stuck and oxen fell as the heavens thundered and strong winds sent the rain swirling about them. The curses of the drivers and the crack of their whips added a Mephisthophelean atmosphere to the scene, lit irregularly by great sheets of red lightning. Many of the plodding troops, who had had precious little sleep during the past twenty-four hours, lacked capes, and the mud and rain had turned their once-scarlet jackets into faded caricatures of uniforms.

Riding ahead with Jenkins, Simon was aware that a large, bearded man riding a horse of gigantic proportions had pulled alongside him. 'God,' said the stranger. 'After this march, I can't see the troops being able to attack tomorrow.'

Simon looked hard at him. The man wore a strange blue naval-type cap wedged on to his head, from which black hair fell nearly to his shoulders. He seemed to be wearing no uniform.

'Sorry,' said the man, extending a hand. 'Russell, *Daily Telegraph*. You're Fonthill, aren't you?' He nodded across to Jenkins. 'Alice Griffith has told me a bit about you both – although not much. That girl likes to keep a good story to herself.' He grinned.

Simon smiled back. 'Presumably Alice is back with the General, is she?' He tried to keep his tone matter-of-fact.

'Good lord, no. She's just back there, with the rest of us scribblers. Somewhere between the artillery and the commissariat.'

'This is no place for a woman, Mr Russell,' said Simon, shaking his head. 'It's bad enough now, but the fighting hasn't even started yet.'

Russell grinned. 'I quite agree with you, Fonthill, but the world's a-changing faster than I can keep up. And I'm supposed to chronicle it. No doubt we shall be having women generals soon. But she's a damned fine journalist, I'll say that.' He paused and wiped the rain from his face with a dirty grey handkerchief. 'What do you think of our chances in the morning? I've told my readers last night that I couldn't see how these troops could go straight into the attack. They're soaked and damn near exhausted.'

Simon shot him a keen glance. This was a man who had reported all of the great wars of the past thirty years: the Crimea, the American Civil War, the Franco-Prussian conflict, the recent Zulu War and numerous colonial clashes. Probably no general had witnessed so much warfare from so close a range as this awkward, paternal-looking figure riding beside him. But he was a shrewd, iconoclastic operator. Was he pumping him? Better be careful.

'Come now, Mr Russell,' he said, 'you know as well as I how capable the British soldier of the line is.' He was forced to shout as another great thunder roll echoed across the narrow valley. 'This is hard, but give him time for a mug of tea and a pipe of 'baccy after the march and he will get up and charge with his rifle and bayonet as though he'd just stepped off the parade ground. There's no one better at slogging through this sort of hell and then getting on with the job. You were at Sebastapol – and think of Ashanti and Rorke's Drift.'

'Ah yes. You were at the last place, I hear. Great deeds. Perhaps you are right. We shall see in the morning. Good luck, Fonthill.' And he let his horse fall behind.

Although the conditions made the march through the long, thin valley extremely difficult, at least the route presented no problems of navigation, for the way lay straight ahead and it was not possible to deviate. The storm also prevented Sekukuni from sending out skirmishers to harass the column as it plodded along, vulnerable to attack from the high hillsides that frowned down upon it from either side. In fact, as dawn neared, the conditions improved and Simon was able to mark quite clearly the gap where the hills to the left swept down, giving access to the main valley. Here, Baker Russell called a halt and gathered his force together.

The lieutenant colonel, slim and worried-looking, had been one of the great successes of Wolseley's Ashanti campaign, and Simon had heard that Wolseley had deliberately stepped back from direct command of the assault on Sekukuni's township to give his protégé a chance for glory. Despite his harassed appearance – and, reflected Simon, who wouldn't look concerned after making a forced march like this? – Baker Russell was precise and Wolseley-like in giving his orders for the attack. The assault would be delivered simultaneously from three directions. That from the south would be led by the charismatic Colonel Ignatius Ferreira, the daring Boer leader who had, it seemed, taken part in every military enterprise that South Africa had seen over the last thirty years. He would be at the head of his eponymous Horse, dismounted for the task, and supported by native contingents. The central attack would be launched by the rest of the colonial troops, most of them of British stock, again backed by native levies, and the northern thrust would be made by the British troops and the artillery. The latter would direct fire on the kopje, which would be the main target for the line soldiers, who, until their turn came to storm it, would stay in reserve. Covington was expected to synchronise his attack over the mountain at the same time.

Quietly, the column debouched on to the plain and the men took up their positions in the darkness, waiting for the dawn. As though awed at the prospect of slaughter, the weather now relented, but it remained cold and Simon found himself shivering as, with Jenkins, he lined up with the southern Afrikaners and mixed black troops under Ferreira's command. They were within rifleshot of the rough stone walls that marked the edge of the town, but no sound came from them and no light shone from within the township itself. It seemed as though the place was deserted – like some ghost town of the American west. Simon fingered the long bayonet on the end of his rifle and looked across at Jenkins. The Welshman's face was alive with anticipation, his black eyes gleaming in the semi-darkness. As ever, the warrior was ready for the battle.

Jenkins grinned and nodded. 'Cleared up nicely for it, hasn't it?' he confided. 'Remind me again what the bastard looks like, 'cos I've never seen 'im, 'ave I?'

'Tall, very tall.' Simon licked his lips. 'About six foot four. Very broad and with long black wavy hair and a pock-marked face. I don't know what we will discover when we get over that wall,' he found that his voice sounded hoarse and he cleared his throat, 'but once we're inside we'll try and make for his hut, and if and when I recognise him, I'll shout, so stay by me.'

'I always do, don't I?'

Suddenly, as the sky began to lighten from the

west, a single shell exploded high on the kopje to their left. The flare of the explosion added to the lightening of the sky to reveal the crouching attackers, and the low line of the wall ahead suddenly erupted into hundreds of yellow flashes as the waiting defenders saw their targets. At the same time a howl went up from the city – a cry of taunting ferocity that sent a shock wave through Simon's body, so barbaric and ethereal was it in pitch and tone. It was as though a thousand lost souls had been unearthed from their tombs to run free among the living.

'Blimey,' muttered Jenkins. 'They've bin waitin' for us. What a welcome. It's like attackin' the gates of 'ell.'

The defenders' volley was too high to take effect, but the howl was enough to daunt even the bravest soldier, and although sounds of attack came from the left, higher up the valley, the men of Ferreira's force stayed crouching, their eyes wide. Then a shout – probably in Afrikaans and therefore unintelligible to Simon and Jenkins – came from the tall figure of Ferreira himself, who stood, waved his hand at the wall and ran towards it alone, the occasional low-aimed bullet tearing up a spurt of dust around his feet.

'Come on,' gulped Simon, and he scrambled to his feet and followed the colonel, with Jenkins close by his side. The firing from the wall was intense but quite erratic and undisciplined. If the rifles lining the wall had sights, they had clearly been set too high and the running men heard the *ping* of bullets flying over their heads. In addition, the single-shot rifles were not being reloaded

387

quickly and there was no attempt at volley firing. As a result the two men were able to gain the wall without injury and scrambled up on to its top alongside Ferreira, who stood there jabbing downwards with his bayonet, seemingly impervious to the gunfire directed at him. All three used their long rifles and bayonets to deflect the assegai thrusts that came at them from below, but they remained terribly vulnerable to the gun of any marksman who had had the sense to remove himself from the mêlée to take cool, deliberate aim at them. Then a yell in Simon's ear told him that the rest of the Colonials had reached the wall, and the crash of fire from Martini-Henrys sent a swirl of acrid smoke to engulf attackers and defenders alike. It was too much for the bePedis and they turned and ran – but only to a second line of defence, a ditch backed by a wall of roughly piled stones. Another line of defenders was waiting there, muskets and rifles levelled, but the fallback of the men from the first wall inhibited the field of fire from the second, and the volley that should have taken its toll of the Colonials was irregular and ineffective.

Following the fleeing bePedis, Simon slipped to the bottom of the ditch and lay there for a moment, his hands clutching his long rifle and perspiration running down his face. He fumbled to reload and then realised that he had not discharged the round already in the breech. He looked around for Jenkins, but all he could see were the backs of the brown uniforms of the colonial troops as they scrambled up the other side of the ditch and then the rough piles of ill-assorted stones that formed the wall. Once again Simon experienced the literal taste of battle – the acrid bitterness of cordite on his lips and the rough, choking smell of smoke from a hundred rifle barrels. He gulped. Oh God! Where was Jenkins?

His prayer was answered in a cascade of stones as the little Welshman tumbled down the slope to crash into his shoulder. 'Sorry, bach sir,' he said. ''Ad to finish a bit of business,' and he gestured to his bayonet, whose tip was red with blood. 'Any sign of 'im?'

'No. Can't see a damned thing in this smoke. He could be anywhere. We'll just have to penetrate further with these men into the heart of the town, then, if we can, we must go to that hut. But I'm sure he won't be there. He could be with the King, which will mean the Fighting Kopje, I would guess. Come on.'

But penetrating the town was easier said than done. The wave of the attack had broken on this wall. After climbing it and sending its defenders fleeing once again, the line of Colonials had been halted by strong and, this time, well-directed fire from yet another set of earthworks ahead. Leaving a littering of dead and wounded brown-clad figures on the earth between the two lines, the attackers turned and scrambled back over the second wall, where they settled to exchange rifle fire with the bePedis, whose heads could just be seen intermittently behind puffs of blue smoke as they levelled their rifles from the top of the trench. Simon nuzzled his rifle stock into his shoulder and released his first round of the campaign. Then he was conscious of a figure at his elbow.

Lieutenant Colonel Baker Russell scowled ahead at the obstruction and then lifted his binoculars towards the summit of the mountain behind the township. 'It's going to be damned hard taking this place wall by wall,' he muttered. 'Where the hell is Covington with his Swazis?'

Simon directed his own gaze to the jagged line of the mountaintop ahead. There was no sign of life. The Swazis should have been swarming down the mountainside by now. He held his hand to his eyes, the better to focus. He frowned and then reached a hand across to the binoculars that now dangled on Baker Russell's chest.

'May I, sir?' He had left his own field glasses in his saddle bag. The colonel grunted assent and Simon focused the lenses. 'I thought so,' he murmured.

He handed back the binoculars. 'Sir, direct your glasses to the break in the line of bush, just below the summit, to the right there. What do you see?'

Baker Russell gave Simon a questioning glance, but then focused his glasses. 'Can't see a bloody thing... No. There are a crowd of natives, by the look of it, standing there and looking down on us. Who the hell are they? Eh? Do you know?'

'I think I do, sir. They are Swazi chiefs – and no doubt Colonel Covington is in there somewhere urging them to move. But they won't just yet.' Simon gave a mirthless smile. 'As I told the General, they have been caught too many times being made to take all the risks against the bePedis while the redcoats and, for that matter, the Boers too stand by and watch them break the back of the resistance and take all the fire. They are waiting to see how well we do down here before they attack. When they are convinced we mean business, they will come down, you will see.'

'What? Can't Covington get 'em to move?'

Simon shrugged. 'Obviously not, sir.'

'Good God.' Baker Russell lowered his glasses. 'Well. We have no choice but to go on. If necessary we'll just clear this place by ourselves. But we're going to lose a lot of men if we can't put pressure on the higher end of the defences, up that mountain there. Why can't Covington stick a poker up the arses of his black men and get 'em to come down from the top?'

'No, no. Look.' Simon gestured to the top of the mountain. As though in response to Baker Russell's indignation – but more likely as a result of the gradual inroads being made into the defences of the town on the valley floor – the mountaintop was suddenly lined with a host of black figures. Even at that distance it was clear that hundreds, probably thousands of warriors, were slowly mounting that ridge line from the other side and descending towards the town. As each line of Swazis crossed the ridge, the tiny, insect-like creatures could be seen to lift their shields, and even above the desultory rifle firing and occasional crump of artillery shells against the stone of the kopje, a low rumble of intent, a distinctive, barbaric war cry, could be heard.

'By jove,' exclaimed Baker Russell, 'the bastards are coming at last. Look at 'em. See how they come!'

'Bloody 'ell,' said Jenkins. 'It's like Zululand again.'

The Swazis were now swarming down the mountainside like a broad stream of soldier ants, spreading out to encircle the walls lining the upper reaches of the township's defences and prompting a rattle of musketry from the walls there. A new sound emerged in the terrible cacophony of warfare: a resonant, deep clicking from the hollow bones that the men from the east carried into battle and beat one against the other. The Swazis were now clearly in view and their great headdresses could be seen nodding and bobbing as their wearers thrust and slashed with their spears against the defenders behind the walls. Behind and up above the waves of black warriors, small rectangular patches of red stood out as the four companies of British soldiers of the line descended the hillside more cautiously.

'Now we shall have them.' Baker Russell lifted his voice. 'Colonel Ferreira. Now is the time to advance. Have your command resume the attack at once.'

Immediately, the Colonials reloaded their rifles and discharged them, then, with a high-pitched shout, scrambled over the low wall and rushed across the intervening space with their bayonets levelled. This time the defending bePedis did not break but manfully leapt to their feet in front of their trench and met the attack, spear to bayonet, knobkerrie to rifle butt. The hand-to-hand fighting that ensued was brutal and atavistic in its medieval ferocity. There was no time for the

392

adversaries to reload their rifles; it was now a matter of brute strength and dexterity, the winner in each individual combat being he who could wield cold steel more effectively. In this, the soldiers of Ferreira's Horse, although fine marksmen and possessing consummate skills in horsemanship, were at a disadvantage. They had received little training in bayonet fighting, and at first, the savage counterattack of the bePedi spearmen drove them back.

Simon and Jenkins fought side by side, using the superior length of the Martini-Henry rifles – some six foot from the tip of the triangular bayonet to the butt of the rifle stock – to great effect. Remembering a tactic from the Zulu War, Simon repeatedly jabbed his bayonet through the centre of his adversary's cow-hide shield to where he estimated he was holding it, spearing the knuckles and forcing him to drop the shield, so that he could follow up with a *coup de grâce* thrust to the ribs. But it was fiercely hard and dangerous work, and there was no doubt that the Colonials were gradually losing the initiative when a volley of rifle shots and a loud cheer announced the arrival of a detachment of red-coated infantry from Wolseley's reserve. Their arrival swung the balance of the conflict. The bePedis broke and the Colonials and the British swept through into the kraal behind.

Simon and Jenkins followed, but with a nod of the head from Simon, they diverted to the left and began running through a maze of little alleys between the huts, moving towards the back of the township and up to the cleft in the hillside where the King's large hut and those of his honoured guests stood. Although they were now well in advance of the attacking force, they saw no one but a few scattered women and children, peering round the open door of one or two huts, wide-eyed in their fear. Simon remembered that the majority of the non-combatants and their cattle would be sheltering in the depths of the 'storage' mountain. As he ran, however, he had little hope of finding Mendoza in his hut. Such a man – if he still remained in Sekukuni at all – would be fighting alongside his client king.

However, there was another problem that occupied Simon's mind as he ran, rifle at the ready, through the deserted centre of the bePedi capital: how was he going to stop Jenkins from killing Mendoza?

He had long ago resolved that, villain that Mendoza was – rapist, gun-runner, diamond thief, would-be murderer and abductor – he could not be killed in cold blood. In retrospect, Simon had been disgusted by the killing of Nandi's guards in the hut, but at least that *had* been a necessity, if they were to escape from the citadel alive. Deliberately seeking out and slaying the Portuguese-Mozambiquan was an entirely different matter. All Simon's instincts, upbringing and training persuaded him that the proper, the *civilised* thing to do would be to capture him, hand him over to the authorities and lay charges against him. Harbouring these thoughts himself, however, was a far cry from persuading Jenkins of the rightness of the course. There was no question but that 352 was determined to kill the man who had abused

394

the woman he loved. As he ran, he cast a quick glance at Jenkins. The Welshman's eyes were black-button sharp as his head turned this way and that. They were the eyes of an executioner.

In the event, as Simon had suspected, the hut next to that from which they had rescued Nandi was empty. Bursting through the low doorway, their rifles cocked, the two men found only a large bed, from which the blankets had been thrown, a table containing dirty earthenware dishes and, hanging from a peg on the wall, a strange sombrero and an old European-style jacket. Simon rifled through the pockets while Jenkins poked under the bed. Their only reward was a faded label inside the jacket that gave a Portuguese-sounding name and an address in Lorenzo Marques.

Simon held it up. 'This must be his,' he said. 'Has that bed been slept in recently, do you think?'

Jenkins nodded expressionlessly. 'Still almost warm,' he said. 'The bastard's around 'ere somewhere.'

Simon rolled up the jacket. 'He could be manning the walls or he could be on the kopje. Let's see if we can find out.'

Cautiously, they left the hut. The sounds of battle echoed from all around, but here, in the epicentre of the storm, all seemed strangely quiet and even deserted. Simon pushed open the door of the King's hut. This, too, was empty – or was it? In a dim recess, he saw something move under what seemed to be a pile of skins. He strode across and observed one small bare foot quietly inching its way back under cover. Simon levelled his rifle and whipped away the top skin to reveal the hunched figure of a little black boy, perhaps six or seven years old, whose wide eyes now regarded the pair of them with fear.

Simon allowed himself a grin and, extending a hand, gently pulled the boy to his feet. 'Dammit,' he said to Jenkins, 'this is where I wish I had a twopenny bun to offer him.'

'Better still...' said Jenkins, and he fished in his pocket for a silver sixpence. ''Ere, Jimbo,' he said, pressing it into the little hand, 'buy yourself a pint of good African beer.'

The boy's eyes grew even wider as he looked at the coin and then from one to the other of the men who were bending at his side. His fingers tightened over the sixpence.

'Now,' Simon addressed him, speaking slowly, 'do you speak English? No, how bloody stupid. Of course you don't.' He picked up the jacket and opened it out. 'Mendoza?' he asked. The huge brown eyes regarded him expressionlessly, but at least they did not now show fear. Simon opened the jacket to show the label and tried again. 'Joachim Mendoza?'

At last an awareness dawned on the urchin's face. He nodded his head quickly in affirmation, happy to know that he was not about to be killed and proud that he understood what he was being asked. He spoke quickly in unintelligible bePedi.

'Yes, but where?' asked Simon. He shielded his eyes with one hand and mimed the action of a man looking everywhere. 'Where Mendoza?' he repeated.

Again recognition dawned. 'Mendoza, Ntswan-eng,' he said, mimicking the slowness of Simon's own speech. 'Ntswaneng.'

'Oh, where the bloody 'ell's that, then?' asked Jenkins, turning to Simon in despair.

'It's the native name for the Fighting Kopje. It's as I thought. He's probably with the King, making a stand in the fortress. Damn, it's going to be difficult winkling him out from there.'

Jenkins frowned. 'Don't worry about that, bach sir. It will be done. I promise you that.'

'We must go. I don't want to be cornered in here.' Simon gave a rub to the curly hair of the urchin, who, as they strode to the door, put the sixpence in his mouth, presumably for safekeeping. The centre of the citadel was still deserted and the problem now arose of how to get through the perimeter, which, by the sound of musketry and shouting, was still a ring of fighting.

''Ow the 'ell do we get out of 'ere?' demanded Jenkins.

'I know.' Simon gestured. 'The way we left the first time. Through the roof of Nandi's hut and on to that rock.'

The door of the hut sagged open and the interior still seemed much as they had left it: dishevelled blankets on the beds, the table still standing under the hole in the roof. The bodies, however, had disappeared, only three dull terracotta-coloured stains on the beaten earth to show where three men had been killed. Leaping upwards from the table, Simon was just able to pull himself through the aperture in the roof and lie on the thatch for a moment to get his bearings.

397

The position gave him a panoramic view of the battle for Sekukuni's city. Below him, down in the valley, the walls of the outer perimeter had been broken, but a screen of blue smoke, gently drifting away along its top, only to be constantly renewed at the bottom, showed where fierce fighting still marked the inner ring of stone fortifications. To his right, the swelling mound of the kopje was isolated, with the majority of Wolseley's reserve clearly to be seen surrounding its base, while the occasional flash of shell bursts threw splinters of stone from the higher sides of the granite pile. The shelling seemed to be having the effect of keeping the defenders' heads down, for no flashes of rifle firing could be seen offering response from the somnolent fortress. Up above Simon, where the huts of the upper town meandered up the mountainside to end in another series of stone-wall defences, he could see that equally savage fighting was taking place. Covington's four companies of red-coated British infantrymen were now mingling with the Swazis in savage hand-to-hand fighting at the walls. It was obvious, however, that the greater numerical advantage possessed by the Swazis was taking effect, and even as he watched, he saw the line break and scores of black warriors, brandishing their assegais and frightening in their leopardskins and plumed headdresses, pour through the gap in pursuit of the running bePedis.

Simon reached down and helped Jenkins to join him on the thatch. Together they crawled to the flat rock and lay side by side, rifles at the ready. At one point, Jenkins raised his weapon to sight on a bePedi warrior running down the track below them, but Simon laid a restraining hand on the barrel. 'No, 352,' he said, 'I think we've done enough killing for a while. There will be more to come. Let's wait for that.' Jenkins gave him a quizzical glance, but then nodded and slowly laid down his rifle.

Their position on the rock, some hundred feet above the valley floor and tucked away in the cleft, above and to one side of the trail leading to the mountain ridge, removed them from the battle itself, or rather from what had now become a rout. The Swazis were pouring down into the town, and even though firing continued along the southern rim of the defences, it could only be a matter of minutes before the last organised resistance broke. As they watched, the first burst of flame came from huts in the centre as the Swazis torched them, and soon great columns of smoke began to rise above the once-proud township. Simon hoped that the little boy had been able to get away, with his sixpence, before the fierce attackers swept through. For the first time for some hours, he thought of Alice and offered up a quick prayer that she had stayed out of gunshot range and that she would be prevented from venturing too close to the kopje.

He looked up at the sun. It was still only mid-morning. The battle for Sekukuni's capital had been won. That for his fortress, the Fighting Kopje, had yet to begin.

Chapter 15

An hour later, Simon and Jenkins – the latter, as always when officers were present, keeping a diffident pace behind his captain – joined the little group of officers milling around Baker Russell on the valley floor just out of rifle range of the kopje. All around the base of the fortress hundreds of the invaders swarmed, forming a motley, seething gathering of blue-black Swazis, brown-corded Colonials and perspiring British infantrymen, their faces as red as their jackets. Behind them all, the Sekukuni township was now well ablaze and Swazis could be seen extracting cattle from their miraculous hiding places in the storage hill. The Colonel noted this with irritation. He beckoned his young aide-de-camp.

'Jackson,' he ordered, 'gallop across to that damned place. There will be bePedi women tending those cattle. See if you can find Colonel Covington, or, better still, Captain Macleod. Tell them that the Swazis can have the cattle but not, repeat not, the women. That was our arrangement with them. Understood?'

'Very good, sir.'

Baker Russell now addressed his staff. 'Now, gentlemen, our battle has only just begun.' He swung round and stared up at the kopje. As he did so, another shell from the horse artillery exploded high up among the granite slabs. 'As you can see, they are quite impervious to artillery up there, in their caves and trenches. Our guns might have managed to keep them from popping off at us as we attacked the town, but once we start climbing we won't be able to use them and they will come out of their holes and give us hell. Now, I shall... Ah, here's the General. Morning, sir.'

Wolseley, erect as ever on his giant grey, cantered up and raised his riding crop in languid acknowledgement of the salutes. 'Good morning, Russell, gentlemen. Well done so far. You cleared the township well enough. Casualties?'

'I have not had the final report, sir, but quite low, I think. Certainly not many of our chaps. More among the Colonials and, obviously, the native levies. But overall, very acceptable.'

Simon exchanged a sardonic raised eyebrow with Jenkins.

'Good.' The General gestured up towards the top of Sekukuni's mountain. 'What delayed the Swazis? Has anyone seen Covington or Macleod?'

'Not yet, sir. Your scout chap ... er ... Fonting-bridge or whatever–'

'He's right behind you. Morning, Fonthill.'

'Good morning, Sir Garnet.'

'Ah yes, Fonthill. Well, Mr ... er ... Fonthill believes that the Swazis were waiting to see how hard we fought before pitching in. Is that right, Fonthill?'

'I believe so, sir. But in the end they seem to have pitched in with a will.'

Wolseley nodded. 'Right, Russell. Make sure that every last damned hut in that township is

401

burned to the ground. I want these bePedis to be taught a lesson that will stop them raiding farms around here for generations. They must realise that they live on land which is under the jurisdiction of Her Majesty and of Her Majesty's Government.'

Baker Russell nodded. 'Of course, sir.' He gestured to where a thick pall of smoke hung over the site of the King's former citadel. 'The job is being done now.'

'Good. No sign of the King, I suppose?'

'No, sir. We believe him to be up on the kopje with his court and some of his best warriors.'

'Right. Well, pluck 'em out, Russell. Pluck 'em out.'

'Very good, sir.' Baker Russell turned back to his staff. 'Right, gentlemen.' He swept his arm around to indicate the mass of warriors and soldiers. 'Sort out this mess and take your units to their positions. Each of you will report to me when you are in place. I want the attack to spring from all points around the kopje as soon as the signal rocket hits the top of the hill. I myself will lead on this side and every member of the staff is free to lead his unit personally.' He smiled. 'There will be a chance of glory for us all this day, gentlemen.'

His remarks were greeted with a cheer and the group broke up. 'Fonthill.' The colonel beckoned Simon towards him. 'You heard those orders?'

'Yes, sir.'

'Well, the officer commanding the bloody Swazis did not. Will you please ride immediately to Colonel Covington and relay them to him. He is obviously somewhere in the township. Both he and Captain Macleod know where these black chaps are to be positioned and he must move them down here immediately. I cannot attack until they are here. If you can't find Covington, give the orders to Macleod. He knows the Swazis better, anyway. You can't miss him, the feller will be wearing a kilt.'

'Very good, sir.'

Nodding to Jenkins to follow, Simon strode off to find his horse, and together they rode towards the base of the smoke. The township, once home to four thousand people, was now a mass of cinders, for the huts, with their brittle, sun-dried timber and thatched roofs, had provided perfect fuel for the flames and nothing could stop the conflagration. As the pair neared the smoke, they were forced to wrap handkerchiefs around their mouths and pull low the brims of their hats as protection against the blown ashes.

A tall Swazi, his spear bloodied and his shield holed, gave them a blank glance as they approached.

'Where is Colonel Covington?' shouted Simon, in the hope that the man spoke English.

His hope was rewarded. 'Don't know him, baas,' came the reply, 'but Captain Macleod, him over there.' He pointed with his assegai to the northern edge of the town, where a group of Swazis were busy fetching and carrying.

It proved to be a casualty clearing station, and they found the captain, with his face, his Macleod tartan and his jaunty bonnet all covered in soot and a spear tear in his once-white shirt, supervising with great care the loading of three wounded Swazi warriors on to stretchers.

Simon flung himself off his horse and gave the Scotsman Baker Russell's instructions. 'Aye,' said Macleod. 'I'll get them along there directly but it may take a while.' He gave a wry smile. 'These chappies can't just be ordered about like that, you know – particularly when there are cattle about.' The smile disappeared. 'Tell the colonel that I will be in command because Colonel Covington has been wounded, I am afraid. He has been taken to the forward hospital and is being well looked after. Now you must excuse me.'

Simon held his arm. 'Wounded? How badly?'

'I've not seen him, but I understand that it's a pretty bad wound, though not life-threatening as far as I know. Now, if you'll forgive me, I must get on. There's much to do.' And he strode away, gesticulating to a group of native warriors who were herding away a cluster of long-horned cattle.

Simon and Jenkins exchanged glances. 'Blimey,' said Jenkins. 'Nothing trivial, I hope.'

'Now then, 352, enough of that. We have work to do. Come on.' But Simon's brain was working hard. A severe wound? How bad would that be, and what would Alice make of it? He shook his head.

They rode back towards the kopje, where some sense of order was being restored to the masses of troops around its base. They eventually found Lieutenant Colonel Baker Russell and Simon gave him Macleod's message. If the colonel was concerned by the news of Covington's wound he gave no sign. 'I just hope Macleod gets here within the next half-hour,' he grunted, and strode off.

Simon now looked for Alice, but as far as he could see, none of the press corps was in evidence on this side of the kopje. No doubt they would be on the far side, probably with General Wolseley. Should he make an effort to find her and tell her about Covington? He cast a quick glance towards Jenkins. The Welshman obviously harboured no concern about their former CO, for he was scanning the upper reaches of the kopje, his hand shielding his eyes. At the moment, Jenkins 352 had only one thought in his mind. Simon sighed. No, dammit, he would not go hunting for Alice among the many hundreds of soldiers now filling the valley floor. She would have enough to do in reporting on the battle and he saw no reason to divert her now with news of her fiancé. She would find out quickly enough. He fumbled in his saddle bag for his field glasses, focused them on the slopes of the conical hill and slowly traversed his gaze along its rocky ledges.

'Any sign of 'im?' croaked Jenkins, wiping the soot from his face.

'No. All I can make out are rows of heads above the rocks and rifle barrels poking through them too. The fact that they have all been quiet up there doesn't mean that they are not going to fight. They're waiting for us all right.'

'Well, the sooner we get started the better. What's the plan then, bach sir?'

405

Simon lowered his glasses and licked his dry lips. 'We've no way of knowing where the hell he is, so I guess we will just have to go up with the first wave of troops. As always, let's stay together. It's going to be a hard climb.'

'It's them bloody bees as is worryin' me, look you.'

They did not have long to wait. Dense masses of Swazis had now joined the British infantrymen, the Colonials and other black irregulars swarming around the base of the kopje, and the British officers, line commanders and staff alike, had forced their way to the front, swords in hand, waiting for the signal to advance. The first rocket, telling everyone to make ready, hissed overhead, arcing over the kopje and what remained of the smouldering township and extinguishing itself against the side of the mountain. The invaders on the valley floor stiffened and waited. Then the second rocket signalled the advance and the artillery sent down a last barrage against the giant rock slabs and grey boulders before falling silent as the attackers began their steep climb. Silence, however, did not reign. The higher slopes of the great hill exploded with rifle cracks and flashes and that demonic, high-pitched howl as the bePedis once again expressed their defiance. It was joined this time, however, by the skirl of Highland pipes as well as the clacking of the Swazis' hollow bones and the thud as these warriors crashed their knees, Zulu-style, against the inside of their shields. And yet the Swazis made no attempt to begin the attack. In a dense black mass, they stood back and watched as the British and Colonials, heavily burdened by their battle packs, rifles and bayonets, began scrambling and slipping among the scree at the base of the steep hill.

Simon looked down as he heard a familiar voice. General Wolseley had ridden up to the Swazis and, riding crop in hand, was shouting at them. 'Come on, you fellows. Come on. Is there no one to make them understand?'

But the General's urging and the sight of the soldiers beginning their climb demanded no interpreting. The Swazis had seen enough. The white men were not going to leave the fighting to the blacks. They surged forward and, carrying only their assegais and shields, their bare feet finding amazingly easy purchase on the rocks, the warriors soon overtook the booted and heavily laden white men and swarmed up ahead, booming their own battle cry.

For Simon and Jenkins the arrival of the Swazis was almost certainly a life-saving intervention. Unhampered by packs, they had made easier work of it toiling upwards, so had left the troops behind and were attracting much of the attention from the defenders up above. Bullets were pinging into the rocks all around them, sending granite chips flying and forcing them to stop every few yards to seek cover as well as to regain their breath. Now, however, the swarming bodies that overtook them, darting like black rams on a mountain, provided some sort of screen for them as they slipped, scrambled and hauled their way upwards. Perspiration was now almost blinding Simon and there was certainly little he could hear above the frightening din of battle. The howling of the opposing warriors' war cries, the crack of the rifles, the screams of the wounded as the bullets found their mark, and above it all the high-pitched skirl of the pipers from down below created a mind-numbing cacophony that he would remember for the rest of his days. His senses shattered, he continued to climb doggedly and blindly, numbly aware that Jenkins was still at his side.

At last the two comrades managed to scramble into a shallow trench that had been scratched out from the stones about halfway up the kopje. It was empty of defenders, although two bePedis were lying on their backs nearby, sightless eyes staring at the sky and blood draining from terrible assegai thrusts in their chests.

'Bloody 'ell,' gasped Jenkins. 'I can't do much more o' this. 'Ow the 'ell are we goin' to find our bloke in all this?'

'I don't know,' replied Simon, his breast heaving, 'but surviving is the main thing.'

As though to emphasise his words, two bePedi warriors suddenly burst from a cleft in the rocks to their right and fired their rifles at them. It was virtually point-blank range but both warriors, hampered anyway by the assegais they carried, fired too hastily and the bullets sang over the heads of Simon and Jenkins. The bePedis had no time to reload their single-shot rifles so they discarded them and, raising their assegais, hurled themselves at the two white men. The abortive shots, however, had given Simon and Jenkins just enough time to scramble to their feet, and although the chambers in their rifles were empty, they were able to present their bayonets to their attackers.

The bePedis carried no shields, which was to their disadvantage, for they had no secondary weapon with which to evade the much longer reach of the white men's bayonets. Jenkins, his short legs giving him a low centre of gravity, easily parried the thrust of his assailant and slipped his lunger's point around the shaft of the spear to rake the warrior's forearm. With a cry of pain, the man turned and ran out of sight around a bend in the trench. His companion, who had been parrying the thrusts of Simon's bayonet with increasing desperation, now found himself presented with two adversaries, and he too suddenly turned and sprinted away, howling derision at the white men.

Jenkins slipped a round into the breech of his rifle. 'I must say, bach sir,' he said, 'you're gettin' to be quite 'andy now with the old lunger.'

'Don't be so bloody patronising. Be careful. There might be more of them round that bend.'

They advanced with care and found that the cleft in the rock was in fact a cave, about five feet in height and some four feet wide. It was black and uninviting and the decision about whether they should investigate its depths was quickly made for them when a flash of flame from deep inside sent a bullet passing between them. At that point, a party of panting men of the 94th came over the lip of the trench.

'Be careful,' Simon shouted to them, 'there are armed natives in this cave. Sorry, we've got to get on.' And, without waiting for a reply, he and

Jenkins recommenced their climb.

The pair were no longer in the lead, and looking up, Simon could see red coats up ahead of them and, further towards the summit, Swazis engaged in fierce hand-to-hand combat with an enemy not in view. Nor had the defenders' fire died away. Bullets now seemed to crash into the rocks around them with greater intensity and boulders came tumbling down the forty-five-degree slope, creating an additional hazard. Bodies were now slipping and sliding down the hillside, some of them crying out in anguish from their wounds, others with the set expression of the dead on their faces.

Pausing to regain their breath on a precious piece of level ground behind a large boulder, Simon and Jenkins were joined by a young subaltern of the 94th, sword in one hand and revolver hanging from a lanyard round his neck. 'Good God,' said the young man, 'this is hard work.' He took a pull from his water bottle and offered it to the others, who accepted gratefully. He stoppered the bottle, wiped his mouth and grinned. 'Well, onwards and upwards,' he said. 'One good thing, though. These Kaffirs couldn't hit a haystack at fifty yards, otherwise–' His sentence was cut off as a bullet smashed into his throat, sending a perfect parabola of blood arcing on to the ground. He stood, wide-eyed for a second, before crumpling and toppling backwards down the steep slope, bouncing and crashing down in a landslide of shale.

'Oh, bloody 'ell,' said Jenkins. 'I don't like this at all. It'll be the bloody bees next.'

And so it was. As they crouched beneath the shelter of the jutting boulder, they glimpsed a series of small columns of smoke from on high to their right. Then they saw several rectangular wooden boxes, smoke rising from them, being tossed high into the air, outwards from the kopje's side, to hit the slope below. As they did so, the boxes burst open and black clouds of insects came buzzing malevolently from the ruins of the hives to engulf the red-coated infantry struggling up the mountain. Disregarding the other dangers, the men took off their helmets and lay on their backs, swatting at the angry bees which surrounded them.

'Come on,' said Simon. 'What was it that poor devil said? Onwards and upwards. Bullets are better than bees.'

'Absolutely right you are,' agreed Jenkins. 'Let's go, quick like.'

Still climbing, Simon and Jenkins eventually came level with a ring of combatants – Swazis, redcoats and colonial troops – engaged in close-quarter fighting with a line of bePedis, who were stabbing desperately with their assegais from the protection of a long, low stone wall. The wall seemed to run at irregular levels completely around the kopje, and the effectiveness of the defence showed in the number of black and, to a lesser extent, brown- and red-clad bodies that lay on the slopes below it. The pair edged along, below the level of the fighting, until they found a gap where, their boots slipping and sliding as they sought to gain purchase on the slope, they could add their bayonets to the spears of the

Swazi warriors fighting on either side of them. They stayed there lunging and parrying, sometimes being able to slip a round into the breeches of their rifles and firing them, and remained, virtually wedged in between the sweating warriors on either side, until, almost miraculously, the opposition seemed to melt away.

From the left came the cry, 'Cease firing. Advance with care. They've gone into the caves.'

A strange quietness descended upon the kopje – not a complete silence, for an occasional shot echoed from various levels of the conical hill, and the moans of wounded men and, particularly, the cries of that section of the 94th who were still being tormented by the angry bees echoed around. But the tumult that had assaulted the ears during the height of the battle had died away. Even the pipers on the plain below had suspended their wailing. It seemed that a strange victory had been won and that the Fighting Kopje now belonged to Queen Victoria.

Jenkins took out a soiled handkerchief, wiped his forehead and slumped to the ground. Simon sat beside him. 'I've seen some fightin',' said the Welshman, 'but this was the most devilish and the most awkwardest, if you know what I mean, bach sir.'

'I know what you mean all right. I suppose that we've won, but it's all stopped so suddenly, I can't quite understand it.' Looking up, he saw the moustached captain of the General's staff gingerly making his way down the steep slope. 'What's up, Jackson?' he called. 'Is it over?'

The young man sat on his bottom and slithered

down to Simon's side. 'Well, actually,' he said, 'it is and it isn't. I'm just going down to report to the General.' He swept back the edge of his moustache with the back of a filthy hand. 'It seems the Kaffirs have bolted down their holes. The mountain is full of them and the bePedis have retreated into them. We are on the summit now and we've won the mountain all right, but how we get the buggers out of these caves I don't know. Perhaps a bit of cheese at the entrances? Eh, what? Sorry, can't stop.'

Simon called out as Jackson continued his descent, 'Any sign of the King or of a big Portuguese who is supposed to be with him?'

'No, old boy. Not a sign. In the depths of this ant hill, p'raps.'

Jenkins made a face. 'What now, then?'

Simon levered himself to his feet. 'Let's search the slopes. Mendoza could be amongst the dead, he could be down in a cave somewhere, or perhaps he has got away. If he has escaped, then...' he looked apologetically at the Welshman, 'I'm sorry, 352, but I don't see what more we can do. He could have gone anywhere, but probably back to Portuguese East Africa. We shall just have to get the General to issue a warrant for his arrest.'

Jenkins made no reply, but his face was set hard.

Together they began the unpleasant business of looking at the bodies which were strewn around the conical hill. It was clear that the bePedis had received the heaviest losses, followed by the Swazis, who had been first up the kopje. The colonial and British troops, it seemed, had got off

413

comparatively lightly, although the forward dressing stations of the 94th Regiment were attracting lines of soldiers in extreme discomfort from bee stings. Simon and Jenkins's search among the dead attracted enquiring glances, but nowhere was there a trace of a large, swarthy Portuguese.

In their search, they encountered Baker Russell climbing the lower slopes of the hill with a party of Royal Engineers, who were carrying slabs of gun cotton. 'He's going to try and blast them out,' murmured Simon. 'Poor wretches, they won't stand a chance down those holes.'

But Simon was wrong. As the day wore on, the sound of muffled explosions came from all parts of the kopje. In some instances they were followed by sporadic gunfire as the defenders in their caves displayed their continued defiance, but there were no surrenders.

Simon met Jackson again. 'We may have to try cheese after all,' said the young captain with a wan smile. 'Many of these devils have worked in the Kimberley mines and they know all about explosive devices. They're just cutting the fuses and staying put. Amazin'. One good thing, though. A captured bePedi has told us that the King is still up there somewhere with his entourage. Plucky old bounder, by all accounts. He says we'll never get him out. Oh, and he's got at least one foreigner with him – that big feller you were asking about.'

Simon smiled gratefully. 'That's just what we wanted to know. Many thanks.' This news, when relayed to Jenkins, brought the biggest smile from the Welshman that Simon had seen for days. He said nothing, but nodded his head and began oiling his rifle.

Towards the evening a large party of native labourers were set to shovelling out a primitive trench all the way round the kopje, about one third of the way towards the top. Lobbing in explosives and direct attacks on the caves had proved abortive and it was clear that Wolseley had decided to invest the fortress and starve out the defenders – or, more likely, force them out of their warrens for want of water. It could, therefore, be a long wait, and an air of impotent frustration had descended upon the British command, denied of what had seemed at first to be a quick and decisive victory.

Simon sought out his friend Jackson but he was nowhere to be found. Instead, he accosted a young subaltern whom he had noticed among Baker Russell's staff and, in as off-hand a manner as he could manage, enquired about Alice. He was greeted with a sharp glance and then a knowing smile. 'Ah yes. The pretty one – not that she's got much competition.' Simon frowned at the familiarity and the young lieutenant composed his features quickly. 'Sorry, old boy. Can't help. All the press johnnies are round the other side of the kopje with the General. All scribbling like mad when last I saw 'em – writing the news of Sir Garnet's great victory, no doubt. Could be a bit premature, don't you know. But we shall see. Complicated business, getting their stuff home. I suppose they have riders to take their dispatches to Lydenburg, where there are cable facilities. Bit of a race against time and each other, I gather. Strange way to earn a living, ain't it?'

Simon nodded and then asked after Colonel Covington. The young man knew no details. 'I gather he's in no danger but there had to be an operation of some sort. Nasty business. Got it coming down the mountain, tryin' to keep up with old Macleod's Swazis. By the way, those bloody natives have refused to guard the kopje higher up. I think they're a bit miffed because they've been prevented from taking the bePedi women. So most of us will have to stand guard during the night. Not much fun after a hard day's fightin', eh?'

That evening Simon and Jenkins ate a lonely meal around a flickering camp fire in front of their bivouac tent. Each was silent: Simon yearning to see Alice and wondering how the news of Covington's wound would affect her, and Jenkins sitting with his eyes rarely leaving the darkening outline of the kopje. Simon once again considered the problem not only of finding Mendoza, but of preventing Jenkins from killing him before the Portuguese could be arrested. Looking at the Welshman's grimly set visage, he realised that reasoned argument would not deter him. It would have to be a case of reacting to the situation when they found the man – *if* they found him, that is.

'We had better join the trenches for the night watches,' observed Simon eventually. 'Just in case they try to break out during darkness.'

Jenkins nodded glumly and they prepared to stand watch.

416

It quickly became apparent that the vigil in the trenches would be less than comfortable. The pair took up their position with a section of the 94th at the less steep part of the hill, where a breakout by the defenders could be feasible, at least, under cover of darkness. They wriggled and squirmed, trying to find some ease among the stones that lined the bottom of the shallow trench and which made lying or sitting down agony after a few minutes. As they did so, an ominous boom of thunder came from the south, the other side of Sekukuni's mountain, and as they lay in the gathering darkness, they heard the thunder growing nearer and began to see the top of the mountain outlined against the red flashes of lightning.

Simon had pulled his ground sheet over his head and was surrendering himself to misery when he felt a tender hand stroking his cheek. He looked up into the grey eyes of Alice, smiling at him from a distance of three inches.

She put her finger to her lips. 'Shush. Don't wake 352.' Awkwardly, because of the voluminous ground sheet, she put her arms around his neck and kissed him. 'Oh, my dear,' she whispered, 'I am so glad you are safe. I have been so worried and I had to be sure. I've spent half the night looking for you, peering under ground sheets and being shouted at by sergeants.'

Simon grinned. 'You, young woman, are not supposed to be halfway up this mountain and halfway through a battle. Wolseley will have you shot.'

She sniffed and kissed his nose. 'And you, young man, are only supposed to be a scout, not a front-line infantryman. You shouldn't be here either.'

They hugged each other, lying on the damp ground companionably. 'How on earth did you get through the lines?' asked Simon.

'Hair tied back, breeches, black mackintosh.' She smiled. 'No one expected to see a woman up here. Everyone thought I was an officer – except the sergeants.'

Simon grinned. 'Typical. Now, really, Alice, you must go. Even if the bePedis don't try and break out you could get drenched soon. Off with you. And stay out of the line, I insist...'

As he spoke, the storm reached them. It began as a few hard spots, and then the heavens opened and rain came thundering down like vertical liquid rods, bouncing from the top of the soldiers' capes and immediately filling the bottom of the trench. Rivulets began to surge down the kopje and the miserable guards ringing the hill bent their heads against the stinging storm and tucked their rifles under their capes.

It was at just this point that the bePedis broke out. The noise of the rain and the thunder of the electric storm provided ideal cover for their escape. A glissade of stones came suddenly down the hill, followed by hundreds of black warriors carrying shields and spears, looking like devilish apparitions in the jagged flashes of lightning as they leapt and slid down to the trench. Many of the soldiers, half dozing in their wet misery under their capes, were speared as they sat. Others were knocked over by shields as the warriors swept through and over them, screaming their battle

418

cry, and streaming down the steep sides of the kopje to spread out on the valley floor below.

Simon had time only to shout a cry of alarm and throw himself over Alice before the first man hit him – literally, for the bePedi, his face contorted with the desperation of battle, leapt into him from above and struck him on the shoulder with both feet. Simon was knocked over and went rolling down the hillside, joining the bePedi in their descent, his hands clutching at rocks to stop his slithering fall. With a crash that winded him, he hit a large boulder and curved around its contours, gasping for breath. His rifle had been left in the trench and he lay defenceless but in no real danger, for the tribesmen were intent on escape, not further conflict. As he lay, trying to gather his breath, he watched as the glistening black figures, illuminated intermittently by the red lightning, came down at him, then bounded away in their frenetic dash for freedom. It was a scene from some lycanthropic ballet, lit by the heavens and choreographed by the very devil himself.

Frantic at the thought of Alice being speared, he staggered to his feet and realised that his Colt was somehow still wedged in its holster at his belt. He drew it and fired at a huge shadow that materialised at him out of the rain. He missed and the man struck him back-handedly as he went by, knocking Simon down and sending the Colt spinning into the mud. On hands and knees he looked up at the descending warriors and froze. Down the hill, leaping and jumping the stones and skidding in the scree, came the incongruous figure of Alice, black mackintosh glistening, revolver in hand, in the middle of the bePedi hordes, who seemed completely impervious to her.

'Alice,' he cried, desperate to make himself heard above the rain and the howls of the warriors. She saw him just before she hit him, and the two went rolling together down the hill, in the shale and mud, locked in an embrace that owed nothing to passion. Together and completely winded, they lay for a moment up against the stunted bush that had stopped their descent. Alice recovered first and immediately fired the revolver that she had continued to grip during their rolling slide at a warrior who had raised his spear at them. They both saw the spurt of blood from his arm, where the bullet tore through, but he carried on running, his face a grimace of determination.

'No.' Simon pulled Alice down towards him. 'Lie still. They'll run past us.'

And so they stayed, perhaps for a minute, curled up to the bush, watching fearfully up the hill until there was a break in the figures streaming down it. Simon scrambled in the mud for his Colt and then they rose to their feet, only to see a huge man rushing straight at them. Simon pulled the trigger of his revolver, but the Colt, jammed with mud, refused to fire and the figure swerved away and rushed by them – not before, however, Simon had glimpsed at close quarters the distorted features of Joachim Mendoza. At almost the same time, Jenkins crashed into him amidst a shower of stones.

420

'Thank God I've found you,' shouted the Welshman. 'I thought you'd gone for good. But did you see 'im? It was 'im, wasn't it? Giant of a bloke, wearin' civilised clothes. It must 'ave been 'im.'

'Yes, it was Mendoza all right.' Simon's chest was heaving as he tried to catch his breath. 'Go after him, I've got to get Alice out of here.'

For the first time, Jenkins noticed Alice crouched at the base of the bush. 'Good lord,' he said. But then he turned and continued to half run, half slide down the hill after Joachim Mendoza.

Simon and Alice followed, jumping as best they could from stone to stone, slipping and sliding and only dimly aware of the black figures that were now once again all around them. Stabs of light in the darkness below showed that some of Wolseley's men in the valley had turned out from their tents and somehow become aware of the situation, and were firing to stem the mass exodus. But the chaos of the night – the pounding rain, the thunder claps and the now less frequent flashes of lightning – did nothing to aid their aim. The running warriors reached the valley floor and streamed through the tent lines and away to the east to the temporary safety of the Lulu Mountains. Simon and Alice somehow reached the bottom of the kopje without turning an ankle or receiving a spear thrust and there they met a sodden, furious Jenkins, who was looking around him, not knowing which way to turn.

'Fuck it!' he screamed – it said everything for his distress that he spat out the invective without a thought for Alice. 'The bastard's gone. 'Es got

421

away. 'Ow we goin' to find 'im now. Eh?' Jenkins was almost hysterical with dismay. 'We'll never find 'im in this bleedin' mess.'

'No,' gasped Simon. 'We'll find him. He'll have nowhere to hide in Sekukuni land, which means he will head for the border. For that he will need a horse. We will get him. But first I must look after Alice.'

Despite her own distress, Alice could not forbear to smile at the woebegone face of the Welshman, black hair plastered over his brow, mud caked into the great moustache, who looked at her as though seeing her for the first time. 'Oh, sorry, miss,' he said. 'Please excuse the language. Under a bit of stress, see. Didn't know that you'd joined the army, look you.'

Trying to smile, Alice turned to Simon. 'Don't worry about me. What are you going to do? Let me come with you, please?'

'I'm sorry, darling. Jenkins and I have got some rather unpleasant business to attend to. Best if you're not with us.'

Simon caught the sleeve of a passing young NCO. 'Corporal,' he shouted, 'take care of this young lady immediately. She is the niece of General Wolseley and there will be hell to pay if she comes to harm. Take her back way behind the lines at once, do you hear?'

The corporal's jaw dropped as he regarded the mud-caked trio, but Simon's air of command and the mention of the General's name were enough for him. 'Very good, sir,' he said, saluting. 'Right away, sir.' And he took Alice's arm.

'No, no,' cried Alice, but the corporal's grip was

firm and Simon and Jenkins were already running towards the horse lines. Turning his head, Simon shouted, 'You must stay out of trouble. Don't worry about me. See you in the morning...' His last view of Alice was of her wet face looking anxiously after him as the corporal led her away.

The horses were tethered under the care of a glistening wet Ndebele.

'Do you speak English?' demanded Simon. The native nodded wordlessly, his mouth open. 'Did a big man – looks like a Boer – just come up and take a horse?'

'Yes, baas. Him say he got urgent message for the General and to give him best horse.'

'Damn. Which way did he go?'

'That way, baas.' He pointed to the north. 'He don't stop for saddle or bridle.'

Simon and Jenkins exchanged glances. 'He's making for Lorenzo Marques,' said Simon. 'If he's stopped he'll bluff his way through our lines. He can't be far ahead. I'll get the horses and you get the saddles. Come on.'

Simon ran down the lines of horses and found their own mounts while Jenkins staggered up with saddles and bridles. They lost several precious minutes in saddling up but then set off to the north, galloping through the milling crowds of colonial troops and British redcoats, all in various stages of undress. Of the fleeing bePedis there was no sign. They seemed to have vanished from the valley as though by magic.

The pair galloped as fast as their horses would take them, Simon setting a course to the north as

423

best he could, taking as guiding marks the dark, lowering blurs of the hills on either side. Eventually they were forced to rein back to a walk to save their mounts, from whose glistening flanks steam was now beginning to rise as the sky grew lighter to the east.

'We mustn't flog the horses,' said Simon. 'We may have a long ride ahead of us. At least the rain is easing off.'

'Yes,' grunted Jenkins, 'but will we find 'im in this country? It's not goin' to be easy.'

'Don't worry. We will find him.' Simon thought for a moment. 'I don't think he would have recognised me on the kopje in that rain and darkness, so he won't suspect that anyone is following him. Why should they? He looks and sounds like an Afrikaner. He will think that he has got clean away. So he won't be pressing his horse now and he will have difficulty anyway in riding without saddle or bridle. So I think we should come upon him soon. But we must find him before he gets on to the plain proper, because if he hasn't got a compass or is not absolutely sure of the quickest way to the border, he could stray across the veldt. I think we had better separate, the better to spot him. But we must keep each other in sight.'

Jenkins sighed. 'Oh, yes please. You know 'ow good I am at gettin' lost, like.'

'Right. Let's diverge here, each to go at an angle. You go that way. Then, after about ten minutes, turn to the left a bit, with the sun on your right, but keep me in sight. Wave your handkerchief if you see anything.'

'Huh, lost it hours ago.'

'Then wave your rifle. But don't let him see you if you can help it.'

'Very good, sir. But don't forget – I want 'im.'

It was Simon's turn to sigh. 'Now look, 352. We cannot kill him in cold blood. We will arrest him and take him back to be charged by the authorities. Is that clear?'

'Oh, very clear.' But Jenkins's voice was cold. 'You don't even 'ave a rifle, look you.'

'No, but I've got my Colt. Go on. Get on with it.'

As the sun came up, the rain ceased and in the growing light Simon realised that they had left the valley and the Lulu range behind and were indeed on the open veldt. The seeming flatness of the plain was deceptive, because it was broken by low scrub and gentle undulations that could hide a single horseman even if he was not seeking cover. But it soon became clear that Mendoza felt he was in no danger, for about a mile away to the south, Simon perceived a thin column of smoke rising into the now blue sky. Jenkins spotted it almost simultaneously, and the two immediately converged.

'It has to be him,' said Simon, 'although he must be a good bushman to have lit a fire on this sodden plain. Now.' He turned to Jenkins. 'No shooting unless in the last resort. We will walk our horses up to him as though we are not looking for him and I will pull my hat over my eyes so that, at first, he won't recognise me. My feeling is that he will not be expecting to be pursued and will just attempt to bluff his way through. I intend to charge him formally, and while I do so, keep him covered with your rifle. But don't raise it until we are near enough to talk to him. I don't want to provoke him needlessly.'

Jenkins made no reply but merely nodded, his face set.

The distant figure could now be discerned sitting by the small fire, his saddle-less horse tethered to a bush a little distance away. Simon raised his field glasses and focused on the man. It was the Portuguese all right, his greasy, wavy hair hanging down and the pock-marks on his face clearly visible in the strong magnification. He must by now have seen the two riders approaching him, but he showed no sign of alarm, for he was munching away, his rifle propped against the same bush to which he had tethered his horse. He could have been out on a Sunday-afternoon picnic. Even when the pair were less than one hundred yards away he still did not raise his head.

'Right,' murmured Simon, swallowing hard. 'Don't do anything rash – and I mean it. Don't threaten him with the rifle unless he makes an aggressive move. Then warn him before you shoot.'

At last, when they were about fifty yards away, Mendoza looked up and slowly rose to his feet. He continued eating something – presumably biltong – from a dirty cloth which he held in both hands. Then he grunted a greeting in Afrikaans, but there was no inquisitiveness in his gaze or his voice.

'Joachim Mendoza,' Simon began, speaking slowly and loudly, 'I am Captain Simon Fonthill of the British Army. This is Sergeant Jenkins. I arrest you on charges of diamond stealing and smuggling, attempted murder and the abduction of Miss Nandi Dunn. It is our duty to take you to the British authorities for trial on those counts.'

Recognition dawned on Mendoza's face, but he looked unperturbed and his gaze shifted from one to the other. Then a smile crept over his face, although it did not reach his eyes. 'Ah, the Zulu girl,' he growled. He looked at Jenkins as though deliberately to provoke him. 'She not a good fook, she rubbish.'

A snarl came from Jenkins, and his rifle barrel, which he had obediently kept pointing at the ground, now came up. But Mendoza was quicker. The rag was flicked away to reveal a revolver, which he fired first at Jenkins and then, a split second later, at Simon. Jenkins cried out and then crumpled and fell from his horse. The second bullet tore into Simon's mount, which reared and toppled over, trapping Simon's leg beneath its body and sending his Colt, which he had just had time to pluck from his belt, spinning away across the damp sand of the veldt. Winded but otherwise unhurt, Simon tried desperately to pull his leg free, but the inert body of the dead horse trapped it firmly.

Unhurriedly, Mendoza walked over to Simon, tucked his revolver back into his cummerbund and stood over him, still chewing. He spat out a piece of meat and regarded the trapped man with no obvious emotion.

'English,' he said, 'you cause me lotta trouble. You take my diamonds, kill my men and take my girl. Now I kill you.' He gestured with his head to the fallen Jenkins. 'But not quick like him. I kill you slow, with this.' He pulled out a knife. 'I cut you up a bit at a time. I hurt you.'

Simon still had both hands free, and as the Portuguese bent down, he lunged forward to grasp his leg. But the big man was quicker. Evading Simon's arm, he stamped on his wrist with his boot and then stood on it, pinioning that arm to the ground. Bending lower, he prised free the fingers of Simon's other hand from round his ankle and, holding the wrist firmly, slowly began working the tip of his knife into the palm of Simon's hand.

The pain was immediate and piercingly sharp as the point of the knife was screwed into the flesh, and Simon screamed. The scream almost, but not quite, drowned out the crack of Jenkins's revolver. The bullet took Mendoza in the thigh and he fell to the ground, clutching the wound, blood spurting through his fingers. He fumbled for his own revolver in his cummerbund but a second shot shattered his shoulder and he lay pawing the ground in pain.

Jenkins rose to his feet, his face a mass of blood from where the bullet had seared along the side of his head. 'You all right, bach sir?' he asked as he staggered towards Simon.

'Watch out, he's got a pistol in his belt.'

'I know.' Jenkins's voice was so low that Simon hardly heard him. 'But 'e's not goin' to use it. In fact, 'e's not goin' to use anythin' else, ever.'

428

Simon grimaced from the pain in his hand and from another abortive effort to free his leg. 'Don't kill him, 352. Let's take him back to hang.'

'Sorry, bach sir,' said Jenkins as he bent to retrieve Mendoza's knife, 'but some things 'ave to be done my way. Now don't you look if you don't want to.'

Knife in hand, he stood over the Portuguese, whose black eyes regarded him without expression. 'Now,' whispered Jenkins, 'this is for the Captain 'ere,' and he plunged the knife into Mendoza's uninjured shoulder. The big man's head went back and he gasped in pain, his mouth open. Jenkins withdrew the knife. 'This, matey, is for poor little Nandi.' The knife plunged again, this time into Mendoza's genitals. 'And this, this, you bastard, is for me.' With one quick sweep of the blade, Jenkins cut the Portuguese's throat. His grim work done, he flung away the knife with a contemptuous gesture, stepped back three paces and then slowly slumped to the ground and put his head in his hands.

Both men stayed silent for perhaps half a minute, the munching of Jenkins's horse as it sought fodder from the barren ground and the soft cry of a martial eagle wheeling high overhead the only sounds, until the buzzing flies found the blood oozing from Mendoza's body. Simon regarded Jenkins with wide eyes, stunned by the ferocity and the suddenness of the violence and by the execution that had ended it all. There was, however, no sign of exultation in the man who sat, head bowed, shoulders drooping, opposite him now. It was as though the prospect of venge-

429

ance had given purpose to the little Welshman for the last few weeks, and now that retribution had been done, the life force had suddenly drained out of him. Simon felt a sharp sense of compassion for his friend.

He broke the silence. 'It doesn't matter about that evil man, 352,' he said. 'He's dead now and that's all there is to it. I should have been much more alert, but thank you. Once again you saved my life.'

Jenkins regarded him with red-rimmed eyes and spoke in a voice hardly above a whisper. 'You know, bach sir, this may surprise you, but I've never killed a man like that before. In cold blood, so to speak. Except that my blood wasn't cold, it was bloody 'ot. So p'raps I'll be forgiven up there.'

'I think somehow that you will. Don't brood on it. Look, no one knows about what has happened here and I am sure that we have not been missed. So we will say nothing about it to anybody. Agreed?'

Jenkins nodded glumly.

'Now, what about your head?'

'Ah, he just winged me.' Jenkins raised a tentative hand to the long red weal running through his thick hair. 'Knocked me out for a second or two but I came round just in time, I think. Couldn't get me rifle, though, so 'ad to use this pop gun. I never could handle these things. That's why I only got 'im in the shoulder, see.'

Simon summoned up a grin and raised his injured hand, into which he had stuffed a handkerchief to stop the bleeding. 'I do see. Now, although I must look very comfortable lying here, with a hole in my hand and a horse lying on top of me, I can't move and I *would* like to get up.'

'Oh, sorry, bach sir. Anythin' broken?'

'No. See if you can ease this poor animal off me.'

Together they extricated Simon and, using strips of shirt tails, washed and bandaged each other's wounds. They found tea, a water bottle and a billycan near Mendoza's fire – he must have equipped himself for the ride before his plunge down the Fighting Kopje – and brewed themselves a hot drink. Simon looked down at the dead man and, on an impulse, searched his pockets. He found a small bag containing about twenty diamonds. He held them up to Jenkins: 'To add to Nandi's dowry,' he said.

'What's a dowry, then, when it's at 'ome?'

'Oh, never mind.'

They dismissed the idea of attempting to bury Mendoza, for they had no tools and under the sandy topsoil, soggy from the recent rain, the veldt was rock hard. They covered him inadequately with the few stones they could find but were under no illusion that his body and that of Simon's horse would escape the ravages of vultures. Then, with Jenkins riding bareback on Mendoza's horse, the two comrades set off back towards Sekukuni, the crisp, healthy air of the high veldt beginning its gentle task of blowing away the smell and memory of the reckoning with Joachim Mendoza.

Chapter 16

Walking through the lines to the General's tent, Alice looked with curiosity and just a touch of apprehension at the note in her hand summoning her to meet Wolseley 'as soon as is convenient'. Could it be that something had happened to Simon? Her heart leapt at the thought. But then, she reasoned, the General would not know that she was in love with this strange scout, so why should he bother to summon *her* with the news? No – and she felt better at the thought – perhaps it was to receive a reproof for slipping through the lines and getting among the fighting on the kopje? But the young corporal had been happy to receive a sovereign 'not to tell my uncle', and had released her at the press compound with a smile. She had rejoined her colleagues without fuss and written her story. Her dispatch reporting on the battle had been suitably complimentary to Sir Garnet and his troops, even though she had taken care to give due credit to the Swazis and other black levies who had borne the brunt of the fighting, and had also praised the bravery of the defeated bePedis. But all of this should not be controversial to a seasoned soldier like Wolseley who himself was not above commending the skill and courage of the enemy. It did, after all, en- hance the scale of his victory. Perhaps he merely wanted to ply her with sherry! She smiled at the unlikely thought.

On arrival at the General's tent, she was ushered into his presence without delay – a fact which did cause a momentary shaft of anxiety. Wolseley looked tired (she had heard that an old wound in his leg was causing him pain), but he leapt to his feet gallantly and pulled up a chair for her.

Smiling her thanks, Alice said, 'Congratulations, Sir Garnet. It sounds as though it has been a comprehensive victory. London will be pleased.'

He nodded. 'Thank you, Miss Griffith. Much of the praise must go to Baker Russell, you know. I put him in command for I felt it was time he had an opportunity to show what he could do. He – and the troops, of course – performed splendidly.'

'What about the King?'

'Yes, well, he did escape with about five hundred of his tribesmen during that damned storm. But most of those, and, indeed, all of the bePedis who were left in the caves, have now surrendered. We have received information about the whereabouts of Sekukuni.' He smiled. 'The old varmint is holed up in a cave, I gather, about twenty miles from here. We have sent a small party to get him and he should be safely in custody within a day or so.'

'Good. May I quote you on that?'

Wolseley's smile widened. 'Of course. My goodness, Miss Griffith, you don't usually ask.'

Alice let the shaft pass with a reciprocal smile as she scribbled on her pad.

The smile gradually faded from the General's

face. 'However, I did not ask you here, my dear, to speak about the battle and its now rather boring consequences – the mopping up and so on. No, I am afraid that I have some rather bad news for you.'

Alice looked up, wide-eyed. 'Oh dear. Pray tell me quickly.' It *was* Simon, after all. She had wondered why he and Jenkins were nowhere to be found, although she had been so busy with her dispatches that she had had little time to search for him. Oh God! To lose him so soon after finding him at last...

'It is Covington, I am afraid, your fiancé. Now don't be upset, because the news is not half as bad as it might have been.' Wolseley looked down at a piece of paper on his desk. 'He has been wounded but has survived and is responding to treatment very well. He is now in no danger, I am informed.'

'Wounded?' Alice's thoughts raced. 'How? In what manner?'

'It seemed that his left forearm was shattered by, of all things, an elephant gun fired at him at quite short range by one of the bePedi as he descended the mountain with the Swazis. I am afraid, my dear, that it has had to be amputated.'

'Oh God!'

'But that is not all, I am afraid.' The General coughed. This was clearly not to his liking. 'Yes. As he staggered away from the force of the shot – luckily his arm was extended so his body was not injured – as he fell away, a bePedi spear caught him in the face. He has lost his right eye and ... er ... I fear that his face has been rather badly

434

slashed. However,' he hurried on quickly, 'as I say, he has been operated on with great success by one of our splendid medical chaps here and has recovered well from both operations. To repeat: his life is not in danger and he will be sent home just as soon as arrangements can be made for him.'

The little man now smiled. 'May I say from personal experience, Miss Griffith, that losing an eye and suffering some ... ah ... facial disfigurement is not the tragedy that it might at first appear. As you can see from the example before you, it can leave a chap positively enhanced.' He gave a chuckle and Alice produced a weak smile in response, but the General was continuing. 'Ralph is conscious now and, in fact, is wondering whether you can spare time from your ... ah ... duties to visit him.'

'Yes, yes, of course. I must.'

Wolseley leaned forward, his face set earnestly. 'My dear, your fiancé will quickly realise that his army career is over, and this will sadden him, of course. I may say that it saddens me also, for I regarded him – I *still* regard him – as an able and gallant officer. But he has the prospect of his wedding to look forward to. Miss Griffith, your fiancé will need you now more than ever. Knowing and ... ah ... respecting your courage and spirit as I do, I know that you will not let him down.'

Alice heard the words as though they came from a distance. She held the General's gaze for a moment without being aware of it and then switched it unconsciously to his glazed, unseeing eye. A silence fell between them. Eventually Wolseley, evincing some embarrassment at the silence, coughed, stood up, and extended his hand. Then he struck it to his forehead in a gesture of annoyance.

'Ah,' he said. 'One more thing. Knew I'd forgotten something. Here.' He picked up an envelope from his table, withdrew the letter from within and handed it to her. 'This concerns you and I think you will be interested in it.'

Puzzled and annoyed at the intrusion into her fuddled thoughts, Alice looked at the bold, scrawled hand and began to read:

Dear General,

I am writing to say that I renounce all claim to the diamonds that you took from me. You are right, they did not belong to me. (Mind you, I don't think they belong to the British Army either, but I leave it to you what to do with them.)

The point is that I have heard from that remarkable woman Miss Griffith, via a black friend she has here in Pretoria, that Fonthill and Jenkins, God bless them, have found my daughter Nandi and that she is under care in your camp. I am riding now to see her. Now that my daughter is freed I have no need for those damned (excuse me) stones, so do with them what you will.

I do not know how to contact Miss Griffith or Fonthill and Jenkins but I hope somehow to find them and to thank them personally for the great service they have done me.

Yours sincerely,
John Dunn

She nodded to the General, distantly, her thoughts on other things. 'Thank you,' she said. 'That is very gratifying.'

'Indeed. All ended happily. Now,' he extended his hand again, 'will you please tell Covington that I will call on him just as soon as I can clear this rubbish from my table. And, my dear, if there is anything I can do for either of you, you have only to request it.'

'Thank you, Sir Garnet, you are very kind.' They shook hands and she turned and left the tent.

Once outside, Alice spun on her heel and walked quickly without any sense of direction, her brain in a spin. Ralph Covington, the brave, insouciant, debonair Ralph Covington, now a one-armed, one-eyed man without a career! Ralph Covington, the fiancé to whom she was about to break the news that she loved another man, now dependent upon her! Ralph Covington maimed... Oh God, it was all too much; too cruel!

Somehow she found her way back to her tent within the press enclosure and flung herself on her narrow bed. She stared at the canvas wall without taking in the green coolness, the heavy stitching so close to her face. What to do? *What to do?* Of course, society – stiff-backed, honourable *society* – would expect her to stand by her man; that was certainly what her parents would expect of her. But her parents and society – bloody hypocritical Victorian *society* – would know nothing of her deep passion for Simon Fonthill and of the true happiness which her love

437

for him had brought to her life. Damn it all and damn them all! She turned on to her stomach and buried her face in the pillow. At that point, a deep sense of shame overcame her and she began to sob, as she realised that she was behaving with extreme selfishness, thinking of herself only and not yet sparing a thought for the handsome, manly soldier who had been so cruelly cut down in his prime and deprived of the career that meant so much to him. This was a man who, after all, she thought she had loved. What would *he* do now? The thought concentrated her mind and the old rationality returned. *Do, do?* He would get on with his life, that was what he would do. He was strong and, in his very own way, selfish too. He would do what he *had* to do, what life forced him to do. That was the way of things.

Immediately, Alice rolled over, sought her handkerchief, blew her nose and sat up. The way of things. Well, indeed – *damn society!* Her deeply nonconformist, rebellious nature now surfaced – a fundamental part of the Alice who had talked her way into a career as a hard-nosed foreign correspondent of one of the greatest newspapers in Britain; the Alice who had ridden with armies and covered a dozen campaigns in two continents; the Alice who had scooped even the great Willie Russell. She would *not* let society dictate to her. She would tell Ralph Covington the truth – and he would be man enough to understand and not insist on her fulfilling her contract.

Her thoughts were interrupted by a diffident cough from outside her tent. 'Miss Griffith?'

She quickly wiped her eyes and put her head through the tent opening. A young medical orderly stood there. 'Sorry, miss,' he said, 'but the General felt that you might like me to take you to Colonel Covington. The lines are in a bit of a mess, see, and it can be difficult to find the hospital.'

Alice swallowed hard. The confrontation so soon! She was not being allowed to escape. 'Of course,' she said. 'How thoughtful of him. Please wait a moment and I will join you.'

She found her still-damp face cloth and wiped away the residue of tears, applied a little face powder, ran a comb through her hair and joined the young orderly. Together they walked through the detritus of an army in the field until they found the large red-crossed hospital tent. There the orderly left Alice and she was met by a bearded army doctor whose face looked even more tired than that of Wolseley. He had obviously had much to do since the end of the battle.

'Ah, Miss Griffith,' he said, giving her a wrinkled smile. 'Good of you to come and see the Colonel. Won't you sit down for a minute?'

'Oh ... well ... thank you, but I would like to see Colonel Covington as soon as possible, please.' *Don't stop me now. I must get it over with before my courage fails me!*

'Of course, I quite understand. But perhaps it might help you if I tell you a little about his injuries first. At least...' the doctor's smile drooped, 'it will save the Colonel from having to acquaint you with the ... ah ... gory details himself.'

'Yes, of course.' *If you must. If you damned well must!*

'Good.' He drew up a chair. 'I am afraid the injury to his arm was very serious. The heavy slug shattered the bone just below the elbow – at least that was good news in that we were able to preserve the joint, as was the fact that, as a right-handed man, it was his left arm. But it was some time before we could operate and the beginnings of gangrene had set in, so I was unable to save the forearm.' His voice, previously so professionally matter-of-fact, now softened. 'It will mean, I fear, that some sort of hook or similar apparatus will have to be fitted eventually, to give him a modicum of digital dexterity, you know.' The doctor's voice now dropped further and acquired the smoothness of expensive velour. 'As his fiancée,' he murmured, 'I felt that you should know that.'

'Of course. Thank you.' *Make it quiet clear what is required of me, you swine!*

'By the same token, you should be prepared for the fact that his face has been ... ah ... mutilated by the spear thrust and will not exactly present a pleasant appearance for, perhaps, the first year. But, of course, the wound will heal, and although he will be scarred, an artificial eye can be fitted, or, if preferred, an eye patch can be worn and the Colonel will look Nelsonically distinguished, if I may say so.' He gave a gruff laugh.

Alice forced some sort of smile. 'It is good of you to tell me all of this. Now, perhaps, I could see the Colonel?'

'Yes, of course. I know he will be so pleased to see you, but don't stay too long. He tires easily.'

They both stood and the doctor led her down between rows of narrow beds containing wounded men, some bandaged, some seemingly uninjured but staring motionlessly at the roof of the tent, until they came to a curtained section at the far end. There, the doctor called out, 'You have a visitor, Colonel,' then bowed briefly to Alice and left.

Alice, biting her lower lip, stared down at Ralph Covington. As she entered, he was lying on his back, with the heavily bandaged stump of his left arm – Alice sucked in her breath when she saw it; *that was where the hook would go, of course* – lying above the bed sheets and his head, equally swathed, turned away from her. Hearing the doctor's voice he slowly turned towards his visitor to reveal the left side of his head and face bandaged whitely, throwing into relief the one good eye that stared at Alice with what at first seemed almost like ferocity. Then the lopsided gaze softened as he attempted to smile, twitching the one end of his moustache that could be seen. He withdrew his good hand from beneath the bedclothes and extended it to her, gesturing to a camp stool by the side of the bed.

His voice was muffled and almost unrecognisable. The spear thrust had, she realised with horror, probably extended down to the upper lip. 'Good of you to come. Knew you would. Do sit. Sorry about all this.'

Alice held his hand, sat on the chair and promptly burst into tears: shoulder-heaving sobs that she could not control as she clutched her hands together in her lap.

441

'Now, now, now.' The words were slurred, but even so, the tenderness was apparent. Alice noted, even in her agitated state, that she could not remember him ever speaking tenderly to her before. 'Do not distress yourself. Where is the tough foreign correspondent now, eh? What would Willie Russell think of his feared opponent, blubbing away there like a little girl, eh?'

She sniffed and smiled at him – at his solitary eye – through her tears. 'I am sorry, Ralph, I must look a wreck.'

'Look marvellous to me. Here, have a blow.' He tossed across a handkerchief. Typically, it was starched clean and white. She wiped her nose and tried to regain some kind of equilibrium, furious with herself for breaking down.

'Now,' said Covington. 'Can't talk very well, as you can hear. Stitches in and hurts a bit. But got something important to say to you and want you to listen carefully and believe me. All right?' What little she could see of his face was contorted in pain.

She nodded.

He spoke now as loudly and as fast as his impediment would allow, as though he had rehearsed the sentences well. 'No question of our engagement continuing, I'm afraid,' he began. 'I have important and difficult things to do in adapting my life and I cannot be tied to a wife. For that matter, you cannot be tied to a one-eyed, one-armed man. Not a brilliant young gal like you.' His eye, which had engaged her so fiercely, now turned to the ceiling. 'You are relieved of your commitment and I shall explain to everyone that you wished to continue but I had lost the will. Which is true. Sorry to hurt you, but I don't want to be married to anyone now. I am sure you understand...' His voice tailed away, rather lamely, so reducing much of the credibility that its earlier strength had given to his words.

At first Alice listened with growing incredulity, and then her heart leapt. *He was releasing her. She was free!* Then, almost as soon as that joyous thought had entered her mind, it was replaced by a sudden deep surge of pity and admiration for the crippled man opposite – the man who was making such a ridiculously inept job of being honourable, of doing the decent thing. He needed her, probably desperately, but he was prepared to sacrifice his need and any prospect of dredging some happiness from his blighted future, so that she could be spared from having to share his disability. Clearly that's what those gabbled words implied, for she knew what she meant to him, not just because of Wolseley's plea but also from the two years of his patient courtship. The immensity of his gesture pierced through the jumble of her thoughts like a lance. Covington, scarred, pain-stricken Covington, was sparing her at the very moment when she was about to hurt him far more savagely than a thrust from an assegai. Could she – could anyone – do this to such a man?

These thoughts tumbled through her mind in split seconds as she looked at the half a face staring at the ceiling. She had to make a decision – and make it now. Of course, she could pretend to believe him, to offer even some semblance of

443

hurt pride at his 'rejection' of her. Then do what: run into Simon's arms? From somewhere deep within her – perhaps springing atavistically from a well of breeding that had been fed for centuries by the drip of education and the constant reminder from parents, clergy and teachers of where the path of duty and honour lay – came the overwhelming realisation of what she had to do. She heard herself answering him as though from far, far away.

'Don't talk nonsense, Ralph,' she said. 'Of course we shall get married.'

'No, no.' His voice was half strangled and he still addressed the ceiling. 'Don't wish to. No sacrifices. Too much ... too much.'

'It is not a sacrifice. We shall be married and I shall look after you and we will live happily ever after.' Once again Alice heard herself speak as though from a different place and time, yet she knew that she was committing herself irrevocably; there would be no turning back, however terrible the consequences. She felt something cold surround her heart.

Slowly Covington turned his head towards her. She realised that his eye was moist. 'Do you mean it? Honestly mean it?'

Alice gripped his hand tightly. 'Of course I do, my dear.' She forced a smile. 'What on earth else did you expect me to say?'

The incipient tear now swelled into his eye and rolled down his cheek. 'Knew it,' he said. 'Always knew it. Wonderful woman. Love you with all my heart. Dammit, bloody cryin' now.'

Alice smiled and leaned across and wiped his

444

eye and cheek with the crisp handkerchief. 'Well, don't,' she said. 'You're going to be all right. But, my dear, I think you should get some rest now. I was warned not to tire you, but I will come and see you again tomorrow. Oh, and Wolseley says that he will come soon.'

He smiled and nodded but couldn't stop another tear rolling down his cheek. 'Rather see you. Off you go. Start planning your trousseau.'

The words sounded like a death knell, but she forced another smile, bent over and kissed his unbandaged cheek. 'Goodbye,' she said.

'Ah. Sorry.' He seemed agitated. 'One more thing. Not terribly important but you should know in case scuttlebutt gets about. You remember Fonthill being left high and dry when we were on reconnaissance with Wolseley?'

She nodded, frowning.

He blinked his eye. 'Well, didn't fire my revolver deliberately, whatever bloody Fonthill might think. Hate the man but wouldn't do that. Stumbled over a tree root and damned pistol went off. Complete accident. Want you to know that.'

'I never suspected anything else, Ralph. Neither, I think, did Simon Fonthill.'

'Good. Just wanted to clear the record, so to speak. Goodbye, my darling. And thank you, so much.'

Alice Griffith walked back to the press enclosure with her head held high, her step firm and her mind now quite clear. *There was no other way.* Happiness with Simon would have been bought at too high a price: that of delivering a terrible blow to a man at the lowest point of his existence, when he needed her – she specifically – to help him rebuild his life. Simon, with his high standards, would understand. He *must* understand!

Back in her tent, Alice sat with her head in her hands, wondering how to tell Simon. For the first time since her interview with Wolseley, she also began to worry about what had happened to him and Jenkins. Could the terrible Mendoza somehow have turned the tables on his pursuers and killed Simon? To lose him at this point, completely, would be too much. Even the God who had played this most unkind of tricks on her surely could not go that far! No. He was out on the veldt somewhere, with the great and good 352 Jenkins to look after him. She lay back on the bed and agonised about how to break this terrible news. It did not take her long to decide that she could not face Simon personally. The sight of his sad brown eyes would be too much for her; she might relent and that would be intolerable. No. She was a writer, after all, so she would pour out her heart to him on paper and explain the reasons for her decision in a way that he could not interrupt in an attempt to dissuade her. He would understand. She pulled paper, pen and ink towards her and began to write.

Simon received her letter that evening, after he and Jenkins had made their slow, sad way back to the camp in the Sekukuni valley. They had first sought out a surgeon to apply proper dressings to

446

their wounds and this delay meant that it was nearly dusk when they were able to locate a quartermaster, who told them which tent they had been allocated at the southern end of the valley, pitched away from the officers' lines among the stores. It was there that a flushed orderly came with Alice's letter, explaining that he had spent half a day trying to find them.

Simon recognised the writing immediately and his throat dried as he wedged his thumb under the flap of the envelope and tore it open. Alice had taken five pages to tell him of her decision. Typically, she had not attempted to dissemble but had explained exactly what had happened, and described the conflict of emotions that she had felt in visiting Covington and in making up her mind. Her decision, however, was irrevocable. Her closing paragraph read:

It would be cruel and dishonest to pretend that all of this has changed my feelings towards you. If anything, this tragedy has made me love you more than ever and I know that, throughout my life with Ralph, I shall always keep that love in my heart. But I could not live in dishonour – I don't mean the opprobrium that my leaving of Ralph would bring from society, you know that I wouldn't give a fig for that – but rather the knowledge that our happiness had been built on the unhappiness of someone who was impaired, both emotionally and physically. I know that you, of all people, will understand. You will also understand why I cannot see you to tell you all of this face to face. I am not as strong as you, my darling, and I know I would break down and that would not help either of us. I am leaving the camp tomorrow to be out of everyone's way (I have to make preparations in Lydenburg anyway for Ralph's onward journey home) and I would rather that we did not meet. Give my love to dear 352 and take my deepest, most special love with you for the rest of your life.

Your Alice

In a typically efficient gesture, Alice had remembered to add a separate PS, giving Wolseley's news about Dunn's imminent arrival and also Covington's explanation of the pistol shot which, to Simon, seemed to have echoed round the Lulu Mountains years, if not centuries, before.

He read the letter sitting on his trestle bed as Jenkins bustled around him, in and out of the tent, preparing a fire and something for them both to eat at the end of an exhausting forty-eight hours. Eventually the Welshman stopped in the middle of his chores, no longer able to avoid the quiet, fixed stare that Simon directed at the beaten earth at his feet.

'Bad news?' he enquired.

Without speaking, Simon handed him the letter.

'Are you sure – not too ... er ... personal, like?'

Simon shook his head, and Jenkins sat on his own bed and began reading Alice's letter, silently mouthing the words as his eyes slowly scanned the pages. It took him all of five minutes. Then he handed it back and the two men sat in silence for a while.

'Blimey.' Jenkins spoke eventually. 'You know,

bach sir, I just can't understand – I never shall understand – the ways of the upper classes. She's a lovely lass, bless 'er, but this is just bloody barmy. Isn't it? I mean, I know the bloke's 'urt an' all that, but you an' I know 'e's a bastard, saving your presence an' all. So why is she takin' 'im an' not you?'

Despite the agony, Simon had to smile. 'Good question,' he said. 'But I think she has answered it in her letter.' He paused for a moment, attempting to put together the conflicting thoughts that had raced through his head during the last few minutes: the initial pain and despair, then the bitterness, and now a deep, melancholic admiration for Alice Griffith and her decision. He hated it and yet somehow his spirit lifted at her passionate and articulate description of the agony she had gone through, and at the thought of his own love for her – a love that he had nurtured for so long and which had at last looked as though it could come to fruition. It had all seemed, in these last few days, too good to be true anyway. Perhaps the disgusting ending to the attempt to arrest Mendoza had been a portent. He sighed.

'It is exactly what I would have expected of her,' he said. 'And she is right. It is the honourable and proper thing to do. And that's the end of it.'

Jenkins shook his head. 'Well, look you, I dunno. I really don't.' He went outside to build the fire and then poked his head around the tent flap. 'I managed to get a bit of mutton from the cook. Thought I'd just boil it in the pot. Is that all right?'

'Of course. It doesn't really much matter.'

449

'Blimey. It does, you know.' Jenkins, his tired, unshaven face looking peculiarly jowly in the flickering firelight, was indignant.

'We've got to eat, even if the whole bleedin' world 'as collapsed around our ears. Life 'as to go on, you know, bach. In a way, you know, that's what *she's* sayin' an' all. We've got to get on with things. I shall boil the bloody stuff, then.'

Simon scowled at Jenkins's retreating back. He hated it when the man slipped into his role of barrack-room philosopher. Banal rubbish ... and yet ... 'We've all got to get on with things.' True. What alternative was there?

Later that night, as they huddled in their blankets by the fire in the cold night air of the valley, drinking strong coffee, Jenkins returned to the subject, albeit hesitantly. 'There's one good thing about all this, bach sir,' he said.

Simon lifted a weary head. 'Oh yes. What?'

'Well,' the Welshman looked away and spoke almost shyly, 'although it wasn't mentioned, I knew, o' course, that you an' Miss Alice were ... you know ... back on course, so to speak. An' I wondered a bit where that would 'ave left me.'

Simon's eyebrows shot up. 'What do you mean? If we had ... ah ... married, as I think we would, you would have lived with us, of course.'

Jenkins squirmed. 'Oh, I wouldn't 'ave much fancied that. I would 'ave been very much in the way, wherever you settled.'

'Don't talk rubbish. Anyway, it's not going to happen and...' he looked up keenly at his comrade, 'aren't you going to get married yourself?'

Jenkins's jaw dropped. 'Bloody 'ell. Who? Me?

450

Not on your life. Who would marry me?'

'Why, Nandi, of course. You love her, don't you?'

Simon was not sure if he had ever seen Jenkins embarrassed, but that look of abject misery, shame and awkwardness, which combined to make the Welshman's face appear even more lugubrious than ever in the half-darkness, seemed as close to embarrassment as he would ever manage.

'Love?' he said. 'Blimey, people like me don't know much about that, see. I'm a bit rough for that sort of stuff, bach sir.' He looked up and shot Simon a quick look, almost of appeal. 'If it 'adn't been for you, look you, I would 'ave drunk myself to death by now. After all, I'm a soldier really, even if, like you, I don't wear a uniform – an 'appy state which I much prefer, as you know. No, I suppose I kill people for a livin' an' that don't exactly lend itself to marryin', now does it? Though...' he looked down at the floor again and his voice dropped, 'I am a bit fond of 'er, as you know.'

'Well, there you are. You ought to settle down. Look, I think you feel a bit more strongly about Nandi than you say, and...' Simon's voice tailed away slightly in some embarrassment, 'I don't blame you. She's a brave, intelligent and very pretty young woman. Also, I think she is fond of you; in fact I know she is. There are those diamonds we gave her and these extra few here that you could bring to the partnership. You could set up home together, in Natal or even Zululand, and you could take up farming or whatever–'

Jenkins sat up immediately and cut in, his voice

expressing high indignation. 'Farmin'! I don't want to go back to bloody farmin' – even with Miss Nandi, God bless 'er. What's wrong with what me and you do together? It's a bit 'ard and downright dangerous at times, but I enjoy it. Don't you want me to stay with you? Someone's got to look after you, particularly now.'

Simon looked hard at his comrade. Was this another case of someone being loyal beyond the call of duty? No. Jenkins couldn't be disingenuous if his life depended upon it. He made one more try.

'Look, 352,' he said, leaning forward. 'This is a golden opportunity to find happiness and do the normal things: marry a splendid woman, have children, build a life together, all that sort of thing; away from violence and death. Of course I don't want to lose you, but I would come and see you.'

'Oh yes. And what would *you* do? Who would look after you?'

'I've told you often enough, I don't need nannying. What would I do?' He mused for a moment. 'Well, you know that originally I wanted to spend a bit of time at home, with my parents. That's where we were both heading when we got Nandi's letter. But I am not sure now.' He leaned over and poked the fire with a stick. 'I don't want to be in England when Alice marries, and because her parents and mine are virtual neighbours, we would be bound to meet. I don't think I could face that just yet.'

He turned back to face Jenkins. 'Anyway, I – we – seem to have built a bit of a reputation with the army. I certainly don't want to take up a formal commission again, but perhaps Wolseley could fix me up with some employment that's interesting – and exciting – on the edge of the army. He owes me something. I sense that this country could erupt in some way soon and there will be plenty to do. I am not sure I want to leave it just yet.'

'Exactly!' Jenkins's joy lit up the embers of the camp fire. 'That's exactly what I want to do. That's settled then. We'll do it together, whatever it is...' he finished rather lamely.

'Oh very well. But you're a bloody fool.'

'Well, it takes one to know one. Oh, sorry, bach sir. Didn't mean to be disrespectful, like.'

Simon gathered up his blanket and crept into the low bivouac tent – the army could find nothing smartly bell-shaped for them. He pulled off his boots and, unwashed, crawled between the blankets on the trestle bed. After much loud washing of the plates outside, Jenkins followed suit and, within a minute, was loudly snoring. Simon looked across in the dim light to the humped figure of the Welshman on the other bed and, amazingly, his deep sadness began to lighten before he too fell asleep.

It was hardly light when a footfall outside the tent woke him. 'Mr Fonthill, sir?'

'Yes.'

'General would like to see you, sir, as soon as is convenient. By which I think he means now.'

Simon sighed and knuckled his eyes. 'Very well. I will be there in ten minutes.' What now? He

453

rolled out from between the blankets and pulled on his boots. The call seemed urgent, so he did not stop to shave, merely splashing water, cold from the night air, on to his face and neck.

Wolseley was hard at work at his trestle table by lanternlight as Simon was ushered in. The General gestured with his pen to the empty camp chair before him and sat back. 'Sorry to get you up so early,' he said. 'But I haven't much time and it was important to see you right away.'

Simon sat down. 'Sir?'

'Look here. One of our patrols has brought back news that a man – a Boer from his appearance – has been found out on the plain, north of here, brutally murdered by the look of it. From what I hear, he sounds like this man Mendoza you have been pursuing. Know anything about it?'

'Yes, General.' Simon thought quickly. There was no use denying the killing. Wolseley would find out soon enough about the pursuit. Yet Jenkins – disadvantaged, working-class Jenkins – must not be put at risk. 'I killed him. I am sorry we couldn't bury him but we didn't have the tools to do so, and, anyway, both Jenkins and I were wounded and, frankly, more or less exhausted. So we had to leave him where he was, under a few stones, and ride back in.'

Wolseley remained silent for a moment, his face expressionless. 'Fonthill,' he said eventually, 'you continue to amaze and – yes – shock me. You had better tell me about it before you and your man are arrested for murder. You are still under my command.'

Simon sighed and related the story of how he and Jenkins had tracked Mendoza down and attempted to arrest him and bring him back for trial. And of how Mendoza had resisted, shot Jenkins and disarmed Simon, and of how the two had fought with knives, with Simon eventually emerging as the victor.

Offering his hand with its bloody bandage as proof of the encounter, Simon concluded: 'He had tricked us, sir, and it was him or me. I had a bit of luck in the struggle and, in the end, it was him – although I had to stick him twice in the fight before I was able to cut his throat and finish him.'

Wolseley listened without interruption. At the end he tilted back his chair. 'And your man, of course, can vouch for this in every way – particularly the fact that this, ah, brute resisted arrest?'

'Yes, sir.'

'Very well.' The General's chair crashed back. 'Then nothing more will be said about this matter. I have far too much to do to worry about the death of one man, when I have to report in detail that of so many others.' A half-smile now crept on to the little man's face. 'I must say, Fonthill, you are a determined sort of chap. You do what you set out to do, don't you? This was your kill. Eh? What?'

Simon ran his hand across his eyes. 'I wouldn't put it quite like that, Sir Garnet. We would have preferred to bring him back and see him hang, but both Jenkins and I felt strongly that this man had to be apprehended and shouldn't be left to rape, cheat and kill wherever he liked. We hadn't intended to kill him. I am sorry if this has caused you trouble.'

'Dammit no. But I had to clear it up. Now,' his tone softened, 'you've heard about Covington?'

'Yes, sir. I am sorry.'

'So am I. Damned good soldier.' Wolseley's eye stared at Simon. 'Just as well, though, that he's got his marriage to look forward to. Damned fine girl, eh?'

Simon tried to keep his face expressionless. 'Indeed, sir.'

'You know her quite well, I think?'

'Yes, sir. We are – were – neighbours in Brecon, and her father and mine served together in the same regiment.'

'Good.' Wolseley's tone softened again. 'Good that she's going to stand by him. No doubt about that, I suppose...?' The question was left hanging and Simon let it stay there, just for a second or two. He had no wish to buttress the sense of propriety of the military ruling classes – but then, he quickly realised, he could not let Alice down.

'Oh, no doubt at all, sir.'

'Splendid. Now, Fonthill, I don't want to keep you too long.' He gestured again at the papers on his table. 'I sometimes think that there's more to do after a battle than before it. But before I get completely immersed and you disappear again off into the depths of Africa, or wherever it is you intend to go next, I do wish to talk about you.'

'Sir?' Simon felt a familiar warning bell jingle.

'Yes. You, young man, are clearly a damned fine soldier. Your appreciation of how to attack Sekukuni's fortress was impeccable, and,' he held up a tattered piece of paper, 'even this sketch you did of the kopje was accurate and most helpful. You must, you really must, come back into the army.'

Simon moved his buttocks on the chair. 'That's extremely kind of you, Sir Garnet, but–'

'I can offer you an immediate majority in whatever regiment of the line you choose – sorry, not the Guards, as you will appreciate – and the rank of warrant officer for my familiar friend, Jenkins. So you two can continue to serve together. Now what do you say to that? You would probably be the youngest major in the British Army.'

'As I say, sir, it really is most kind, but I fear I must decline. I am just not a line officer any more, I fear. However, if we can be of service to you in a less conventional capacity here in Africa, perhaps ... something which will not bind us to strict army discipline and that sort of thing. Perhaps as scouts, wherever there is trouble. I don't know. But not a formal commission, thank you, sir.'

Wolseley puffed out his cheeks and shook his head. 'Well, you're a peculiar one, Fonthill. No doubt about it. I won't attempt to argue with you because I've got too much to do. But you are right. The army shouldn't lose you completely. What do you intend to do now?'

Simon smiled. 'Not quite sure yet. But perhaps we might escort Mr Dunn and his daughter back to Natal to Zululand and help them to set up wherever it is they wish to settle.'

'Good.' Wolseley stood and offered his hand. 'Make sure you contact me at my headquarters in Durban when you get down there. Now, be off with you – and for God's sake don't go killing any more Thugs or Portuguese rapists until I'm out of this damned country.'

They exchanged grins and handshakes and Simon walked out into the warmth of another dawn in the Transvaal. He stopped for a moment and looked around at the familiar signs of an army camp beginning to stir itself. He sniffed the crisp, clear air. Perhaps life *could* go on, after all. Dammit, of course it could! And he strode off to find Jenkins and demand breakfast.

Author's Note

The Sekukuni campaign earns only a small footnote, if that, in the history of British colonial warfare. But most of those historians who have noticed it seem to agree that, by putting down this previously invincible chieftain, Wolseley did impress the Transvaal Boers sufficiently to delay the onset of the First Boer War. It was a complete victory for 'the Very Model of a Modern Major General' and, as Wolseley predicts at the end of the novel, Sekukuni was found hiding in a cave within a few days of the end of the battle and was put into captivity and later exiled. The King was murdered by his brother in 1882 and the bePedi power was destroyed and the people scattered. In fact, the once-proud citadel of Sekukuni, with its population of more than 4,000, had been reduced by the year 2003 to a few scattered huts on the sandy floor of the valley. The town, these days, is spelled Sekhukune, but I have followed the 1880 spelling, as shown in the old map which illustrates this story.

I have described the battle, with its two distinct phases, as best I can, basing the details on respected accounts at the time and on the folk memory of local residents now. However, I must confess to setting back the date of the battle by a few months into 1880, to allow Alice, Simon and Jenkins to see the end of the Second Afghan War and arrive in the Transvaal in time to take part in the conflict. I hope studious scholars of the period will forgive this modest time-switch. I should also report that contemporary records seem infuriatingly imprecise about the exact locations of Wolseley's forward camps from which he launched the final assaults. I have therefore been forced to make what I hope are intelligent assumptions on these points.

Most of the characters in the novel are fictional. But Wolseley, of course, was not, and was probably the most skilled exponent of colonial warfare in British history. He went on, as did General Roberts, his great rival from the Indian Army, to become a field marshal and a great reformer of the army. Wolseley's attack on Gladstone and his eulogy on the desirability of dying from bullet wounds, made in his first meeting with Simon in Durban, are taken from the General's letters home to his wife. Similarly, the startlingly jingoistic diatribe delivered by Cecil Rhodes to Simon in Kimberley is based on Rhodes's 'Confession of Faith', a document he first drafted in the mining town in about 1877. I have included extracts from both because they do help, I feel, to illustrate the attitude of the British ruling classes towards the Empire at its apogee. Rhodes, of course, went on to become one of the most influential and controversial figures in late-nineteenth-century Africa. *Inter alia*, he tightened his grip on Kimberley to build de Beers into the leading mining company in South Africa, from which it has become the commanding force in today's international diamond industry.

As I have stated in those earlier adventures of Simon, Jenkins and Alice, *The Horns of the Buffalo* and *The Road to Kandahar*, there are precedents for women serving the great British newspapers of the time as war correspondents. Alice, then, though perhaps uniquely feisty, was not alone.

If Alice's decision in the last chapter strikes some readers as less than credible, I can only insist that adherence to codes of honour ran strongly through the middle and upper classes of nineteenth-century Britain (as did strands of huge immorality – but that's another story!). For instance, Arthur Wellesley, later to become the great Duke of Wellington, proposed to an Irish lady when he was an impecunious young officer. Her parents refused to let her marry a man with such poor prospects. He remained unmarried but went on to make his name and his fortune in India. Although they had not met in the interim and he had long since fallen out of love with the lady, Wellesley felt that he had to honour his proposal all those years later. It proved a disastrous marriage, but they stayed 'together' until she died. *'Autres temps...'*

Baker Russell, Captain Macleod, Willie Russell (who *did* tell his readers on the eve of the battle that he doubted if the invading force had the strength to attack the next day), the German missionary Merensky and John Dunn are all real figures, as was Piet Joubert, the tough Boer leader. His brief defence of the Boer position given to Alice in Pretoria is based on the record of a meeting he had with Wolseley at roughly that time. But Dunn seems to have disappeared from the pages of history after the break-up of the Zulu nation, and I hope that any descendants of his will forgive my manipulation of him for the purposes of my story.

This Large Print Book for the partially sighted, who cannot read normal print, is published under the auspices of

THE ULVERSCROFT FOUNDATION